BY SUSAN RIEGER

Like Mother, Like Mother

The Heirs

The Divorce Papers

Like Mother,
Like Mother

Like Mother,
Like Mother

| A NOVEL |

Susan Rieger

THE DIAL PRESS
NEW YORK

Published in the United States by The Dial Press, an imprint of Random House, a division of Penguin Random House LLC, New York.

THE DIAL PRESS is a registered trademark and the colophon is a trademark of Penguin Random House LLC.

LIBRARY OF CONGRESS CATALOGING-IN-PUBLICATION DATA
Names: Rieger, Susan, 1946– author.
Title: Like mother, like mother: a novel / Susan Rieger.
Identifiers: LCCN 2023050450 (print) | LCCN 2023050451 (ebook) |
ISBN 9780525512493 (hardcover; acid-free paper) |
ISBN 9780525512509 (ebook)
Subjects: LCSH: Mothers and daughters—Fiction. | Family secrets—Fiction.
LCGFT: Domestic fiction. | Novels.
Classification: LCC PS3618.I39235 L55 2024 (print) |
LCC PS3618.I39235 (ebook) | DDC 813/.6—dc23/eng/20231107
LC record available at https://lccn.loc.gov/2023050450
LC ebook record available at https://lccn.loc.gov/2023050451

Printed in the United States of America on acid-free paper

randomhousebooks.com

2 4 6 8 9 7 5 3 1

First Edition

Book design by Susan Turner

For my grandchildren, Eliza Pouncey, Felix Miller,
and Dominic Miller

Don't look back. Something might be gaining on you.

—Satchel Paige

Contents

PART I

Lila

1

Death

LILA PEREIRA DIED ON THE FRONT PAGE OF *THE WASHINGTON GLOBE.* She also died on the front page of *The New York Times,* astonishing and gratifying *The Globe*'s publisher, Doug Marshall. Lila had been *The Globe*'s executive editor, the female Jim Bramble, who'd out-Brambled Bramble, her predecessor during Watergate. In 2018, Lila and her Pirates, a gritty band of cutthroat reporters, exposed President Webb's pay-to-play scheme and brought down him and his two hapless sons. Webbgate gave Watergate a run for its money. The Pirates collected two Pulitzers and a George Polk. Lila picked up honorary degrees from Stanford, UVA, and Georgetown.

Lila had retired on January 31, 2023. It was company policy for top editors to step down the year they turned sixty-five. Doug offered her a seat on the editorial board, but she declined. "I've never seen the point of the opinion pages," she said. "All Talmud, no Torah. I want the facts, the red meat. I'll die of boredom and aggravation." Two months later, she was dead from Stage IV lung cancer. Everyone asked if she'd been a smoker. She had smoked in college, at parties. "I was a drinker. I should have gotten cirrhosis. Give it a rest. Bad luck."

Lila was buried in Congressional Cemetery. She didn't want a funeral, only a memorial service. "Hold off a bit," she told Doug, who wanted to make sure she got the send-off she deserved. "You need to give people time to think about what they want to say. I wasn't the GOAT. Remind them."

Lila's husband, Joe Maier, unstooped at sixty-nine, spoke at the memorial service, along with two of their three daughters, the virtual twins, Stella, thirty-six, and Ava, thirty-five. Her youngest daughter, Grace, twenty-nine, sat mute, in the reserved section, alongside Ruth, her best friend since their freshman year at the University of Chicago. Grace had visited Lila regularly during her illness, but their relationship, never easy, had become increasingly fraught for Grace ever since she published her novel, *The Lost Mother*, in the fall of 2022. The day Lila died, Grace sat with her for two hours, racked by sadness and sorrow. *What was I thinking*, she thought. *Why did I write it.*

"You can talk to her," the nurse had said, looking in briefly to see how her patient was doing. "She can still hear."

Grace nodded. "Thank you." She laid her head gingerly on Lila's chest and wept.

THE MEMORIAL SERVICE WAS MOBBED. Everyone in D.C. who wasn't a Webbite, and even some who were, wanted a ticket. There was a guest list and a standing room list and a wait list. Rupert Murdoch was invited, over Lila's dead body, but he wasn't seated down front. Joe drew the line.

Doug had thought the funeral should be in the National Cathedral. Lila reminded him she was Jewish. "Isn't there a cross over the pulpit?" She squinted at Doug. "Who would say Kaddish?" She decided on the Kennedy Center's Eisenhower Theater.

Doug was disappointed. "Why not the Concert Hall or the Opera House?"

"They each hold over two thousand people," Lila said. "The Eisenhower holds a thousand. Grand is okay, not grandiose."

"Do you think I'm on the guest list," Grace asked Ruth as they walked inside the theater. "Just kidding."

"You're going to have to make it up with Lila, dead or alive," Ruth said. She had loved Lila. As with all of her daughters' friends, Lila had been at her most charming, most engaging with Ruth.

"I thought she'd like *The Lost Mother.* It was funny, people said it was funny. She was the book's hero."

"Lila was a hero in life," Ruth said.

There were ten speakers, each held to seven minutes, Lila's hand from the grave. "I want stories, funny stories," Lila had written in the instructions. "No tear-jerking the congregation." Her sister, Clara, recited the Kaddish, memorizing it for a second sad time. The first time had been at their brother Polo's funeral. He died in 2000, jolting Lila into a fury of mourning.

"I hate this feeling, like it's the end of the world," she had said to Joe at Polo's funeral. "Is this the way regular people feel?"

"Yes," he said.

"He was only forty-seven, three months away from retiring." She blew her nose. "I guess he saw he was running out of time."

For a month after his death, she had walked five miles a day, getting up at 6:00 A.M. so she'd be done by 8:00.

"What do you think about on your walks?" Joe had said.

"I don't think. I walk. You know I can't multitask."

"How do you not think?"

"I don't want to think, so I don't. I walk to breathe. If I can just keep breathing."

If she could have just kept breathing, Joe thought, as Clara finished the prayer.

Over everyone's objections—Covid was still lurking—Joe's mother, Frances, attended the service. "It keeps her alive for me," she told Joe. "The day she died was the saddest day of my life."

The virtual twins, both visibly pregnant, had also been discouraged from coming, everyone weighing in—Joe, their obstetrician, the airlines. They wound up leasing a plane, picking up Frances on the way.

"It's sad Lila won't know our babies," Stella said.

"Sad too they won't know her," Ava said.

Doug Marshall was the first speaker. He had taken up the role of master of ceremonies. He was used to bossing people and he looked the part. Six-three, once blond, now graying, he was, as Lila often said, "an echt WASP and an echt mensch."

He told the story about the midnight meeting the day the president's counsel was fired, when Lila's Pirates were working the phones, trying to find a second source for the rumor that Webb was going to let his younger son take the fall for the pay-to-play scheme. "Webb is a gerbil," Doug said, gleefully, his voice rising for the peroration. "He eats his young."

All the *Globe* stories were funny and fierce and first-person, as much about the eulogists as the deceased. None of them cried openly. Lila had forbidden it.

Felicity Turner, one of the Pirates, talked about a trip to Detroit she had taken with Lila, shortly after the cancer diagnosis. "We drove around her old neighborhood, which had been the site of the worst of the 1967 riots. Lila opened the window and pointed to a run-down brick house, with broken front steps and a sagging front porch. The houses on either side were in better repair, their lawns mowed, their front doors brightly painted. 'I grew up there. Little House on the Prairie.' She closed the window. 'Detroitus.'"

Sally Alter was cleanup, the youngest last. As she opened her mouth to speak, tears trickled down her cheeks. "Lila treated me like a daughter." She dabbed at her eyes with a tissue. "Allergies."

Grace folded her program. *This is satire,* she thought.

Sally told the story about the press conference in early 2018 when Webb attacked the stories in *The Globe*. "I never sold an ambassadorship. Never. Lila Pereira is a lying— You can finish the rest of that sentence." Sally had been twenty-four, a guppy then. She wanted to catch Lila's eye. "I called her to see if she wanted to comment. I was interning at Politico. I needed a break. 'What's he going to do about it,' Lila said, 'put my tit in a big fat wringer?' I put it on Twitter and the trolls went wild. Lila hired me six months later."

Joe and the twins had been affectionate. Joe told the story about Lila's first day at her first job at *The Cincinnati Courier*, writing obituaries about "sainted" Irish grandmothers. "'I thought at first the survivors were taking their revenge,' Lila said. 'I thought "sainted" was code for "drunk."'" He smiled, waiting for the laughter to die down. "Lila was like no one else. I never knew what she'd do or say next, but whatever she did or said, it seemed inevitable. She was Detroit to the end. She always had your back."

Stella and Ava told the story of their first swimming lessons ages two and three. "Lila threw us in. We sank. She fished us out, disappointed. 'I saw it on television,' she said to Joe. 'They were supposed to burble to the top.'" They spoke alternately, taking only a single speaker's slot, one voice blending into the other. Lila had called them the Starbirds, synching their names translated into English. They had Lila's last name, Grace had Joe's. It made sense on the surface. The Starbirds looked like Lila, Grace like Joe.

"I don't think anyone can tell them apart," Grace harrumphed, "except, of course, Joe, and maybe their husbands."

"Lila's doing, I take it," Ruth said.

Grace nodded. "For someone who did so little at home, she did so much."

Grace and Ruth ducked out on the reception.

"I can't face all the accusatory looks." Grace shook her head. "I didn't know she was going to die when my book came out. It's a first novel. Everyone pillories their parents. Who else is there to write about."

"I wondered why you didn't want to speak at the service."

"I'd have been booed from the podium. I hate D.C. When's our train?"

Ruth put her arm through Grace's. "Tomorrow," she said. "What would you have talked about?"

"Maybe the real story of the swimming lesson, the one in *The Lost Mother.*"

• • •

WHEN GRACE WAS THREE YEARS old, Stella and Ava threw her, fully clothed, into the deep end of a swimming pool. They were at the tennis club. It was Memorial Day weekend. The grown-ups were drinking in the clubhouse. The children, at loose ends, were wandering the grounds looking for small animals to torture. Grace couldn't swim. She sank like a stone. Her sisters stood at the pool's edge, watching. Neither one jumped in to save her. They knew how to swim, they were eight and nine, but they didn't want to get wet. They were wearing new party clothes, Laura Ashley dresses and patent leather shoes. They dressed alike. They looked alike. Grace didn't try to tell them apart.

When Grace didn't bob up as they expected, the Starbirds ran screaming to find a parent. Recognizing their panicky voices, Lila sprinted from the clubhouse. Several other parents followed more slowly, drinks in hand, vulture-like. Without waiting for the lifeguard ("Where the hell was that cretin," Lila said later, back in the clubhouse, finishing her margarita), she jumped into the pool and fished Grace out. She was wearing a navy off-the-shoulder cocktail dress and stiletto heels. She walked to the shallow end, thumping Grace on the back.

Her sisters told Lila that Grace had fallen in. Wriggling, red-faced, and spitting water, Grace yelled in fury, "No. No. No. No. They tossed me. They said you tossed them."

Stella and Ava were bad liars. Caught in the prisoner's dilemma, each worried the other would break first and confess. They looked down. They knew to show remorse the moment they'd been found out.

"She followed us out here. We told her to go back to the clubhouse," Stella said. "She wouldn't listen but kept following us."

"We asked her if she wanted to learn to swim," Ava said. "She nodded."

"We said you had thrown us in a pool when we were two and three," Stella said. "We said that's how we learned to swim."

"We asked her if she'd like that," Ava said. "She nodded again."

"I've told you before, you may not kill your little sister," Lila said. "Why didn't one or both of you rescue her?"

They looked down at their brand-new Mary Janes.

"Take them off and give them to me," Lila said.

They unbuckled their shoes, dread in their hearts, and gave them to her.

She threw them into the middle of the pool.

The vultures applauded.

"Mikado justice," Lila said.

LILA'S STYLE OF MOTHERING WHEN the girls were young was nonchalant and intermittent, nothing like her spiky and seductive *Globe* personality. She left the girls almost entirely to others. She hadn't fallen in love with them as babies and didn't spend much time with them. She relied on Joe, nannies, and au pairs.

"I only want for them what they want for themselves," she said to Joe at dinner one evening. They'd been married a dozen years. The Starbirds were in preschool. Grace had yet to make her appearance.

"What if they want more of a mother?" Joe said.

"They have you. They don't need me to look after them. They need me not to harm them."

"That's it? That's . . ." His voice trailed off. *I was warned,* he thought.

"What do I know about mothering? I didn't have a mother, and my father . . ." Lila's voice faded. She never characterized Aldo's behavior. She told stories about him, what he did, not what he was. She had no interest in soul-searching, her own or other people's. She rarely read memoirs. "What do they want from us, our pity, our admiration? I can't tell." She only read the tough-minded stories, *Memories of a Catholic Girlhood, Memoirs of a Dutiful Daughter.* No one pitied Mary McCarthy or Simone de Beauvoir. She wouldn't be pitied either.

"Being pitied is almost as awful as being scared." She put down her fork. "It's insulting. I don't feel sorry for me. No one else is allowed to." She paused. "Same thing with hurt feelings. No one hurts my feelings. I don't allow it. I won't give other people that power." She knew she was an outlier on this. She didn't think, *Get over it, people.* She understood they couldn't. What she couldn't fathom was the search for catharsis and closure. "There's no walking into the sunset," she would say. Aldo could die, but not her hatred.

She didn't ask Joe to understand her, only to put up with her. "It's not personal. I never much cared for young children, not even as a child, except my brother and sister. They were the best. They had my back, I had theirs." Her voice faded, summoning, unbidden, her wretched childhood. "I couldn't wait to grow up and get out of Detroit." She shrugged. "Spilled milk."

Lila had grown up on Grand Street, off Linwood, in Detroit's old Jewish enclave. Her family was a relic. After the Second World War, the middle-class Jews, lawyers, accountants, teachers, nurses, had begun moving north of Eight Mile Road, part of the white flight to the suburbs. The Jews who remained, like Lila's father, were tied to their jobs and businesses.

Joe, gently nurtured in Bloomfield Hills, seethed at Lila's stories of her childhood. "Your father was out of Dickens, part Fagin, part Bill Sikes. Mostly Bill Sikes."

Lila took a swallow of wine. "We could have lived in a better house. Aldo worked on the GM assembly line. He belonged to the UAW, he made decent wages. He installed engines, a more interesting job, he'd say, than installing hoods and wheels. He never talked about his work except to curse it and us. 'Today, I broke my balls installing three engines an hour for eight hours, so you stinking kids can have a roof over your heads and a meal at this table. Are you grateful? No. You take it for granted.' I tried once to thank him for working for us. I must have been eight or nine. He smacked me. 'Enough of your sarcastic remarks.' I protested that I meant it. He smacked me again. There was no winning with Aldo." She stopped, caught in a wayward thought. "His father worked the line too . . . and beat him regularly. 'It made a man of me,' he'd say." She shrugged. "I suppose it made a man of me, too."

Lila and her siblings had belonged to the Linwood Gang. They weren't active members, they avoided the gang fights, staying in at night, but they carried double-action switchblades and knew how to use them. They practiced stabbing small trees. "You had to belong, it wasn't optional. They'd beat you up or rob your house if you didn't. We carried the knives as signs of belonging, like wearing your colors now. Baby Mafiosi."

In the winter of 1980, during a prewedding visit to Joe's mother in Bloomfield Hills, Joe and Lila drove into Detroit for dinner. As they got out of the car, a kid, fourteen or fifteen, pulled a small kitchen knife on them and asked for their money and jewelry. Lila reached in her pocket and pulled out her switchblade. It sprung open, almost twice the length of the boy's knife. He leaped backward. She did a quick slashing movement. "Wanna rumble?" The boy fled.

Joe leaned against the car, his heart thundering in his ears. "What were you thinking?"

"He didn't even have mustache hair."

"It's only money."

"'Only money' to you. Money is never 'only money' to me."

Six years later at a showing of *Crocodile Dundee,* Lila watched Dundee pull a knife on a mugger. "He stole that move from me." She turned to Joe, poking him in the ribs. Joe grunted. "The bowie knife was a nice touch," she said, "but too big for anything but skinning a moose."

To the end of her life, Lila carried a switchblade, testing its action monthly. She was on her seventh when she died. She liked new models, the way Joe liked new cars. "You're kidding me," she said to him when he asked her to give it up. "I'd feel naked."

The girls, when they heard about her knives, were astonished.

"What did you do with a knife when you were thirteen?" Stella was stunned. She was thirteen.

"Mostly, I played Stretch with Clara," Lila said. "She was taller but I'd win. She hated the knives. She isn't competitive. She's a good sport."

"What do you do with it now?" Ava spoke hesitantly, not sure she wanted to know.

"I carry it in a pocket. All my clothes have pockets. I like to have a knife on my person. You never know when you might need one."

"Have you ever sliced anyone up?" Even at seven, Grace went straight to the point, asking the question her cautious big sisters shied from.

Lila considered her answer. "Knifing someone is so personal, so intimate. Not like a gun, easy as pie."

ON THE MORNING OF LILA's burial, Joe went with Grace to the funeral home. He brought Lila's seventh switchblade with him. He liked the weight of it in his pocket, like the change he used to carry before the ubiquitous cellphone. He'd gone to say his final goodbye, also to make sure they hadn't embalmed her or made her up to look like an aged starlet. His instructions had been overexplicit.

"We're Jewish," he told the funeral director the day she died. "We bury them quickly. No viewing." He handed him his business card. *I'm a lawyer,* he thought. *He might as well know it.*

Lila had been refrigerated. She looked like herself, her cancer-ridden self, only thinner and more tired.

Joe asked the director to leave them alone. "We'll be a few minutes."

"What are we doing?" Grace looked in the coffin, then looked away, her face wet with tears. *Why did she have to die? I needed more time.*

"I'll never see her again," Joe said. Stroking her head with one hand, he reached into the coffin with the other and smoothly, stealthily slipped the switchblade into the side skirt pocket of her suit, a navy Armani, Frances's gift, like all her suits. He leaned over to kiss her. *It's in his kiss,* he thought, remembering.

"They'll find it, you know." Grace stifled her tears.

"Odds are, but she'd have appreciated the gesture."

At the burial, Grace looked around to see if Aldo had come. She had never seen her grandfather but she figured she would recognize him. She scanned the grounds. He wasn't there, unless he was skulking behind a tree. She was disappointed. She'd have liked to confront him. She'd have liked to punch him out. As the other mourners walked slowly back to their cars, she approached the open grave. She picked up a handful of dirt and threw it in, along with one of the older switchblades Lila had kept in a shoebox in her closet. *I can't leave you unarmed.*

2

Motherlessness

ALDO HAD COMMITTED HIS WIFE, ZELDA, TO THE ELOISE ASYLUM, THE old Wayne State County Poorhouse, in 1960, when Lila, the youngest of their three children, was two. Lila never saw her mother again.

"'Mental,' my father would say, pointing at his head." Lila pointed to her forehead. She looked sideways at Joe to see if he was repelled. It was the late spring of 1977. They were on their second real date. "I couldn't tell if she was padded-cell-deranged or yellow-wallpaper-depressed." Whenever she talked about her childhood, Lila's voice went flat, losing its snap and its rhythms. Grace called it her "dead voice."

Lila's immigrant grandmother ran the house for Aldo, her only child. "Bubbe liked Clara best," Lila said. "Then Polo. I came third if I came at all."

On April 1, 1968, Aldo told the children that Zelda had died the day before. They were at dinner. Polo, fourteen, sat, stunned, not knowing where to look, what to say, how to feel. Clara, twelve, began to cry.

Lila, ten, stood up, furious. "Is this an April Fool's joke?"

"What are you talking about?" Aldo said.

"When is the funeral?" she said.

"She's already buried."

"Where is she buried?"

"In a cemetery, the other side of Eight Mile Road."

"What did she die of?"

Clara, shaking her head, put her hand on Lila's arm.

"She died. She was nuts. Electricity couldn't cure her. She ruined my life." Aldo wiped his mouth with his napkin. "Go to your room or I'll get the strap."

Lila shook off Clara's arm. "Did you kill her? You used to hit her."

Aldo reached over and smacked her so hard she fell on the floor.

She got to her feet, stumbling. "You'll be sorry someday you did that."

Aldo pushed her down. "You can finish your dinner on the floor, like the vermin you are."

Lila reached in her pocket and closed her hand around her switchblade.

"March thirty-first, 1968, is the most important day of my childhood." Lila looked sideways at Joe. It was the first time she'd spoken of her mother's death to anyone other than Polo and Clara.

He nodded. "Go on."

Lila took in a deep breath. "That day, President Johnson said he wouldn't run for a second term. The two events—Johnson's resignation and my mother's death—collided in my mind, as if Zelda were a casualty of Vietnam."

Aldo never remarried. He liked living with his mother. He had girlfriends, all of them *shiksas*. None stuck around for long. He was always complaining to them about Zelda. "You rant against her as if she walked out on you yesterday," one of them said over her shoulder as she was leaving.

Zelda's death spurred Aldo to purge the house of her remaining possessions, including the photographs the children had in their rooms. Bubbe pocketed her daughter-in-law's jewelry and donated her clothes to the YMHA.

Zelda hadn't had much jewelry: a wedding ring, a cameo pin, a delicate gold chain, a gold watch. Aldo had bought the ring, the rest had belonged to Zelda's mother. Orphaned at sixteen, Zelda married Aldo at seventeen, unable to imagine an independent life. She had been an only child of lower-middle-class parents, Jewish shopkeepers who stayed in the neighborhood to be near their store, a kind of precursor to 7-Eleven. She came with a small inheritance, an attraction for Aldo, along with her looks. She was blond, blue eyed, bosomy, slim, with a creamy complexion. Other men admired her. Aldo moved first.

Zelda was useless as a homemaker. She had never done housework. Her family had had a maid in twice a week. Bubbe fumed at her daughter-in-law's incompetence but pitied her too. Zelda spent her days recumbent and pregnant. In four years, she had three children.

"The doctors fried her brains," Lila told Joe. *Get it all out there,* she thought. *Get it done with.* "Bubbe said Aldo was willing to pay extra for the shocks, and if someone would pay, they'd do it." Her voice was flat. "She was only thirty-four when she died. Aldo didn't sit shiva. He didn't say the Kaddish. No minyan. I don't know what Bubbe did. Maybe she went to the synagogue."

"Aldo's glad she's dead," Lila had said to her sister and brother the night Aldo told them she died. "I don't remember her. It's as if she never was."

"She was pretty," Polo said. "She cried a lot. She wanted her mother and father. When she was around, he didn't hit us. He only started hitting us after he put her in the loony bin." Polo stopped, his voice choking. "She was like a prisoner. She would spend the day lying on the couch downstairs, watching television. She loved *The Guiding Light.* At exactly four forty-five, she'd go upstairs to the bedroom. Aldo got home at five. First thing he'd do is go up to see her. He'd come down for supper at five-thirty. Sometimes, she came too. She often had bruises. She said she fell down a lot. She said her big belly made her wobbly."

"Did she tuck us in?" Lila said.

"No, Aldo kept her in the bedroom after supper."

"Did she ever leave the house?"

"Only to go to doctors." Polo lowered his voice. "She told me once she liked going to the doctors. I thought that was crazy. 'Don't they give you shots?' I said. She held her finger to her lips. 'Aldo's afraid of them.'"

Two days after Zelda's death, Bubbe came downstairs wearing her daughter-in-law's jewelry. "She would have wanted me to have it," she said, "for looking after you three."

"No, she wouldn't," Lila said. "I don't think she liked you. No one likes you."

Bubbe cuffed her on the side of her head. "You think you're so smart, Miss Lila. Watch out or Aldo will put you in the Eloise."

"I didn't think you cared if anyone liked you." Lila rubbed her ear. "You don't act like you do." Bubbe cuffed her again. "You don't learn, do you."

"Do you like us?" Lila dug her hands into her pants' pockets, feeling for her knife.

Bubbe lowered her hand, which had been poised for a third cuffing. "I feed you, I keep you in clothing, I take you to the doctor, to the library. That will have to pass for liking you." She looked hard at her granddaughter. "Do you think I wanted to spend my old age taking care of three children and their do-nothing mother. Do you think I like cleaning, doing the laundry, cooking meals, all day long, day after day."

"Why do you do it?" Lila said.

"My grandmother took care of me after my mother died. It's what you do." Bubbe leaned down to plump a pillow. "My generation, we didn't have choices. I had to drop out of school in sixth grade to work. I worked as a maid." She stood up stiffly. "I'm still a maid."

"I wish you had a nicer life," Lila said.

"Wish, wish. Wishes make nothing happen." Bubbe plumped another pillow. "You need to watch your mouth."

"Do you ever buy yourself something?" Lila said. Bubbe had four cotton everyday dresses she wore in strict rotation and one shiny black dress for synagogue.

"Who do you think I am, Henry Ford?" Bubbe lowered her voice. "Aldo's cheap."

Lila lowered her voice as if they were conspiring. "Was Zelda really insane?"

"There was something wrong. Crying, crying, crying, and the shock treatments didn't help." Bubbe plumped the pillow again. "She said Aldo was a beast. It's true. What could I do."

"Was she insane from the beginning?" Lila kept her voice low.

"No. She had a bit of a smart mouth, not as smart as yours, but Aldo didn't like it. He showed he was the boss. At the end, she never talked, she only cried."

"How did she die?"

"I don't know." Bubbe shook her head.

"Did you ever visit her?"

"No." Bubbe looked away. "Aldo had told them no visitors, except him. The last day you saw her was the last day I saw her."

"Maybe they electrocuted her."

"That's enough," Bubbe said. "Go do your homework."

The day she left for college, Lila stole back her mother's jewelry. She didn't take the ring. Aldo had bought that. She gave her sister, Clara, the watch and cameo and told her to hide them. "Let Bubbe think I have them," she said. She kept the necklace. She wore it all the time, never taking it off. In moments of distraction, she would run her fingers along the delicate links.

In the early weeks after Zelda's death, Lila spent Saturdays looking for her grave in Hebrew Memorial Park. She was systematic, walking the original synagogue allotments, Beth Joseph, Pinsker, Zhitomer, B'nai Moshe. *This is religious, I'm being religious,* she thought, as she wandered among the tombstones, many inscribed in

Hebrew. No one in the family went to services except Bubbe, who went on the High Holy Days and sat upstairs. Her brother hadn't been bar mitzvahed, a local scandal. Aldo wouldn't pay the fees. At Bubbe's insistence, he'd been circumcised.

"Who are you to break the chain going back to Abraham," she had said to her son.

Lila read Exodus three times. That was the aleph-and-tav of her Jewish education, Jews who fought back.

To take the bus to Hebrew Memorial, she stole a dollar from Aldo's wallet. Her grandmother would have noticed if she'd stolen from her. Bubbe kept her money in her brassiere during the day, under her pillow at night.

The cemetery was in Oak Park. Lila had never crossed Eight Mile Road before. Later she thought of it as a rite of passage. "Literally," she said. In that first crossing was the final one, the day she left home for the University of Michigan and turned her back on Grand Street.

After eight weeks of searching, Lila gave up. She never asked the caretakers for help. She was afraid they'd ask her name and call her father. Some months later, she asked her grandmother if she'd ever been to Oak Park or the other northern suburbs.

"Why would I want to," Bubbe said. "So many *goyim*."

Bubbe spoke for the community. Most of the old people in the neighborhood had never crossed Eight Mile Road. "We have everything we need here," they said, their mouths tight. "Getting above yourself, aren't you?"

"I'm blowin' this town first chance I get." Lila spoke in her James Cagney voice. She lifted her chin and hitched back her shoulders as if to say *Whadda ya gonna do about it*. She had seen *Angels with Dirty Faces* on TV. Already, at eleven, she was an avid movie watcher. At night when everyone else was asleep, she would sneak downstairs to watch *The CBS Late Movie*. She loved the old black-and-white movies, from the thirties, forties, and fifties, especially gangster movies and movies with tough-talking dames—Rosalind Russell, Barbara

Stanwyck, Bette Davis—but she'd watch anything that was on. Sometimes Polo joined her. She didn't like the baby doll actresses who surfaced in the late fifties and sixties, the Sandra Dees and the Tuesday Welds. She thought them a terrible comedown, like Shirley Temple after Mae West.

"Cute as buttons, dumb as rocks." She squinted at Polo.

"I wouldn't be so hard on them," he said. "You and Clara look just like them. So did Zelda."

Lila gave a low hoot. "You know who Aldo looks like?"

Polo closed his eyes to think. "Little Caesar in *Little Caesar*?"

Lila shook her head, smiling. "Quasimodo in *The Hunchback of Notre Dame*."

Listening to Lila's stories, Joe felt his blood rising, his mind reeling. *What would I do if I ever came face-to-face with Aldo. How did she survive him. Who lets this happen to children.*

"Are you okay?" Lila said.

"Are *you* okay? That's the question," he said.

"I upset you."

"I'm as angry as I've ever been in my life. Aldo is a monster."

"He doesn't stand in my way."

"Was there anything good in your childhood, besides your brother and sister?"

Lila smiled. Joe's heart flipped. "Movies. I was saved by movies."

LILA LOVED MOVIES TO THE end, and, to general amazement, she passed her love on to her daughters. "My legacy, for what it's worth," she said to Joe. Starting when Grace was seven, at least once a week, she would get the girls up at night to watch an old movie on TV. She'd check the TCM listings after she got home from work, and when she spotted "a classic," she'd rouse them. Grace was in ecstasy. The Starbirds were game but they thought she was insane.

"Tell me again why we are watching a movie at two A.M.," Stella said the first time. "We can rent movies."

"We can watch them anytime we want to," Ava said. "We're living in the twenty-first century."

Lila slowly shook her head. "Serendipity. I know what you rent on your own: *Titanic, Home Alone, Forrest Gump,* maybe *Dirty Dancing* or *Back to the Future* if you think you want an 'oldie.' You never heard of the midnight movies." She served refreshments, hot chocolate, popcorn, and peanut M&M's.

Lila invited Joe to join them but he turned her down. "Too late for me. And anyway, I think of it as Girls' Night." He smiled. "You're almost motherly, watching movies with them," he said.

"Curatorial. More Miss Jean Brodie. 'Putting old heads on young shoulders.'"

Over the next several years, until Grace went off to college, they watched scores of movies. Lila started with her favorites: *All About Eve, Born Yesterday, The Third Man, Sunset Boulevard,* and, not to be overlooked, which could so easily have happened, most of the Torchy Blane, Girl Reporter, movies. Stella and Ava liked Katharine Hepburn best. *The Philadelphia Story,* they thought, was perfection, especially the clothes. Grace liked Judy Garland, not in *The Wizard of Oz,* but in *A Star Is Born.*

"What do you like about these movies?" Grace said.

"The women had shoulders," Lila said.

"And faces." Grace looked sideways at Lila.

"Exactly."

WHEN GRACE WAS NINE AND the Starbirds fourteen and fifteen, Lila took the three of them to the Eminem movie *8 Mile.* She cried softly, intermittently throughout. The Starbirds were shocked. They had never seen her cry, not even at *Casablanca.* They had been thrilled to be taken to the movie. It was R-rated. Grace cried along with her mother, riveted and confused.

"They said 'fuck' a hundred times," Stella said, loud enough for her mother to hear.

"What does 'fuck' mean?" Grace poked her sister. "I mean, really mean, besides a curse word."

"Copulation. Sexual intercourse," Ava chipped in. "Having sex."

Grace looked confused.

"Like a man and woman making a baby," Stella said. "Without the baby."

Lila ignored them. "The 'sixty-eight riot in Detroit, in April, after Martin Luther King's assassination, was in my neighborhood." She spoke in her dead voice, as she wiped her eyes. "I walked to school past burnt-out buildings. The house next door to ours was torched." She got up from her seat. "Jews lived in the south then. As Blacks moved in, Jews moved out, resegregating." She blew her nose.

Stella wanted to shake Lila. "Why are you crying?"

"You're nothing like Eminem," Ava said. "You can't sing."

A scary thought ricocheted across their brains. *She's having a nervous breakdown, like Zelda.*

Wanting to join in, Grace burst out, "You don't have any tattoos. You don't rap."

"Borrowed nostalgia," Lila said. "Crossing Eight Mile was a big deal."

Stella and Ava exchanged a look.

Lila saw it. "C'mon. Give me a break. People cry at new movies. It's the throbbing music. They mean for you to cry, not like the oldies, where the actors break your heart." She turned to Grace. "Why were you crying?"

"I was embarrassed for you," Grace said. "I thought if two of us cried, no one would think you were weird."

"I am weird," Lila said. "You too, kiddo." She looked at Grace appraisingly. "'Where the going gets weird, the weird turn pro.'"

The next morning at breakfast, yesterday's pizza, Grace asked her mother what it was like growing up in Detroit. It was not even six. Dawn was their time. They were the early risers, light sleepers, sufferers of recurring bad dreams.

"Better than Beirut," Lila said. "Better than Southeast Asia."

"Were you ever mugged?" Grace said.

"No. Local code of honor. No mugging girls, not even the gang members, except not always."

"When did you last see your father?"

"The day before I left for college. That night, he beat me, a going-away present to remember him."

"Why?"

"There was no 'why' with Aldo. He hit me so hard, I slammed into a door and broke a tooth."

"Did he just hit you, out of the blue?"

"What are you?" Lila laughed. "My biographer?"

"I want to know what happened before he hit you."

"I said I saw the *shiksa* take a hundred dollars from his wallet, which she did. Not that I was one to talk, but I was blood."

Grace opened the notebook she carried everywhere and wrote down *Shiksa?* Then she wrote down *Delicate Gold Chain*. "Why do you do that thing with your fingers?" she said. Between coffee swallows, Lila had been kneading the chain on her neck. "You have funny fingers."

"Do I?" Lila said.

"Yes." A disciple of Harriet the Spy, Grace took in everything Lila did. She kept track in the notebook. Years later, she'd say to Ruth, "I wasn't so much spying on Lila as majoring in Lila." Ruth gave her a long look. "I think you were spying."

"It reminds me of how much I hate my father," Lila said.

"How much do you hate him?" Grace wondered what she'd say. *How much can you hate someone, to the moon and back?*

"If he was standing next to Hitler and I was told I could only shoot one of them . . ." Lila pointed her fingers, gun-like, at the clock on the wall. "I'd have to kill Hitler, I know that, but I'd be torn."

"Did he beat you a lot? Did he use a belt?"

"Until I was thirteen, he beat me maybe once a week, hand, belt, chair. He tapered off then. Polo had had it. He was still living at home, but he was out most evenings, night classes. He'd gotten big, strong, angry. One night at dinner, Aldo smacked me for mentioning Zelda. Polo leaped up from the table and punched him in the head, pop, pop, pop, like a boxer. 'You hit her again,' he said, 'I'll beat you to a pulp.' After that, Aldo picked his moments carefully."

"Why did he beat you? You were the littlest. Were you the scapegoat?"

"When I was really little, he hit me about the same as the others but by the time I was seven, eight, nine, your age, I'd goad him when he was in a lousy mood so he'd take it out on me and not Polo or Clara. He needed to hit someone. I stepped up. After a while, it became a habit, for both of us." She took a swallow of coffee. "Polo and Clara were scared of him. They'd known him longer. They saw him beat Zelda. Polo said it was like beating a newborn puppy. He left marks on her skin. I didn't want to be scared the way they were. Better to be beaten than scared. A beating stops, being scared doesn't. Take it and get on." She fiddled with her chain. "You have to remember to breathe. You have to focus on the breathing. Don't think, just breathe. It gets you through."

"'What doesn't kill you makes you stronger,'" Grace said.

Lila stared at her daughter. "Who's been feeding you that drivel?"

"Nietzsche. He went mad. The Starbirds read it in Bartlett's *Quotations*."

"What does not kill you makes you furious. If you're going to quote, quote poetry."

"'Nevermore.'" Grace shot Lila a sly smile.

"Attagirl. Time for school."

Grace took a last bite of pizza. "Doesn't the necklace remind you of Zelda too?"

"I don't remember her. I was too young." Lila ran her fingers along the chain. "I sometimes wonder if she really was crazy. Maybe she just needed a job. Maybe she didn't want any more children. So many years ago."

"Maybe she ran away like Dicey Tillerman's mom in *Homecoming*. She left Dicey and her other children in a parking lot at a mall. She was catatonic." Grace gave a sharp nod, a mental exclamation point.

"The Case of the Disappearing Mother," Lila said. "It sounds scary."

"It was very scary but it worked out at the end. Did you ever visit Zelda at the mental hospital?"

Lila shook her head. "No. We weren't allowed."

"Did you go to her funeral?"

"No. Aldo didn't tell us she was dead until she was buried."

"Wasn't that suspicious." Grace's eyebrows took a dive. "Do you think she was really dead?"

Lila nodded. "Dead as a doornail."

Grace stood up, excited. "Maybe she isn't. Maybe she's been watching you, from a distance, never letting on she's alive."

"That sounds more like a fairy godmother than a mother."

"Amnesia," Grace said. "Maybe she had amnesia."

Lila shook her head again. "Dead."

Grace's eyebrows dived again. "I'll tell you what I think. If she's dead, Aldo killed her."

"Interesting theory," Lila said. "I see why you could think that."

3

Love

LILA AND JOE MET IN LATE SEPTEMBER 1976, AT THE START OF HER freshman year at Michigan and his first year in the law school. He was her TA in Modern European History, moonlighting to escape the boredom and drudgery of Civil Procedure. She liked him. He had no edge. He liked her. She was all edge.

They often talked after section, in the hallway.

"How come you get to teach history?" she said to him the first time they spoke. He leaned over slightly. He was tall and lanky, a good ten inches taller than she.

"Graduate school dropout. I couldn't face the thesis," he said.

"What were you planning to write about?"

"The German resistance in World War Two."

"Germans resisted? You mean like the generals who plotted to kill Hitler?"

"Ordinary people, like those French farmers in *The Sorrow and the Pity*. Some were antisemites. Anti-Hitler antisemites."

"How many could there have been?" She looked at him sideways. *Is he putting me on?* she thought.

"You'd be surprised," he said. "There were as many German resisters as French. The best estimate is half a million."

"You're Jewish, right?" she said. "The Maier part threw me off, the 'i' instead of a 'y.' Very classy."

"My grandfather Meyer changed the 'y' to 'i,' also the first 'e' to 'a,' when he turned twenty-one. My grandmother said he was 'unshtetling' himself. She was German Jewish. He married up." Joe's eyebrows rose and fell. "He left the Orthodox synagogue the same year. He wanted to spend his Saturdays at the track." He gave her a half smile. "Are you Jewish? Pereira?"

"Sephardic," she said. "Portuguese." She smiled. His heart seized. "I've never been to synagogue. I've never said a Hebrew prayer. I know many Yiddish words, insults, curses, and complaints. From my grandmother. She spoke Yiddish as if it were a language and not a Catskills joke."

At the end of the term, Lila asked him if they were ever going to go on a date.

"Are you taking the second semester course?" he said.

"Yes," she said.

"Then, no," he said.

"Why not?" she said.

"The others in the class will think you're getting special treatment. They'll hate us both."

"It sounds like you've been burned."

"Well, you're not the first student to ask me out, though you're the only one who waited until grades were in." He smiled. "You're not like other people."

"You don't know the half of it," she said.

By the time they went on their first date, in May, they'd talked about everything but sex and Lila's childhood. They liked each other before they loved each other, although Joe was smitten from the beginning.

Lila insisted on paying half the bill on their first date. "I don't like to be indebted. If I had enough money, I'd pay the whole thing, and then you'd be indebted to me." Her face grew serious. "I grew up poor. I still am, though not as poor as I was." She smiled. "I have a benefactor. An anonymous donor sends money every month. I'd have to work twice as many hours without it." Her face grew serious again. "They take the poorest students, from the worst high schools, the ones who never took an AP test or prep course for the SAT, and make them work. It's as if they're setting us up to fail." She gave a slight headshake, as if swatting away a mosquito. "If I didn't have a bene-factor, I'd have to work twenty hours a week."

"Do you know who it is?" he said.

"No."

"Do you have an idea who it could be?"

"Henry Ford."

Joe looked confused. "Family joke," she said.

"Do you think it's a relative?" he said.

"My mother is dead. My father would burn money before he gave it to me. My grandmother has no money."

"Don't you want to know?"

Lila shook her head. "I don't want to have to give it back."

"Save your money," Joe said. "I've got money, my family has money. Not from Henry Ford. Alfred P. Sloan." He shrugged. "But that's beside the point. I'm going to marry you."

"How can you know that?" she said. "We've never kissed."

"I knew it the day I met you," he said. "It was in the stars."

LILA AND JOE WERE AN odd couple, physically and temperamentally. He was tall, six foot two, lean, rangy. She was five foot three, curvy, compact. He was easygoing, thoughtful, slow to anger, forgiving. She was decisive, tough-minded, unafraid, driven. He said he tempered her steel. She said she raised his ruckus.

On their twenty-fifth anniversary, Grace, eleven, asked Lila why she had married Joe.

"You're so different," she said. "What do you have in common?"

They were at a restaurant, celebrating, the five of them. The Starbirds sat up straight, waiting to see what Lila would say, *in front of Joe, no less.*

Lila smiled. "Isn't it obvious? Don't you all want a partner like Joe? The best."

"It isn't obvious," Grace said. "You're too different." She bristled at being put off.

"He's smart, he's interesting, he's generous, but that could be said about other men." Lila ran her finger along her necklace. "The *sine qua nons:* I trusted him from the minute I met him. He told me how the world works. I knew nothing of the world when I met him. And then, like the song, 'It's in his kiss.'"

"What about his family's money, did that figure?" Grace said.

Faced with a hostile question, Lila always answered straight, no use even getting annoyed. "I fell for him when he was driving an old Chevy station wagon and wearing cords and Michigan sweatshirts. I thought he was middle class, upper middle class. What did I know about the rich, except from the movies. He said his family was 'comfortable.' That's the word the rich use. I didn't know he was really rich until he took me home sophomore year to meet his mother. It was a shocker."

Lila's first trip to Bloomfield Hills had been eye-popping. As they drove up the driveway, she had burst out, "You grew up at Tara," half in jest, half in astonishment. The house had eight sixteen-foot columns along the portico. "I asked him if a butler would open the door for us. He didn't answer."

"I should have warned you," Joe said. "The other girls I dated knew more or less what to expect from Bloomfield Hills." He gave a glimmer of a smile. "It's an embarrassment of riches."

Out of the presence of Joe's benevolent mother, Lila fell into calling the house Tara. Years later, her daughters would take up the name sincerely, loving it for its trapdoors and hidden rooms, its back stairs and pocket doors, its canopy beds and feather comforters, and, best of all, its huge center hall stairway with fleur-de-lis carpeting, "the wedding runway," they called it.

Lila took a swallow of wine, a full-bodied red. She never drank white. "There wasn't a butler but there were two maids, a house-keeper, and a cook." She put down the glass. "The food was what got me. Mayonnaise was a revelation. I'd only ever eaten Miracle Whip, which tasted like lemon marshmallows. Then there were the foods I'd never seen or even heard of: artichokes, asparagus, endive, avoca-dos, oysters, goat cheese. And those weren't even the main dishes." She took a bite of her miso cod. "What is miso?" she said.

"Fermented soy," Grace said. Everyone stared at her. "What," she said, exasperated with them all. "Everyone eats Japanese food these days. Sushi is my favorite food."

"I was forty before I ate sushi," Lila said. "I like it, but not as much as fresh oysters, which I also didn't eat until I was forty."

"I can't eat them. They look like wads of spit," Grace said.

Stella stared at her. "Oversharing."

Ava made a face. "Yuck."

"No they don't," Lila said. "I know from spit. Aldo was a spitter. He spit everywhere, the street, the kitchen floor. 'Man of the house, does what he likes,' he'd say."

Grace took out her notebook, always about her, and started writ-ing. *Aldo was not only mean, he was disgusting.*

In time, Lila became used to Tara as she became used to the other trappings of the rich. As *The Globe*'s executive editor, she had a car with a driver who drove her to and from work every day. She had an expense account that included a clothing allowance, and a salary beyond her needs or desires, though not as large as Joe's, which hit seven figures. At fifty, he was elected managing partner of his law firm, Sanger, Booth, Benett & Zimmerman, his low-key style scut-tling the competition.

"First time they elected a criminal lawyer," he said, laughing when he called Lila to tell her. "We bring in so much business these days."

"I hope they don't raise your salary," she said.

"You sound like my mother," he said.

Lila was discomfited by the Maiers' wealth. She feared her daughters, GM heirs, would become entitled, spoiled, showy. The year after she was named executive editor, she set up trusts for Grace and the Starbirds. "I want them to look out for other people," she said to Joe. Starting when each girl turned eleven, she had them give away 10 percent to charities of their choosing. "It's called tithing, a way of thinking about our great good luck." Stella and Ava gave to animal rescue organizations. Grace gave to food banks and abortion rights organizations.

"Can you believe it," she said to Lila. "There are people who would make an eleven-year-old girl have a baby."

Joe spent money, when he spent it, on things: high-end audio systems, cars, and sports equipment. His parents had bought him his first suit at Brooks Brothers, and he never left them. Lila spent money on activities: dinners, movies, books, and theater. Frances bought her the expensive suits. Lila thought of Joe's interests, "hobbies" he called them, as signifiers of the rich. Her interests were aspirational, the working-class girl pressing her nose against the candy store window.

"The differences between us weren't simply economic, though those were huge," she said, twirling her wineglass, as if to say, *case in point*. The wine tasted expensive. Joe always ordered the wine. "They were cultural, political, social." She spoke deliberately, accentuating each word. "In short, anthropological." The girls looked confused. "The rich aren't different from the rest of us simply because they have more money. Don't fall for that old canard. They're different in almost every way." Holding the wineglass by the stem, she swirled the wine. "Of course, the money makes the other differences possible."

"What are you talking about," Stella said.

"I don't get it," Ava said. "It's not the money, it is the money."

Grace turned to them. "You're not listening." She sounded annoyed. They stared at her.

"For example," Lila said. "Joe grew up skiing and rowing and playing squash and lacrosse and tennis, activities as foreign to me as avocados. I learned to swim in high school. I didn't know how to ride a bike when I got to Michigan." She took a swallow of wine. "Joe taught me, the way he taught you three."

Grace opened her notebook and wrote: *Lila married the man who taught her to ride a bike.* In her seventh-grade English class, her teacher had said, "In books, characters say the most important thing first, unless it's a mystery. In real life, people hold back, saving the important thing for last." Grace continued writing. *Lila doesn't get scared, she doesn't feel sorry for herself, she doesn't cry except at movies with pounding music. What else does she doesn't?*

JOE AND LILA AGREED THEY'D marry, after her Michigan graduation, at Tara. It was a huge pile, over eight thousand square feet, with twelve bedrooms, sixteen bathrooms, a conservatory, a saltwater pool, a cabana, and a tennis court. The front windows on the portico, behind the columns, were two stories high.

"What's a conservatory?" Lila had said to Joe, during her first visit.

"A greenhouse with furniture, a kind of indoor-outdoor living room," he said. "It has special windows, jalousies. They're windows that look like Venetian blinds." During their Michigan years, Joe would tease that he'd become the Village Explainer. On their third date Lila had said to him, "You need to tell me everything you know. I only know Detroit. I'll never get on unless I get smarter."

"You're smart enough," he said. "Don't confuse money with brains."

"I knew your folks had money," she said. "I didn't know they had loot."

"My mom's family. Her father was the comptroller of GM, for forty years, Henry Fieldstone, originally Feldstein," he said. "The money was nothing like it is today, but houses were much, much cheaper. Everything was much, much cheaper."

"Did you drive GM cars then?"

"Buicks and Pontiacs. Cadillacs were too showy," Joe said. "My first car was a muscle car, a neon blue Firebird with fins. So sweet. It's somewhere around here." He waved his hand toward the woods beyond the tennis court. "We have a big garage over there, filled with our old cars. A sort of GM museum. We had a Corvette and a Corvair." He smiled. "No one in the family works for GM these days. My mother drives a Mercedes."

"Why did you drive an old Chevy wagon?" she said.

"No loss if it was stolen," he said.

What would have been a loss for him, Lila thought, *Tara burning?*

With Lila's and Joe's encouragement, his mother, Frances, had taken over the wedding planning. It was a godsend for a woman with no daughters, and Frances did it tactfully and lavishly. Early on, she asked Lila who she wanted to invite. "No limit," she said.

"My siblings and a few friends from Michigan," Lila said.

"You're not inviting your father?" Frances said.

"He's dead," Lila said. *Not a lie. Not entirely. Aldo's dead to me.* "We should invite my grandmother." *I owe her,* she thought. *She didn't call the police on me for stealing Zelda's jewelry.*

"I hope she can come. Family is important," Frances said. She nodded sympathetically, then went looking for Joe. "You might have given me a heads-up," she said. "I knew her mother was dead. I didn't know about her father. She's an orphan."

"Like all heroines," Joe said.

Lila called Clara over Christmas break. "I'm getting married at Tara this summer. It was that or City Hall. The Maiers are very excited. Don't tell Aldo."

"Bubbe is very sick," Clara said. "She had a stroke yesterday. I was going to call. She's incontinent. 'God's final humiliation,' she said. "She's not eating."

Lila didn't know what to feel. Bubbe had had a terrible life, harsh and loveless. They never really talked a second time after the day

Bubbe came downstairs, bedecked in Zelda's jewels, but Bubbe never cuffed her again.

Bubbe died five weeks after her stroke. Clara called the next morning, crying this time.

"Bubbe's dead," she said. "She died yesterday. Aldo wanted to bury her today. Polo and I insisted on a funeral. She had paid for it."

"You always cry for the dead," Lila said.

"I am the designated mourner," Clara said. "She gave me a wedding present for you. A crystal vase that was Zelda's mother's. She said it was worth 'fifty dollars, easy.' She kept it on her dresser, with artificial flowers. She said it was good you didn't know about it, or you'd have stolen it too. She was so happy to be invited to your wedding. She had hoped to be invited. She had seen the engagement notice in the newspaper. She showed it to Aldo. He spit on it. 'Do you think she ever thinks of all I did for her.' He works on the GM assembly line and you're marrying GM royalty."

"God bless America," Lila said.

"I'm so glad you invited her. She got so little from life," Clara said. "She left us, Polo and me, cash money. Seventy-five hundred each. She gave it to us maybe two months ago. You could have knocked us over. She told me we should buy a house with the money. 'Leave,' she said. A week later, we bought a house north of Eight Mile. We each put three thousand dollars down. Polo moved in the day we signed the contract. The owners wanted to be gone. I stayed to be with Bubbe. I only left today. I think Aldo expected me to take over the housekeeping. He came by the new place today, to fetch me home. Polo wouldn't let him on the porch. 'If you come by again,' Polo said, 'you'll go home in an ambulance.'" She laughed. "We didn't take anything from Grand Street, except a box of Bubbe's papers and photos. We didn't have to. We're heirs. We bought new beds and down comforters." She stopped, suddenly remembering. "Bubbe said she had looked out for you. Actually, she said she looked out for 'that smart mouth too.' Do you know what she meant?"

Clara's question was a sucker punch. Lila almost dropped the phone. Against all reason, she had thought, secretly, hopefully, delusionally, that Zelda had been her benefactor. *You idiot, you stupid sentimental fantasist,* she told herself, flattened, gutted. *Zelda's dead. Dead as a doornail.*

"I think so," Lila said, breathing out slowly. "Someone's been sending me $150 every month, since I've been at Michigan. Fifty months, $7,500. Had to have been Bubbe. I didn't know who it was. I thought of it as the low-end version of that TV show *The Millionaire,* a mysterious benefactor. It never occurred to me it was Bubbe. She didn't like me."

"Are you okay?" Clara said.

"Knocked me off my pins," Lila said.

"She didn't want us to thank her," Clara said.

"Does Aldo know?" Lila said.

"He's suing us." She laughed. "He's not suing you, as far as I know. He doesn't know if you got money too, and he's afraid of the Maiers."

"Where did she get the money?" Lila said.

"Aldo gave her a salary. She called it her allowance. After Zelda was hospitalized, Bubbe insisted on being paid weekly, 'like the housekeeper you'd need to hire,' she told Aldo." Clara paused to gather her thoughts. "She talked a lot at the end. She said her husband, Guido, Aldo's father, was worse than Aldo. He died of encephalitis at fifty-two. Mosquito bite. She said she went to the burial society to make sure he was dead, then she went to his funeral, to say 'thanks be to God for smiting him.' She saw God's hand in his death. 'Jewish God likes to do the punishing Himself,' she said. 'Guido stepped on God's toes. I think Aldo too.'"

"How'd she save twenty-two thousand dollars?" Lila said.

"She stole from Aldo, like the rest of us, for pocket money," Clara said. "She invested her salary in Procter & Gamble and Kimberly-Clark. 'Always buy stocks in companies that make goods you throw away or use up on a daily basis,' she said to me, almost her final words. 'Toilet paper, Kleenex, all your sanitary pads, Tide. I went through a box of Tide a week.'"

"This is hilarious," Lila said, slowly regaining equilibrium. "Bubbe's secret life as an investor. Did she always mean to give us the money?"

"I asked her," Clara said. "She said, 'Who else would I leave it to? Henry Ford?' I asked her if she had regrets. She said, 'My life is one long regret.'"

"Did she talk about Zelda?" Lila said.

"I asked her once. She shook her head. 'Don't ask.'" Clara sighed. "Bubbe knew she should have stopped Aldo from beating us, she admitted as much, but she was afraid of him. 'Too much like his father, too much like my father,' she said. 'I thought all fathers beat their wives and children. Jews no different from Christians that way. If they tell you differently, they're lying.' Then Bubbe said something very upsetting. She said Polo was 'a ticking time clock.' She said he was upset you were always the one who got the beating. He talked about it a lot, his baby sister taking the beatings for him. He hated what it said about him." Clara's voice broke. Lila waited. "I'm worried about him. He's taking a lot of chances at work, rushing into buildings, totally in flames, that sort of thing. He rescued two children a few weeks ago, from the second floor. He went in a window, black with smoke. They told him not to go. He got a citation and a picture on the front page of the *Detroit Free Press*. I asked him what he thought he was doing. 'You'd be surprised,' he said, 'how many parents run out of a burning building, leaving the kids.'"

FRANCES INVITED EVERYONE IN HER address book to the wedding, including the second cousins once removed. She held it in the back garden, under a tent. *Gatsbyesque,* Lila thought, gazing up at the chandeliers Frances had had installed. Lila had agreed to the chan-

deliers, also the lobster and the ten-piece band. Joe had thought Lila
might bristle at the excess.

"Let her have her wedding," Lila said. "She's so happy."

Lila drew the line once, at the synagogue. The Maiers belonged
to Temple Beth-El in Detroit, the oldest synagogue in Michigan. Joe
had had his bar mitzvah there. Frances was secretly relieved. With a
temple wedding, she'd have had to order buses to ferry the guests to
and from the house. *Too much mishigas,* she thought. *Lila's Jewish.
She's pretty. She's smart. That's enough to stop the yentes.*

"I'm agreeing to a rabbi for you, this once," Lila said to Joe. "My
plan is never to step foot in a synagogue, except for funerals. Not
mine, of course." They were lolling on lounge chairs at the side of the
pool, talking over the wedding plans.

"Won't we raise the children Jewish?" Joe said.

"What children?" Lila said, her stomach rising to her throat. "Are
we having children?" She sat up straight and stared at him.

Joe stared back, "I'd like two," he said. "I was an only child. Most
married people have children."

"No sane person would have children with me." She sank back
into the chair, her mind somersaulting, not wanting children, not
wanting to disappoint Joe. *How could he not know I wouldn't want
children,* she thought. *All the Aldo stories.*

"I'm stunned. I never expected this," she said.

"You would do it right," Joe said. "You wouldn't beat them."

She shook her head. "I know nothing about being a mother."

"You'd come to love them," he said.

"I can't do it." She shook her head. Joe looked as if he'd been
slapped. "I could do pregnancy and childbirth, my body could take it,
but I can't see myself raising them. You'd have to do it on your own."
Joe's shoulders slumped. "With help of course," she said, her insides
churning. "They can each have their own nanny. I'll read to them at
bedtime."

As a child, Lila had always wanted someone to read to her. Polo said that Zelda had sometimes read to him, not children's books, but the books she was reading. "She had a book called *Marjorie Morningstar.* I stole it from their bedroom after she went away. I still have it."

Joe took in a deep breath and let it out slowly.

"Okay," he said. "Me and nannies."

"I won't breast-feed." After her first concession, her willingness to accommodate subsided and her position hardened, as with the rabbi and the synagogue.

"Okay," he said. "Formula."

"I won't take them to the doctor except in emergencies, I won't hire the help." Joe nodded. "I can drop them off at school in the morning." She lowered her voice to press the point. "I'm not fit to be a mother. I'll make sure I earn enough money to pay for the nannies and everything." She took his hand. "You'll be a wonderful father. You'll be enough. In the nineteenth century, lots of men brought up their children alone. Women died in childbirth all the time." She nodded, more to reassure herself than Joe. "I'm floundering. I feel awful. I can't do it."

"We'll talk more," he said, squeezing her hand. "Money isn't an issue. The GM trust fund will take us to 2050 at least and then there'll be the disbursement." He let go of her hand and sat back in the chair. *Why am I surprised when I shouldn't have been. The question is: Do I want to do it alone?*

"We'll have two, close together," Lila said, "so they'll have each other." She brightened. "Maybe I'll get lucky and have twins."

Instead of Dr. Spock, Joe gave Lila Don Marquis's *The Lives and Times of Archy and Mehitabel.*

STELLA WAS BORN IN 1987, Ava in 1988. Lila thought she was finished. Grace, born in 1993, was an accident.

"Fine by me, I'd like a third," Joe said. "Maybe it will be a boy, maybe it will look like me." He laughed. "I think I've got the hang of it now. Take nothing personally. Five- and six-year-old girls, all over the country, are stamping their feet and bossing their dads, in between the marriage proposals."

"Are you sure you want it? I don't have to have it," Lila said. "I've been as good as my word, really as bad, and I'm not going to improve."

Lila had an easy birth with Grace: two hours of labor, two pushes.

"I should have known it was a bad omen," she said to Joe, after one of Grace's adolescent flare-ups. "Easy birth, hard child."

She took two weeks' leave, sleeping in between telephone calls. Morning and night, she looked in on Grace. "She looks like a baby," she said to Joe, who spent his evenings holding Grace and cooing to her. "I forgot how generic they are. Those puffy cheeks and recessive chins."

"Do you want to hold her?" he said.

Lila took Grace into her arms and walked around the room, holding her at arm's length, as if she were the Thanksgiving turkey. "I'm so bad at this," she said. "Are you sorry she's not a boy?"

He shook his head. "I got a Maier, the eyebrows."

Grace proposed to Joe when she was five. She didn't ask, she assumed. "We'll get married and Lila can live at *The Globe*."

Joe was expecting the proposal. At five and six, the twins had proposed, though less confidently.

"Could you have two wives?" Stella said. "Like olden times."

"What about Lila?" Joe said.

"She'll be the grandmother," Ava said. "We won't call her Grandma or Nana. She'll still be Lila."

From the get-go, Lila had her daughters call her Lila, not Mom or Mommy. She'd point to herself and say, "Lila, I'm Lila." They caught on quickly. Soon, they were calling Joe Joe.

Lila never spoke to her daughters in mommy-speak. She never said, "Mommy will be late tonight. She has a meeting." She said, "I'll be late tonight." *Who refers to themselves in the third person, besides royalty.*

Not long after the proposal, Grace, confused and suspicious, took up the matter with Lila. "Why do we call you Lila instead of Mommy?"

"I don't pick up on Mommy," Lila said.

"Are you my real mommy?" Grace said.

"Yes."

"You never call yourself Mommy like the other mommies," Grace said.

"Why would I do that. I know who I am."

"What did you call your mommy?" Grace said.

"I didn't have one." Lila spoke slowly. "I'm making it up as I go along."

"How did you get born?" Grace stared at Lila, her eyes wide, her eyebrows hoisted. "You can't get born without a mommy."

The literal-mindedness of children, Lila thought. *I keep forgetting.* "My mother got sick when I was two. She went to a hospital. I never saw her again."

"Did Clara or Polo call her anything?" Grace said.

"Nothing that I remember when she was . . . around," Lila said. "After she went into the hospital, we called her Zelda. It felt too weird to call her Mom, Mommy, Mother, even my mother. We didn't know her. She was a stranger, a dead stranger."

"What did you call your dad?" Grace said.

"We didn't call him anything to his face. Behind his back, we called him Aldo," Lila said. "I aways wondered what Stalin's children called him."

When she was ten, Grace started calling Lila Mommy.

"Getting my goat, are you," Lila said, after a week.

Grace shook her head. "I was wondering if I'd feel closer to you if I called you Mommy."

"Is it working?" Lila said.

"No," Grace said. "I'm thinking of trying Mama or Mother or"— she looked at Lila sideways—"Mommie Dearest." They'd watched the movie on TV a few weeks earlier.

Lila was silent for several seconds. "If you don't want to call me Lila, you can call me Ms. Pereira."

THE STARBIRDS NEVER THOUGHT TO call Lila anything but Lila. They accepted her as she was. Grace couldn't. Joe sympathized, to a point.

"I know you love her, but I'm not sure Grace does," he said to Lila. They were getting ready for bed. Lila had missed dinner four days running, fallout from her recent appointment as executive editor. Grace kept count. When she was seven, she had started keeping a ledger. In two years, the number of consecutive missed meals grew incrementally but steadily.

"How do you show it to children? I'm not a hugger, or even a head patter. I talk to them, like they're people worth talking to, which they are." She kicked off a shoe. "I want them to thrive. I need them to outlive me. I love watching movies with them." She kicked off the other shoe. "I worry about Grace."

"She'll be a happier adult than child," Joe said.

"She's like me, except prickly and sensitive," Lila said. "She finds me deficient mother-wise. Also defective, which I am."

"She wants a more conventional mother," he said.

"I don't know what those mothers do . . ." She weighed whether to go on. "I like being their mother, platonically speaking. I don't know how to 'mother' them." She fiddled with her chain. "I hate the verb 'parenting.' I'm waiting for 'fathering' to catch hold."

JOE THOUGHT GRACE MIGHT GIVE up her grievance against Lila once she hit puberty. Most teenagers wanted less attention from their mothers. Not Grace. "I know she knows my name," she said to Joe, "but does she love me?" They were having dinner, sushi takeout for the third night in a row, the two of them. Stella and Ava were at Stanford, Stella was a junior, Ava a sophomore. Lila was at *The Globe*. At fourteen, Grace had given up snooping on Lila. It hadn't provided answers. "Does she even like me?"

"She loves you and she likes you," Joe said. "She doesn't know why every conversation she has with you has to be a dogfight."

"Why doesn't she ever come home for dinner?" Grace said. "I have the same dream. I'm drowning. Lila is standing on the side of the pool, watching."

"A bit of a rewrite," Joe said.

"Duh," she said. "I'm talking feelings, not facts."

"You two are too much alike," he said. "You have her humor but not her charm." He ate a piece of sushi. "She wasn't exactly charming when I met her, but she had the potential. Freshman year at Michigan mellowed her a lot." He took a swallow of beer. "Hers is a cultivated charm, a tactical charm, to counter her native ruthlessness." Biding time, he took another swallow of beer. "You might think about cultivating a bit of charm."

"I don't approve of it," Grace said.

"You're angrier than your circumstances would seem to warrant," Joe said.

"There's a hole in my life," Grace said.

"Much smaller than the hole in Lila's," Joe said.

"An absentee mother can be as bad as no mother," she said. "Zelda didn't decide to be a bad mother."

"But Lila has?"

"You know what I mean."

"Keep your anger," Joe said, "but use it to some end. Lila rarely shows anger though we know it's there. Lashing out, unless you're hugely talented, is a losing strategy. Even then . . ."

"I'm going to be a raging, wrathful writer," Grace said. "The second Charlotte Brontë, without that sappy ending."

"I would suggest getting angry on behalf of something other than Grace Maier."

Grace jumped up from her chair. "Why are you lacing into me?" she said.

"You get to reinvent yourself when you go to high school, not entirely of course, too many people know you, but enough to make a difference."

"What do you mean?"

"You might start by easing up on Lila." He nodded, encouragingly. "Give it a try. See if you like it. I'm a great believer in changing from the outside in."

Grace harrumphed. "Lila is all outside."

4

Reporter

DURING HIS THIRD YEAR AT MICHIGAN LAW, JOE LINED UP TWO CLERK-
ships. The first, during Lila's senior year, was at the Federal District
Court in Detroit. The second was at the Sixth Circuit Court of
Appeals in Cincinnati.

"Cincinnati," Lila had said when Joe told her what he'd like to
do. "Who moves to Cincinnati?"

"That was my best shot at a circuit court clerkship," he said.

"How long?" she said.

"Two years," he said. "After that, I follow you."

Lila took stock of the situation and got a job writing obituaries at
The Cincinnati Courier. She started July 7, 1980. She was twenty-
one, green and ambitious. As she walked to work the first day, she
talked to herself, an old habit she called "fronting." *I can do this*, she
thought. *I can write stories about dead people.* She hadn't written for
her college newspaper. She had shelved books in the library and
answered the phone in the English Department.

She arrived at *The Courier*'s offices early. No one was there to
meet her. She sat on a hard bench off the lobby waiting for her new

boss, Frank Quinlan. She spent the time reading *The Courier's* real estate and job ads. *Who lives here?* she thought. *Who reads this paper?*

Quinlan strolled in, smoking a cigar, at 9:40. "Eager are you," he said. "Good."

As they walked to the office—"a mouse hole," he said, "not even a rat hole"—he explained the importance of the department. "The department is a cash cow, second only to the classified pages," he said. "It brings in paid death notices and subscriptions. The citizens of Hamilton County want to die in the pages of their local paper."

The department had two employees—Quinlan and Lila.

"House Rules," Quinlan said as they sat at their desks, side by side.

"First Rule: No pussyfooting. We use 'died,' not 'passed' or 'passed away,' or, God help me, 'passed on' or 'passed over.' Occasionally, a local celebrity will have 'passed away' on the front page, but everyone 'dies' in Obits. Soldiers die. Accident victims die. Children die. It's not a job for the squeamish. Got it?" He gave a sharp nod. "The paid notices are something else. 'You are one of God's Angels.' 'I hope to see you soon.' 'Put in a good word for me.'

"Second Rule: Don't be a patsy. Call the funeral home, make sure the person is dead." Lila started. Quinlan gave a slight nod. "We'll get four or five notices a year for people who haven't died or never lived. Some people's sense of humor.

"Third Rule: No throat clearing. 'Newspapers are written in a hurry, to be read in a hurry.' Get to the point. Quick. First sentence: who, what, where, when, and how. Order doesn't matter. Bang, bang, bang. 'Frank FitzGerald, 93, died at home, on Tuesday, May 12, watching the Bengals lose to the Raiders.' Save the metaphors for your memoir. Use a cliché if you must, but nothing in French. Ate like a pig. Fell like a log. Died like a dog. The last, not in an obit.

"Fourth Rule: Ask questions, don't chatter when you interview the families. Take notes. Tell them you're taking notes. On the phone, ask them to hold on a second while you write it down. It makes them feel heard. It makes them feel important. It loosens the tongue.

Silence always works to the reporter's benefit. It unnerves civilians. They rush to fill it. Vacuum abhorrence.

"Fifth Rule: Play it straight. No sarcasm. No jokes. No puns.

"Sixth Rule: One-syllable words are best. Use one-syllable words over two-syllable words, two over three, three over four.

"Seventh Rule: Around here, we're only rude up, never down."

Lila spent most of the first day filling out forms, touring the building, meeting other staff. Toward the late afternoon, Quinlan assigned her a small obit, Patricia O'Rourke, a retired teacher at Mount Notre Dame High School.

"Time to get your feet wet," he said.

Lila called the family.

"They were very happy I called," she said. "They told me 'Gran was sainted.'" She shook her head slightly. Catholics were a mystery. "Do I say that in the obit? Won't they think I'm making fun?"

"Oh no," Quinlan said. "All Irish grannies are 'sainted.' The other Irish grannies, the living ones, like to read it. They expect their children to say the same of them. Put it in quotes." He looked at her closely. "You're not Irish, are you," he said. "Obituaries are the Irish sports pages, the first section in the paper they turn to in the morning. Who beat the reaper, who didn't." He coughed. "I'm betting Mr. O'Rourke proposed marriage by asking Patty if she wanted to be buried with his people. She had better be sainted." He shook his head. "The best parties I've been to have all been wakes."

On her second day, Lila left home at 9:15, barely beating Quinlan in. As he walked to his desk, he called to her to get him a cup of coffee. She stared at him and went back to her work. He came and stood over her. "I could fire you," he said.

Lila got up, grabbed her purse, and started walking toward the door.

"I didn't say I would, I said I could," he said.

She came back and sat down. "I'm a reporter," she said, "not a waitress. If you want a waitress, repost the job."

"Who do you think you are," he said, "His Girl Friday?"

"Close," she said. "Torchy Blane."

Quinlan pulled his chair next to hers and sat down. "You're too young to know Torchy Blane. I swooned over Glenda Farrell." He leaned back in his chair. "Miss Blane, 'did you know Mr. Craig very well?'"

"'Not well enough to stab him,'" Lila said.

Quinlan roared with laughter, almost tipping over. "I loved that dame."

"I love all dames," Lila said. "I saw *Blondes at Work* when I was ten. After that, I was Lila Pereira, Girl Reporter."

"You're one tough broad," Quinlan said.

"You don't know the half of it," Lila said.

From then on, he called her Hildy and she called him Burns. It was a kind of love story, like the original.

QUINLAN WAS OLD SCHOOL, DOWN to the bourbon bottle in his bottom desk drawer. He rolled up his shirtsleeves, like reporters in the movies. His tie was always loose. He had started in the news business as a copyboy, in 1925, when he was fifteen. "We wore hats then, like G-men," he said. "JFK killed hats. The one thing I can't forgive him for." At *The Courier*, he was an institution, its longest serving reporter and its living memory. He had been a crime reporter, a City Hall reporter, a sportswriter, the sports editor, the city editor, and finally at seventy, unable to face retirement, the editor of the Obits department.

A lapsed Catholic, a lapsed Socialist, and a lapsed husband, Quinlan believed in nothing except newspapers. God was MIA. Life was unfair. People were disappointing. Money was the root of all evil. Lila collected his sayings in a notebook. After he died, she often said them aloud to herself, to hear his voice in her head. "I never met . . ." he would begin.

"I never met a compound complex sentence that didn't show off."

"I never met a good reporter who didn't tip big."

"I never met a real reporter who called himself a journalist."

"I never met a real reporter who consorted socially with the folks he covered."

"I never met a pol who walked past a store window without looking at his reflection."

"I never met a pol who used the urinal in the gents' room without looking left and right, sizing up the competition."

"I never met a rich workingman."

"I never met a boss who didn't think he'd done it all by himself."

MOST OF LILA'S REPORTING WAS on the phone. Quinlan could hear everything she said. During the calls, he'd shake his head and pass notes. Afterward, he'd debrief her.

"You know, you're not interviewing Mrs. Roosevelt," he said when she had stayed on the phone forty minutes, listening to the grieving, garrulous widow of a recently deceased alderman. Twenty minutes earlier, he'd handed her a note.

"What do you know," she said. "If I'd hung up when you started pulling your ear, I'd never have learned he had a slush fund at Hamilton Savings." She picked up her steno pad. "I suppose I can't put that in the obit."

"I'll pass it on to City," he said. "Did she mention any names, bank officers, the like."

"Hey," she said, standing up to stretch. "The City Desk can hire me if it wants my story."

"Did she say anything else?" Quinlan said.

"A young man from Norwood is contesting the will."

"You're annoying me," he said.

"Well, your note to me was rude," she said.

"Not all your long calls pay off like this." He picked up a pencil and examined it. "I'm sorry you thought I was rude."

"He claims he's the son of the alderman," she said. "Mrs. Alderman said he was a nice-looking, well-spoken young man. James Connor. OU grad. 'Not a boy to be ashamed of.' Her own sons, I take it, are a disappointment." Lila looked at her notes. "Young Mr. Connor has letters Mr. Alderman wrote to his mother. He hasn't formally filed yet." She lowered her voice. "I didn't think you were rude. You were rude."

He'd written: *If you're going to waste your time and, incidentally, mine too, do it in the toilets.*

"I should have written 'the Ladies,'" he said.

LILA SPENT TEN MONTHS IN Obituaries under Quinlan's rigorous tutelage. Four weeks after she started, he told her to take ideas to other departments.

"You've got to work on your Obit-exit strategy. I feel I'm a failure if my people don't advance. I'm the best hirer at *The Courier*. The assistant managing editor and the editorial page editor and about twenty others on staff started with me when I was the city chief. Try Features first. They're the most flexible and forgiving. Not Society or Fashion. No lipstick shades, no debutante balls. Stick with shenanigans, stories about local cranks, corrupt politicians, larcenous bankers, high-living preachers." He tapped the side of his nose. "Stay away from the restaurant linen and carting businesses. Got it?" He tapped his nose again. "Keep submitting ideas. Don't argue about the ones they reject. Give 'em new ones. Wear 'em down. After Features, do Sports. The same kind of men own sports teams and newspapers."

Lila made the front page on October 18, 1981, after eight months of "wearing 'em down," when she interviewed the brother of a nurse at Mercy Hospital accused of murdering seven patients. "I'm not surprised," his brother said. "When he was fifteen, he drowned a litter of kittens." The headline was NO ANGEL OF MERCY.

In her last week in Obits, Lila wrote up the death of a local celebrity. Quinlan let a quote go in even though it violated the Fifth

Rule. "Janie Buckley died in the arms of her grieving third husband. 'I was sure I'd die first,' he said. 'Me, too,' she said."

Lila loved everything about *The Courier,* except her salary, not a sticking point for a rookie. She loved the dingy offices, the down-at-heel reporters, the down-at-mouth editors, the flashy coverage, the seventy-two-point headlines, the endemic gallows humor. *I was born to do this,* she thought.

Quinlan dropped dead of a heart attack walking home from work on August 3, 1982, a week before Lila decamped for D.C. Earlier in the day, they had had lunch at Smokey's, "the only lunchroom in this town an honest newsman drinks in," he said. His wake went on for twenty-four hours. No one knew how the paper got published the next day. Lila was one of three reporters on the paper to give a eulogy at his funeral. Quinlan had left instructions. "No crying. Got it?" Her heart ached but she didn't cry. His obit ran on the front page, below the fold. They gave him a photo. He was wearing his hat pushed back on his head.

AFTER THEIR TWO YEARS IN Cincinnati, Lila and Joe moved to D.C. Joe had a job in the Solicitor General's Office. Lila didn't have a job yet, but she had two interviews lined up, one at *The Washington Globe,* one at *The Washington Times. The Washington Post* had passed, earning Lila's lifelong enmity. Quinlan had made calls. "The best young reporter I've ever raised up. She has the nose," he told the city editor at *The Globe.* "She doesn't cross any lines, but she could report for a Murdoch paper." He paused. "Don't judge her on her looks."

Lila was a knockout. She was Brigitte Bardot without the pout, short, blond, shapely. Well into her forties, she made heads turn. The twins' boyfriends swooned over her. "A MILF, if I ever saw one," Stella's high school steady said. Stella and Ava had their mother's looks, but like most copies, they were dimmer. Clara looked like her too, a wholesome, athletic version. Grace was Joe's child.

Lila's first interview was at *The Globe*. She wore a beautiful navy Armani pantsuit. Frances had bought it for her. "Dress for the job you want," Frances had said. Lila accepted it as graciously as she could. "Wow," she said. "I didn't think he made clothes for short people." Lila had trouble thanking. Also apologizing.

The interview with the city editor, Mike D'Angelo, was short.

"Quinlan didn't tell me you looked like Goldie Hawn, the girl I'd never get." He held up his hand, palm forward, as if backing away from the comment. "I say this because from what he said about you, I expected Lois Lane."

"Camouflage," Lila said.

"What kind of name is Pereira?" he said. "It's not Italian. Is it Spanish?"

"Portuguese," Lila said.

"And the blond hair?" he said.

Who can be bothered with these cretins, Lila thought. "Swedish mother," she said, telling a lie she'd tell the rest of her life.

Mike held up his hand again. He was the kind of guy whose conscience was always a step behind his mouth. "You have to meet the big guy. Not too many women in our operation. He's comfortable around men. Big mouth. Dirty mouth. Funny as hell." He gave her a smile bordering on a leer. "He likes blondes."

Lila didn't find Jim Bramble funny, then or ever. "He's one of those men who like 'fuck' jokes," she said to Joe. "'On the fuckin' couch in the fuckin' office, the fuckin' fucker had sexual intercourse.'" Lila never told jokes, she had a fast comeback. "Guerrilla humor," Joe called it.

"Mike gave you the thumbs-up," Bramble said. "You'll be our fifth female reporter." He looked briefly at her résumé. "So, what's your strength?"

"I'm Woodward and Bernstein. I can interview and I can write," she said.

"How do you interview?" he said.

"I ask then I wait," she said.

He looked at her résumé again. "What job do you want? What department?"

"Now?" she said. He nodded.

"Congress. The House," she said. "Careless men. Good copy."

"And in, say, ten years?" he said.

"Sports editor," she said. Bramble raised an eyebrow.

"I want to expose the NCAA," she said, "then the International Olympics Committee, then FIFA."

Bramble laughed.

"And in, twenty years," he said.

"Your job," she said.

LILA KNEW THE EFFECT SHE had on men, not only the crass ones. "Gentlemen prefer blondes," she would say, shrugging, acknowledging the foolishness and usefulness of it.

"You trade on your looks, don't you," Grace said to Lila one morning. They were having one of their 6:00 A.M. breakfasts: black coffee for Lila, warmed-over pizza for Grace. Fifteen was a hard age for Grace, also for her parents. She regularly started the day spoiling for a fight. "Some feminist."

"My looks may have gotten me interviews," Lila said. "They didn't get me jobs." She took a swallow of coffee. "I suppose I have relied on my looks. Some people had connections, I had blond hair." She took another swallow. "I can't help my looks. I had nothing to do with them."

Grace glared at her mother, offended and disgusted. She was reading *The Beauty Myth*, her first incursion into feminism.

"That's disgraceful," Grace said. "It's so unfair. Genetics roulette." Tall and gawky, she was opinionated and angry, mostly at Lila but also at the patriarchy.

"It's racist," Lila said, "part of the preference for light people over darker ones."

"Intelligence should count for something," Grace said.

"Brains are inherited too," Lila said. "You got a first-rate brain from

Joe. I got mine . . . probably from Zelda. Aldo's as thick as board." She took a long swallow of coffee. "I know I got her looks. Clara, too."

"I got Joe's looks and brains," Grace said. They were the outliers, Joe and Grace, tall, thin, brown haired, and gray eyed, with high cheekbones and swashbuckling eyebrows, like Frida Kahlo's but less aggressive. "Stella and Ava are third-generation petite blondes. I'm the un-Pereira," she said. "Also, the anti-Pereira."

"I love your looks." Lila ignored the barb. "I love Joe's."

"You're, you're . . . missing the point." Grace stumbled over the unexpected compliment. "Women torture their bodies to please men. Look at all the women's magazines, article after article on breast implants, face-lifts, liposuction, diets, thousands of diets. Your newspaper too." She stopped to catch her breath. "Every year hundreds of women die of anorexia, trying to look like models."

"Hold on a minute," Lila said. "Anorexia is an illness. It's no more a beauty regimen than obsessive-compulsive hand washing is a hygiene one. Those women and girls need medical help." She took a sip of coffee. "It's not so easy starving yourself, kiddo. It takes dedication." She shook her head. "What is it with women, it's always their doing, their fault." She picked up the book and pointed to the author's photo. "Naomi Wolf is beautiful. Only a beautiful woman could have written that book. A plain woman would have been accused of sour grapes."

"That is so reductive, so dismissive." Grace squinted at Lila, her eyebrows lowering in pique.

Lila was quiet for several seconds. "If I got in the door at *The Globe* on my looks—which I didn't, Quinlan got me in—I got the job because Bramble said I 'clanked' when I walked."

"What does that mean?" Grace said.

"'Iron balls.'"

IN LILA'S SECOND YEAR AT *The Globe,* during a department meeting on sexual harassment in the Senate, one of the men standing behind

Lila put his hand down her pants and stroked her bottom. She reached behind her, caught his hand, and held it up.

"Does anyone know whose hand this is," she said loudly so everyone could hear. "I found it on my ass."

The men in the room laughed nervously, the women, all eight of them, gasped, then applauded.

The reporter who'd been caught out pulled his hand free. "I was making a joke," he said. "Irony."

"You've got a problem then," Lila said. "Everyone knows women don't have a sense of humor."

The meeting was suspended, along with the reporter. The men in the room, gropers and nongropers alike, were caught off guard. They counted on women not making scenes in public.

"That was funny what you did, but also embarrassing," the chief said.

"It was insulting," Lila said. "I wasn't embarrassed. Why were you? Who were you embarrassed for?"

DOUG MARSHALL TOOK OVER AS publisher on January 1, 1990. Lila first came to his attention six months later with a pair of stories on a glossary of invective, *Language: A Key Mechanism of Control*, published by GOPAC the summer before the 1990 elections. The Republican minority whip, Newt Gingrich, had drawn up a list of his choicest slurs and insults. Members who wanted to "write like Newt" were encouraged to consult the list. Lila got a copy off a staff assistant.

The original story included a short paragraph using thirteen of the words. She wrote it straight, abiding by the Quinlan rule forbidding sarcasm.

If we didn't know how **sick** they are, we might think Democrats were simply **bizarre** and **pathetic.** In fact, they're **selfish, greedy,** and **shameless liars** who feed on rotting **decay.** Their

platform is to **destroy** the American way of life, **corrupt** its
shining youth, and **betray** our freedom and our flag. They are
radicals and **traitors.**

THE GLOBE PUBLISHED THE STORY in the Sunday edition, in a box on
the front page of *The Weekly Review.* Two days later, at a town hall in
his home district, a Republican congressman used Lila's paragraph
as his opening remarks. The crowd gave him a standing ovation.

She wrote a follow-up article, which appeared the next day on
the front page. The header read: GLOBE REPORTER "GHOSTWRITES"
CONGRESSMAN'S SPEECH.

Doug sent her a note. "Newt owes you one."

Eight years later, Doug noticed her work for a second time. He
called her in. She was on the White House beat. The story was going
around the newsroom that Lila had heard about Monica Lewinsky
and had passed the information to a colleague who made the front
page three weeks later.

"How'd you get the story?" Doug said.

"When Lewinsky was moved over to the Senate, an aide there
gave me the scuttlebutt," she said. "Men are the worst gossips."

"Why didn't you cover the story?" he said.

"I'm not interested in sex scandals. I made sure the story was
covered, just not by me."

"Because you're a woman?" he said. "You passed it on to a man."

"I knew it was a big story," she said. "I didn't want to spend the next
year interviewing young women who had had exploitative sexual relations with their aging bosses." He gave a slight nod. "It told us nothing
about Clinton we didn't already know. Ditto Hillary. Ditto starstruck
twenty-one-year-olds." Lila shook her head. "Also, because I'm a
woman. I could see getting pigeonholed, the way a man wouldn't. Sexual assault, sexual harassment, they're not my beat. I'm a political
reporter and this story isn't political, whatever the political repercussions. I'm talking facts, I'm talking plot. This story is not so different

from one about a female student teacher and a male school principal, or a young actress and a big-time movie producer. If I'm going to break a big story, I want to break one like Watergate or Abscam."

"You're ambitious," Doug said. "Tough too."

"You don't know the half of it," she said.

After this meeting, Doug started having monthly lunches with Lila, taking her measure. Bramble would retire in three years. Doug needed to find a successor, preferably an insider. A woman might be the ticket, an outsider-insider. Within a year, Lila became the front-runner. She understood. She would show Doug her mettle. *I'm front-ing now, but I know I can do it. I want it more than . . .*

They began meeting weekly. He talked to her about running the paper. "A lot of people have the skills the job requires, but few have the temperament." He sat back in his swivel chair. "Good judgment is essential but also decency and fearlessness." He almost smiled. "Mike D'Angelo said you outed a groper, in front of the City staff. Wish I'd been there. Mike thought you shouldn't have done it."

"What do you think," she said.

"Spot-on," he said. "Much more effective than those online sexual harassment courses."

"I don't have an inner life. I do therefore I am. Socrates blinked. The examined life isn't worth living. Look what happened to him." She smiled. "My husband, Joe, says it's genetic. My sister is an ER triage nurse. My brother is a fireman."

5

Editor

POLO DIED JANUARY 1, 2000. THERE WERE FIRES ALL OVER THE CITY. HE called Clara a little before midnight to wish her Happy New Year. "Candles, drunks, space heaters, gas stoves, arson," he said to her. "Busy night." He was on the third call of the evening. Everyone was exhausted, wrung out. The second fire had been fatal, an old man. At the third house, a woman in a nightgown and bare feet was sobbing on the street. "My children are in there, on the second floor," she said. "I couldn't get to them, the stairs were on fire." Polo told the engineer to raise the pompier to the second-floor window. "I'll get them out the window." The captain grabbed his arm. Polo shook him off. He climbed the ladder and went in. He was carried out dead the next morning, his arms around two dead children.

A week later, after the funeral, the department held a memorial service. Firefighters came from all over Michigan. An honor guard stood duty during the vigil, the station bells tolled three times. Clara said the Kaddish. Polo was the first Jewish firefighter in Detroit to die in the line of duty.

The next day, his picture was on the front page of the *Detroit Free*

Press, along with an article on his exploits. "He took chances no one else would," the chief was quoted as saying at the service. "He would say, laughing, 'I'm Asbestos Man, I walk through fire and smoke.' He threw off any notion he was heroic. 'If I were a hero, I'd be dead,' he said. 'I'm an escape artist.' We called him Houdini."

"He wanted to die," Clara said to Lila a day later. "Always, every time, he was saving you." They were at the Detroit Athletic Club. Frances Maier was a member. They'd invited Polo's battalion for an improvised postburial shiva/wake. They all showed, many with members of other companies. There was food and drink for all. One older club member, wandering in, quickly retreated. "I knew they weren't members," he said. "They were too handsome."

Polo left his share in their house to Clara. "Lila would kill me all over again if I left anything to her," he had said, laughing.

Aldo didn't show up. Clara had called him New Year's Day. "You're not invited to the funeral, or the memorial service, or the shiva," she said. "If you say anything to a reporter, I'll set Polo's battalion on you."

Lila took a week off from work. "It's my fault," she said to Joe. "I shouldn't have taken the beatings."

Joe took her hand in his. "You were not even four the first time Aldo beat you. You had a mouth on you. You still do. He didn't hate the others the way he hated you. He couldn't beat you into submission."

"I'm too much like him. Why isn't he dead instead. I don't love that many people." She started counting on her fingers. "You, Stella, Ava, Grace, Clara, Frances. I can't lose any more. I'm going first."

TWO YEARS LATER, LILA WAS appointed executive editor of *The Globe*. She had risen from covering D.C. politics, to covering the House, to covering the Senate, to covering the White House. She never got to Sports.

"What are you thinking?" Doug said. He knew not to ask, "What are you feeling?"

"It's what I wanted. Top Dog," she said. "I won't let you down." She nodded, her way of saying thank you. "I wish Quinlan were here to see it."

"What are your plans?" he said.

"I want more women, more people of color writing for the paper. I want to keep the print edition," she said.

"Is it in danger?" he said. "Subscriptions are holding."

"How do you read *The Washington Post, The New York Times, The Wall Street Journal*?" she said. "Online."

"Any other things I should know about you," he said, "other than, at heart, you're a tabloid creature."

"I'm not rude down, only up," she said.

THE ANNOUNCEMENT WAS A SURPRISE to almost everyone. The men sulked. The women danced in the aisles. The also-rans, all men, groused loudly. Josh Morgan, a State Department reporter, CNN commentator, and Pulitzer Prize winner (shared, one of eight), was enraged. He thought the job was his. He thought he was Marshall's golden boy. When he heard the news, he went down to Doug's office, barging in without knocking, jaw out, hands clenched. Doug was at his desk, reading copy. He waved Josh to a chair. Josh stayed standing.

"Of all people, Pereira," Morgan said. "I can't believe you picked that lightweight over an admired, famous, I'll say it, prizewinning journalist and eminent talking head. Other reporters call me for the lowdown." He took out a small black book and smacked it on Doug's desk. "Telephone numbers of everyone who counts in Washington. I've been to dinner parties at Joe Scarborough's. Also, Al Gore's and Colin Powell's."

"I picked Pereira," Doug said.

"You made me think I was going to get it," he said.

"I let you think that, along with some others," Doug said. "To keep you from sabotaging each other."

"I told my wife, my in-laws, my parents, my children, my friends," Josh said, "even my enemies."

"Stupid thing to do," Doug said.

"Son of a bitch," Josh said.

"Look," Doug said, ignoring the insult. "You're not a bad reporter, but Lila has the better nose for stories. You go deep. She goes wide." He looked at Morgan appraisingly. "She's a better writer. She has better taste, better sense."

"It's because she's a woman, isn't it," Josh said.

Doug was quiet for several seconds. "You were never a serious contender," he said. "You're not editor material. You lose your temper easily. You only look out for yourself. You treat the administrative and custodial staffs like crap. You have lousy judgment." He warmed to his topic. "Lila's tough, tougher than you. She never yells at people." He leaned forward. "You shouldn't have groped her. Everyone remembers. If you go after her, if you try to bring her down, I'll fire your ass. Or she will." He stood up. "Now I'd like you to leave my office."

Five minutes after his extemporaneous interview with Doug, Josh Morgan walked into Lila's office without knocking.

"You ratted me out to Doug," he said.

"Mike D'Angelo ratted you out, though he thought he was ratting me out," she said.

"You don't deserve it," he said.

"Are you resigning in protest," she said. "You'll need to put it in writing."

Josh started. "No, no," he said. "I thought I'd get it."

"You're not a newspaperman," she said. "You were made for TV." She tilted her head, as if picturing him on the small screen. "You need a better haircut. Who does Anderson Cooper go to?"

"'Whom,'" Josh said, "not 'who.'"

"*For Whom the Bell Tolls*," she said, "Otherwise 'who.'"

Later that afternoon, Lila dropped down to Doug's office to tell him about Morgan's visit.

"I didn't fire him," she said. "He didn't say I slept with you to get the job."

JOE WORKED HARD BUT NOT as hard as Lila. It was a choice he made, both as a parent and a husband. The parent part had been negotiated at the start. The husband part was improvised. Joe didn't need success as much as Lila did, and he thought she deserved hers more. *I suppose,* he thought, *I'm the fairy godfather, sending Cinderella off to the ball.* Cinderella was on his mind. He'd taken the three girls to the Disney movie at a retrospective film showing.

"You take them to R-rated movies and I take them to Disney," he said after the girls were in bed.

"I didn't much care for Cinderella," Lila said. "Who wants to go to a ball?"

"That's what Grace said. She also said she didn't like that Cinderella was blond." Joe raised an eyebrow. "The Starbirds thought the animation was second rate. I tried to explain that every cel was hand-drawn. They didn't care."

"Prince Charmings come in handy," Lila said. "You're a Prince Charming."

Joe smiled.

"No, really. You make everything I do possible. If I weren't married to you, I couldn't be married. No other husband would put up with me."

"I put up with you because you always surprise me. And you don't chatter."

"No small talk, only big talk," she said. "The thought of having to ask: 'How are the twins, Mrs. Bush?' when you want to ask, 'Are you anti-abortion, like your husband?'"

"I'm small-talked out from the school runs," he said. "I've become boring."

"You're not boring," she said.

"Definitely bored. I should have stayed in government. When I left for Sanger, Booth, I had this idea that I should make money. So stupid. I had money. I never had to work a day in my life if I didn't want to." He scratched his chin. "I loved the SG's office. I loved arguing appellate cases."

"Has that door closed? What about looking for a government job at Justice, or as counsel to a committee? What about working as outside counsel on arguments?"

"I'd have to work terrible hours."

"The girls are old enough for you to be home less often. Why do we have all this help?"

"A parent has to eat dinner with the children five nights a week," he said. "That was Frances's cardinal rule on raising children. 'So long as you eat dinner with them, they'll turn out right enough.'"

"Did Frances actually eat dinner with you?" Lila's eyes lit up. "I thought you lived like posh Brits. High tea at five for the kiddies. Black-tie dinner for the grown-ups at eight."

He shook his head. "Where do you get your ideas from. Oh, right, the thirties movies. Most nights, it was Frances and me eating lamb chops and salad. Dad worked late." He gave a half smile. "She never minded. 'A man who has been the indisputable favorite of his mother keeps for life the feeling of a conqueror . . .'"

"There must be some job you could conquer," she said.

"I wouldn't be my own person, someone else would be calling the shots, deciding what cases to take, what side to take," he said. "I don't think I can be a subordinate anymore. I don't like being in charge but I want to be, as Grace used to say, the boss of me."

"Do you want me to be home more?" As a reporter, Lila had taken most weekends off, or parts of most weekends, and she had made an effort to be home for dinner, though often she went to work afterward. Joe wondered how long she'd continue to keep to that schedule in the new job.

"Is that my real complaint," he said.

"Could be," she said.

"I rattle around in this house," he said. After living in a small three-bedroom apartment for ten years, they'd bought a townhouse on Capitol Hill in '93, shortly after Grace was born. It was pretty and prettily furnished, but stunningly generic, *House Beautiful,* except for the girls' rooms and the playroom. A decorator had done a very good job. The furniture was comfortable, the wall colors soothing. It looked like a stage set, after the curtain had risen but before a character had entered.

"I'm compulsive," she said.

"You have the job you've wanted from the day you set foot in the *Courier,*" he said. "Quinlan saw it. Everyone saw it. I want that more for you than I want you around." He shrugged. "Yes, I want you around more."

"I'll try," Lila said. Joe's heart sank.

IN HER FIRST YEAR AS executive editor, Lila put in nine-hour days, weekends included. The next year, she put in nine-and-a-half-hour days. The year after that, she worked ten hours a day, the year after that, ten and a half. Her workday kept growing incrementally. In her sixth year, the 2008 campaign pushed her into twelve-hour days. She rarely came home for dinner. After Obama's election, if she was awake, she was at work. The reporters started calling her FILO, first in, last out. She lived for the job. She couldn't do it any other way.

Joe had his fill when she started sleeping in her office once or twice a week, during the 2012 campaign. On October 2, the day after his fifty-ninth birthday, he told her he was moving out. She hadn't shown up for dinner the evening before. He found her tiptoeing in at 6:00 A.M., to take a shower.

"We need to talk," he said. "I'll see you in the kitchen."

Lila came down fifteen minutes later, in new clothes exactly like the ones she'd taken off. "What's on your mind?" she said.

"I want a separation," he said. "We haven't had dinner together this year, or last year, or the year before, or . . ." He shrugged. "You don't go to Bloomfield Hills for Thanksgiving. You missed my birthday dinner yesterday."

Lila started. "It's been overwhelming. Covering the campaign is exhausting," she said. "I sent flowers. Didn't you get them."

"Were they the peonies?"

"Have you met someone?"

Joe shook his head in annoyance. "It won't be hard."

"The job is engulfing."

"You want it that way. It's your life. You love it."

"I'm not really a wife, more like a husband."

Joe was silent.

"I don't want a separation," she said.

"I kept asking if we could have dinner, at home, at a restaurant. You didn't answer. With the Starbirds in law school and Grace at Chicago, there's nothing holding me here. I like my work. I don't want to do it round the clock."

Lila poured a cup of coffee and sat down at the table. "This makes me sad," she said. "I love you, more than anyone."

He shook his head, weary in disbelief. "Dinner isn't the only thing we never do. We never go to the movies. We never go on vacations, you never go, I go. We never have conversations about anything but your work. We never see Stella and Ava here. They don't see the point of coming home, I go to see them without you. Then there's all the ways you let us all down." He organized the list in his head. "You didn't take Grace to college as you promised. You didn't go to Grace's high school graduation, and you didn't go to Stella's and Ava's Stanford graduations. You don't take my calls at work. You don't answer your daughters' emails."

Lila felt a wave of panic. She thought she remembered Joe saying Stella was engaged. *Could I have missed her wedding? No. They wouldn't let that happen.*

"Stella and Ava call you Godot," he said. "They were at Stanford when you started working twenty-four/seven. It's been hardest on

Grace." He cleared his throat. "In middle school, Grace used to ask me 'Where's Lila?' Now she says, 'Who's Lila?'"

"No one told me," Lila said. "You all seemed fine, going about without me."

Joe stared at her. "We asked, all the time, if you could do this, go there. You'd say, 'Yes, of course,' and then you wouldn't show. You'd email or leave a phone message. Lately you haven't even bothered to make excuses. You just say, 'I'll do my best,' and then add, 'You know I want to.'" Joe lowered his voice, suppressing the desire to raise it. "You don't want to. You don't want to do anything but work, and I don't want to be married to you."

Lila stirred her coffee.

"What if I came home for dinner a few nights a week," she said. "I'd have to go back to the office . . ." Her voice trailed off.

"I haven't found a place. I haven't packed. I'm not moving out tomorrow. I wouldn't do that to you."

"I should be the one to move out. Like Grace's marriage proposal when she said I could live at *The Globe*. Children see everything."

"I want to leave," he said. "I don't want to stay here. We'll sell the house if you don't want to stay in it."

"You're the best husband, the best dad." She took a swallow of coffee. *Ever since Cincinnati,* she thought, *I've come first. I never made a pretense, at home, of putting anyone ahead of me.* Without bidding, she remembered a baffling line in *The Secret Garden,* a book she'd never returned to the library, loving it too much. The "two worst things that can happen to a child, is never to have his own way—or always to have it." At ten, she was enraged at the equivalency. *How can they be the same awfulness,* she had thought. *Never is worse than Always.*

Lila took another swallow of coffee. It was warm, bitter. "Have you told the girls?"

"No," he said.

They had been married over thirty years. She couldn't imagine life without him. He was her ballast, her "there." She had never lived alone. She couldn't work the washer or the TV remote. She'd never written a check. *If I had had to choose between Joe and* The Globe . . . Her thought trailed off. *He thinks I've chosen.*

"The paper means . . . a lot to me," she said.

"It means everything to you," he said. "Your sister and brother loved you. They made you human." He stopped for several seconds. "You were a better wife, before Obama's first election. You were good enough. Now you're not."

THE 2008 AND 2012 POLITICAL campaigns were the high points of Lila's first decade as executive editor. The 2008 primary, Obama vs. Clinton, was a win-win from her point of view. The country would likely elect its first woman or its first Black president. McCain couldn't win. "Maybe if he'd been a general as well as a hero," Lila said to Doug. "Colonels don't run for office; they overthrow the government. They're never elected. They lead coups."

"It was his voice," Doug said. "Too high. You can't have a president who sings tenor."

"Lincoln apparently had a very high voice," Lila said. "Sharp, shrill."

"He was a foot taller than Douglas," Doug said.

"You're a foot taller than me," she said.

"That much?" he said. "You don't present petite. Your older daughters do, but not you. I'd have said you were medium height."

"Big head and stilettos," she said.

In 2012, *The Globe* endorsed Obama. They had endorsed him also in 2008, but this time he had a record. He had passed the Affordable Care Act. He had reversed the Bush torture policies. He had protected dreamers. He was smart and witty and charming. He read novels as well as nonfiction. He was handsome. He had beautiful manners when he chose. Lila didn't think he had been an outstanding president, but he was "good enough," a category she and Joe both applied liberally, admiringly. After reading Winnicott, she had decided that if the "good enough" mother was "good enough" ("which I am not," she admitted), "good enough" was "good enough" for everything else except *The Globe*. "I need it to be good," she had said to Joe.

Careless mistakes were a constant low-grade aggravation. Every night between 2:00 and 3:00 A.M., a courier delivered the morning paper to the house. Lila stayed up to read it. It was the same story night after night. The presses had started their run before Editorial had finished proofreading. She'd wince at a confusing headline— POST OFFICE ADDRESSES A DISASTER. GINGRICH ATTACKS MEMORY OF GREAT MAN—or a misidentified photo— invariably someone Asian or Black, Aretha Franklin for Gladys Knight—then turn the page and summon the voice of consolation, Quinlan misquoting Gide. "Not to worry," he would say. "Every newspaper is less interesting tomorrow than it is today."

Quinlan had never thought of newspapers as the first draft of history. "The best ones report plausible hearsay," he said. "The rest make it up." He pointed at an article, marked up with pencil, lying on his desk. "Twelve hundred words, at most three credible facts." He gave her a sharp look. "Every adjective, every adverb is a lie. All those 'analysis' pieces, they're just 'opinion' pieces in tuxedos."

Once the paper confused Paul Ryan and Rand Paul. Lila wondered if it had been done deliberately.

DOUG AND LILA GOT DRUNK together the night of Obama's reelection. It had been a long day without any solid food, and between them they'd drunk a liter of scotch. They were sitting next to each other on the sofa in Doug's office, talking and laughing, happy and excited. The lights were dim, the building empty. They'd somehow gotten the paper out while everyone was crying and watching television.

"I'm proud of the country for electing a Black president twice," Doug said.

"I think Romney lost when he put his dog on the roof of his car," Lila said. "This is a godforsaken country, full of cranks and misfits, genetically contrarian, descendants of people who couldn't get along in the old country and can't get along here. Like my father."

"My people got on swimmingly," Doug said. "They owned half of Fairfax County." He came to a full stop. "That and a hundred human beings."

"Whoa," Lila said.

"There was a kind of reckoning, not that it helped the enslaved," he said. "My great-great-grandfather was a colonel in the Confederate Army. He went off in 'sixty-one and never came back. In March of 'sixty-five, the Yankees, on their way north, torched the house, the barns, the fields. My great-grandfather, who was five at the time, watched, riveted. Nothing remained except the great chimney. His mother, standing next to him, was steely-eyed. She had managed to save the silver, burying it in the family graveyard, next to her mother-in-law. They moved to Delaware after Appomattox. She had cousins there and wanted "the safety" of living in a Union state. She remarried and had four more children. My great-grandfather went to Princeton, instead of Mr. Jefferson's university, launching a legacy. I was fourth generation." He shrugged. "My son went to Yale. He refused to apply to Princeton. 'The family acts as though it's our birthright,' he said to me. 'Granddad said it was my safety school.' Yale assigned him to Calhoun College." Doug half-smiled. "You can't outrun your history."

"Mine is the untold Jewish immigrant story, a violent and abusive father." Lila took a sip of scotch. "When I was two, he had my mother sectioned. He said she was crazy. I never saw her again. She died— he said she died—when I was ten. I tried to find her grave in the Jewish cemetery. I went eight times. I couldn't find it." Her voice was flat. "I gave up."

"Did you try later to find out what happened?" Doug said.

Lila shook her head. "Suppose she didn't die. Suppose she ran off. I didn't want to know that she had abandoned us to Aldo." She ran her finger along her chain. "Of course, I abandoned my children, but to Joe."

Doug poured the last drops of scotch into their glasses. "To us," he said. He leaned over to kiss her on the cheek. She turned her head, her mouth meeting his. He pulled her toward him.

Lila hadn't kissed anyone but Joe since freshman year at Michigan, when he wouldn't date her. Kissing Doug was beyond exciting. *This is lunacy,* she thought as they slid onto the floor, wrapped in each other's arms.

Afterward, they lay quietly for several minutes.

"We were drunk," Lila said. "At least I was."

"We were drunk and happy," he said.

"It was my doing," she said.

"Oh, I was very willing," he said.

"I'm not sorry."

"I'm never sorry for sex."

She laughed. "You were great."

"You, too."

"Back to before," she said. "Back to work."

"I like you very much," he said.

"I like you very much," she said.

He stood up and pulled her to her feet.

"We took a detour," she said. "Better to stick to the main road."

"I always thought Frost's poem on taking the less traveled road was gnomic hogwash. Every choice makes all the difference."

"Back to the crossroad," she said.

"I'll always remember."

"Our Paris interlude."

JOE AND LILA DID NOTHING to make their separation official, no agreement, no distribution of property and assets, no separate bank accounts. They continued to file their taxes jointly. Joe paid the bills for the both of them.

Their first year apart, they spoke occasionally on the phone, mostly about logistics. The second year, they began having monthly dinners at restaurants they had never been to. Lila would ask him out. She could get a reservation anywhere in D.C. She always asked for a table in the main room in the quietest corner. Neither told anyone. Their daughters were confused. The gossips were in the dark.

In the third year, they began having late weekly meals, at dives and bars. Lila did the inviting. They talked about their work and lives. They never said if they were seeing anyone else.

"It's the geriatric replay of the year we met at Michigan," Lila said. "I'm chomping at the bit. You're shying."

"You'd think I'd know better," Joe said.

As Joe warmed, he began to push Lila to connect with her daughters, especially Grace, who had told her father that if she never saw Lila again, it would be soon enough. Lila began to woo Grace. She visited her at Chicago, she took her out to dinner when she was home. To everyone's surprise, she went to Grace's Chicago graduation.

The night Charles Webb was elected president, Lila showed up at Joe's place at 2:00 A.M., in a state of despair.

"It's too awful," she said.

"I'm glad you came," he said. "Here, have a swig." He handed her the bottle of gin he was holding.

They drank until 5:00 A.M., falling into bed together.

The next morning, still in bed, Joe told Lila that Grace was thinking of writing a novel, a roman à clef, "not now, in a couple of years. She's interested in your mother's story," he said. "Was she hospitalized at the Eloise? Did she die in 'sixty-eight? Is she buried in a pauper's grave? Grace thinks she scarpered."

"This is an old story with her," Lila said. "When she was ten, we had a conversation about this. As she was spinning her theories, I remember thinking that when I was ten, I also thought Zelda might have run away."

"She wants me to prepare you," Joe said. "She didn't say that, but that's my guess."

"I've never gone there," Lila said, "not after my skulkings in the

Jewish cemetery. I could have done it when we were living in Cincinnati, but I didn't see any good coming of it. If she was alive, I'd hate her. Grace only sees the romance of the runaway Granny. She doesn't have a dog in this hunt."

"She thinks Zelda's disappearance and its repercussions made you who you are today." Joe gave a slight headshake.

"'Motherless Detroit,'" Lila said.

"I don't think she'll write a hatchet job," he said. "She said she wouldn't turn you into Sophie Portnoy."

"Grace has never accepted, after years of disappointment, that I will never be the mother she wants." Lila kicked off the blanket.

"I think it's the mother she needs," Joe said.

"Want-need," Lila said, "what's the difference with children." She got out of bed and put on Joe's robe. "Grace is a lot like me. I'm nothing like her."

6

WebbGate

LILA HAD A PARTIALITY FOR STORIES OF CORRUPTION AT THE HIGHEST levels. "Teapot Dome, Watergate, Iran-Contra, stories to kill for," she said to the staff her first day as executive editor. "May the gods deliver one of those to us." The gods came through.

In 2016, Charles "Chick" Webb, Jr., aka the Spider, won the presidential election by electoral college votes. He lost the popular vote by the largest margin since John Quincy Adams. Out of 136 million votes, he won 60 million. His opponent, the former governor of New Jersey, won 70 million votes. Webb was unabashed and unapologetic.

"I won the all-American states," he crowed to a roaring crowd at the Dallas Hilton on election night. "I got the best votes." He did his cheerleader move, arms akimbo, thumbs up, Nixonesque but more athletic. "A win is a win if it's one vote or ten million votes."

The one-vote reference wasn't strictly rhetorical. His margins of victory in some states, notably Virginia, Georgia, North Carolina, and Arizona, were so narrow, the Democrats cried foul and contested the outcomes. The U.S. Supreme Court, in a 5–4 decision, halted the recounts on December 12, the same day it had halted the Florida recount in 2000. The headline in *The Globe* the day after ran in thirty-six-point type: BUSH V. GORE HAS LEGS AFTER ALL.

"It's our electoral college system doing what it should," Webb told Anderson Cooper a week after the election, "giving the victory to the best person for the job." He looked into the camera. "The governor didn't win the popular vote. The Democratic Party jiggered the voting machines in California and New York."

Cooper looked confused. "If they were into jiggering," he said, "wouldn't they have done better to do it in Virginia and Georgia, to nail down their electoral votes."

The president-elect laughed. "They're like that Colombian soccer player who scored an own goal against America in a World Cup game. America wound up winning." He looked into the camera again. "America won this time too."

Webb, a two-term governor of Texas, had been a dark horse candidate at a brokered convention. He had a lot of money from his daddy, an oil and gas man, and a lot of swagger. A good ole boy, he surrounded himself with friends and relations, the Spiderlings, who came to Washington with their hands out.

Webb made forty-two appointments in the first three months of his term, thirty-five of them interim. The reporters called them the Psycho-phants, "which would have been funny," Lila said to Doug, "if they weren't running the federal government."

Webb described himself as an Evangelical libertarian. "Not like some presidents," he told the crowds at campaign rallies, "I cling to my Bible and my guns." He floated the possibilities of repatriating Muslim immigrants with green cards and resuming drilling in the sacred lands of the Blackfeet Reservation in Montana. As he grew comfortable in the job, he began holding back funds from the agencies he didn't like: the Post Office, the IRS, the EEOC, the NLRB, the FTC. He'd restore the money, in dribs and drabs, after Congress grew restive.

"What's the matter," he said to the Republican Speaker of the House. "I thought you liked trickle-down economics."

Webb had started taking bribes when he was sheriff of Alamo County, his first elected office. He auctioned off deputies' jobs. As governor, he sold judgeships and sheriffs' offices. By the time he got to 1600 Pennsylvania, he had offshore accounts in countries he'd never heard of.

The presidency offered new and mouthwatering opportunities for payoffs, and within days of the inauguration, friends and friends of friends started lobbying Webb for positions in the White House and Departments. They came with their checkbooks. A major donor, a fellow Texan, familiar with Webb's shake-down schemes, wanted to be the ambassador to Brazil. In a private meeting, he offered, without winking, to pay four million dollars "to the charity of your choice." Rocking back on his heels, Webb slowly shook his head. He hated to turn him down. "I can't. You're too notorious," he said. The donor had been indicted for tax evasion and though he would likely plea and avoid prison, the publicity would be too damaging to the new administration. He thought for a second or two. "Are you interested in something that doesn't need Senate approval?" For five hundred thousand dollars, Webb appointed him to the National Science Board. "That should put you in like Flynn with the UT eggheads," Webb said. "I'll also invite you to the first White House dinner."

The NSB appointment launched Webb's presidential pay-to-play scheme. In his first year as president, he sold the ambassadorships to all the embassies in western Europe. The going price was six million dollars. European ambassadors' jobs had always gone to rich men who covered the expenses of running the embassies. No one realized for two years that in the Webb administration, the jobs came with hefty application fees. Three paid with Bitcoin.

The scheme started unraveling when a candidate for the Canadian ambassadorship, an investment banker, Government Witness No. 1, was asked to pay seven million dollars. The president's younger son, Robert, made the offer over lunch at the Sherry-Netherland Hotel. Robert was the outside man, the dealmaker; his older brother, James, it was said, was the inside man, the money launderer.

"How does this work?" No. 1 asked. "How does one pay?"

"Donations to SpiderPAC," Robert said, showing his teeth. "We'll take cash, Bitcoin, personal checks from offshore banks. You can pay in installments. No credit cards."

No.1 went straight from lunch to the office of the U.S. Attorney for the Southern District of New York (SDNY). An hour later, he called Doug. They played golf in the summer on Martha's Vineyard. "I've informed the U.S. Attorney's Office," he said, "but I'm worried the attorney general will find out and kill the story." He laughed. "Does this make me Deep Throat? I taped the conversation, probably illegally."

Doug and Lila mobilized. They pulled together a team of ten reporters, men and women with proven investigative chops, deep D.C. sources, and driving ambition. At their first meeting, after hours, Lila swore them to secrecy on the *Associated Press Stylebook.*

"No joke," Lila said. "Closest thing to a Bible we can agree on. I'll fire anyone who leaks. That includes telling your partners. You're swearing to each other as well as to us."

"You'll get your assignments on Monday along with your covers," Doug said. "We'll take care of your bosses. They won't know what you're doing, only that you're working on a special project for the paper, something like the Pentagon Papers." He surveyed the room, making sure he had their full attention. "Last thing. No drinking. No drugs. No sex with strangers. For the duration."

"What do you think," Doug said after they left. "Can they all keep a secret?"

"They're pirates," Lila said. "They'll scuttle the ship before they surrender it."

"I'm not sure. There may be too many to keep it under wraps," Doug said. "Pillow talk. Bragging. They were so excited, too excited."

"Webb had to be doing this when he was governor," Lila said. "You don't start an operation like this when you're president." She sent three reporters to Texas and five to Europe. Two stayed in Washington with forays to New York.

Within days, the Texas crew found three judges and four sheriffs who said they'd made offshore campaign contributions. In every case, Robert Webb was the person they'd done business with. They all said they never heard from the governor until he offered the job. "I assumed Webb was behind the scheme," one of the sheriffs said, "but he left no fingerprints."

The European Pirates had a tougher time making contact. They started by asking politely for private appointments with the ambassadors. The deputies balked. They said they couldn't schedule an appointment without knowing the topic. After a week of ballroom dancing, one of the Pirates broke step. "I need to talk to the ambassador," she said, "about conversations he may have had with Robert Webb."

The ambassador to Country No. 4 was the first to break. "I paid in four installments," he said, "out of an account I set up in Luxembourg. I assume the others—I assumed there were others—did something similar. I didn't use any U.S. lawyers. I was told not to. Robert said they might 'get prickly' about the arrangement. I was told the money was a campaign contribution, to a PAC. I only spoke to Robert."

His story set the pattern for the ambassadors who'd paid with dollars. The ones who'd paid in Bitcoin had an awkward time explaining. "I'd sold a Rothko and been paid in Bitcoin," one of them said. "The money was just sitting there. Everyone takes Bitcoin these days."

In Washington, the investigation stalled. The president was "too busy" to meet with *Globe* reporters.

"Son of a bitch," Lila said. "He's going to throw Robert under the bus."

Two days before Lila planned to break the story, Josh Morgan called her. "I've heard rumors you're doing an investigation of Webb," he said. "Big story. I'd like in."

"Too late, it's wrapping," Lila said.

"Is it true?"

"You can read it in the paper."

Josh hung up.

Lila called Doug.

"Josh Morgan just called. He heard about the Webb investigation," she said.

"I bet he's sleeping with one of the Pirates. A young one. He does that. Female, under thirty, recent hire, hasn't heard the stories about him." He sighed heavily. "He doesn't have friends, only contacts. Try a Pirate first."

Lila called in the likeliest woman, Felicity Turner, twenty-eight, the youngest Pirate. Felicity had been at *The Globe* almost two years, after four years at *The Baltimore Sun*. She'd done a first-rate job on the Webb investigation.

She was visibly nervous when she arrived. "I feel like I've been called to the principal's office," she said.

"Do you know how Josh Morgan found out about the investigation?" Lila said.

Felicity gasped, then started tearing.

I should have fired his ass that first day, Lila thought.

"He promised he wouldn't say anything," Felicity said. "He kept complaining that I was in Texas all the time." She began sobbing. "I'm so sorry. What do I need to do?"

"I need you to resign after the article breaks," Lila said. "I want the letter today, dated the end of the week. Make it simple." She nodded. "You're a good reporter. You made a mistake. Don't make another." She sat back in her chair. "Don't say anything to Morgan until you're gone. I will recommend you for other jobs but not if he finds out you're resigning. Got it?"

Felicity looked down and nodded. "I won't say a word." She wiped her nose. "What if you sent me back to Texas until the story breaks. That would make it easier. He'll badger me." She blew her nose. "I'll go tonight and, once I'm there, I'll tell him I'm finishing up." She teared again. "I never told him who was involved or what jobs. I think he thinks it has to do with Webb's years as governor."

"I'm on it," Lila said. She scribbled a note.

"I thought we were in love," Felicity said. "What a sucker I am."

Lila's phone rang. She ignored it.

"Don't you want to answer it," Felicity said.

"No," Lila said, silencing the ringer. "I'm talking to you. Why would I answer my phone. With one tuchus you can't dance at two weddings."

"What if it's an emergency?"

"Is that why you answer the phone when you're out to dinner with friends?"

"We all do it, my generation. FOMO."

"What would you have missed," Lila said. "Your dentist. A car warranty scam. Josh Morgan."

The Globe went with the European Embassy stories the next day and nailed four diplomats. The headline shook Washington: WEBB'S SON RAN A PAY-TO-PLAY OPERATION WITH U.S. AMBASSADORS.

The president was outraged. "The story is a total invention," he said at an afternoon press conference, "and a libel against my son Robert. *The Globe* is attacking him to get to me." He pointed at the *Globe* reporter in the audience. "You're a lying sack of— And your newspaper is garbage. I wouldn't wipe my ass on it." He stood up straight, throwing back his shoulders, the way he'd seen "my generals" do it. "The American people won't stand for it. They know me. They love me. I'm the most popular president since Roosevelt, bigger than Reagan. Children write me letters. Women propose to me. Men want to be me." He pointed at the reporter again. "You're trying to ruin a good man's reputation. Robert would never do anything dishonest. Never, never, never. He's not going to stand for it." He pointed a third time at the reporter. "See you in court, Benedict Arnold."

Robert panicked. He hired a well-known D.C. white-collar criminal lawyer, a former U.S. Attorney (SDNY) and a registered Democrat.

Lila suspended Felicity for three months, telling her to say she was taking a break to recover from investigating WebbGate.

• • •

THE NEW YORK TIMES LEAPED into the investigation. Having broken the story, Lila wasn't interested in competing with the Leviathan. "Let them have Webb. They'll do a great job," she said to the Pirates, who groused about relinquishing the big story. "They'll write about the 'death of kings' while they dig his grave." She smiled. "No 'death of kings' palaver in *The Globe*. They're fencers. We're street fighters."

Webb hung on for a year before resigning. On his last day, he pardoned his sons, Robert and James, his wife, his ex-wife, and himself. "Sort of like Napoleon crowning himself," Lila said to Doug.

Two days after the pay-to-play story broke, Lila called Josh Morgan into her office. She wanted him to resign. "It's time you talked to CNN."

"What is this," he said. "Belated Me Too?"

"I'd rather keep Felicity Turner than you," Lila said. "She told me she told you."

"Are you blaming me?" he said.

"Yes," she said.

"You can't do that," he said.

"Do you want me to fire you instead," she said.

"This is a vendetta," he said.

"Hold it," she said. "I'm giving you time to get another job. Here's the offer." She handed him a large envelope. "Don't come back to the office. Tell them you're working from home."

"That twat," he said. "She was bragging to me about working on the Big Case."

"I'll call Security and have you escorted out if I have to," she said.

"You've always been jealous you didn't go to an Ivy school."

"I think you mean 'envious.'"

He stood up. "For Who the Bell Tolls. You'll hear from my lawyers."

Lila called Doug to let him know she was axing Morgan.

"I offered him four months to find another job," she said. "I'm going to check out his credentials with HR. He said something when he left my office that set bells ringing." She paused. "Do you know anyone at MSNBC or CNN who might hire him?"

Lila called the director of human resources. "I want you to pull up Josh Morgan's file. Where did he go to college?"

The director called back a few hours later. "He's precomputer. We had to go down the mines to find his file." She rifled through the folder. "It says he graduated from Harvard, Class of 1982."

"Call them," Lila said, "and if he didn't go there, find out where he did go."

The director called back the next morning. "Morgan went to UMass, Class of 1983. His application says he worked two years at Investigations, Inc., after graduating. Do you need more?

"Yes. Check out his high school record, his summer jobs, his job reviews, his vacation records, his expense accounts, and anything else with his name on it," Lila said. "I want to know him better than his mother." The HR report came in the next day. It read, in part,

In his latest job review, the Political Editor describes Morgan as "arrogant, rude, and randy, nothing new, but a good reporter, dogged and thorough." By various accounts, he's had affairs with several women on the paper, the latest, Felicity Turner. Four years ago, Sally Alter complained after he made passes that bordered on harassment. He hung around her desk, sent her flowers at home and at work, asked her out repeatedly. She kept saying no. "I warned him I would report him if he didn't stop." When he didn't, she filed a complaint. "I have to work with him. Make him stop." He was spoken to. He moved on to a news assistant. None of the other women identified complained, though the news assistant left. In her exit interview, she said there was "too much testosterone," in the newsroom. Morgan's expenses are more expensive than most. They've been questioned but never denied. He's the biggest spender in Politics, not counting editors. Lunches, dinners, equipment.

He went to Hawaii and expensed it. He wrote two stories that were published after he came back. They hadn't been assigned. He did the same the year before in England, again two stories."

After reading the report, Lila called the assistant managing editor, one of her direct hires, a "Quinlan grandkid."

"Do you have any reason to think that Josh Morgan made up sources or quotes in his articles or embellished his own experiences, contacts, credentials? I'm thinking specifically about the two recent trips he took to Hawaii and England. They look like vacations. He filed expenses for articles that weren't assigned but later published in the paper. Would you mind running a check on the stories."

The AME was silent for several seconds. "He's bent," she said. "I keep telling the others but they think I'm prejudiced against him because he's such a lech." She paused. "I'd like to tell the ME I'm doing this. He doesn't like back doors."

"Do a quick search and find out if there were similar articles in Hawaiian and English newspapers and get back to me. It shouldn't take long. Then we'll tell your boss."

An hour later, the AME appeared at her door. "I always think the ME reads my email." She handed Lila copies of stories from Honolulu and London papers along with the *Globe* stories. Morgan had used the same facts and the same quotes, pretty much verbatim, but mixed up the sentences and paragraphs and used different names. "How did you know he did that?" the AME said. "I'd never have guessed."

"It's so blatant, no one would guess," Lila said. "My first boss, Frank Quinlan, schooled me on bad reporters. Morgan fits the bill. He's a schnorrer. He writes long sentences. He goes to sit-down dinner parties with the pols he covers." She rifled through the pages. "I've always thought he cut corners but your boss always sticks up for him." She laid the pages on her desk. "Go downstairs. I'll take care of everything."

Agnew of Libby, Rove, Kushner & Agnew called Lila the following week "on behalf of our client Joshua Morgan."

"I was expecting to hear from Mr. Morgan's lawyer. Let me tell you the problems." Lila, coached by Joe, laid out the case against Josh, the fake Harvard degree, the plagiarized articles, the false expenses.

"Thank you, Ms. Pereira," the lawyer said and hung up.

Josh resigned. Lila called Doug to give him an update.

"I wanted to fire Josh the day you were appointed," Doug said, "but I didn't want to step on your toes."

"So what do I do about the 'testosterone' problem in the newsroom," Lila said.

"Start with the ME," Doug said. "Men need to clean up their messes."

7

The Lost Mother

THE LOST MOTHER WAS PUBLISHED AFTER THE MIDTERM ELECTIONS IN November 2022, less than three months before Lila's retirement. The preceding spring, Grace's publisher sent Lila the galleys, worrying she might sue for defamation. Calling a book fiction didn't make it fiction.

Lila read it in a single sitting.

"I'm trying to figure out what I'd think of the book if someone else's daughter had written it." She laughed. "If someone else's daughter had written it, I wouldn't have read it."

She handed the book to Joe. "It's a good story. She's a reporter. She did what reporters do, she went with the story, except . . . she wrote it as a novel."

"She's been talking about this book since she graduated," Joe said. "Time to fish or cut bait."

"Why didn't she investigate?"

Joe fanned the pages of the galleys. "Maybe she doesn't want to know what really happened any more than you do. Your version is as much a fiction as hers. My guess is she's protecting you and her relationship with you. She wants her story out there, but she doesn't want to attack you. She doesn't want to say you didn't try to find out the truth."

"My version is Aldo's version. I've always hated that."

"On that ground alone," Joe said, "her suspicions were justified."

"If she'd done an investigation, if she'd found out what really happened, I'd have praised her, however it turned out."

"You know that. I know that. She doesn't. Not yet."

Lila never thought of suing. She couldn't imagine the circumstances under which she would sue a daughter. "Even if she accused me of child abuse, I wouldn't do it," she said to Joe. "I was surprised I came out so well." Grace's stories were entertaining. The only publicly combustible one, and then, only in D.C., was the story of the affair between the editor of *The Globe*—called *The World* in the book—and its publisher. Lila knew people at *The Globe* who would be angry and hurt if they believed she and Doug had had an affair. She worried about the Pirates especially. *They'll think it's true,* she thought. *They'll take it personally—not the affair, we were Mom and Dad—but the secrecy. As if we would have told them.*

Lila sat back to consider the book in terms of its appeal. *On the plus side, a good title, Elena Ferrante echo, lively writing, and a messily fraught relationship between a well-known mother and her daughter. On the minus, not enough suffering to propel the book into bestsellerdom. Except in D.C. It will sell like hotcakes here.*

Grace had made up names for all the characters, but they were so similar to their real names, the changes seemed pointless. Joe was Sam Shriver, Lila was Ana Monteiro, Zelda was Zelina, Grace was Hope.

"It suits her better than Grace," Lila said to Joe.

"So far," Joe said. "She's a work in progress."

"Lila Pereira sounds like an opera singer in a thirties movie. Ana Monteiro sounds like an opera singer in a Bugs Bunny cartoon." She smiled. "What do you think, Sam?"

Joe raised an eyebrow. "What do you think of the Zelina/Zelda story?"

In the last chapter, Zelina/Zelda had decamped. She was never hospitalized. She was alive, in ill health, widowed, and living in an assisted living facility in Ann Arbor.

"She doesn't say Zelina spied on me when I was at Michigan. She pulled her punches."

Lila called Grace.

"The publisher sent me your galleys," Lila said. "Congratulations. I know you've been working on it for a long time."

"Not quite forever," Grace said. "Almost forever."

"You're talented, you're a real writer. I recognize you and me and your sisters and Joe but not all the events. What is it exactly? Is it a novel, a memoir?"

"It's an amalgam, a hybrid. It's a novel with intuited facts from real life."

"Intuited facts?"

"I believe everything I wrote is true in terms of the novel. I don't know if it's true in life." Grace cleared her voice.

"I'm not on the same page here."

"I describe situations that might have happened, could have happened, that I find plausible, true to the moment, true to the person."

"Ah," Lila said. "The fiction part."

"You might call it fictional nonfiction or a real-life novel. I got the idea from *The Bell Jar*. Sylvia Plath called herself Esther Greenwood."

"Congratulations," Lila said. "When is it coming out?"

"Before Thanksgiving, in time for Christmas. My editor wanted to give you lots of notice. She was worried you'd sue. I knew you wouldn't. I didn't know but I knew."

"I didn't know about your affair with the older, married reporter," Lila said. "But then parents tend not to know about those things."

"It was lovely. He was lovely. I didn't expect it." She paused for several seconds. "Josh Morgan."

"What do you know," Lila said. "Where was he working?"

"CNN, here, in the city. He said he was 'a very trusted' anchor and I should trust him. I did."

"How did you meet?" Lila rifled through the galleys. *Josh Morgan*, she thought, *I never saw that coming.*

"He cold-called me when I was writing about the Russian oligarchs for *The New Yorkist*. He said he could help. 'Older reporters help new, younger ones,' he said. And he was helpful." Grace took in a deep breath and let it out slowly, not wanting to sound embarrassed. "It went on for a long time. And then it was over. I got a call from Felicity Turner. She pushed what I knew had to happen. He said to ask you about him. I don't want to know." She took in another deep breath. "Felicity worships you, like all the young women at the paper."

"The Zelda story," Lila said. "Did you interview Aldo?"

"No," Grace said.

"Have you ever met Aldo?"

"No," Grace said.

"Did you talk to Clara about the book?"

"No."

"Wouldn't that have been useful?"

"I wanted my truth, not yours, not hers, not Aldo's."

"I suppose the doctor could have helped Zelda escape . . ." Lila's voice faded.

"You don't like it, do you. You're sorry I wrote it, aren't you."

"It's a good book," Lila said.

"I never believed she was dead," Grace said. "Didn't you ever wonder why Aldo didn't marry again?"

"I don't think he was afraid to commit bigamy. He liked *shiksas*, and Bubbe would have moved out if he'd married one of them."

"You wanted Zelda dead. You refused to look beyond that," Grace said. "I really think she's alive or was alive after 1960."

"Are you coming for Thanksgiving?" Lila said.

"No. I told Joe I was staying in New York. Ruth's doing it."

"Maybe Christmas then," Lila said.

Lila called Doug. "Grace wrote a book. The publisher sent me the galleys. I'll give them to you. Joe's almost finished reading them. She writes that we had an affair, from 2012 to 2016, at the Hay-Adams, in the afternoons."

"Does she?" Doug was quiet for several seconds. Lila could hear his breathing. "Don't send me the galleys. I don't care what she wrote." He paused. "The Hay-Adams, really?"

Grace's book made Joe uncomfortable. "I found myself feeling guilty and embarrassed, as if I'd opened my father's underwear drawer, looking for a clean pair of socks, and found his condoms instead. Who was the affair with?"

"Josh Morgan," Lila said. "It was different from his other trysts."

"Did he do it to get back at you?" Joe said.

"If he did, it backfired," Lila said. "I think he was in love with her. Last call." She shot him a quizzical smile. "She was circumspect in the book, protective of him, of both of them. He sounds like a completely different person. Human."

"Did you have an affair with Doug?"

Lila shook her head. "We could run the paper or have an affair, not both."

Joe phoned Grace. "The book is wonderfully written but difficult to read. It made me squirm. Your story is our story. Can't you postpone publication a few months, until after Lila retires? It's thunder stealing. Her retirement is a big deal."

Grace didn't answer for several seconds. "The publishers want it to come out then, to take advantage of the hoopla surrounding her retirement. 'Borrowed publicity,' they call it."

"And you agreed?"

"Yes."

"How true is the story about Zelda/Zelina? Did you find her?"

"No." Grace gritted her teeth. "I wrote what I believed to be true. It's true to the book."

"And Lila's affair with Doug? I didn't like reading that."

"You were separated then."

"How do you know it happened? You were never home then."

"She was never home." Grace cleared her throat. "I didn't 'know' know."

"Didn't you think I would mind?" Joe said.

"I knew she wouldn't mind. I assumed you wouldn't either. Is it true? Was I right?"

"Truth. Whose truth? Everyone will think it's true. Whether it's true is irrelevant."

"I don't come off so well. Sulky, angry."

"That's also irrelevant."

"You could sue," Grace said.

"You know we won't do that," he said. "I'm talking to you."

"It's a roman à clef, though no one says that anymore. Recognizable persons, recognizable events, embroidered."

"I wish you hadn't done it," he said. "It interfered with the pleasure I might have gotten from the book."

"You never seemed to mind anything she did."

"Are you being deliberately obtuse? It's what you've done. You made me look like a cuckold."

Grace's throat closed.

"Okay," he said. "I got it off my chest. We'll talk again soon."

He hung up. Grace burst into tears.

At supper that evening, Joe told Lila he'd talked to Grace about her novel.

Lila shook her head. "I wish she'd kept you out of it. It's one thing if it's me, but you." She touched his hand. "'Sharper than a serpent's tooth.'"

"We've grappled before," Joe said. "She doesn't apologize."

"I don't apologize," Lila said.

"I know."

"The Zelina story is fantasy," Lila said. "If Zelda didn't die—big IF—she didn't live the life in that book." She picked up a piece of sushi. It fell back on her plate. She had never gotten the hang of chopsticks. Clumsy hands, she'd say. She hated buttons. Her hand-writing was terrible. "Since I was ten, I told people my mother was dead. Grace has written the only life of Zelda. People will think it's true." She took a swallow of beer. "It's not my truth. If she's not dead, why isn't she?"

She picked up the sushi again and dropped it again. "I need a fork," she said.

Joe took her hands in his. "What's the matter with your hands?"

"Arthritis," she said.

"How so?" he said. "You don't have it anywhere else."

"Injuries," she said.

"Aldo?" he said.

She gave a half shrug.

"What did he do?" Joe could feel his anger rising.

"He stepped on my fingers. I was twelve or thirteen. I was lying on the floor, doing my homework. He walked around me, going somewhere, then came back and stepped on them. Bones were bro-ken. I could hear the crack. By the time I saw a doctor, they were a mess. It was too late to try anything. It might have been too late in the beginning. There are fourteen bones in the fingers, times two is twenty-eight."

"Oh, God," he said.

"I yelled but I didn't cry," she said. "It was painful, for weeks. Polo called Children's Protective Services. They never showed up. Aldo was in the union."

"You never told me this before. I thought you had hands like Aldo's."

"His hands were a mess. Maybe his father stepped on his fin-gers." She half-smiled. "There were accidents all the time on the assembly line. No one reported them unless the injuries were major. A severed hand would get reported."

"The first time she met you, my mother said you must have had a rough childhood," he said.

"Frances said that? How would she know? I never said anything."

"That's how she knew. She said most children complain about their parents. You didn't."

"Quinlan's childhood was straight out of *Angela's Ashes,* the Cincinnati edition." Lila ran her fingers around her necklace. "He'd tell his stories, maybe one a week. After he'd told me five or six, he said, 'You know what I'm talking about, don't you? You don't cringe.' He gave me a small salute. Just remember, 'The happy childhood is hardly worth your while.'"

She stabbed a piece of sushi with her fork. "I wouldn't be where I am if I'd been raised by Frances."

"I think about that," Joe said, "How come Clara turned out . . . almost normal."

"Magic," Lila said. "She's a nurse, she's a saint, a real one, not a *Cincinnati Courier* saint. We used to joke, if we were comic characters, Polo was the Knight, Clara was the Guardian, I was the Hoodlum."

"I told Frances, Aldo wasn't dead dead, only dead to you," Joe said.

"What did she say?"

"She said she knew."

"How?"

"A GM acquaintance told her, unsolicited," he said. "She had 'gonnections.'"

STELLA AND AVA BOTH FOUND *The Lost Mother* a hoot. Grace had sent them advance readers' copies, autographed.

"She got everyone just about right," Stella said to Joe.

"We're ridiculously inseparable," Ava said, "but it's too late to change."

They called Joe from their office in Los Angeles to find out how Lila was taking it. After Stanford, Stella and Ava had gone to Stanford Law. They were divorce lawyers, in practice together, Pereira & Pereira.

Joe wished they'd move back East.

"They'll never do it. They're natural Californians, cheerfully uncanny: Diane Arbus by way of Walt Disney." Lila laughed. "It was always thus. When they were little, they liked tutus and crowns and purple and horses." She closed her eyes, trying to picture herself wearing a tutu. "I supposed I might have liked those things too if I hadn't been raised by Aldo. It's amazing the things you don't know when you grow up poor. Of course, when you grow up rich, you miss out too. They shuddered the first time I showed them my switchblade. Not Grace, for the record."

"They're easy," Joe said. "Not Grace." He blamed himself more than Lila for the Starbird meld. *I should have separated them, given them their own rooms, sent them to different schools,* he thought. *A real mother, not Lila, of course, would have known to do that. I was grateful they were so close. It made my life easier.*

The call was classic Starbirds.

"One of our friends read the advance readers' copy," Stella said. "She asked us if we were hurt by it. We asked her if she could tell us apart at twenty feet. She giggled."

"Grace wrote we were *Legally Blonde* squared," Ava said. "I couldn't tell if she wrote that descriptively or derisively."

"Mixed," Stella said. "I think she envies us, the way we look like Lila. It's an advantage, being short and blond. People underestimate us."

"Lila knew it," Ava said. "She called it 'Dolly Parton camouflage.' She said: 'Don't run away from it. Use everything you've got.'"

"We were lucky we had each other," Stella said. "Gretel and Gretel."

"Grace was on her own," Ava said. "Still, she's twenty-nine. Someone needs to tell her the statute of limitations has run."

"No more blaming the parents for childhood wrongs," Stella said. "Spilled milk, as Lila says."

"Unless they beat you," Ava said. "Lila gets a bye."

"Except . . ." Stella said. "She doesn't blame Aldo."

"She hates him," Ava said.

Joe hung up, reeling from the ping-pong of his older daughters' conversation. *Is it intuition,* he thought, *or telepathy?* Midway through, he'd lost track of who was speaking. *I wonder what their husbands make of it,* he thought. Their husbands had played football for Stanford. They were best friends. They didn't go pro. They went to Stanford Business School. Afterward, they worked together, "in real estate." Joe assumed they made a lot of money by borrowing and not paying taxes. Hulking over their diminutive wives, they worried they'd have sons too short for football. As a backup, they settled on soccer. Game of the future, they agreed. They were happy men married to happy women.

A MONTH BEFORE THE BOOK'S publication, Grace hand-delivered a copy of *The Lost Mother* to Ruth. Ruth had refused to read it in its earlier iterations.

"I'll wait for the book itself," she had said to Grace. "I don't like the whole idea of it, and I don't want to be ornery with you for the next however many years it takes you to finish it."

"You could make it better," Grace had said. In college, Ruth read everything Grace wrote and made it better.

"No thank you. I don't even want to be in the acknowledgments."

Four years later, sitting on the sofa, Ruth took the book in her hands. It had a pale, pebbled jacket, the color and look of parchment.

"I like the cover," she said. It was a faded pencil sketch of Rochester's wife, in a long nightgown, her dark hair long and wild, setting fire to bed curtains. The title was in red. "I get it, *Jane Eyre.* The madwoman in the attic."

"This attic." Grace pointed to her forehead.

"Southerners don't hide their crazy people in an attic. They bring them out. They show them off. No one cares. They only want to know whose side of the family, mother's or father's."

"I had to write it," Grace said.

"I know you believe that," Ruth said.

"I've been trying this whole year to explain to myself why I felt I had to do it. I've been made to feel disrespectful and perverse. 'Nepo Baby Skewers Mom.'"

Ruth waited.

"I've never believed, not for one second, that Zelda died and I never believed ever, ever, that she died in the mental hospital." Grace said. "When I was ten, I told some other ten-year-old girl that I never knew my grandmother, that she died years ago when my mother was exactly our age. Seconds later, I felt terrible. I felt like I had lied, to show off, to feel important, touched by tragedy. I swore I'd never do it again." She looked intently at Ruth to gauge her reaction.

Ruth nodded. "Go on."

Grace started tearing. "Easier said than done. Whenever I tried to say to people outside the family circle that Zelda might be alive or could be alive, I choked. I could hear what they were thinking. 'What's it to her. It's not her mother.'"

Ruth handed Grace a tissue.

"Part of it is because I feel in my bones I'm right, but that's only a part." Grace wiped her nose. "Lila saying Zelda's dead doesn't make her dead for me, or Joe, or the Starbirds, or even Clara. It's like the family, for Lila's sake, is living under a collective delusion."

"We all live with delusions," Ruth said. "That's how we are able to go on. Why do you want to overthrow Lila's?"

"If Zelda decamped, she was a monster, not as great a monster as Aldo, but still, a monster. She abandoned her children to save herself." Grace wiped her cheeks with her sleeve, the way a small child might. "Lila would never have done that. For all she didn't do, Lila couldn't have done that. She'd have died for me and my sisters." She stopped, thought-struck. "She'd have killed for me and my sisters."

8

Exit

WHEN LILA RETIRED IN JANUARY 2023, D.C. WENT TO TOWN. TOTALED, there were fourteen farewell parties, including one at the White House hosted by President Biden. *The Globe* threw three parties: the first in the Great Hall for everyone who worked in the building, including the cleaners and cafeteria workers; the second for the *Globe*'s board and senior editors at the board chairman's mansion on Capitol Hill; the third for the Pirates at Doug's house in Kalorama. The party with the Pirates was a romp. Lila and Joe stumbled home at 4:00 A.M. The board's party was annoying beyond measure. The man on Lila's right talked about all the changes at *The Globe* as if he'd made them. The staff party was a throat choker. Doug's toast had everyone sniffling and blinking, except Lila, who stood next to him, shifting impatiently from one leg to the other and whispering to him to get on with it.

"Lila is leaving because all senior editors must retire the year they turn sixty-five. I'll be following her out the door in a couple of months. We've had a great run and the new editor deserves a new publisher, not one who would invariably judge them against their brilliant predecessor." He paused. "Newspapers are dying everywhere, even big city papers, the victims of shrinking markets, rapacious investor-owners, Covid, and, of course, the internet and its social networks. How did *The Globe* escape this fate? Lila. Brandishing carrots and sticks, she brought us, me especially, foot-dragging, into the twenty-first century. I was Watergating, wallowing in our glorious past.

"In my time as publisher, there have been four things *The Globe* did that count as groundbreaking achievements: One, diversifying the staff, bringing on women and persons of color. Forty percent of our reporters are now women, a total of three hundred. Twenty-two percent are people of color, up from two percent when Lila arrived. Two, making the paper profitable, going all out online. *The Digital Globe* has over 3 million subscribers. Last month it recorded 75 million unique visitors. Three, tackling the Covid pandemic—from the ICU at Johns Hopkins—by instituting work-at-home arrangements, which were a huge success, to my surprise. Four, breaking the story on Webbgate and bringing down the president, a giant-killing feat which won us Pulitzers and Polks and the gratitude of the country." Doug raised his glass. "To Lila Pereira, indomitable, unstoppable, incomparable, unforgettable. My friend, my colleague. We shall not look upon her like again."

Lila shook her head. "Now see here," she said. "Our essential job is to cover the government's sausage-making apparatus. That's why *The Globe* is protected by the First Amendment. We don't deserve that protection if we don't do our job." She scanned the audience. Knowing the drill, the Pirates were all grinning, waiting for the shoe to drop. "So, here's a heads-up for someone nosy. I've heard recently that Supreme Court Justice Frederick Malcom may have flown on private planes to Palm Beach, Palm Springs, Kiawah Island, Saint John, Maui, Easthampton, Nice, Agadir. Beach towns. He may have visited courthouses there. He may have stayed at very expensive hotels or villas rented by the planes' owners. He never filed expenses. My last assignment, a parting shot. You've all been great. I couldn't have done it without you."

After the seventh party, Joe asked to be excused from further attendance. "More farewell tours than Sarah Bernhardt."

Lila coughed and nodded. Joe shook his head.

"This cough has been going on too long. No one has bronchitis for a year. I asked you last spring to see a doctor. You need to see a doctor. You're going to cough up your lungs."

"Long Covid," she said. "Phlegm and mucus."

Lila didn't go to doctors for regular checkups, only to get vaccinated. "I believe in preventing diseases, not 'managing' them," she said. The last time she had a checkup, for the *Globe* Company's insurance policy, the doctor said she was prediabetic and prehypertensive. He wanted to prescribe glucose inhibitors and statins. "I'm also pre-dead," she said to him. "What do you have for that?"

"I wish you'd go," Joe said.

A week later, after coughing blood, Lila went to Joe's doctor. The diagnosis was dire. She had Stage IV small-cell metastatic lung cancer, which had spread to her liver and brain.

"I wish you'd gone sooner," Joe said.

"If I'd gone the day after you told me to, I would have had the same diagnosis, and not have had these last carefree months."

"What do they recommend?" he said.

"Chemo and immunotherapy," she said. "I told them I only want palliative care. It will spread to my bones, if it hasn't already. I'm going to die in two or three months without treatment. With it, I might last an additional three or four months, tethered to machines in the ICU." *He'd keep me alive if I were a brain in a jar,* she thought. "Clara says never to go into an ICU with Stage Four anything. 'They'll do everything they can think of to keep you alive. Your kidneys go and before you know it, you're on dialysis. Then with lung cancer, you're on a ventilator and dialysis.'" Lila shook her head. "This is why I never went to doctors. I couldn't find one who didn't see death as the enemy."

Clara's advice didn't change but she was heartsick. "I cannot bear it," she said to Joe in a phone call. "We are cursed. 'And I only am escaped alone to tell thee.'"

Until the last month, Lila took afternoon walks with Doug in Kalorama Park. Joe welcomed the break. He was gutted by grief. The last several years had been good for their marriage. Without talking anything through, they had drifted back together. Neither had any interest in rehashing the past. "Spilled milk," Joe said to Lila. They moved into a larger apartment, five bedrooms for all the children and prospective grandchildren to visit, and hired a decorator.

Lila changed as much as she could, more than Joe expected. She came home for dinner at least three nights a week; they went to the movies on Sunday afternoons. She looked into buying a small-town newspaper when she retired.

Joe continued practicing law. He thought about taking golf lessons. "Will you wear those white shoes," Lila said. He took piano lessons instead and made good progress. He'd played as a boy but stopped after college. Often in the evenings, he'd play Berlin and Sondheim for her. "I like music for the words," she said to him. "Classical music singes my nerve endings."

Doug was bereft at the thought of Lila dying. "You've been my friend for over twenty years, my closest friend, my favorite friend," he said on one of their last walks. "I don't want to think about a future without you. I feel cheated. You're not even sixty-five. I thought we'd walk into the sunset together." His voice broke. "I love you."

Lila tucked her arm in his. "I am glad I'm dying while there are still printed newspapers and printed money."

"You are an odd duck," Doug said. "Any regrets?"

She shook her head. "I've been lucky, luckier than I deserved." She squeezed his arm. "The thing I hate most about dying, do you want to know? Aldo will outlive me."

Lila died at home. Hospice arranged for nurses and painkillers. Clara moved in. She'd retired a few years earlier though she often subbed on weekends and holidays. On alternate weeks, Stella and Ava flew in from Los Angeles. Grace went back and forth weekly between New York and D.C. On the nights she couldn't sleep, she lay awake berating herself for publishing *The Lost Mother*. It had been reviewed in all the national papers. The bad reviews weren't harsh, they were prurient or disapproving. The favorable reviews saw Lila as a hero for the twenty-first century. A good number wrote about the affair. *The Globe*'s book editor had asked Zadie Smith if she would write an essay on the roman à clef, including *The Lost Mother* and any other books she thought of. "Say anything you like about it," the book editor said. "Lila's insistent on that point." Many reviewers thought Grace should have waited until her parents were dead.

"Betraying the dead is preferable to betraying the living," one of them wrote, "though perhaps not as much fun."

The end was hard. Lila was in terrible pain and heavily sedated. She had a morphine pump and morphine patches. Clara sat with her in the morning, talking about their childhood, pulling up memories of their high crimes and misdemeanors. None of them ever stole money, except from Aldo. Lila regularly shoplifted bread and peanut butter, for afternoon snacks, and now and then a Three Musketeers bar. Clara and Polo thought she shouldn't, but they ate the sandwiches and split the candy bar three ways. Joe spent the afternoon, sitting in her room, reading Dickens to her. In the evening, if she was awake, he read to her from Chekhov's diaries.

"He was a peasant, like me," she said. "By some miracle, I made a life." Her voice was hoarse. "Because of you."

The last two weeks of her life, Lila spent mostly unconscious, breathing raggedly. When the hospice nurses said the end was coming, Joe called Grace in New York. "Last trip," he said. "She hasn't long." Grace caught the next train. For two hours, she sat weeping by Lila's side, holding her hand, touching her cheek, resting her head on her chest. As she straightened up to leave, damp and stiff, she kissed Lila's forehead. Lila blinked unseeing.

"I always loved you," Grace said.

"Ditto, kiddo," Lila said, in a whisper, so faint Grace wondered if she made it up.

9

The Quest for Zelda

A WEEK AFTER THE MEMORIAL SERVICE, GRACE RECEIVED A PACKET from Joe. Inside was a letter from Lila, written in her barely legible hand.

March 1, 2023

Dear Grace,

A letter from beyond the grave. Joe said he'd send it after the memorial service.

I'm sending you on a quest. It is difficult as quests always are.

Find out what happened to Zelda. Did Aldo commit her to the Eloise in 1960 and did she die in 1968? Or did she run away (in 1960? 1968?) and make a life for herself? Find her or her death certificate and then find out the kind of life she had, wherever she lived, and what kind of death she had, however she died, if she is dead.

Talk to Clara and Aldo. Move quickly on Aldo. He's very

old, ninety-four or five. He knows if Zelda died or disappeared. He will not help you, still, an encounter would be interesting, deep background. Meet on neutral ground. He'll ask you for money. Have DNA testing. Second cousins may turn up. Joe has a lock of my hair somewhere.

I was a better wife than mother, also a better friend, a better sister, a better editor, a better boss. I knew nothing of mothers. I loved you as much as I could, as best as I could. I gave you the best father.

Find Zelda, for both of us, and share her story.

You'll be a good mother, if you have children. You'll be good at anything you turn your hand to.

Here's looking at you, kiddo.

Lila

PART II

Grace

10

College

GRACE COULD COUNT ON ONE HAND THE MEMORIES SHE HAD OF LILA before she was seven. "There were only Joe and the babysitters," she said. "Sounds like a high school garage band." She was explaining her family to Ruth. It was the second night of freshman year, September 22, 2011. They had settled in, unbunking the beds and hanging their posters, RBG and Obama.

Ruth's account of her family had been eye-popping for Grace.

"I grew up in the Florida panhandle, the only child of an unwed mother who is the hardest-working person I know. After I was born, she put herself first through a GED program, then community college, then Florida State twice. She took two courses a term, six a year. I was raised by my grandmother." Ruth looked directly at Grace, trying to see what she was thinking.

"Say more." Grace nodded.

"Mom worked all the time she was in school, first as a nurse's aide, then as a licensed nurse, then as a registered nurse, then as a nurse-practitioner, saving as much money as she could for my college. Education was the world to her. By my senior year, she'd saved enough for me to go to the University of Florida, *not* Florida State, for four years, tuition and room and board. 'No commuting for you,' she said. 'You're going away to college.' When I got a full scholarship to Chicago, she was as proud as a peacock. Embarrassingly proud. 'They want you so much, they're paying you to go there.'" Ruth paused. "I never did anything wrong growing up. I couldn't bear to let her down. She used the college money to buy a house, to make a down payment on a house. Both my gran and mom worried that I'd get pregnant, third generation. I'm a virgin. I couldn't take that chance."

"Why Chicago?" Grace said. She knew within minutes of meeting her that Ruth was brilliant. She was taking third-year physics and reading *The Second Sex* on her own.

"We moved to Tallahassee when I was going into ninth grade, so I could go to Chiles High School. I'd grown up south of Tallahassee, in Vestry, population five thousand, ninety percent white, a hundred percent ticks. We called our neighborhood Bus Stop because that was all there was. There wasn't even a dollar store or a 7-Eleven." Ruth shook her head, sensing Grace's incredulity. "Ninth grade was a terrible year in a hundred million ways, starting with the fact that I sat alone at lunch, I dressed like a hick, and I read books. Nobody else did. Chiles was the best high school in Tallahassee. The neighborhood was too rich for us. The rent took most of Mom's paycheck." Ruth gave a slight nod, as if pleading guilty. "But I had this great English teacher, Mrs. Goldsmith, starting sophomore year. She lent me books and CDs and took me to plays and movies. Junior year, she talked to me about colleges.

"At Chiles, the football players were gods. Most of the students stayed in state for college, except for those who went to Alabama. 'Roll Tide Roll.'" Ruth rolled her eyes. "I think I was partial to Chicago because it didn't have a football team. Mrs. Goldsmith said that I was very smart and that I needed to do well so I could go to a good university, not a college, and find people like me to talk to. She went to Chicago, English major. She so-called lent me airfare so I could

have a campus interview and tour. I worshipped her so much I practiced speaking like her. She grew up in New York but doesn't have a
New York accent, not to my ear, and she never picked up a drawl.
Southerners drop their 'g's. 'Lookin' real good, girl' is a major compliment. I'm good with languages. At the end of my senior year, Gran
said I was talking 'like a Yankee.'" Ruth smiled. "She didn't say I
talked 'above myself,' which was pretty much what everyone else
said. People would tell her I was too smart by half. 'Oh, no,' Gran
would say. 'She's smarter than that.'"

"You don't have an accent," Grace said, "not a Southern accent.
You speak slower than a Northerner, but not as slow as Midwestern-
ers."

"I speak in tongues," Ruth said. "Mostly I talk Northern, except
when I'm with Mom and Gran. Then I automatically slip into Southern. I can't not. It's like humming a tune without knowing you're
doing it." She looked sideways at Grace. "Most Northerners think
Southerners are stupid, which is an iniquitous prejudice. Southerners speak in metaphors, Northerners in euphemisms." Ruth looked
almost fierce, as if smarting from an insult. "Southerners say 'he
kicked the bucket.' Northerners say 'he passed away.' Southerners
say 'she's poorer than a field mouse.' Northerners say 'he lives below
the poverty line.' Southerners are funnier than Northerners." She
gave a half smile. "I'm not funny, but I like funny people. My gran is
funny."

"Is Mrs. Goldsmith funny?" Grace said.

Ruth shook her head. "Mrs. Goldsmith is bighearted."

"She sounds like a real mensch," Grace said. "Yiddish for a stand-
up person."

"The most stand-up ever," Ruth said. "She saved my mom's
career, her life really. A baby was born at the hospital with cerebral
palsy from oxygen deprivation. They said it was Mom's fault. Mrs.
Goldsmith got her husband to look into it. He's a hotshot lawyer in
Tallahassee, and also a . . . mensch." Ruth laughed. "He went to
Chicago too. You must know people like him. He's on the hospital's

board and the Tallahassee school board and the Florida Bar Board and every other board. He's the smartest person I know but he doesn't let on, except when he does, and then he's terrifyingly smart. He saw right off the bat what was going on. The hospital thought they could pin it on Mom, blaming the least important person in the room. They didn't think she'd defend herself, and she might not have on her own. They put her on unpaid leave. Mr. Goldsmith got the charges dismissed in two months. It took longer, but he also got the obstetrician fired. Well, not exactly fired. He lost his privileges. The hospital apologized to Mom, one of those unapologetic apologies. 'Regrettably, mistakes were made.' Mr. G. made them do it in writing. Mom resigned with a good severance package, back pay, and a recommendation, and then went to work in a doctor's office. It's a family practice. She has her own patients." She paused. "I'm going to be a doctor, a GP. Mom thinks GPs are the princes of medicine."

Grace was quiet for several seconds. "Are you doing that for your mom?" she said. "You don't have to answer it, or any question. A Lila rule: Just say, No thank you."

Ruth shook her head. "When I was eleven, I had this horrible sore throat. Gran took me to the doctor. He was in a foul mood. He was usually short with people like us, but this time he was mean as a junkyard dog." She squinched her nose. "I wanted to leave but I didn't know where else we could go. We were on Medicaid. He was it in Vestry."

"What did he do?" Grace said.

"He said he lost money on Medicaid patients and if she had any decency or pride, she'd pay another fifty dollars for the visit. He said most Medicaid patients were drug addicts or hypochondriacs." She paused. "I knew what that word meant. I'm a nurse's child."

"What did your grandmother do?"

"She was amazing. She's always amazing. She touched him gently on the arm and said, 'You're having a tough day. I can see that. Too many sick and unhappy patients. Have this.' She reached into her handbag and she handed him a cranberry muffin. She always carried muffins with her. Carefully wrapped. 'For rainy days,' she'd say." Ruth paused. "He sat down at his desk and took a large bite. 'I haven't eaten since breakfast,' he said. 'Let me write you a prescription.'"

"What kind of doctor do you want to be?" Grace said.

"A family doctor who eats lunch," Ruth said. "Don't you get cross when you're hungry and don't know it?"

"I'm always on the cusp of cross," Grace said. "Joe says I'm like a horse with a burr under my saddle. It makes me mad, but I don't balk or try to throw the jockey. I finish the race." She took a swallow of water. "He says I'm my own best enemy."

"Was it hard growing up in D.C. with a big-shot mom?" Ruth said.

"It was hard growing up with a mom who was never home," Grace said. "When I was in third grade, a friend asked me in a whisper, 'What happened to your mom? Is she dead?' I wanted to kill her, killing off Lila like that. I hissed back at her. 'My mother has the biggest job in Washington after the president. She doesn't have time for the PTA.'"

Grace reached for a bag of chips. She had a stash of snacks in a side cubby. Lila had sent them. "What happened to Lila was Aldo, her father. I didn't know that then. A story for another day. Do you want some chips or pretzels or M&M's?"

Grace shrank at the thought of talking about Lila's childhood. *I'm going to look like I'm competing, setting Lila's miserable childhood, and mine by association, against Ruth's.*

Ruth took the pretzels. "You don't look like her. I mean you don't look like her pictures," she said. "I googled you when I found out you were my roommate. Are you on Facebook? I'm not. The church said it was the devil. Now, I could join, but what then do I do, post selfies and look like an idiot."

"I tried to find you on Facebook, and when I couldn't, I googled you," Grace said. "I found your yearbook picture. You were the valedictorian. We didn't have rankings, thank heavens. Quaker school."

"I don't look like my mom either," Ruth said. "I suppose I look like that lowlife"—she paused—"the 'progenitor,' lying in the grass like a snake." Ruth was willowy, with shoulder-length, straight, dark blond hair, gray eyes, and high cheekbones. The combination was arresting. "Much better than pretty-pretty," Gran said. "Keeps away the riff-raff."

"I've looked like Joe from the get-go," Grace said. "My sisters are short and curvy and blond, like Lila, with cornflower blue eyes and rosebud lips." Grace made a fish-kiss mouth. "They're on the Barbie–purple princess spectrum. They're not stupid, far from it, but you might be fooled unless you listened very, very, very carefully. Physically, they're indistinguishable, cute as buttons."

Joe had taken Grace to college. Lila didn't have time. In the runup to the 2012 election, she was working fifteen hours a day. She had taken the older girls to Stanford, Stella in 2005 and Ava in 2006. "I took them because I had interviews with Jobs and Zuckerberg," she had said to Grace. "I wouldn't have gone otherwise. Don't take it personally. I'll go to your graduation." She hadn't gone to the older girls' graduations.

Lila thought Chicago was a good fit for Grace, especially since she refused to apply to the Ivies. Grace didn't like the D.C. kids who went to them. She called them "the carnivores." Lila shared the prejudice. "Too much entitlement," she said. "They think they should have the White House beat after six months." At the paper, she preferred state university graduates. "Their schools publish real newspapers. They don't let 'class' or 'old boy' connections—Skull and Bones, Hasty Pudding, that sort of thing—get in the way of their coverage." When Grace mentioned Stanford, thinking she might follow her sisters, Lila was leery. "Stanford was fine for the Starbirds," she said. "They're sorority girls, football fans, econ majors. They'll probably stay in California after they graduate. That's not you." She looked out the window. The day was dark and overcast. "You need weather, the way I do. Chicago has weather. Northwestern has weather. UVA, Johns Hopkins, Georgetown, MIT have weather. California only has climate: fires and mudslides, earthquakes and droughts." Grace applied early to Chicago. Joe had gone there and loved it.

"Don't do it for me," he had said to Grace.

She had laughed. "That would be so unlike me."

"Your dad is so nice," Ruth said. "I never went to a restaurant like that. I don't know what I ate." Joe had taken the girls to Topolobampo, Chicago's famous and famously expensive Mexican restaurant. "I called my mom and gran afterward and tried to explain it. They only got it when I told them the prices."

She was quiet for several seconds. "You know, if your dad was your mother, and your mother was your father, you'd have no complaints against her. You'd take it as the natural order." She looked at Grace to see if she was making inroads. "I'm sort of in the same position. Gran was really my mother. Mom was more like a father."

"Aren't you curious about your . . . 'progenitor'?" Grace said.

Ruth shook her head. "Answered prayers."

Grace started. "What do you mean?"

"Beware them," Ruth said. "He could be a drug addict, a deadbeat, a wife-beater, an Evangelical hypocrite. Most of the dads in Bus Stop lived with their girlfriends. Didn't you have friends with moms with big jobs?"

"Yes, but they showed up for soccer at least once a season," Grace said. "They went to teacher-parent meetings. They ate dinner most weeknights with their children."

"And did their dads show up?" Ruth said.

"When she showed up, my friends all thought my mom was the greatest." Grace took a handful of chips. "It's hard to be the child of a famous person. I know, I know, first world problem. Still . . . it was always, Grace Maier, the daughter of Lila Pereira, et cetera, et cetera, et cetera. On top of that, Lila was born in the equivalent of a log cabin. She came from nowhere." She caught herself. "I can't believe it. I've known you ten minutes and already I'm whining."

"You ask good questions," Ruth said.

"Is your last name your mom's?" Grace said.

Ruth nodded. "McGowan is my last name, my mom's last name, and my gran's last name. There have been no dads for generations upon generations, parthenogenesis." She gave a half laugh. "Gran jokes that the last man in the family was a Confederate Army veteran."

"My sisters have Lila's last name," Grace said. "I have Joe's."

"Do they have a different father?" Ruth said.

"No," Grace said, "Joe is their father too. It was his idea to give them Lila's name. He thought it might arouse her motherly instincts. He'd given up that illusion by the time I came along."

Ruth laughed. "You're your dad's daughter, like Athena, bursting from Zeus's brain," she said.

"Joe's great."

"You won the Dad sweepstakes, I won the Mom," Ruth said. "Gran always says, 'Know your luck.'"

"Lila always says, 'Better to be lucky than smart.'"

THE NEXT NIGHT, GRACE AND Ruth talked until 4:00 A.M. They made instant hot chocolate and caramel popcorn from Lila's care package.

"When's your birthday?" Ruth said. "Mine's March twenty-first, the first day of spring."

"We're exactly six months apart," Grace said. "Mine's September twenty-first, the first day of fall. I just turned eighteen barely."

"Why didn't you say anything?" Ruth said. "I'd have bought you a cupcake."

"We just arrived. Next year."

"I'm eighteen," Ruth said. "My mom is thirty-five. My gran is fifty-four."

"Lila is fifty-three," Grace said.

"I thought so," Ruth said. "You went to private school, didn't you. The students with 'old' moms went to private school. The ones with the old dads are from second marriages."

"Wow," Grace said. "Heavy sociology."

"Didn't you catch it?" Ruth said.

Grace shook her head. "Now, yes, but not before you said it. It just seemed normal to me." Grace smacked her forehead. "I went to Bethesda Friends. They told me I have a light inside me. You have one too."

"That's good to know since I'm not saved," Ruth said. "Mom and Gran are Baptists. I refused to be baptized when I turned twelve. It was, literally, a Come to Jesus moment and I balked. I wasn't going to be born again, not as Baptist. It's painful for all of us, but we know we're all good people, so we don't talk about it."

"Do you think of yourself as a Christian?" Grace said.

"I reckon if you woke me from a deep sleep, in the middle of the night, and asked me my religion, I would say I was Christian." Ruth took a handful of popcorn. "I wouldn't say I was *a* Christian except in the 'feed the poor,' 'love thy neighbor' way. And Christmas. I love Christmas, I love everything about it, even the Baptist Church."

"I'm Jewish, like most of the kids at Bethesda, but not at all practicing," Grace said. "My family doesn't celebrate any of the holidays, not even Passover, which has sort of become the Jewish Thanksgiving. I love Christmas too, except"—she winced—"the King of the Jews bits. My Christmas is gifts, a tree, and the movie *White Christmas.* Chanukah is to Christmas as, as . . . I'm working on my metaphor." Grace lowered her eyebrows. "As a pigeon is to a peacock."

Ruth laughed. "The Goldsmiths are Jewish," she said. "They upside-downed Mom and Gran's feelings about Jews. They used to be antisemitic without ever knowing a Jew."

"I've never had any religious education. Neither have my sisters." Grace gave a half shrug. "My grandmother says one of us has to say the Kaddish at her funeral. Joe was bar mitzvahed. He could probably do it. His Jewish is bagels, Groucho Marx, and Philip Roth. Lila's is *Survival in Auschwitz,* Irving Berlin, and Meyer Lansky. Which just goes to show how patriarchal Judaism is for their generation even for those who don't observe."

"What's your Jewish?" Ruth said.

"Leonard Cohen's "Hallelujah," *Are You There, God, It's Me, Margaret,* and RBG," Grace said. "Does Jewish mean anything to you?"

"Let me ruminate on that," Ruth said. "Off the top of my head, Anne Frank, *Seinfeld,* and Bernie Sanders." She frowned. "Growing up, Jewish meant Christ killers. Ugly." She shook her head. "Your name threw me. Grace is New Testament. But then I have an Old Testament name."

"There was a Jewish boy named Christopher at Bethesda. True," Grace said. "I went to his bar mitzvah. When the rabbi called him up to read his portion, people in the audience gasped, the ones who didn't snicker." She took a handful of popcorn. "There was a Jesus too in our class, though the 'J' was pronounced like an 'H.' He used his middle name, Antonio. Tony. No one knew his first name until graduation. When the head called his name, everyone in the class looked around. 'Who?' He was smart. He knew what would have followed. 'Hey, Jesus, walk on water for us.'" Grace scowled. "The boys at Bethesda were such jerks. They mocked everything about everyone, except being Jewish or Black."

"Were you mocked?" Ruth said. "Weren't you in the cool crowd?"

"It wasn't everyone, just the assholes." Grace jerked her head. "You don't curse, do you? I won't if you hate it. The other thing about Bethesda. We all had filthy mouths."

"I don't curse out loud," Ruth said, a faint smile appearing, Cheshire Cat–like, "but my thoughts are in the gutter."

"I can't believe that." Grace took a swallow of hot chocolate. "I wouldn't have minded the mockery, if I'd liked my name," she said. "The worst was 'I feel the Grace of God upon me.' It came with rutting gestures. Quaker nonviolence in a teacup." Her eyebrows furrowed. "Lila says the only thing to do with childhood memories is to embalm them, make stories about them. Anything bad happens, move on. Spilled milk. Joe says Lila is pre-Freudian."

"I like the name Grace," Ruth said. "What's wrong with it?"

Grace took another handful of popcorn. "It's so plain, so short, so monosyllabic," she said. "No music to it, not like my sisters' names. They have beautiful names. Stella and Ava Pereira. I'm Grace the old, gray Maier. I wish it wasn't a word."

"I've always liked my plain, short, monosyllabic name. Like RBG. Also, like my gran," Ruth said. "It's a word, too, meaning pity or sorrow, but no one uses it anymore except in the negative. Ruthless. The jokes where I come from are fart and boobie and belch jokes. Your jokes were much more sophisticated." She took a handful of popcorn. "You know you were named not only for a word but for a virtue. That's where Christianity comes in. Think of the virtue names you dodged: Patience, Faith, Prudence, Mercy." Ruth nodded, the way a schoolteacher might nod. "In the Baptist Church, we were taught that grace wasn't a little prayer you said before dinner. It was a way to live."

Grace's eyebrows took a deep dive. "When I was ten, I asked Lila why I didn't have a beautiful name, like hers and my sisters'. She didn't argue with me. She didn't say Grace was a beautiful name. She asked if I wanted her to call me Grazia. I thought she was making a joke, but I think now she was sincere. She never teases."

Grace ate the last pieces of popcorn in her hand. "Joe talked to me a few days later. He said he had picked my name, not Lila. He said he was sorry I didn't like it. He thought it was beautiful."

Grace picked up her mug. "I told him the stupid boys at school asked me if I lived in D.C. or the state of Grace. He said boys were obnoxious. And then he said something that almost reconciled me to the name. He said, 'Courage was Grace Under Pressure.'" Grace took a swallow of hot chocolate. "If I ever write a memoir, I'm going to call it *Grace Under Pressure*." She put the mug down. "When Lila offered to call me Grazia, I told her she was ten years too late. She squinted at me. 'I better watch my back around you,' she said. I was so insulted. 'I'm not a sneak,' I said. 'Watch your front.'" Grace lowered her voice, almost to a whisper. "I'm a virgin too."

11

Thanksgiving

THE DAY AFTER HALLOWEEN, LILA SENT GRACE AN EMAIL: "I'M GUESS-ing Ruth has only two round-trip tickets home, Christmas and summer. Invite her to Tara for Thanksgiving. You can rent a GM car—Frances will arrange it—and drive to Bloomfield Hills. It's four to five hours, any way you cut it, plane, train, car. Ruth wouldn't let you buy her a plane ticket. No hitching."

Grace had assumed Ruth would go home. *I am so blotto,* she thought, grateful and ashamed for Lila's intervention. *The Scholarship Sisterhood.* She trashed the email.

That evening, over dinner, Grace invited Ruth for Thanksgiving. "If you're not planning on going to Florida," she said, "you should come with me to my grandmother's house in Bloomfield Hills, Michigan. We could drive there. They all want to meet you."

Ruth's face lit up. "What a special invitation. Thank you. I hope I get to meet Lila and the Starbirds."

"My grandmother's house is called Tara," Grace said.

"Like *Gone with the Wind*?" Ruth said. "Really?"

"You'll see," Grace said.

. . .

GRACE AND RUTH LEFT CHICAGO at 1:00 P.M. the Tuesday before
Thanksgiving, planning to make it to Bloomfield Hills before dark. As
they closed in on Ann Arbor, Grace introduced "the Matter of Frances."

"'The Matter,'" Ruth said. "What Matter?"

"My grandmother, Frances, has too much money and only Joe
and me and my sisters to leave it to," Grace said. "Her father left her
a huge pile—she was an only child too—and compound interest
made it huger. She gives to charities and Democrats, but the donations never seem to make a dent. Joe calls it her Miltonian sin, 'a
huge heap increasing under the very act of diminishing.'" She
laughed. "Which is the right metaphor since Frances thinks it's a sin
to be so rich. She used to say, 'If we can't spend it or donate it, we
need to lose it.' For years, she spent two hundred dollars a week on
lottery tickets. She called it virtuous gambling because the money
went to public schools. But then she won five grand. She was so
annoyed. She didn't understand. She'd been told the chances of winning were one in a million. Joe said she was one in a million. She
didn't claim it."

"Is that 'the Matter of Frances'?" Ruth said.

"Sorry, no," Grace said. "Frances will want to buy you things, and
when she takes you shopping—she'll insist—you'll have to go." Keeping her eyes on the road, Grace nodded several times, a series of
physical exclamation points. "She'll buy you something you'd never,
ever have thought of buying. Lila wears nothing but Armani. Frances. My Birks and my Moncler puffer. Frances. The Starbirds' Mano-
los and Hermès scarves. Frances." Grace shook her head. "She'll
corner you and she'll kidnap you and the ransom will be the gift she
buys you. There's no getting round her, at least none of us has managed it."

"What does she buy Joe?" Ruth said.

"Cars. A new car whenever he's driven over fifty thousand miles,"

Grace said. "The only time he put down his foot was when he was at Michigan. He kept his old Chevy at a friend's in Bloomfield Hills so she couldn't junk it. When he graduated from law school, she bought him a Mercedes. Joe told her it was an old lady's car. She kept it for herself and bought him a BMW. He traded it for two Volkswagens, one for him, one for Lila." Grace laughed. "Of course, in her generosity, she's imperious, like a regular rich person."

"My mom would die of shame if she bought me anything other than lunch," Ruth said.

"I can talk to Joe," Grace said, "but I don't know that he can stop her. Lila capitulated the day they met. She said Frances didn't do it charitably, she did it bountifully, to everyone. No sting. Lila learned the sting of charity early. All her clothes came from the Salvation Army. She says she never had anything new except underwear. She refused to wear someone else's underpants. Their wedding, Lila and Joe's, is known as Frances's wedding. My aunt Clara is still in recovery. 'All that money,' Clara said. 'You could buy a house with it.' She was maid of honor. Frances bought her a Vera Wang dress, a gorgeous confection of satin and tulle that looked nothing like a bridesmaid's dress, more like a ball gown. 'So you can wear it again,' Frances told her." Grace did an umpteenth headshake. "As if Clara wore dresses like that. She gave it to one of those programs that give away free prom dresses."

"The Goldsmiths have bought me things," Ruth said, "but we keep a running tab. I owe them four hundred and forty dollars." She laughed. "They'll probably find a way not to take my money—Mr. G. said if I repaid the loans, he'd donate the money to the Southern Baptist Church—but Mom and I would feel better about it."

"Lila won't buy you anything," Grace said. "She'll charm you. She's irresistible. Don't worry. Don't resist. I'm so used to it. Growing up, I often wished Clara was my mother, and Lila was my aunt. It would have been so easy to love Aunt Lila."

"Do you think you're easy to love?" Ruth said. "I find you lovable, but others might find it . . . stonier ground." She looked out the window and caught sight of the sign for Bloomfield Hills. "Here comes our exit."

Grace turned off. "You'll love Clara," she said. "She's a miracle. No one knows how she turned out the way she did. Whenever we're in Detroit, she stays at Tara with us unless she's subbing for nurses with children. Frances is voracious. She's absorbed all the Pereiras, except, of course, Aldo, who she always refers to as Lila's 'nasty, brutish, and short' father. Frances is loyal." She gave Ruth a quick sideways glance. "I'm not impossible to love. Joe loves me. He says Lila loves me."

GRACE AND RUTH PULLED IN at 5:30. Ruth's reaction, like Lila's, was jaw-dropping. "I thought Tara was a joke," Ruth said.

"Wait till you get inside," Grace said.

Frances came out to meet them. "Call me Frances," she said to Ruth, smiling. "Everyone does, except Joe who, against the tide, has persevered in calling me Mom. At least to my face," She pointed to Ruth's suitcase. "I'll take that." At eighty, she moved quickly, with the ease and vigor of someone younger. "You carry the book bag." Ruth stood still, unsure what to do, her Southern manners upended.

An old friend of Joe's had recently called Frances "spry." She turned on him. "Intended, no doubt, as a compliment," she said, "but it is sexist and belittling." Joe's friend flinched. "I beg your pardon," he said.

"You must have noticed by now—what are you, fifty," she said, "that only 'old ladies' are ever called 'spry.' No one ever said, pointing to Einstein, 'What a spry old gentleman.' Old spry men are called 'amazingly youthful.'" She looked hard at him. "How would you like to be called 'dapper'?"

Frances was tall and lean, like her son and youngest granddaughter, and had their slashing, expressive eyebrows. She wasn't mean in any way, only bracingly direct, like so many rich people. "Money corrupts even more than power," Joe would say. "I'm tainted too."

Frances nodded sharply and stretched out her arm. Ruth handed her the suitcase. *It's begun,* she thought. *The "Matter of Frances."*

"I told the cook to make something delicious," Frances said. "There's only the three of us for dinner tonight. Only five for Thanksgiving dinner. Joe comes tomorrow. Lila comes when she comes. Clara has to work. Correction. She volunteered to work. Giving thanks her way." Frances shrugged in resignation. "The Starbirds are having Thanksgiving with their prospective in-laws. Who are those people to make such demands on them." She put the suitcase down, beyond Ruth's reach. "With Lila, there was never the problem of 'in-laws,' only the job, and then, only in the last decade or so." She picked up the suitcase. "I think Polo's death killed holidays for Lila and Clara, not only New Year's."

"Who's Polo?" Ruth said, looking at Frances, then at Grace, then back at Frances.

"Polo was Lila's older brother, the oldest of the three," Frances said. "A lovely human being. A swashbuckler. He was a fireman. He died in a fire. January first, 2000. Impossible to forget the day. It was our own personal 9/11."

"I didn't know she had a brother," Ruth said.

"It's hard to talk about Polo," Grace said. "I don't remember him very well. I was only six when he died. Lila was grief-stricken. I remember that. She blamed herself. I didn't recognize her. It didn't fit with the rest of her." She picked up her suitcase, swinging it away from Frances, who had reached for it with her empty hand. "About two weeks after Polo died, we were having dinner at Marco's, the five of us. Lila didn't say a word throughout the meal. She moved the food around her plate. We were all subdued, also scared. We didn't know if we'd ever get Lila back. I couldn't take this new, broken Lila." She took a deep breath. "As Joe was paying the bill, she finally spoke. 'None of you are allowed to die before me. Got it.'"

RUTH WOKE AT SEVEN. GRACE wanted to sleep in. Walking down the wedding runway, Ruth mentally squared her shoulders. *Time to get the march on Frances,* she thought.

The cook had laid out breakfast on the sideboard. It looked like the breakfast buffet at a deluxe hotel: hot cereal, hard-boiled eggs, scrambled eggs, bacon, sausage, sliced tomatoes, muesli, toast, orange juice, cranberry juice, mixed berries, yogurt. Dazed by the display, Ruth turned toward the dining table, a huge rectory table, at least fourteen feet long. *Like the table in* Citizen Kane, she thought, *but longer, grander.*

Frances, who rose every day at dawn, was seated at the far end, reading the paper. She looked at Ruth and beamed. "Oh good," she said, "I have you to myself." She pointed to the chair next to her. "Take what you want, then come sit by me. Tomorrow we'll have bagels and lox."

Ruth took a glass of juice and some scrambled eggs and toast. She saw that Frances was eating a fruit plate. *It's true,* she thought. *The really rich don't eat.*

"Is anyone else coming to breakfast, besides you and me and Grace?" Ruth said.

"The groaning board, I know," Frances said. "Holiday breakfast, the way my parents did it. I'm sure my father died of a surfeit of something, like someone in Dickens. He started life in America as an immigrant, eating a poor man's terrible diet: potatoes fried in pools of schmaltz. He ended on the top rung, eating a rich man's terrible diet: rib eye steaks slathered in butter." She pushed her plate away. "I used to eat like a plowman. Now everything . . ." She shrugged. "Tell me all about you, only what you want to tell me. I won't probe. I won't be intrusive in our first encounter."

"I'd like to probe intrusively," Ruth said. "May I?" *Frances has been direct. I'll be direct too.*

Frances laughed. "Cheeky," she said. "Go ahead."

"How did you meet your husband?" Ruth said.

Frances leaned back in her chair. "No one's asked me that question in fifty years," she said. "There's the Tracy-Hepburn version or the Bette Davis."

"Bette Davis, please," Ruth said. "I just saw *All About Eve.* Grace has me watching old movies in the middle of the night."

Frances smiled. "It was an unlucky-lucky encounter, the kind Jane Austen specialized in," she said. "My father, after he became comptroller of GM and started making real money, became suspicious of my dates, my 'suitors,' he called them, thinking they were all after his money. 'No fortune hunters for you,' he'd say. I didn't understand what he meant until I read *Washington Square* freshman year at Wellesley, but even then, I was puzzled. I'd always had nice boyfriends from 'good' families, and I wasn't plain like Catherine Sloper. Everyone we knew was well off. I thought he was paranoid." She poked distractedly at a strawberry. "I was tall, too tall for insecure men, but that was only to the good."

"Same here," Ruth said.

"We'd moved to Bloomfield Hills when I was starting high school," Frances said. "That way, I would only meet the right sort of people, which meant specifically well-off Jewish boys, who were the sons of prosperous businessmen. Best-laid plans. I had a gentile boyfriend in college. Well off, businessman father. I was crazy for him. He was at MIT. His name was George." She sighed. "When my father found out, he flew into a rage. He called me a *nafka*, a whore in Yiddish, and a *shande,* a disgrace to the community. It was the summer before my senior year. I was stunned. I had always been his darling. My mother grabbed our sweaters, took me by the arm, and pushed me out the front door. She had left before, when my father became 'overbearing,' she called it, but she'd never taken me, knowing she'd return at some point." She smiled at Ruth. "I haven't told this part of the story in years. The *nafka* part. I still find it enraging and humiliating. He was more like a jealous husband than a worried father." She took a hankie from her pocket and blew her nose. "Excuse me," she said. "I find it so easy to cry these days."

"Where did you go?" Ruth said.

"We went to friends, the Maiers, who used to be the Meyers, M-E-Y-E-R. We stayed two weeks, the longest my mother had ever been gone. The Maiers had a son, Martin, Marty, a senior at Dartmouth. Two weeks is a long time for two young people thrown together. We got engaged Thanksgiving of my senior year. He was in his first year of Harvard Law School. We got married the Sunday after I graduated."

"How did your mother and father make up?" Ruth said.

"He said he regretted his words," Frances said. "My mother said next time he was abusive, to either one of us, she'd leave for good. That was a real threat. He'd lose his job, important as he was. No divorces at the top of GM."

"Did your father like Marty?" Ruth said.

"He thought he was better than a gentile." She poked another strawberry. "My father didn't have a college education, only an accountant's training. He thought college was for lazy, weak men who didn't have the drive and guts to make it on brains and will-power. He'd wanted a businessman for me. He thought lawyers made things unnecessarily complicated. 'I had a good deal,' he'd say, 'until the lawyers stuck their noses in.'" Frances gave the slightest of nods. "The Maiers weren't wealthy, they were comfortable, but that was less a sticking point than their 'pretensions.' They were educated, cultured. They subscribed to the symphony. My father thought they were snobs. Marty's father was a Polish Jew, but his mother was a German Jew. She was a Steiner. A big name in Detroit. Her family came to America in the 1840s. My father thought they looked down on him. He called Marty a *shaygets,* a gentile."

"What happened to your relationship with your father?" Ruth said.

"I still loved him, but . . ." Frances shook her head. "But I stopped taking him seriously. His feelings were hurt. He didn't understand what he'd done wrong. He'd apologized only so that my mother and I would return." She moved the food around her plate. "I got married when I did because I couldn't have lived with him."

"Did you love Marty?" Ruth said.

Frances was quiet for several seconds. "I didn't love him the way I'd loved George," she said. "I didn't have sex with him until our wedding night. He thought I was a virgin." She turned toward the window. "He died when Joe was eleven, suddenly, a congenital heart condition, like those young football players who drop dead during practice."

"Did you ever see George again?" Ruth said.

"That's a story for another day," Frances said. She reached over and took Ruth's hand.

"What would you like to do today?"

"I'd like us, you and me, to take a walk, first on the grounds, then through the house and outbuildings." Ruth squeezed Frances's hand. "I want to see everything. I want you to tell me all the stories."

The day after Thanksgiving, Frances took Ruth and Grace to the club for lunch. She never took Ruth shopping.

LILA ARRIVED AT TARA AT 1:00 P.M. on Thanksgiving. "To the minute," she said as she walked in the house. The limousine driver who met her plane ate dinner with the cook and the waiter. She left at 4:30, to catch her 6:30 flight back to D.C. She talked to Frances, to Joe, to Ruth, to Grace. *Spreading the fairy dust,* Grace thought.

Ruth wasn't prepared for the first question Lila asked her. They'd barely sat down. "If two weeks ago," Lila said, "you had won a prize of five hundred dollars for your essay on Simone de Beauvoir, what would you have spent it on, not a need but a want?"

Ruth blurted the answer. "A plane ticket home for Thanksgiving." She turned to Frances. "This is second best. If I can't be home, this is where I want to be." She then turned to Lila. "What would you have done with the money when you were a freshman?"

"I did win a prize junior year, not five hundred dollars, but the equivalent for its time." Lila smiled. "I blew it in an afternoon. I was nineteen. I slunk into Detroit the day after Thanksgiving and took my sister and brother to lunch at the Dakota Inn, German despite the name. It was famous then, still famous now, dirndl skirts and lederhosen, like a setting from *The Student Prince.* Every twenty minutes, the sound system would play 'Drink, Drink, Drink.'

Mario Lanza." She smiled at Joe. "We'd never been to a nice restaurant. Aldo never took us to any kind of restaurant, and he didn't let us go with friends and their families. We took cabs both ways. Polo was twenty-three. Clara and I had fake IDs. We drank beer and ate schwein schnitzel and potatoes fried in lard. All *treif*. So delicious. My grandmother kept kosher. We agreed it was the best meal of our lives. Nothing could top it." Lila smiled. "The dean asked me what I had done with the money. I told her I was saving it for a plane ticket to England after I graduated. She wouldn't have understood the lunch."

Ruth squinched her nose. "I don't know if I could lie to a dean," she said. "I have lied and not been found out but it was always a surprise, not being found out. I thought my gran could read my mind."

"Did your gran think you should never lie," Lila said.

Ruth shook her head. "She would say, 'You don't owe the world the truth, but lies have a way of creeping up from behind and biting you on the keister.'"

Lila laughed. "Aldo said, 'You don't owe anyone the truth.'" She then turned to Grace. "Why do you think they put you two together as roommates? What was the housing dean thinking?"

"Height," Grace said. "Also straight hair and high cheekbones."

Ruth stared at Grace.

"I am five eleven. Ruth is six feet. 'Like Michelle Obama,' she says. We're the two tallest girls on the floor," Grace said. "Short people are friends with short people, tall with tall. All my friends at Bethesda were tall, at least five seven." She looked around the table at the startled faces. "You never noticed?"

"No," Lila said. "I don't have women friends, or men friends either, except for Doug. I have family and colleagues."

After dinner, Lila left and the party moved to the library. Frances served port, B & B, and marc. Ruth asked for a glass of marc. "I know what it is. The Goldsmiths have it, but I've never tasted it." She took a sip, then a second, then a swallow. "This is delicious," she said. "Smooth and burning. How does it do that?"

Joe was drinking beer. "I've always liked beer best. Good beers but really any beer darker than . . ." His voice trailed off.

"I saw Lila smile at you when she mentioned Mario Lanza," Ruth said to Joe.

"Lila loved *The Student Prince*. It was her favorite schlock movie." He took a swig of beer. "We danced the first dance at our wedding to 'Drink, Drink, Drink.' To the band's dismay, we piped in the Lanza recording. When the music started, we stood up. Clara and Polo joined us. We'd all gone to dancing school and learned how to dance the Viennese waltz." He summoned the memory. "We twirled around the room in huge swoops. The guests went wild. Even Mom." He smiled at Frances. "Lila had insisted on the dancing lessons. 'I don't know any dance steps,' she said. 'I have to learn to ballroom-dance before our wedding.' We started with the two-step, then the fox-trot, then the Lindy, then the waltz, then the Viennese waltz. After that Lila wanted to learn to tango, but I refused. Our height difference would have made us look ridiculous, like a stork dancing with a chicken."

At bedtime, Grace asked Ruth how she'd rate Thanksgiving at Tara, "being your first, with no basis of comparison." They'd taken up rating events. Grades mattered so much at Chicago, they'd decided to grade everything.

"I'd give it an A minus. The Starbirds and Clara weren't here, a disappointment to be borne, and Lila didn't stay long enough. Frances, standing alone, was A plus. Like my gran."

Joe left on Friday. Ruth and Grace left on Saturday. Frances wanted them to stay until Sunday, but they begged off. "We have papers to write, books to read," Grace said. "Sometimes I wish I'd gone to Michigan. Everyone is so serious at Chicago, so studious. 'The place where fun goes to die.'"

On Friday night the three of them watched *Desk Set* with Tracy and Hepburn. "A rom-com with middle-aged people," Grace said.

"Much better than *Guess Who's Coming to Dinner*," Ruth said.

"I had a Jewish friend who married a gentile," Frances said. "Her parents sat shiva."

The next morning, Grace and Ruth took off early.

"You must come every year. I'm counting on it," Frances said to Ruth. "Of course, if you win a prize and buy a ticket home, I'll understand." They hugged.

"Frances never bought you anything," Grace said as the car pulled out of the driveway, "not even a plane ticket home."

"No," Ruth said. "She knew I couldn't have refused it, much as I would have wanted to. Too high a ransom."

12

Florida

AFTER THANKSGIVING BREAK, RUTH INVITED GRACE TO VISIT HER IN Florida. "You must come in June, before the mosquitoes take over," she said. "You can meet my mom and Gran and the Goldsmiths. They've heard so much about you."

"Thank you. I'd love to," Grace said. Ruth was teaching her manners by example. Pre-Ruth, she would have said "Sure, awesome."

"Mom and Gran will die if they find out I called your parents by their first names," Ruth said. "I suppose if I call them Joe, sir, and Lila, ma'am, they wouldn't mind so much." She laughed. "You don't have to worry about sirring and ma'aming. Mom thinks Yankees have bad manners and Gran thinks they have no manners. But they already love you for taking me to Tara for Thanksgiving."

"You have to come to Tara for spring break. Frances insists," Grace said. "She's crazy about you. What did you two talk about?"

"I asked her how she met your grandfather. She told me. Boom. It was a 'strangers on a train' moment." Ruth stopped to consider what to say next. "It's always easier talking to a stranger than to kin. Gran says kin only hear what they want to. Your brother says: 'Ma was mean.' You're thinking: 'Ma loved me best.' All family life is *Rashomon*." She nodded. "I believe everything Frances said. Hers is the only version. I didn't know her father, who, by the way, didn't get a name. I thought that was telling."

"His original name, off the boat, was Hyman Feldstein," Grace said. "When GM recruited him, he changed it to Henry Fieldstone. He'd say, 'People call me Hank.' So they called him Hank. Frances said he hated the name Hyman. The sexual homonym made him squirm."

"Frances never called him anything but 'my father,'" Ruth said. "She's eighty, he's been dead, I don't know, forty years. He's still taking up a lot of acreage in her brain."

"I'll never get over Lila," Grace said. "If I have children, they'll never get over me."

"Did you notice," Ruth said. "Frances looks backward, Lila looks forward. Joe must have seen that. He must have wanted that."

Grace started. "The things you think of never cross my mind. I don't know if it's because I'm unimaginative or inattentive. There are other explanations, which I don't care to entertain."

"I want to be fair," Ruth said.

Grace laughed. "I want to be right."

THE SECOND WEEK OF JUNE, Grace flew to Tallahassee. Ruth, her mom, and her gran met the plane. Grace was excited and nervous. *I'm meeting real Southerners,* she thought. *Will they invite me to go to church with them.* She had asked Ruth what she should call her gran and her mother.

"Southern style would be Miss Ruth and Miss Ann," Ruth said, "but that sounds too hokey, plain old Ms. McGowan and Ms. McGowan will do."

The McGowans' house, purchased with the University of Florida money, was a three-bedroom, off the Count Turf Trail.

"We bought it for the trees, for the shade," Ms. Ann said. "And the kitchen. All electric. Built-ins." She pointed to a computer on a built-in desk in the corner. "We read *The Globe* online. Would you say it's a . . . liberal paper?"

"The editorial pages are, but the publisher runs those," Grace said. "Lila doesn't like opinion pieces. She fired someone, early on, for repeatedly sticking his opinions into news stories. 'Analysis,' he called them. She gave him two warnings. The message got through to the others."

"I'm confused. I thought your mother was the editor," Ms. Ann said.

"Oh, sorry. Lila is my mother," Grace said. "My sisters and I call her Lila. Her doing. We call our dad Joe, for symmetry." Grace shrugged. "Lila's on a first-name basis with just about everyone but President Obama and doctors. If a doctor wants to be called Dr. Podsnap, and not plain Bill, she'll tell him to call her Ms. Pereira. She likes mutuality. She's on a first-name basis with all the *Globe* employees, from the porters to the publisher."

"Is that a Yankee custom?" Gran said.

"No. It's Lila. She's a small 'd' democrat. She got into trouble her sophomore year at Michigan. She called her English professor by his first name. He got his back up. 'I'm Professor Podsnap,' he said. She almost laughed. 'Do you need to be called "professor" to know you're the professor,' she said. He reported her for insubordination." Grace laughed. "Lila had a conversation with the dean of discipline. She agreed not to call Podsnap by his first name. She didn't call him any-thing. Two years ago, she got an honorary degree from Michigan. Podsnap came to the reception. 'Lila,' he said. 'You've done us proud.' 'Ms. Pereira,' she said. Lila can hold a grudge forever."

"Were they both the doctor and the professor Podsnaps?" Ms. Ann said. "What an odd name. And two of them."

Grace shook her head. "Sorry about that. Joe came up with the name. Lila was using real names in her stories. 'Just call them all Podsnap, unless they're recurring characters,' he said. 'We'll know where you're heading.' He didn't want to know their real names. He doesn't hold grudges and certainly not by proxy."

"Does a Podsnap ever have a first name?" Ms. Ruth said.

"Oh, no," Grace said. "Lila's never on a first-name basis with a Podsnap. Someone in her bad books loses first-name privileges for eternity."

"She is a character, your mother," Ms. Ann said.

"She is," Grace said. "Someday, I'm going to write about her."

The McGowans were struck by Grace's confidence. "She speaks right up," Ms. Ann said to Ms. Ruth in private, not sure she approved. "Not like a Tallahassee girl."

"Piffle," Ms. Ruth said. "Tallahassee girls singsong or giggle. You like that better?"

"There sure were a lot of Podsnaps at the hospital," Ms. Ann said. "It's like the Army. All the doctors are generals, and all the nurses are sergeants."

THAT NIGHT AT BEDTIME, RUTH said softly, "I think the 'progenitor' is a Podsnap."

"Do you know his real name?" Grace said.

"Robert E. Lee Bates," Ruth said, "known about Vestry as Bobby Lee."

"Is he a real Lee?"

"No," Ruth said. "The parents named the sons after Confederate heroes. His brother was Jefferson Davis Bates. It's just as well they didn't have a hand in raising me up."

"How do you know their names?"

"Google and the genome. I took a DNA test in March, when I turned nineteen. There's a company called Genealogies. A birthday gift from me to me. Mom always said it wasn't rape. 'I was drunk,' she says. 'I liked the way he smelled. I think it was Old Spice.'"

"Does he know about you?"

"He didn't, but he does now. His brother, Jeff Bates, did Genealogies, too. I popped up as his niece."

"Couldn't your mom have told you Podsnap's name?" Grace said.

"She thought he was named for Robert E. Lee," Ruth said. "She pushed the 'event' out of her mind. She was four months pregnant before she told Gran. She didn't remember much. I'm guessing, the earth didn't move." She squinched her nose. "But, hey, here I am, lucky and grateful to be alive. Mom and Gran both say I was the best thing that ever happened to them. Mom says I made her turn her life around. Gran says at thirty-five, she was finally the right age to raise a baby."

"How come you took the test? Answered prayers and all that."

"I'm a new Ruth, bad Ruth. I've been wanting to know for a while, but Mom and Gran didn't want me to test. I thought about it for a month, every day, but I didn't think it through. It was 'should I or shouldn't I.'" She shrugged. "It was my first act of rebellion."

"What do you want out of it, and don't tell me it's his medical history."

Ruth was quiet for several seconds. "I want him to know I exist," she said.

"Do your mom and gran know about the test?"

Ruth nodded. "Here's where it gets truly weird. The day I got the result, Mrs. Bobby Lee Bates called Mom. She asked if it was true that her husband, Robert E. Lee Bates, was Ruth McGowan's daddy. Mom said she believed so. The name sounded right. Mrs. Bobby Lee said her brother-in-law had taken a DNA test and I had popped up as his niece. She said she was very upset, 'as you can imagine,' and she didn't want any trouble from 'Little Ruth.' She hoped I wasn't 'after anything' from their family. Mom was fit to be hog-tied. 'Don't you worry,' she said. 'Ruth is at the University of Chicago on a full academic scholarship. It's the fourth best university in the country according to U.S. News. You have a nice day, now.'"

"One proud mother," Grace said.

Ruth smiled. "When I came down for breakfast, Mom asked me if I had taken a DNA test. I said I had. She wanted to know why. I said I wanted to know who provided the sperm. She winced. I winced. It was awkward. I said, 'What should I call him? I can't call him Daddy or Pa or Father.' I handed her the results. They showed the uncle and an assortment of cousins. I googled Jeff Bates and found an obituary for his father. Bingo. There was Podsnap."

"Do you have their address?" Grace said. "Don't you think we should drive down and look at the house, maybe catch a glimpse."

Ruth shook her head. "I'll stick to Google for now."

"I can't see naming my children after generals or presidents, not even Lincoln," Grace said. "Poets and novelists, maybe. Or maybe fictional characters. Jo March Maier, Nancy Drew McGowan."

"I grew up with a girl named Scarlett O'Hara Murphy," Ruth said. "She was named for the movie, not the book."

"Do you want children?" Grace said.

"I don't know. It's so far in the future. I can't wrap my mind around it," Ruth said.

"I'd only have children if I married someone like Joe," Grace said. "I can dimly see myself being a mother but not a good one."

Ruth had a summer paralegal job working at Mr. G.'s law firm. He thought she should be a lawyer.

"You're a natural," Mr. G. said. He had offered her the job over Christmas break. "You don't have to do what I do. You can go the high road. Clerking, U.S. Attorney's Office, teaching." They had been sitting in his office, drinking coffee and eating coffee cake.

"I want to be a doctor," she said.

"Work for me in the summer," he said. "I pay well."

"Everyone says I need to work in a lab, to show I'm serious," she said.

"That's shortsighted thinking," he said, shaking his big head. "Two reasons. One. The pay is crappy in labs, if they pay at all. I'll pay much better. Build a nest egg. Two. No one should go to med school straight out of college. You should wait, at least three years." He leaned back and put his long legs on the desk. "I have four reasons for waiting." He pointed at her again. "One. You need to live where you are now. Don't waste your time at Chicago taking premed courses. Take them at FSU, after you graduate. Two. You need to take a break. You've been a student your whole life, and you've been living in a teenage bell jar this year. You need to mix with children, old people, people who haven't been to college. You need real-life experience. Three. You need to grow up, mature. You need perspective. Twenty-six, you're an adult. I'm talking physiology and neuroscience. Until then, your judgment sucks. Four. You need to look deep inside. Find out who you are before you decide what you're going to be. I think you're too smart to be a doctor. You may even be too smart to be a lawyer."

"Did you go straight from college to law school?" Ruth said.

"Yes," he said. "I'm saving you from my mistakes."

"What did you want to be?" she said.

"A cartoonist," he said.

"I'd never have guessed," Ruth said. "Why did you give it up?"

"I wasn't always like this, throwing my weight around, telling people off if I wasn't suing them. My parents wanted me to go to law school, but they said they'd pay for it only if I went directly. I was just twenty-one, immature, insecure, cosseted. I buckled. I got into Harvard. I went. I told my kids I wouldn't pay for graduate school until they were twenty-five. They had to go do something else first, I didn't care what it was. They took me at my word. They hiked." He hooted. "They turned out fine. Nico just finished his first year of medical school. Xander's working in a writers' room in Hollywood. Something called *Suits*."

"If I work for you this summer," Ruth said, "how much are you paying?"

"Enough to cover your books and spending money for sophomore year," he said, "and two round-trip airplane tickets home. We'll work it out."

He made good on his word. Ruth's starting pay was seven hundred dollars a week, three hundred less than the regular paralegals made. After three weeks, Mr. G. jumped her to eight hundred a week, with the promise of another jump in a few weeks.

"I told him he couldn't go higher than nine hundred dollars,"

Ruth said to Grace. They were sitting in Ruth's bedroom, snacking on tortilla chips. "I told him it would be terrible for the regulars' morale. He pooh-poohed it. He said they wouldn't find out. I said they'd find out before I did. Someone should write a book, *What the Boss Doesn't Know*."

"And you're liking the work?" Grace said.

"For eight hundred dollars a week, I think it's great."

"I'm getting three hundred a week at *The District*. At eight hundred a week, I'd still hate copyediting. Who reads an internet paper for D.C. employees? And who writes for it?" Grace raised her eyebrows. "I don't mind so much that the writers can't spell, punctuate, or keep their verb tenses straight. They don't have topic sentences or paragraphs. They write like bots. Or vice versa." She shook her head. "I don't see how anyone can break into journalism if they don't have parents with money."

THE GOLDSMITHS INVITED RUTH AND Grace to dinner at Vinegar Hill, a new farm-to-table eatery the locals either loved or hated.

"Organic, no GMOs or antibiotics, free range," Mr. G. said. "They explain what you're eating. As if you didn't know what you ordered. Last time I told them I didn't want to know. I wanted to be surprised."

"I'm trying to go meatless," Mrs. G. said. "Most of the local restaurants take it as an insult."

"I thought Florida was where your Jewish grandmother moved in her seventies," Grace said. "A nice condo near the beach. Early bird specials."

Mrs. G. shook her head. "North Florida is really south Georgia. Cracker country. Tallahassee had huge cotton plantations worked by slaves. Well into the sixties, segregation was endemic—schools, hospitals, libraries, buses, stores, you name it. Floridians likened the day *Brown v. Board of Education* was decided to Pearl Harbor." She fiddled with her fork. "Native New Yorker, here." She gestured with her fork toward her husband. "Native Floridian."

"I grew up here, son of a Chicagoan," Mr. G. said. "My father was stationed at Camp Gordon during the war. He met my mother, a local girl, moved to Tallahassee, and married her in 'forty-seven. I was born in 'fifty. He went to Florida Law and hung up a shingle the same year. My grandfather, my mother's father, owned a dry goods store. He sent his customers to my dad. First, the Jews came, then the rest." Mr. G. laughed, a real guffaw, loud and throaty. "It took a lot of sweet talking to get Kathy to move to Tallahassee. The town was pretty much segregated throughout my growing up. There was knee-jerk antisemitism—golf clubs, neighborhoods, that sort of thing—but nothing like the hostility and animosity shown to Blacks."

"Some of the antisemitism was based on Jewish support of Blacks," Mrs. G. said. "Not in Richard's family."

"My father thought Kathy was 'a dangerous influence' on me, or as they used to say 'bad for the Jews,'" Mr. G. said. "He was always waiting for the next pogrom."

"Why did you come back?" Grace said.

"I got a clerkship with the first Jewish justice on the Florida Supreme Court.

Grace turned to Mrs. G. "Why did you move here?"

"He asked me to give it a try. 'Come the year I clerk,' he said. 'If you hate it, we'll move.' I got the job at Chiles because I flew down for the interview, instead of phoning in. 'We appreciate the effort you made, coming down,' the committee chair said. I wore heels and makeup, which in Florida then wasn't optional." She gave a slight headshake as if to say, *Welcome to the South.* "I found I liked teaching. I liked the kids. I got tenure after three years, though Florida tenure is like Florida snow. Evanescent. I taught for almost twelve years before our boys, the twins, were born, in 'eighty-seven. I went back to Chiles when they were six months. I've been teaching ever since with a few mini sabbaticals." She smiled. "I get along easily with people."

"Like Ruth," Grace said. "I get along uneasily with people."

"Don't put yourself down," Mrs. G. said. "That's a job for other people."

"How's this instead," Grace said. "I don't try to get along with people. I barely get along with myself."

"You're interested in people, the things they know and say," Mrs. G. said. "You ask questions. And then you ask follow-up questions. It's interesting watching you and Ruth. She's a remarkable listener, but you're the remarkable questioner." Grace sat back, embarrassed by the praise. Mrs. G. continued. "Ruth asks one big question, smack on point, then waits. You ask one off-kilter question after another, until the person spills."

"What do you talk about with your parents?" Mr. G. said to Grace.

"We talk about everything, but politics mostly. Joe tries to keep me thinking in a straight line. He says I zigzag. Lila doesn't care. She's interested in the ideas, the connections. She can follow someone's jumbled thoughts down a rabbit hole and ask exactly the right follow-up question. She'll disagree but she doesn't argue and she never pigeonholes people. She thinks anyone might say something interesting. She'll talk economics with the porters and the secretaries, medical ethics with the sportswriters. 'People surprise you,' she says. 'Always ask.'"

"You are not a Southern girl," Mr. G. said. "No makeup."

"No makeup, no perfume," Grace said. "No pantyhose, no high heels."

"I never wear makeup at school," Ruth said. "I gave it up on the second day. I was the only one wearing it." She smiled. "Mom made me put it on tonight. But I'll never wear foundation again."

"Does your mother wear makeup?" Mrs. G. said.

"Eyeliner, mascara. She says her eyes look like poached eggs without it. She's very fair, hair the color of straw, skin the color of parchment, eyes the color of Wedgwood china." Grace half-smiled. "She's beautiful," she said. "I look like my father."

"He must be handsome," Mrs. G. said. Grace rocked back in her seat.

"It took me a while to see how pretty the Chicago girls were, without makeup and big hair. Kathy called it 'topiary.'" Mr. G. laughed. "I didn't know the girls in Tallahassee wore makeup all the time, even to bed. Waterproof and sweatproof." He laughed again. "There were some very smart girls in my high school class but they didn't let on. I think that's changed." He gestured toward his wife. "Kathy sends the smart girls, and the smart boys too if they'll listen, up north to college." He turned to Ruth. "Are you still premed? What are you majoring in?"

Ruth turned to him. "I'm thinking about classics. I had four years of Latin at Chiles and I loved it. Now I'm taking Greek and more Latin. I can do a premed postbac after I graduate."

Mr. G. hooted. Other diners looked at him. "Did you actually take my advice. You don't need to answer, my ego is big enough."

Mrs. G. turned to Grace. "You're majoring in English, no? I think Ruth said that."

Grace shook her head. "I'll take at least one English course every semester, but I've decided to major in history, ancient history, Roman, which is also art history. I write lousy English papers. I don't mind getting bad grades. I mind doing bad work." She smiled. "I can write history papers, I love facts, and I've taken lots of Latin, too, which gives me cred with the department."

"I'm surprised," Mr. G. said. "You strike me as thoughtful, also observant."

"I'm not observant," Grace said. "I notice. Magpie brain. Something catches my eye or my ear, I perk up. It's not that I don't think—when thinking's demanded—but my default is reporting what I heard and read."

Later that night, as they were getting ready for bed, Ruth called Grace out.

"You're observant," she said. "All that spying you did of Lila. Wasn't that observing?"

"No," Grace said. "I carried my notebook everywhere in case she said or did something Lilaesque. I was looking for the gotcha moments."

"How would you rate the evening?" Ruth said. "I say, being back home with the Goldsmiths, hog heaven."

"A plus. They're terrific, both of them," Grace said. "Mrs. G. may be a saint, Jewish division. Jewish sainthood doesn't require martyr-dom or miracles, just insane generosity and kindness." She stopped to pull together her thoughts. "As for Mr. G., I look at him, with his loud voice, his cowboy boots, his wild hair, his guffawing laugh. He's Sacha Baron Cohen."

Ruth smiled. "They're always A plus," she said, "but you were A plus, too. The way you talked about Lila tonight was amazing. You only praised her." She smiled slyly. "I'm not an easy grader."

"One of Lila's iron rules," Grace said. "'No whining in public. The story gets lost. All they remember is that you're a whiner.'" Grace gave a half nod. "I liked them so much, I wanted them to like me." She paused to find the exact, right words. "They mean a lot to you, and they love you."

Ruth blinked back tears. "I love them, too."

"Another Lilaism," Grace said, "her daily-life take on Newton's third law. Life tends to be reciprocal."

13

Interviews

THREE WEEKS BEFORE THE 2012 ELECTION, JOE, PUSHING AHEAD WITH the separation, put the house on the market. He told Lila he was doing it but he wasn't sure she'd taken it in.

A few days later, Grace came home, arriving after midnight. Taking advantage of the long Columbus Day weekend, she had hopped a plane to belatedly celebrate her nineteenth birthday.

"I'm glad you're here," Joe said to Grace the next morning at breakfast. "Lila and I are splitting. I wanted to tell you in person." He was setting the table. *It's easier saying it standing,* he thought. *I can move around.* "My plan is to move the first week in January. The house is for sale. I bought an apartment in the Wyoming." He stood still, his eyes meeting hers, his face grim. "I'm sorry I'm ruining your birthday."

"Where is she?" Grace said, deadpan, the way Lila responded to car crashes and train derailments.

"At work," Joe said. "She came in later than you but left a little after seven."

"I never expect to find her at home," she said.

"Are you okay?" he said.

Grace shrugged. "You've been living separate lives for years," she said. "I couldn't understand why you stayed."

"My life was with Lila and the three of you," he said.

"How did the Starbirds take the news?" she said.

"I had to tell them separately, on the phone," he said. "That was hard. Untethered, they didn't know how to react at first. They said they were sorry. They didn't cry." He stirred his coffee. "Stella said she wasn't surprised. Lila wasn't wife material. Ava said she was surprised. She thought I would stick it to the end. It's funny how they said the same thing so differently. Standard Starbird: point, counterpoint."

"Are you sad?" Grace said.

"Yes," Joe said.

"Will you get divorced?"

"I don't know."

"She's feral." Grace took a bite of bagel. *I wonder if I'll ever eat cold pizza with Lila again.* She felt a pang.

Joe didn't answer.

"Why did you ever marry her?" Grace said.

"If you're angry, get angry. I don't like this guerrilla skirmishing," he said.

Grace mumbled an answer. Joe took it as "sorry."

"Sometimes I regret we're on a first-name basis, and not good old 'Mom' and 'Dad,'" he said. "The boundaries blur. Except when you're sick or broke, you think you're a grown-up, entitled to know what the grown-ups know. Functional only child syndrome. Your sisters never think of themselves that way."

"Ruth and I stay up late talking," Grace said. "Before freshman year, I never shared a room with anyone. We ask each other anything and everything, with the proviso that we don't have to answer. I despise Truth or Dare. You don't play games with the truth." Joe gave a slight nod. "I've told her almost everything about me and the family. I understand now what the Starbirds have. We don't look alike, Ruth and I, but we're the same type." She grinned. "Tall, dark, and handsome."

"I'm detecting traces of charm in your humor, not only barbs," Joe said.

Grace lowered her head, unable to face him, unspeakably pleased. "I'm still a feminist," she said.

"Me, too," he said.

GRACE CALLED HER MOTHER'S OFFICE. She asked her assistant if she might make an appointment to see her later in the day, anytime between 5:00 and 7:00 P.M.

Her assistant said she should come at 5:00. "Late afternoon lull."

Lila was amused. She hadn't known Grace was coming home. She had sent a birthday gift to school, a pair of small Georg Jensen silver earrings. Grace had told her parents and grandmother she didn't want big, fancy gifts sent to Chicago. She'd feel awful opening the box around Ruth.

Lila was good at gifts, so long as they were things and not events or activities requiring her physical presence. The best gift Grace ever got was a pair of red Wonder Woman boots that Lila gave her for her fifth birthday. They were soft red leather, not plastic, and looked exactly like the comic book ones, with the pointed rim at the knee and the white stripe down the front. Grace opened the box and threw herself on the floor in ecstasy. She wore them every day until she outgrew them. She didn't throw them out but had Joe make a display box for them, which she set on a bookshelf facing the door to her room, the first thing everyone entering saw.

"It has an uncanny religious vibe," Joe said.

"Sort of like reliquary boxes in St. Marco's," Lila said.

When Grace started middle school, she moved the box to the floor and used it as a bedside table. She still had it.

Lila called the local deli and asked if they could send round a chocolate babka. Grace, like Joe, didn't like cakes with icing.

"I like chaste cakes," Joe said.

"Sahara cakes," Lila said. She preferred icing to cake. "The best desserts are baby food," she would say as she dug into a mousse, a pudding, a crème brûlée. "No teeth required."

The babka arrived at 4:30. Lila opened the package and sliced off a small piece with her switchblade. *They make a good babka, not a great one,* she thought, *but then no one makes great babkas anymore, not since Bubbe.* Lila started as if slapped. *What do you know, an affectionate memory of Bubbe.*

Grace arrived at 5:00 P.M. sharp. She smiled when she spied the babka.

"What can I do for you," Lila said.

"Joe said you're separating. I came to find out how you're taking it." Grace picked up the switchblade and sliced the babka.

"I'm taking the long view," Lila said. "We're not getting divorced, for now. I'll wait him out. I want to stay married to him even if I'm no good at it."

"He could find someone." Grace sat down.

"He could find dozens of someones," Lila said. "I'll keep my eyes open. I don't think he's stopped loving me. I haven't stopped loving him."

"Where are you going to live," Grace said. "Joe said you're selling the house."

"I've rented a place in Adams Morgan, with all the Gen Xers," she said, "It has three bedrooms. I rented it furnished."

"You never made any effort at home," Grace said. "If something required effort, you didn't do it."

"I've gotten worse with this job," Lila said, ignoring the barb. "I'm in its thrall."

"That's not fair to Joe," Grace said.

"I know that," Lila said. *Children, employees, all the same, needy and aggressive.*

"You don't love him enough, or the right way," Grace said.

Lila was silent for several seconds, the old Monty Python joke jingling in her brain: *No one expects the Spanish Inquisition.* "It's a compulsion," she said. "I worked hard at all my jobs, but this job has consumed me."

"You love your work more than anything," Grace said.

"No," Lila said. "I want it *now* more than anything. I need it *now* more than anything. I love you and Joe and Stella and Ava and Clara and Frances more."

Grace sat back, stunned. She couldn't remember her mother ever saying she loved her. Joe had said Lila loved her, but Grace had been too scared to ask Lila directly. *What if she stopped to think about it.*

Grace stood up. "I'm going now. Thank you for sending the earrings. I wear them all the time." She held her hair back so Lila might see. "When do you have to retire," she said.

"In ten years, at sixty-five." Lila stood up too. "Of course, Doug can fire me anytime."

"Will you stay enthralled until then?"

Lila shook her head. "It started in 2008 with the Hillary–Obama primary. It seemed the world hung on the election. Then, there's this election. World still hanging."

Grace walked toward the door. As she reached for the handle, she turned toward Lila. "Are you having an affair with Doug?"

"Are you saying only a lover explains why I'm never home, always at *The Globe,*" Lila said. "Sex, not work."

"No, no," Grace said. "I don't know what I meant. It just came out."

Lila walked around her desk, picked up the babka, put it in its bag, and handed it to Grace. "Happy Birthday," she said. "Maybe I can make it home for dinner tonight or tomorrow."

Grace lowered her eyebrows. "'When the clocks strike thirteen.'"

THE NEXT DAY, GRACE DECIDED to call the Starbirds. She wanted their take on the separation. She arranged to call them at their office.

They'd be together. She wanted the duet. She loved the swing between them, the clarinet and the flute. They almost drowned her, then they saved her. *I suppose that's all you can expect from older sisters,* she thought. She'd heard much worse from friends at Chicago, though more about parents than siblings. No one's father was as horrible as Lila's, but some came close. She had been sickened by the story Ruth's boyfriend, Artie Brinkman, told. Artie came from a family of hard-core practical jokers. "They were so good at it," he had said. "If pranking were an Olympic event, they'd have medaled."

He was sitting on the bed in his room, along with Ruth, Grace, and a few other friends. It was their second night back from their post-freshman summer. They were so happy to be together. "This is home, now," Artie said. "I'm done with them."

On his return to Allentown in June, Artie had found the family house empty and abandoned. A For Sale sign stood on the front lawn; the windows were shrouded in sheets; the garage was empty, the locks changed. He rang the bell, he banged on the doors, he walked around the house several times. He called his parents' numbers. He got their voicemail. He called his brother's number. The same. He sat on the front steps for two hours, then walked several blocks to the home of an old high school friend. "I forgot they were going on vacation," he said to his friend. "I left my keys at school." He shrugged. "At school, they just buzz you in." He spent the night at his friend's. The next day he walked back to the house. The For Sale sign was gone, the windows were open, the cars were parked in the garage, the locks worked.

"I went in the side door. My parents were eating breakfast in the kitchen," he said. "'We thought you were coming yesterday,' my mother said. 'We were starting to get worried,' my father said. I didn't know what to say. 'This is batshit,' I thought. And then the light went on. This was one of their jokes, the best or the worst, depending on your way of looking at the world. I was angry, really angry. I'd had a terrible time the last twenty-four hours." He was breathing heavily, as if reliving it.

"I didn't say anything for a long time, at least a minute, thinking how I would respond. They began twitching with excitement. They couldn't wait to spring the joke. I sat down at the table. 'I stayed an extra day at school,' I said. 'My girlfriend's pregnant.' They sat still, in shock. I took a piece of bacon. 'We'll probably get married.' My father's face turned beet red. I thought he'd have a heart attack. My mother started crying. 'Unless she gets an abortion.' My mother started wailing. She's pro-life, if it's fetal. They sat there looking crushed, as much for their lost victory as for my bad news. I stood up. 'Just kidding,' I said. 'Prank for prank. Gotcha good, didn't I?'"

Artie slumped. He had tried to bury the experience. He felt his anger rising again. "They were mad at me for ruining their joke. I can't forgive them. I hate myself when I'm mean like that. I'm not going home this coming summer, or the next, or ever again. I'd taken part in some of their jokes against my brother. I apologized to him. He didn't understand. He'd drunk the Kool-Aid."

GRACE WENT INTO HER BEDROOM to call her sisters. *Artie's parents were the meanest,* she thought, *but some of the others had rotten parents too. Not Ruth, of course. And, let's be honest here, not me. I'm luckier than I'm able to admit. Why can't I hold the thought?* She lay back on her bed. *Why am I so angry at Lila? Did she want an abortion? Did Joe talk her out of it? I don't like to think of that. Is it because I don't look like her? Is it my personality? Is it me or is it her? Why aren't the Starbirds the tiniest bit mad at her?*

Grace called their law office.

"What's this about?" Stella said. "Lila and Joe splitting?"

"Yes," Grace said. "Are you upset? Surprised? Disappointed? Relieved? Indifferent?"

"Is this a question or a multiple-choice test?" Ava said.

"Do you want them to stay together?" Stella said.

"I don't know," Grace said. "I guess so. At least for logistics."

"They've given a name to what's been going on for years," Ava said. "They were separated before they separated."

"You haven't answered my question," Grace said.

"Sad, not surprised," Stella said.

"They're sad, or maybe unhappy," Ava said. "One of those."

"Lila's not sad or unhappy," Grace said. "She's regrouping."

"You don't know that," Stella said. "She doesn't show her feelings."

"What feelings?" Grace said.

"You always want Lila to be different from who she is," Ava said.

"Joe said they're not getting divorced, at least not now," Grace said.

"I don't think they'll ever get divorced," Stella said. "Neither can imagine life without the other."

"They'll never fall in love with anyone else," Ava said.

"Are they still in love?" Grace said.

"Unquestionably," Stella said. "Their relationship is the most important one of their lives. Joe has always come first with Lila, and Lila with Joe."

"Where do we fit in?" Grace said.

"We're transients," Ava said. "We're already gone. You're almost gone."

"Where is this conversation going?" Grace said.

"You're acting as if this is happening to you," Stella said, "when it's happening to them. What do you want from Lila?"

"I want her to pay attention to me," Grace said. "I had to make an appointment with her secretary to see her."

"Oh, Grace," Ava said. "You're still longing for the mother who picks her children up from school. Isn't it enough that you were picked up."

"She could have done it once," Grace said.

"Did you ever ask her how her day at *The Globe* went?" Stella said. "Are the printers still on strike? Did someone threaten to fire-bomb the building?"

Grace was silent. The Starbirds waited.

"I was a kid," Grace said, immediately regretting it. *Whine, whine, whine,* she thought.

"Our parents' marriage is pretty normal," Ava said, "except that Lila is the dad and Joe is the other dad. Sort of *Heather Has Two Mommies,* but the opposite."

"Do you think Joe will date?" Grace said.

"Maybe if he gets really lonely, but probably not," Stella said. "I think he's shaking the rafters. Telling Lila to shape up."

"The problem is the new place will give him no consolation, no pleasure," Ava said. "He just should have moved into the Jefferson."

"Lila won't date," Grace said.

"No," Stella said. "She's not interested in other men, and loneliness doesn't get to her. But then, she's never alone."

"Do you think she was surprised?" Grace said.

"Gob-smacked," Ava said.

"Do you think Zelda died," Grace said, "or do you think she ran off?"

"Whoa," Ava said. "Where is that coming from?"

"I was thinking about abandonment," Grace said.

Neither Starbird said anything.

Grace persevered. "If her mother died, that was sad. If she ran away and left her children behind, that was heartless."

"Are you saying Lila is heartless?" Stella said. "Are you saying she abandoned you?"

"You're not taking Aldo into account," Ava said. "Lila didn't know anything about being a parent so she left it to Joe. Safer that way."

"You need to let it go," Stella said. "She doesn't do what she can't do. She's damaged. We know that."

"But she's also heroic," Ava said.

Grace didn't say anything.

"Time to go," Stella said.

"Until next," Ava said.

Grace hung up. *They never say they love me,* she thought. *I never say I love them. Do we love each other? In a Pereira way, I guess.*

Stella and Ava looked at each other.

"We were lucky, having each other," Stella said.

"We didn't miss Lila," Ava said.

"I thought Grace would have let up on Lila by now," Stella said.

"She doesn't seem to have noticed that Lila never hit us," Ava said, "never yelled at us."

14

Graduation

GRACE GRADUATED CUM LAUDE. IT WAS EASIER THAN IT SOUNDED though not easy. Nothing at Chicago was easy. "The competition in history has thinned out," she told her parents. Joe had graduated magna, when history was one of Chicago's biggest majors. Lila said she'd done "good enough" at Michigan. Scores and grades didn't have any particular weight with her. They needed only to be good enough to land the job she wanted. Quinlan had dropped out of Ohio State. The family needed his paycheck. "You would have dropped out for a job, too," he had said to Lila after her first week at *The Courier*. "I like that. Feet on the ground."

Ruth soared through Chicago. She was dean's list all eight terms, "which goes without saying," Grace said. She was also a Robert Maynard Hutchins Scholar, a Georgianna Simpson Scholar in the Humanities, and a Harpers Award winner. Saturdays, she worked as a lifeguard at the pool.

"You swept the field," Grace said to her.

"I didn't do this for fun," Ruth said. "They paid me to come here. I felt I owed them."

After freshman year, Ruth knew she didn't want to be a doctor. As Grace suspected, she had been doing it for her mom and gran. She liked her science courses well enough; it was the thought of spending day after day with sick people that flattened her.

"I don't have the stomach for it," she said, her shoulders slumping. She dropped biology and chemistry and declared classics for her major. In a lecture freshman year, a European eminence on the Committee on Social Thought said there were only two majors worth pursuing, Greek and physics. "Rigor," he said.

"Why didn't you major in physics?" Grace said. "I thought that was your favorite."

"I love physics, math too, but I'm not good enough at either of them," she said. "Physics is harder than Greek."

In her junior year, her mom and gran noticed that she had stopped taking premed courses. She told them it made more sense to do a postbac year later. Chicago had so much else to offer.

"They were sorry and sad; they saw where it was leading, but they felt they couldn't argue with me. They hadn't paid for my education." She straightened her shoulders, shaking off their disappointment. "They're country people. They grew up without money, 'without handouts,' they'll say, and 'proud of it.' They also grew up working-class Republican. They believe you only get what you pay for, and what you don't pay for, you can't expect to get." She shrugged. "They'll come around. They love me."

"What are you going to do with all your prizes?" Grace said. "I'm talking short run and long run." For months, Ruth hadn't wanted to talk about what she would do after college. If Grace asked, Ruth would shake her head. "It's simmering on the back burner," she'd say. The last week of school, with her prizes in her pocket, she announced her plans.

"In the short run," she said, "I'm going to make money and play."

"And then?" Grace said.

"I'll set my shoulder to the wheel," Ruth said.

"What wheel?" Grace said.

"Podcasting." The word burst from her.

"Podcasting?" Grace said. "How's that?"

"It's all come together, my life and my work." Ruth gave a slight head nod. "I'm going to have a show where I interview people about 'turning point' experiences. The conversations will be personal but not intrusive, Terry Gross meets *StoryCorps*." She nodded again. "I've been thinking about this since I had that conversation with Frances, during my first visit to Tara. Now I think of nothing else."

"I'm reeling," Grace said.

"I feel happier and freer and looser than I've ever been," Ruth said. "It's a miracle."

Ruth's imagined future was carefully mapped out. She wanted a weekly, half-hour show, where she'd put the same question to two people, one celebrity and one civilian, "Kim Kardashian and my post-man in Tallahassee," she said. "I'll ask questions like the one I asked Frances."

The show's name was *Elephant Memories*. "I think it works," she said. "Elephants remember and the group remembers too. They're almost Jungian. Then, there's the elephant in the room, 'the obvious unspoken.' I'm not looking to expose people or pry into their private feelings. I want to call up memories that meant something once and likely mean something different now."

"Are you still going to paralegal with Mr. G.?" Grace said.

"I think so, at least while *Elephant Memories* is incubating," Ruth said. "Then, I'm going to learn to ski."

"Ski," Grace said, her voice rising in astonishment.

"I need a break," Ruth said, "and I want to learn something I've never done, something you don't learn from books, something physi-cal, something that has no purpose beyond the pleasure it gives you."

"I just want to graduate," Grace said. "Then, after two years of moping, I'll write my plaintive memoir, *Grace Under Pressure*."

"I'm going for maximum happiness," Ruth said. "But I have to graduate. I have to have my own place. I have to be completely finan-cially independent. I don't know what to do if I work for Mr. G. I don't want to live at home but they'll be so hurt." She squinched her nose. "I'll never have sex if I move in with them."

"Come to D.C.," Grace said. "Live with Lila, work for Joe."

At graduation, Joe had offered Ruth a paralegal job in D.C. Lila had offered a room in her apartment.

"Do you think I could?" Ruth said. "I thought your parents were simply being kind."

"My parents are kind but not kind in that way," Grace said. "They know how smart you are." She gave a laugh that had a grunt behind it. "Not that it's a job qualification, but they think you've been a 'steadying' influence on me. Joe's word."

"Not academically," Ruth said, "and certainly not sexually."

Grace's eyebrows lowered. She had had a number of sexual relationships with guys she liked well enough, but none had been serious. "I wasn't looking for a boyfriend," she said. "I was looking for a sexual virtuoso. I wanted great sex, for its own sake. Sex with someone you love may be 'earth-moving' but sex with someone talented should at least rattle the windows. I haven't found him yet. One came close."

Ruth had wanted romance without sex. She graduated a virgin. She and Artie had broken up over sex. He couldn't understand why she wouldn't do it with him.

"I love you," he said. "I'd never hurt you. I'm not the progenitor."

"I couldn't do it," she said to Grace, "not until I was independent. My memoir would be *Virgin Territory.*"

GRACE CAME HOME FROM CHICAGO to her monk's cell in Joe's apartment. Home was Joe; he was expecting her.

After spending the summer in Tallahassee, working for Mr. G., and living at home, Ruth took the job with Joe and moved into the sunny, spacious second bedroom at Lila's. Gran and her mom were sad she wasn't staying on but they didn't press. "We raised her to think for herself," Gran said. "She took us at our word." Mr. G. understood. Mrs. G. pushed it. "Don't look back, lest you turn into a pillar of salt."

Grace was secretly envious. To her surprise, she preferred Lila's apartment. It had come decorated, not to Lila's taste but to someone's. Joe had bought a few basic items, beds, chairs, a sofa, but his heart wasn't in it and the space was unwelcoming, like the lobby of a midlevel suburban Hyatt. There were only two decent reading lamps, one by Joe's armchair in the living room, one by the side of his bed.

"I never thought a place this clean could be depressing," Grace said to Ruth.

"It reflects its owner," Ruth said.

In September, Grace got a permanent position as the NYC correspondent for *The Town Crier,* a weekly Washington rag. She had worked on *The Crier* for two summers and had done "very decent work," according to its cranky editor, Jim Duffy. He offered her the position, knowing she was burning to get out of D.C. A *Globe* alum, Duffy had started the weekly paper on GoFundMe. Investors got a year's subscription and a T-shirt with the paper's legend: THE LOW-DOWN ON THE HIGH UPS. Her salary was thirty thousand dollars.

Despite the low salary and tabloid slant, Grace was grateful to Duffy. *I'll work there a year, and then I'll move on,* she thought. She rented a tiny studio apartment in Williamsburg. Her parents gave her fifteen hundred a month. "You need to eat," Joe said.

Grace planned to move to New York on the first of October. As much as she had longed to graduate from Chicago, she dreaded life without Ruth. *Ruth makes friends easily. I do not. Ruth likes lots of different kinds of people. I like Ruth, Artie, and two or three others. How will I cope?*

She talked to Joe about it. "Ten days to New York, then I'm going to be Ruthless." They were having a late dinner in the kitchen, take-out tandoori chicken and beer. The sun was still shining but the autumnal slant threw the room into shadow and the trees lining the street had turned black-green, matching Grace's mood.

"I don't think that's the way to start a new job, a new life," Joe said. "Can't you settle for 'professional.'"

"No, I mean literally," she said. "I'm not going to have Ruth and she's not going to have me. Ruthless and Graceless."

"Ah," Joe said. "Word names. Both of you. Serendipity." Without getting up from his chair, he reached sideways to open the fridge door and plucked two more beers.

"We've never once eaten in the dining room," Grace said, "even though you brought the old dining table."

"I'd have to move the fridge into the dining room," Joe said.

"The old house was homier," Grace said. "I don't know who did it—neither of you paid attention or had friends over—but it was a nicer place to live in. How can you stand living in this mausoleum."

"Any place without Lila would be gloomy," Joe said.

"You could buy a few more lamps," Grace said. "Maybe a rug or two. A poster for the walls."

Joe shrugged. "What about your apartment in New York?"

"It's the size of the foyer here," she said. "The fridge is in the dining room, also in the living room."

"So you're going to be a reporter, a newshound," Joe said.

"It looks that way," she said. "I thought I wanted to be a writer-writer, a novelist, a short story writer, but I have trouble making up worlds. I don't think that way. I could write about our family, I could embroider and exaggerate, but I need the rootedness of real people, real places, real conflict, to write. As Lila likes to quote, 'I never met a fact I didn't like.' My thought exactly." She took a swig of beer. "Book writing is also too solitary a life for me. Reporting gets me out of the house. I have to talk to people. I think a lot of nonfiction books are too long because the writer realized the research was more interesting and engrossing and she didn't want to go back into a room of her own—by the way, a completely overrated sanctuary."

"What kind of stories do you want to cover?" Joe said. "Not gossip, I realize, but then Lila started in Obits and was happy to get the job. You start where they hire you. Then, you show them your stuff."

"I think I could make a story out of almost anything," Grace said. "Most people will answer the questions you put to them. They don't like saying no. They may lie but they'll talk."

"Is there a beat you want?" he said.

"Organized and disorganized crime, corruption at any level, family dynasties run amuck or aground, adulterous preachers. Money, basically. Money lucre. I'm not a news junkie like Lila. I might like writing the long obits." Grace smiled.

"It sounds like magazine writing," Joe said.

"A website might publish it," she said. "Everyone says print magazines are dying."

"'Let's start a magazine the hell with literature,'" Joe said.

"You're the best," Grace said.

"No, you're the best."

A WEEK AFTER SHE GRADUATED from Chicago, Ruth's photo appeared on the front page of *The Tallahassee Register,* alongside an article on her stellar college career. The header read: TALLAHASSEE WHIZ KID TAKES TOP HONORS AT UCHICAGO. The university's PR office had sent out a notice and a reporter on the paper had followed up, flabbergasted that a local girl would go to a college that didn't have a football team. He interviewed Ruth, her mother, and her gran, and quoted them generously.

"I had a great education, at Chiles as well as Chicago," Ruth said. "Mrs. Goldsmith always made us think before we wrote. She set aside 'thinking time' with all in-class assignments, even exams. 'The test of an idea,' she'd say, 'is its written expression. If you can't write it clearly, you're not thinking clearly.' Those words are tattooed on my brain."

Ruth's mom picked up an earlier theme of hers. "Ruth won a full scholarship to Chicago for all four years, books and airfare included," she said. "We're so proud of her."

Gran bubbled over. "Ruth read the *Iliad* in ancient Greek. Can

you believe it? Most people in the world haven't read it in any language. I haven't read it, but Ruth bought me a copy in English. She
said I'd like it. I'm a bit daunted but I'm going to give it a try. I know
three words in Greek, *summa cum laude,* with highest honors."

Congratulations poured in from friends, neighbors, colleagues.
Mr. Goldsmith sent two dozen peonies, with a card signed by everyone at his office. Mrs. Goldsmith sent a thank-you note that made
Ruth cry. A boy who'd been in her AP English class called to ask her
out.

A week after the clamor subsided, Ruth received an email on her
Chicago account from Jeff Bates. *Why didn't Bobby Lee write,* she
thought. Resisting the urge to trash it unopened, she waited three
days before reading it.

June 15, 2015

Dear Miss Ruth McGowan,

My name is Jeff Bates. I saw the article in *The Register.* I did Genealogies
two years ago. The results said you were my niece. I have one brother,
Bobby Lee Bates. He must be the father. I'm writing on behalf of the family.

Bobby Lee was only 16 and a young sinner when you were created. He
didn't know you existed until I got the test results, but even if he did know,
he couldn't have been a father to you. He was working two jobs to support
our mom and me. Our father died when Bobby Lee was 14. He dropped out
of high school to go to work. He was wild in those days, lots of girlfriends,
lots of drinking. The pressure of being the family wage-earner got to him.
He regrets he had sex with your mother, though he says he didn't rape her.
She was willing.

Bobby Lee met his wife Jacqui when he was twenty-one. She took him
in hand. He's a Christian now, born again. He has two children, a son 14
and a daughter 15. He's glad your mother didn't have an abortion but he
doesn't want to be known as your father. He has talked to his pastor who
supports him. His wife Jacqui spoke to your mother back when I got the

Genealogies results. She worries now that she was rude. She wouldn't change what she said only how. She would have been nicer. She was very upset. She said your mother was not interested in having a connection. With all your achievements, I'm thinking you don't need support from Bobby Lee or his family.

We hope you're a good Christian. Bobby Lee would be sad to have sired a child who wasn't a good Christian.

On behalf of the Bates family, I wish you a pleasant life.

Jesus loves you. We will not be replaced.

Jefferson Davis Bates

Ruth read the email quickly, her pulse racing, her breath ragged. *I expected something like this,* she thought, *but not this.* She closed her computer and burst into tears.

At breakfast, she showed the email to her mother and gran.

"They are not what I would call good Christians," her mom said. "When they meet their Maker, they're going to have a lot of explaining to do."

"They're embarrassed and afraid," Gran said. "They don't want their children to know. I'll bet he teaches chastity at the teen Sunday school."

"Some pastor," Ruth said.

Gran took Ruth's hand. "That's a hard letter to get."

Ruth nodded, fearing Gran's sympathy would open floodgates.

"I have to feel sorry for them," Gran said, "not knowing you."

RUTH'S FIRST DAY AT SANGER, BOOTH, Joe took her to lunch. He did that with all the new paralegals and associates.

"Someone said you wanted Trusts. Is that true?" Joe said. "Even they were incredulous. No flash."

"Mr. G. said I would have the most responsibility and independence there," she said. "There must be some interesting, terrible cases, blue-blood patriarchs disinheriting their Anarchist children, grannies persuaded to give all their money to the Church of Everlasting Life, *Bleak House*."

"Ah," Joe said. "Spite wills. One last chance to screw over everyone. I hate them. We recently had a case of a married couple where the wife changed her will without telling her husband—or us. All of her insurance and two-thirds of her retirement funds, most of her estate, were distributed to friends without his knowledge." He paused. "Another client, a miserably unhappy person, rewrites his will every six months, disinheriting one child or another in favor of some right-wing charity. He's a Republican, all his children are Democrats. He's free to do that, of course, but you wind up feeling you've crossed a line you didn't want to." He took a swallow of water.

Ruth sat up straight and took in a big breath. *Carpe diem,* she thought. "I need to cross a line," she said. "You can fire me if you want to." She took in another big breath.

Joe sat back, startled.

"You need to get back together with Lila," she said. "Everyone thinks so. They say things to Lila but not to you. You're alone too much."

"'I can't go on, I'll go on,'" he said.

"It's three years, at least, since you moved out," she said, "and nothing has happened. Your apartment is a mausoleum. You've never gone on a date. You eat takeout every night, you don't even go to a restaurant. If you knew someone like you, you'd be worried about him."

"I'm not angry," Joe said. "I left when I couldn't take it anymore. I decided I'd rather be unhappy without Lila than with her. More depressing, less painful." He twirled his fork. "I can almost sympathize with Grace."

"Grace will never give up on Lila," Ruth said. "She's like Lila, a battering ram."

"We've always stayed in touch. Lately, we've been seeing each other, maybe five or six times a month. We have dinners. We go to the movies. We take walks. She makes the dates and reservations. She buys the tickets. She calls on the phone. I stopped answering her texts and emails when I moved out. I don't get my hopes up. They rise by themselves." He sat forward. "You don't need to tell me that Lila loves me, or that I love her. Love is not enough. Love and work are not enough." He sat back. "There's no one like her. She could have had anyone. She picked me."

Ruth started tearing. *Oh, Joe,* she thought. *You break my heart.*

Grace went home to D.C. for her birthday. She stayed with Joe and invited Ruth to stay there too. Ruth flinched. "He's my boss now," she said. "I can't stay there."

"I forgot where I was. It's not a problem in New York," Grace said. "Quite the opposite. Everyone sleeps with the boss, or rather the boss sleeps with everyone."

They were sitting in Joe's kitchen, eating ice cream from the container. The provisions were sparse. There was milk and butter in the fridge, ice cream and bread in the freezer, and coffee pods in a jar next to a small espresso machine.

"Joe's refrigerator is almost as bad as Lila's," Grace said.

"No," Ruth said. "No one's fridge is worse than Lila's. She told me she wouldn't have a fridge if it didn't come with the apartment."

She showed Grace the email from Jeff Bates.

"So mean," Grace said. "He wanted to make sure you'd never get in touch."

"I thought I didn't have fantasies of being welcomed," Ruth said. "It was a real gut punch."

"He's missing the best thing that ever happened to him," Grace said. "Show it to Joe."

They found Joe in the living room, reading *The New Yorker.* Joe read the email slowly. Then he reread it. "I wonder if he had a lawyer help him write this," he said. "It's too good. It's too calculating. Will you go along?"

Ruth shrugged.

"Show it to Lila," he said. "She'll know."

The next morning, Ruth got up at six, hoping to catch Lila before she left for the office. Stumbling into the kitchen, she found her standing at the counter, reading the paper and drinking coffee.

"Can I pour you a cup of coffee," Lila said. "You look shot."

Ruth nodded. "I'd like you to read something," she said. "There was an article about me in *The Tallahassee Register,* this year's local whiz kid. It provoked this email." She handed it to Lila.

Lila sat down at the table, adjusted her glasses, and read. When she'd finished, she sat quietly for several seconds. "Dreadful person, this Jeff Bates," she said. "Bobby Lee and Jacqui too, probably, though it's hard to say who or what prompted him to write. Does Bobby Lee even know about you." Lila took off her glasses. "It's a hurtful letter, designed to hurt. He knew what he was doing. Have you responded?"

Ruth shook her head.

"Take your time," Lila said. "I'm betting he's hoping you'll say something like 'I wouldn't cross the street to spit on Bobby Lee.' That's why he wrote such a cruel email." Lila put her glasses on again and scanned the email. "I wonder why Bobby Lee didn't write. He doesn't want to be the bad guy? He wants plausible deniability? Maybe he had nothing to do with the email?" She took a swallow of coffee. "Do you want to respond?"

"Not now," Ruth said. "Maybe never."

"Why not?" Lila said.

"I don't know what to say," Ruth said. "I don't know what I want."

"How do you feel?"

"Bruised."

"Not answering is an answer, often taken for consent," Lila said. "I find it usually means at best indecision, at worst fear. I always press for a yes or a no. I like things settled."

"I'm not afraid exactly," Ruth said. "I was raised 'to let things go.'"

"I don't know what that's like," Lila said.

"I think Mom and Gran were unhappy that I did Genealogies," Ruth said. "They don't want the Bateses in our life."

"Do you want to keep Bobby Lee's identity a secret?"

"It's not a secret," Ruth said. "Jeff was the closest identified relation, but Genealogies found other Bateses."

"What about your side?" Lila said. "Did anyone turn up?"

"None that I knew, and all very remote, fourth cousins twice removed," Ruth said.

"Why keep a secret that's not a secret," Lila said. "What's in it for you?"

"I'm sorry I did it," Ruth said.

"Spilled milk," Lila said.

"I thought it wouldn't matter, knowing. It was stupid of me. You knew better than to find out what happened to Zelda."

"I assume she's dead. I take the position she's dead"—Lila took off her glasses—"and I want to keep her dead. Why did you do the DNA test?"

"I wanted to know who . . . 'sired' me." Ruth took a swallow of coffee. "Who does Jeff Bates think his brother is, Secretariat?"

"Now that you know and they know you know, are you willing to act as if you don't know?" Lila took a swallow of coffee. "What's in it for you?" She reached over and laid her hand on Ruth's.

"Years ago, we were living in D.C.," Lila said. "Frances took me to lunch at the club. She asked me about my family, 'if I was willing to talk about it.' I told her what it was like growing up with Aldo. She didn't say she was sorry or sad or stunned or shocked, the way everyone but Quinlan did. She said, and I've always remembered her words, 'You are the hero of your own life.' I was blasted sideways. 'You stood up for yourself,' she said. 'You must always stand up for yourself. Every time you stand up for yourself, you feel better. Maybe not in the moment, maybe not for months, but down the line.' She looked sad as she spoke. 'When I was twenty-one,' she said, 'I didn't stand up for myself. I was a pampered ninny, inexperienced, conventional, docile, gutless. I lost my chance for real happiness.' After lunch, she bought me a Bottega Veneta wallet."

15

Real World

A FEW DAYS AFTER TALKING TO LILA, RUTH ASKED JOE IF IT WAS ALL right if she used the firm's online investigatory service to find the email addresses for Jacqui and Bobby Lee Bates.

"Of course," he said. "Look up their criminal records and bankruptcies too. Look up anything you want. Good practice. You need to see how it works," he said. "You don't want a client giving away money that isn't his."

Ruth stared at him.

"Oh, yes," he said. "Most clients lie to their lawyer, usually a small, self-serving one, but some tell whoppers. Somehow, consulting a trusts lawyer generates feelings of grandiosity."

Ruth spent an hour exploring the service. She found the email addresses quickly and the criminal records and bankruptcies almost as quickly. Jeff Bates had a sheet. He was a small-time grifter. He made up to widows, then pinched their jewelry. He had served eleven months and twenty-eight days. Jacqui had a driver's license suspension and an arrest for battery. Road rage. Community service. Bobby Lee had gone bankrupt ten years earlier, trying to make a go of his father's pool-cleaning business. He currently owned a plant nursery and lawn care company. He had an associate's degree from Tallahassee Community College.

At home that evening, Ruth started writing her response to Jeff Bates. Each iteration was shorter and more abrupt than its predecessor.

After three hours, she had a draft she didn't hate. She decided to sleep on it.

June 20, 2015

To: Jefferson Davis Bates

I am unwilling to keep Bobby Lee's identity a secret.
    If anyone asks who "sired" me, I will tell them.
    If anyone suspects his paternity, I will confirm it.
    Why would I lie on Bobby Lee's behalf?

I recognize no obligations to him or his family.

Ruth McGowan

In the morning, she woke in a fury. *Who is Jeff Bates to write to me?* She started slashing her response, taking it to the bone. She sent it off before leaving for work. She didn't show it to anyone. *My mom and gran are probably praying for them,* she thought.

June 21, 2015

To: Jeff Bates
Cc: Jacqui Bates
From: Ruth McGowan
Subject: Genealogies Results

I am responding to your June email. See below.
    I will not discuss the matter with you or Jacqui.

I will discuss it only with Bobby Lee.

Ruth McGowan

Ruth didn't hear from Bobby Lee, or his brother or wife. Months went by. After a while, she almost forgot.

RUTH AND ARTIE BRINKMAN GOT back together briefly, long enough for them to have sex.

Artie had come to D.C. on a pilgrimage. He had a new girlfriend, one who had sex with him, but he couldn't stop thinking about Ruth.

They had sex the first night he was in town. He went straight from the airport into her bed. They had some trouble in the beginning. She was a virgin. He was excited. Over the next several hours, they worked it out.

"It only gets better," he said, afterward, tired and happy. They were lying in bed, on their backs, looking at the ceiling, the easiest way to talk about difficult things.

Ruth didn't say anything.

"We're finished, is that it," he said. "Was this a mercy fuck?"

Ruth was stunned. Artie never used bad language.

"I couldn't imagine having sex for the first time with anyone else," she said. "I didn't want a zipless fuck."

"You won't marry me, will you?"

"No," she said. "I'm too young. I'm not ready."

"I need to get married," he said. "I need a family. I need to belong to someone." Ruth squeezed his hand. Artie hadn't seen his parents since the summer after freshman year.

"I'll never love anyone the way I love you," he said. "I love Jenny differently. She wants to get married. She's three years older. Third year med school." He gave a slight head nod. "I'm not made for consulting. I can't believe anyone hires us. We have no experience, no judgment, no tact, no manners, only good hygiene and top grades at top schools. We tell them what they want to hear and charge them a fortune to hear it. I've applied to med school. Jenny encouraged me." He turned his head toward her. "How are you doing?"

"I'm liking the work much more than I thought I would," she

said. "There's something very intimate about making a will, as if money were the currency of affection, regard, respect." She turned to look at him. "We have this one client, he rewrites his will at least twice a year. He cried in my office, sobbed really. 'My children don't love me. My youngest daughter called me King Lear.'"

"People talk to you, not only me," Artie said.

"Yes," she said.

He sat up. "I've got to go. It's too hard." He turned his body toward her. "'Once more into the breach.'"

GRACE FILLED HER DAYS WITH WORK and many of her evenings too. She was lonely. She was *The Crier*'s only NYC employee and while she had met other reporters on the flashy-money beat, they were too competitive. Outside of work, she saw a few Chicago friends who hadn't yet unwound. They were killing "it," whatever "it" was, law school, Deutsche Bank, Bain & Company. "They all say their jobs are A plus when I ask them," she said to Ruth. "But when they leave, they say they were only building their résumés."

She hadn't dated anyone since she started at *The Crier* except for a Chicago friend with benefits who she saw occasionally. She wouldn't go online, like everyone else.

"I don't want to date if I have to do that," she said to Ruth. "I'm not pretty enough anyway. And I'm too tall."

"Of course you're pretty enough," Ruth said. "Stop fishing for compliments. If you want a boyfriend, you'll find one somewhere. You need a job with other people."

Ruth was asked out all the time by the younger lawyers in the firm. She turned them down. "Too awkward," she said. "Nothing personal." The older, married lawyers might have asked her out too if she hadn't been under Joe's protection. Firm policy forbade partners from fraternizing with secretaries, paralegals, or associates, but it was never enforced unless there was a complaint from the straying partner's partner.

"I'm glad you had sex with Artie," Grace said. "You're over the hump, though the second one can be more awkward. You don't know the person as well. You haven't made out with him for hours."

"I didn't think of that. I was thinking 'piece of cake,'" Ruth said. "Does a guy expect you to have sex with him on the first date?"

"On social, most people do it on the third date," Grace said. "Of course, on social, most people are lying."

"I'm not bringing someone who's not Artie to Lila's apartment," Ruth said. "I'd die of embarrassment."

"Lila wouldn't care," Grace said, "so long as he didn't walk around naked or pee on the floor."

"I thought they didn't do that after college," Ruth said.

"Twenty-two is the new sixteen," Grace said.

Ruth spent two years at Sanger, Booth, a respectable period for a first job out of college. Living rent free with Lila, she saved over seventy thousand dollars, enough, she guessed, to ski for two years. She wanted to go out West. She wanted powder. She'd rent a studio apartment. She'd wait tables if she ran out of money. Off the slopes, she'd write up the business plan for *Elephant Memories*. She went back to Tallahassee to cement her plans.

Though she'd gone back to Florida every summer since she left for Chicago, Tallahassee didn't feel like home anymore. *I feel like a Yankee carpetbagger,* she thought. The city seemed both small and sprawling, backward and proud of it. She thought her mother had voted for Webb, but she didn't ask her. Her gran hadn't voted. "I'd vote Republican," she said, "if one had been running."

Her second night back, she had dinner at the Goldsmiths'. Her gran drove her over. Mrs. G. answered the door. Ruth fell into her arms.

"I shouldn't say this to you of all people," she said, "but I hate Tallahassee."

"Now, now," Mrs. G. said. "Compartmentalize. Don't hate all of it."

They went into the living room and sat down. Mr. G. came in from the kitchen, wearing an apron and carrying limes.

"How y'all doing," he said. "Drink? I'm serving margaritas."

Ruth nodded.

"I keep trying to talk Richard into moving to Miami, since he won't move to Chicago or New York. He won't move anywhere he wouldn't feel 'right' wearing boots."

"Isn't it her turn," Ruth said to Mr. G. "Don't you owe her for living here all these years?"

"I love Tallahassee," he said. "No one knows who I am in Miami."

Mrs. G. turned to Ruth. "Miami, Tallahassee, it really doesn't matter. Our boys won't live here. Nico's in New York, Xander's in L.A."

"Nico's eating with us tonight," Mr. G. said, "if he gets back from the gym in time. He's in town for a week." He looked at his watch. "In two weeks, he starts his third year of residency at the Hospital for Special Surgery. Orthopedics. Knees. Never have surgery in July. Everyone's new. No one knows how to put in a catheter."

The Goldsmiths' sons, Nicholas and Alexander, were fraternal twins. Everyone called them by their nicknames except their Tallahassee grandfather, their zayde, who used their real names to exasperate his son. "You named them for Russian royalty," Zayde said. "I'm going to call the princes by their names."

Ruth had met the Goldsmith twins when she was in high school and they were in college. She had liked them, but she was shy and awkward around them, not having shaken off Vestry. In preparation for escaping the South, she was doing exercises to get rid of her accent. "I sound like a hillbilly," she'd said to her mom and gran. "Northerners think all Southerners are stupid." She squinched her nose. "Racist too."

The twins were six years older than Ruth. Real twins, they were competitive with each other and united against the world. They looked like brothers, same rangy build, same dark hair and eyes, but no one confused them. Xander was talkative, unreserved, jokey, jumpy. He kept his accent and wore Levi's and cowboy boots everywhere. Nico was serious, though not without humor, sometimes sharp. He'd never had a Southern accent—"I didn't want it," he said. He wore running shoes and khakis. They had gone to Columbia, where they were athletes on the track team, Nico, distance, Xander, sprints. After graduation, they spent two years hiking. Xander came through unscathed. Nico broke his ankle and his wrist. When they tired of hiking, they dispersed. Xander went to L.A. to write for television. He rose quickly. He was currently the showrunner for a show he had written, *Florida Men*. Nico went back to New York, to Columbia Medical School. "I'm doing what I want," he told his parents after graduating. "It's interesting. It's not fun. I don't know if it ever becomes fun." He shrugged. "Xander's having all the fun."

Mr. G. brought the margaritas. "I used Grand Marnier, not triple sec. Only the best for Chicago grads," he said. "I'm making dinner so I can eat meat. She's gone pescatarian." He gestured toward his wife, then looked at Ruth. "Nico still eats meat. You too, right?"

Ruth nodded. "I've always eaten what was served to me. I didn't know you had a choice."

As she was speaking, Nico came in. He was larger than she remembered, filled out, as Gran would say. He and Xander were shorter than their dad, but tall by any reckoning. Nico said they were six-two, Xander said six-two and a half.

Ruth stood up. They shook hands. "You're different," he said.

"You too," she said.

"You've purged Vestry and your accent," he said.

"I've been purging where I could my whole life," she said. "I gave up the Baptist Church and the Republican Party long before the accent."

"Mom sent me the article about you in the paper," he said. "The picture didn't do you justice."

"Is that a backdoor compliment?" she said.

"You're very pretty," he said.

"You're not half bad, yourself," she said.

They smiled at each other, then caught themselves.

"He's flirting with me," she said to his parents.

"She's flirting with me," he said.

"Young people," Mr. G. said. "Let's eat. The steaks are ready."

Nico drove her home. They sat in the car and talked for an hour, until Gran started flicking the front door light.

"My signal to come inside," she said. "Not having seen me grow up these last six years, they treat me like I'm still sixteen."

"I know you're not," he said. "I'd like to kiss you."

She smiled and leaned toward him.

They kissed for the next fifteen minutes.

"I have to go," Ruth said. "Gran is flicking the lights again."

"Can I see you tomorrow, lunch, dinner?" he said.

"Lunch."

"I'll pick you up at twelve-thirty. We'll talk about your plan to go skiing."

"McGowan means 'blacksmith' in Irish," Ruth said. "We're Goldsmith and Blacksmith."

16

Real Life

AFTER FIFTEEN MONTHS ON *THE CRIER*'S GOSSIP BEAT, GRACE WAS ready to move on. She was gossiped out. She had worked hard writing junk; she felt she was becoming stupider daily. "Make something of it," Lila had said, when Grace started the job. "Do your best work always. You gain nothing doing second-rate work."

Her job search foundered. With Chick Webb's election in 2016, it seemed everyone under thirty wanted to be a journalist, if not in D.C., then in New York.

"I've been aced out four times by people with more experience, at 'real papers,'" she said to Ruth. They talked on the phone most days before bed. "Time to pivot. I'll keep covering the goings and comings of very rich people—I want to keep my job—but not the celebrities famous for being famous." She paused. "I'll cover the new billionaires, the publicity hungry, big spenders who pay sixty million dollars in Bitcoin for Jeff Koon's balloon dogs and hundreds of millions on megayachts that cost more than aircraft carriers. I don't know who's keeping track but some of them made multimillion-dollar contributions to TarantulaPAC, the campaign war chest run by Big Chuck's friends in Texas." She paused. "Then there are the geeks, Gates, Tesla boy, Zucks, Bezos, getting revenge on the football players who bullied and mocked them in high school."

"Like us," Ruth said, "except we're female."

"I wasn't a geek," Grace said, "not smart enough."

"Will your boss go for it?" Ruth said.

"Lila's rule, 'Never say no to yourself. Make someone else do it.'"

After thinking a day about her proposal, Duffy gave her a qualified okay. "No Saudis. The stories will only provoke anti-Muslim feelings among our readers." He picked up a pencil, a yellow No. 2. "Light on politics, heavy on money and girlfriends and ex-wives." He tapped his forehead with the pencil. "You might also interview the people who work for them. Sociology."

Grace's new direction paid off. She broke out of the gossip grind by breaking a story on the exorbitant services of a freelance, independent school counselor. He was getting children into kindergarten at first-rung NYC private schools by advising parents to make annual donations starting the year the child was born. Grace wrote in part:

> "It's the American equivalent of what wealthy English people have done for generations," Marcus Teller said. "They call it 'putting a child's name down at birth'—for Eton or Winchester or St. Paul's. It's a kind of early registration. The Brits don't, of course, pay in advance. The quid pro quo is assumed."
>
> His fee staggered even his richest clients. "Look," he told them. "How much would you pay to get your daughter into one of these schools? You'd easily pay a million or more for her wedding. Amortize it over thirteen years." He had a flat rate, augmented by a bonus if the child was admitted into one of the schools.
>
> "I'm like no other counselor," he told them. "I run a boutique company. I perform multiple services, most of them delicate."
>
> Like all counselors, Teller recommended the schools to

apply to, but in addition he helped the parents calculate the size of the donation, anywhere from a year's tuition to $200,000, and articulate their motives for donating.

"The schools know what's going on," he said, "but that doesn't mean we wink and poke. No, we are respectful of their standards and values."

Many of his students applied to girls' schools. "For one of those applicants, I might tell the parents to say something like: 'We believe strongly in girls' education and want to ensure its continued existence for all girls, not only our own daughters.'"

He told the parents to give to at least three schools and to designate the money for scholarships. "Diversity is important for these schools," he said. "Scholarships help."

The arrangement isn't illegal, only unsavory. The shocker was that Teller persuaded the parents to donate the money years ahead of time, in hard cash. There was always the risk the child wouldn't get admitted and all that money would be gone, poof, spent on the poorest students. "The tax deduction for charitable donations softens the blow," he told his clients. He made no guarantees. His record was excellent, not perfect. "The schools owe you nothing but their thanks."

Grace's source was a disgruntled customer whose son was rejected after she'd donated almost two million dollars to three schools over five years, "and paid his gigantic fee." She gave Grace names, but no other parents would speak to her. Teller offered no additional comments. "As you wrote," he said in an email to Grace, "I perform multiple services. I wish her son had gotten into one of the schools. A delightful boy. I advised her to keep giving. The boy could transfer." After the article appeared, he opened a satellite office in Los Angeles.

The Crier article on the school counselor got noticed.

"Time to move," Lila emailed. "You'll find a job. That was a first-rate piece." Grace kept the email in her Special Correspondence file.

She had wept the first time she read it, and whenever she read it again, which she did almost daily during her job search, she'd find herself fighting tears.

She applied to more than a dozen publications in New York. *The Pereira name would have come in handy,* she thought with some embarrassment. *I hate the work-arounds.* Duffy had offered to write recommendations for her. "I'll casually drop Lila's name, after I've said all the good things about you, a kind of footnote in the text. I was thinking something along the lines of: 'You might say she comes by her talent naturally—she's Lila Pereira's daughter—but that would be underselling her.'"

After eight months and seven interviews, Grace got a job at *The New Yorkist,* not to be confused with *The New Yorker* or *New York* magazine. The insiders' nickname was *The New Yuckist*: Yuck, Yuck, that's funny, Yuck, Yuck, that's gross. Grace's tabloid experience persuaded the editor, Chuck Kane, she had the chops for the job. The interview had been excruciating.

"Are you anything like your mother?" Kane said as she walked into his office. He pointed to a chair across from his desk.

Grace sat down. "Have you met Lila?" she said.

He shook his head.

"No one's like Lila, no one comes close," Grace said. "Maybe Arnold Schwarzenegger."

"I like it," he said. "Just the kind of hyperbole we like here."

"It's not hyperbole," she said. "If anything, Arnold falls short."

"Very good," he said, drawing out the words. "Using the first name. I like it."

The rest of the interview was more of the same, Kane asking questions bordering on the inappropriate, Grace parrying with pop culture snappers. At the end, he asked her if she had any questions.

"Are you anything like your namesake, Charles Foster Kane?" she said.

He leaned back in his chair, squinting at her. "How'd you know that? Most people your age don't have a clue." He sat up. "The job's

yours if you want it. I'll have HR, aka my assistant, send you a letter."
He stood up. "You're a tough cookie. Chip off the old block."

"Thank you," Grace said, rising from her chair. He looked at her,
downcast. "I got the cookie pun," she said. "I didn't think I should
groan the first time we met."

"Tact, too," he said. "She's got tact and brains."

The job paid $900 a week to start. If one of her stories was picked
up by another publication, she'd get an extra $50. She was expected
to average eighteen hundred publishable words a week, setting her
price per word at fifty cents and her annual salary at $47,000.

Out on the street, walking home, Grace called Lila. *Who else will
understand how I feel?* she thought.

"It's very important," she said to Lila's assistant. "Please, put her
on the line."

Seconds later, Lila picked up.

"What up?" she said. She had been in a meeting. She ended it
when her assistant came in, saying she needed to take a call. Everyone rose, like schoolchildren, and left. Lila never explained interrup-
tions other than to say, "Something's come up." She thought fifteen
minutes was long enough for any meeting, and the one she was in
had overstayed its usefulness.

"I got a job at *The New Yorkist,*" Grace said. "The pay is better."

"Don't undersell it," Lila said. "It has a decent reputation. You'll
be able to move again, if you want. Will you like the work?"

"I like interviewing," Grace said. "I'm not so good talking to people I know, but I'm good with strangers." She paused. "Nothing like
Ruth, though."

"It's different, what you do," Lila said. "She goes deep, you go
wide. And then, you're funny. She isn't. I don't mean she's earnest,
she isn't, she's serious. You're playful. Your writing has zing." She
paused. "She doesn't write. She only talks. You're very good at the
writing game."

Grace blinked, fighting back tears. *Praise.* She coughed. "I know
that, but she gets people to say things they never told anyone else,

and not by forcing a confession. She's not punishing, or envious, like that wretched Barbara Walters person, who was always trying to make celebrities cry, to make them 'just like us.' People don't trust me the way they trust Ruth." She paused. "Still, they're almost always willing to talk about themselves."

"I tell reporters, interviewing isn't complicated; it's listening and waiting. Empathy is for shrinks." Lila's voice softened. "I like to start slow: how old are you, where did you grow up, what's your family like, and when they've gotten used to me and my questions, I move in carefully. I'll use the third person: when did it all start going south? No 'you,' no accusations, no confrontations, no fault assumed."

"I love third person, also the passive voice." Grace laughed. "I once asked a question like that, and the perp said, 'In the womb. She was a boozer. Not that I would have grown up to be a rocket scientist, but maybe a decent mechanic.' I felt bad for him. Briefly. He'd done terrible things to people he didn't know. He did everything but eat them."

"I'm never sure what I'm looking for," Lila said, "which I think is to the good. With so many of the people I interview, no one had ever listened to them."

Grace laughed. "Not a problem with billionaires. Sometimes— this is embarrassing—I lean in when they're talking and make sooth- ing, humming noises, the way people talk to babies and puppies. They don't notice. They're so used to being sucked up to, they expect it." She hummed. "If only they ate the way they consume everything else. People could then see how grotesque and revolting their excesses are. Like *La Grande Bouffe*." She could hear her mother listening. "I make them think I'm on their side. You don't do that. You make them feel you're not against them. You could say that's a mar- ginal difference, but it makes a difference. I'm working on it."

"I swing both ways, good cop, bad cop," Lila said. "You're doing what you should be doing. You're the real thing. Aren't we lucky. There's no better job better than ours. Good work." She paused.

"Someone's pounding on my door. President Webb is throwing a tantrum. I'm off."

Grace put down the phone. *We talked shop, like real colleagues,* she thought. *It was great and yet, and yet . . . I wish she'd said "Love you," before hanging up.* She closed her eyes, blinking back tears. *Then again, she didn't say I was a chip off the old block, she didn't take any credit.*

At Stella's high school graduation dinner, Grace, then eleven, had asked Lila why she never said she was proud of her daughters. They were at a restaurant, the five of them, toasting the graduate and cataloging her achievements: salutatorian, math prize, captain of girls' tennis.

"It seems to me that taking pride in your child's achievement is a way of taking credit," Lila said. "I'd rather say, 'Good work.'" She laughed. "Easy for me to say. I'm in no position to take credit for any of your successes. All credit goes to Joe."

The three girls picked up their water glasses. "Hear, hear," they said. "To Joe, Guinness Book of Dads." Joe, pleased and embarrassed, smiled his aw-shucks smile.

"It may look like I threw you all to the wind," Lila said, "but, in fact, I have a theory of mothering." She held up her thumb. "First, do no harm. Second, give them rope. Third, keep in mind, they're smarter than you know."

"What about helping them with their homework, making them dinner, taking them to the doctor," Joe said.

"Ah," she said. "I was talking theory, you're talking practice."

GRACE HAD STARTED THINKING ABOUT her Zelda novel in the dog days of her time at *The Crier*. With her job search going nowhere, her love life in the toilet, and her salary barely breaking the poverty line, she needed a project. She complained to Ruth, trying not to sound like she was complaining.

"Why don't you moonlight?" Ruth said. "Write an article on spec for some other paper. Write an Agatha Christie. Write *Grace Under Pressure*."

"I can't write a memoir at twenty-four," Grace said. "I haven't had a life."

"Write a novel," Ruth said. "Write about someone with a life."

"I've thought about writing a nonfiction novel about Zelda, my runaway grandmother. I've made a few notes."

"Isn't she 'officially' dead," Ruth said.

"I don't believe it," Grace said.

Ruth was silent.

"You think it's a bad idea," Grace said.

"What are you going to write?" Ruth said.

"I don't know. I only have the Big Idea," Grace said, coughing. "I have named the characters. The first task, like Adam. I also have the title, *The Lost Mother*."

Grace had picked names close to the originals. Those in the know would know, those not, not. The Pereiras would become the Monteiros, *The Washington Globe*, *The Washington World*. Lila would be Ana. She would be Hope. *Even I see the irony in that name*, she thought. She gritted her teeth and went on. Instead of writing a memoir called *Grace Under Pressure*, Hope would write one called *Hope Against Hope*. She closed her eyes and shook her head. *Beyond irony*.

The frontispiece would be the opening lines of Dickens's *David Copperfield*: "Whether I shall turn out to be the hero of my own life, or whether that station will be held by anybody else, these pages must show." *Not possible*, she thought. *No one can compete with Lila*.

When she got the job at *The New Yorkist*, she put the novel on hold. *I have plenty of time*, she thought. *I'm not an infant prodigy*.

17

Oligarchs

GRACE STARTED HER NEW JOB AT *THE NEW YORKIST* THE FIRST WEEK OF November 2017. *Thank God, not an election year,* she thought. She liked working with Chuck Kane. He knew his job and his reporters' jobs too. He was fair, he was honest, he was blunt, he was flexible, he was inappropriate. After six months of reporting on the real estate moguls, she asked if she might cover the Russian oligarchs. They were crass, tasteless, extravagant, and corrupt, tabloid gold.

"They're all in Putin's pocket," Grace said to Kane. "Picking it and lining it. They don't care what he does with Chechnya or Crimea so long as they get their share. They were the ones who hired that school counselor."

"Are you going political on me?" he said.

"Obliquely," she said. "I'm curious about the source of their wealth, their yachts, their children, but also things money can't buy."

"What things," he said. "I'd like to know."

"I'm looking into U.S. citizenship," she said.

"If Rupert Murdoch got it, they can get it," he said.

"They don't own Fox News and *The Wall Street Journal,*" she said.

"Not yet," he said.

"What about a president of their own," she said. "I'm pretty sure they supported Webb. Webb was on *Anderson Cooper* the other night. 'I'm greatly admired abroad,' he said. 'Erdogan, Orban, Maduro, Putin, especially Putin. He says I'm the greatest living leader.'"

"Do you think they funneled money to his campaign," Kane said.

"Is that a yes, then," she said.

"Let's see what you come up with," he said.

THE RUSSIAN OLIGARCHS WERE NOT discreet, only secretive. Grace was impressed by their largesse. They were spreading their money around town, like all out-of-towners, at the obvious, showy places: both Mets, MoMA, Carnegie Hall, the Whitney, Columbia, NYU Langone, NYPresbyterian, the American Ballet Theatre. None of them gave to the City Ballet. *It must be their Russian roots,* she thought. ABT was like the Bolshoi, ballets with stories. *They're sentimental. Like all plutocrats and gangsters.*

Her first article didn't say much that wasn't known, but it said it more sharply and more humorously, passing off facts as gossip, as was *The New Yorkist*'s style. It appeared on April 2, 2018. They held it a day so no one would think it an April Fools' prank.

The oligarchs living in the United States don't give money to politicians. They host them lavishly, on their planes and mega-yachts, in their townhouses and clubs, and they flatter them even more lavishly, praising them for their weaknesses: Lindsey Graham for his lofty principles, Ted Cruz for his animal magnetism, Ron Johnson for his dazzling intellect. They leave it to their wives and ex-wives, if they are U.S. citizens, to donate to campaigns.

Fyodor Semonov's ex-wife, the glamorous and multilingual Daria Molotova (the cocktail's greatgranddaughter), was a bundler for John McCain and Mitt Romney. In the run-up to the last election, rumor had it she was bundling for Chick Webb. "Mummies the word," she says, "Wait for the reports." The only Democrats she has ever supported were Schumer and Gillibrand, her Senators. "New Yorkers won't elect Republicans," she says. "Suicidal craziness, except, of course, when it comes to abortion and the subway."

MOLOTOVA TALKED WILLINGLY TO GRACE. Her divorce was finished. She had gotten less than she wanted, more than she needed. Gazprom had been very good to her ex.

Molotova is as astute as she is frank. Most Russians living in this country are Republicans, the ones with money, but even those without. "We are natural capitalists," she says, tapping her long fingernails on the side table. "The Russian intellectuals, of course, are Democrats or worse, but the rest of us are hardheaded. We lived under Communism. We know better than to believe in a Workers' Paradise. Yes, we are rich, but so are many Americans." Left unsaid was Putin's preference. He liked Republican regimes and they saw no point in upsetting him. He didn't care how they actually voted. "'In American elections,' Putin said to my former husband, 'money is more important than votes. It is possible the Democrat may catch on one day, but unlikely. They stand on their principles and fall on their swords.'"

THE ARTICLE GOT A LOT of attention. Molotova loved it and told all her friends Grace Maier was the best reporter she'd ever talked to. Doors opened.

Some weeks later, Josh Morgan called her up, inviting her to lunch. He had seen the article "floating around the newsroom." He knew some of the Russian oligarchs, he said, the ones investing in media. He thought he could get them to talk to her. "Say they're handsome or strong or piercingly intelligent in the first article, and they'll call you."

She had lunch with him at Moustache, off Sheridan Square. He had suggested the Union Square Cafe. She had declined.

"I don't know you," she said. "I'll pay my own tab at a dive."

Grace was early. Morgan was late. He was good looking in that TV anchor way, older and shorter than she expected, every day a fresh haircut.

"Sorry I'm late," he said. "I'm always late."

"I'm always on time," she said.

"Like your mother," he said.

"How do you know her?" she said.

"I was at *The Globe* for years. I left recently," he said. "I stayed too long. I was unhappy there for a long time. I thought I should have been made editor when Marshall picked her. I let her know. Him too. I thought it was antisemitism. Jews never got above assistant managing editor. Marshall's WASP fiefdom." He shrugged. "When I didn't get to work on WebbGate, I decided I'd give television a try. A newbie. CNN, the four P.M. roundup."

"What are you talking about," Grace said. "Lila's Jewish."

Josh started. "Where'd she get the fancy name?"

"Sephardic," Grace said. "She's Jewish and she married Jewish."

"Whadda ya know," he said. "No wonder she's so tough. I married Methodist. Less friction." He looked at her carefully. "So, you're Jewish. You tough too?"

"Toughening," Grace said, "but I'll never be as tough as Lila." She lowered her eyebrows. "She can fire people to their face."

Morgan laughed. "I bet she has."

He gave her the names of two oligarchs who would talk to her. "Don't write them up together," he said. "They'll feel compared and they don't like comparisons to other Russians, to other oligarchs. If you're going to compare them, compare them to Jamie Dimon or the Sage of Omaha or, if they're not Jewish, a Rothschild. Say nice things about them, then make a mistake, not an important one, an incidental one to anyone but them. The size of his yacht, make it shorter; his office's floor, make it lower; the name of his tailor, make it only the second most expensive. He'll get in touch with you."

"You are cunning," she said.

"Young reporters don't understand the usefulness of a status mistake," he said, "especially with the rich, famous, and powerful. Everything's a competition with them. Who walks through the door first. Who gets a window table at Jean-Georges, never Nougatine. They have much more money than they need. They want more only to beat the others." He took a bite of pizza. "This isn't bad."

"Any other tips, ones I'm more likely to follow," she said.

"All the *New Yorkist* reporters are very high-minded," he said. "Wait till you get to *The Times*."

Grace sat back in her chair and folded her arms. "I can see why you and Lila scrapped."

"Another ploy, a variation on the status mistake, the out-of-touch insult." He smiled. She liked his smile. "The oligarchs got rich the old-fashioned way. They took government money. Lots of it. They cozied up to Putin and so long as he got his cut and the gas and oil flowed, he let them take what they wanted. A lot of Americans have gotten rich with government contracts too. Those guys are the real Welfare Queens, but I digress." He took another bite of pizza. "Here's my point. The oligarchs don't understand the new media. They don't understand making things. They think Mark Zuckerberg is a jerk, but they envy him. They don't know how he did it. That goes for Steve Jobs and Bill Gates, too, and the Google gang and that obnox who makes the beautiful electric cars. See what I did, I said he was obnoxious, but his cars were beautiful. You can do that. He'll eat out of your hand." He grinned at her. "If you say that the Russians don't have any stake in the new media except as stockholders, they'll get their backs up. It's a sore point because it's true and it shows they're out of touch. Twentieth-century moguls."

"Do you deliver out-of-touch insults?" Grace said.

"On television, never," he said. "We're Caesar's Wife, above reproach. Also, instantly recorded and YouTubed. Excepting the Fox conservatives, of course." He took a swallow of coffee and smiled. "Fox is very popular with a narrow demographic, white, middle-class, red-state Christians who think America has gone to the dogs. I don't say they're racist. They're very touchy about that label. Some of their best friends are Black."

"Why did Webb win?" she said.

"The Electoral College works as our founders intended," he said. "Fox's voters are more powerful than MSNBC's. Wyoming's are more powerful than California's."

They split the bill, Grace insisted. "Business lunch," she said. He charged the whole tab, she paid him her share in cash. *I'm not going to think about how he expenses that,* she thought.

"Why are you helping me?" Grace said.

"You're going to be successful." He leaned forward. "You're ambitious, you're smart, you're literate, you're well connected." Grace flinched. "Go with it. Go with everything you have." He sat back. "You can go to journalism school or you can learn on the job, from older reporters. Kane is smart. I'm smarter. Think of me as a mentor."

"How old are you," Grace said.

"Too old for you," he said.

The waiter brought the check. Morgan left a tip that was, by Pereira-Maier standards, too small. As she was leaving, Grace put down a five-dollar bill. He saw her do it.

"A big tipper," he said.

"The smaller the bill," she said, "the larger the tip, percentage wise. Didn't they teach you that?"

"You tip big, and then really big, when you've made it," he said, "not before."

"Haven't you made it," she said.

"No," he said. "I want Anderson's slot. I dream of it. I'll never get it."

Morgan called Grace two days after their pizza lunch, again inviting her to lunch at the Union Square Cafe. "My treat," he said. "Put aside at least two hours. Okay?"

On the day, he sent two dozen mixed tulips to the office.

"What's this for?" Kane said. "Who's the guy?"

"Josh Morgan. He knows my mother," she said. "Maybe he's sucking up to me to get to her."

"He'd have sent roses if that was the case," Kane held up a warning finger. "Bounder. Watch out."

"He said he wanted to mentor me," she said. "He said you were a good reporter."

"I am a good reporter," Kane said. "Better than him."

Grace had a very good time at lunch. Morgan told funny stories. He asked her questions about Chicago, her job. They talked more politics. He was smart. He walked her back to her office. At the entrance, he kissed her on the cheek.

"Same time, same place, next Friday."

Grace nodded.

He called her the next morning. They talked for an hour. He called her on Tuesday evening. Again they talked for an hour.

"On Friday, we'll need four hours," he said. "At least."

Grace had never been so smoothly propositioned. *Do I want to do this,* she thought.

Against reason, she did. She was attracted to him. He made her laugh. He said she was great looking. "I love tall women," he said. "Eye to eye always works out best, especially when other things are uneven."

Their second lunch at Union Square was even better than the first. He ordered the food for them. "Let me do this," he said. "Last time, you went modest. Blowout time."

As the second hour wound down, he grew serious. "With hope in my heart, I made a reservation at the W Hotel. Not far from here." He leaned in. "Would you come with me."

Grace looked at him without saying anything for several seconds.

"Say something, please," he said. "You can say no, I'll understand."

"I'll come with you," she said.

He reached across the table and touched her hand.

"You won't regret it," he said.

She didn't regret it. His body was older than the bodies of the other men she'd slept with, but he had moves. *It used to be a drink before and a cigarette after. Now it's Viagra before and Ativan after.*

They stayed the night. After breakfast they parted.

"I hate to leave you," he said. "I have to see you again. Soon." Grace nodded.

"Tuesday," he said, "then Friday. Okay?"

Grace nodded again.

"Let's skip Union Square and have room service here. One P.M. Overnights only on Fridays. I have my show on Wednesday."

Neither of them told anyone. He was married. She knew better.

They carried on for a year. Every Friday he recommended a book. Sometimes he brought one.

"It's all part of the mentoring process," he said. "Read some of the male swaggerers, Philip Roth, the Zuckerman novels, Cheever, the stories. They've gotten a bad rap lately. David Foster Wallace's essay. You must have read it." She nodded.

Because of Morgan, she read during the year they were together: Forster's *Howards End.*

"I liked the movie," she said.

"The book is better," he said.

Dalton Trumbo's *Additional Dialogue.*

"The blacklist laid bare," he said. "Wonderful jokey letters with Ring Lardner."

The Autobiography of Alice B. Toklas and Hemingway's *A Moveable Feast.*

"Stein is the better writer, IMHO," he said.

Didion's *The White Album,* and Mailer's *The Executioner's Song.*

"Don't read their novels," he said.

Anything, everything by Eudora Welty, but especially "Why I Live at the P.O."

"Perfection," he said.

18

Next Moves

ON CHRISTMAS EVE 2018, ON A WINDY SLOPE IN JACKSON HOLE, SNOW falling softly, a year and a half after they re-met, Nico and Ruth agreed they'd get married "sometime."

"Are we engaged?" he said.

Ruth shook her head. "You have to meet my mom and my gran first," she said. "They confuse you and Xander. There are snags."

"Like my being Jewish," he said.

"The Jews are the Chosen People, the Bible says so, and Jesus was Jewish. That goes a long way with them," she said. "They're not antisemites, not now. Your parents did that. What they don't understand is why the Jews haven't accepted Jesus as their savior. 'They've been waiting for the Messiah for five thousand years,'" Ruth twanged, channeling her gran, "'and it's right before their eyes.'" She looked serious. "They're worried I won't be saved."

"My parents love you. They saw it coming, that first night. They were almost giggling when I got back from driving you home." He blinked to clear the snow from his eyes. "Most of their Jewish friends' children have married non-Jews. 'The grandkids are half-and-half. Only to the good,' Dad said. 'Christmas without guilt.'"

"They'll like that you're a doctor," she said.

"Can we get married this summer?" he said.

"We can't marry until I've launched *Elephant Memories,* and you've finished all your schooling."

"You've thought about this," he said.

"I've overthought about it," she said. "It's what I do. Joe calls me 'Belt Suspenders.' The only spontaneous thing I've ever done is this ski trip, and it took me two years to plan it." She smiled at him. "I didn't overthink us. I knew it within a week."

"I knew it the first kiss," he said.

"I want to finish my skiing year," she said.

"Will we move in together when you're done?" he said.

Ruth shook her head. "That would be too much for Mom and Gran. Anyway, your hours are impossible. It'll be better when you've finished the postdoc."

"Maybe for the best," he said. "Something's come up. Something interesting." He smiled. "Better than interesting."

"What?" she said.

"Biomedical engineering. Robotics. Prostheses. They're doing the most amazing things. I did some research but I wanted to talk to you first. I could probably do the Ph.D. in three years—I'll start while I'm doing my postdoc. I'll be Doctor Doctor." He wiped the snow from his mouth. "I'd rather make things than fix them."

"Me too," she said.

"I think I could get funding," he said. "If not, I've some savings. My parents would chip in."

"I have money, too," she said. "I'm not cheap, but I'm frugal. I have thirty-five thousand bucks in a savings account."

"The last person with a savings account," he said.

She leaned her head against his shoulder. "I'd kiss you but I'm too cold. No feeling in my lips."

They went into the bar. Nico ordered a bourbon on the rocks.

Ruth ordered a negroni. She only drank cocktails, never hard liquor straight, and she never had a second. She still worried she'd get drunk and do something stupid and calamitous. Her mom never drank after Ruth was born. Gran drank beer on July Fourth and sherry at Christmas.

"Family news," Nico said. "Mom's running for the state legislature. She's so tired of all the Florida Men running the show. She's worried about abortion rights, gay marriage, gun control, Webb contagion, the stuff of Xander's show."

"Abortion is hard for me," Ruth said. "I'm officially pro-choice, but I don't know that I could ever have one."

"Rape? Ectopic pregnancy? Terrible deformities?" he said.

"If I had an ectopic pregnancy, I'd abort. No question. I could die. Rape, too. I couldn't do that to you, to us. In the case of deformities, I don't know." Her mouth drooped. "If my mom had had an abortion, it's almost unbelievable she didn't—sixteen years old, a high school junior—I wouldn't be here."

"She never had any other children," he said. "Or a husband. Or even boyfriends. Do you think she feels she missed out?"

"Mom believes that things are meant to be," she said. "The gospel according to *The Sound of Music*. When God closes the door, He opens a window. Gran says I'm the basket she put all her eggs into."

"My mom had an abortion, the year before we were born," Nico said. "Dad told us first, Mom later. They'd been married more than ten years. He started messing around. They separated. She went back to New York, to stay with her parents. She didn't know she was pregnant. Dad was devastated, guilty and devastated. They got back together and eleven months later, Xander and I popped out." He shrugged. "If Mom hadn't had an abortion, I wouldn't be here."

"I guess 'choice' works," Ruth said.

"Everything hangs on a thread," he said.

By the end of the skiing season, Ruth was an intermediate skier. "I've conquered sharp turns, and I'm not scared, except of moguls," she said to Grace in a phone call. "I'll get better." After the last snow, she got a job in town waitressing. Nico came out once a month.

In late spring, they told their families they were marrying. The Goldsmiths were thrilled.

"What we wished for," Richard said to his father. "Are we lucky, or are we lucky. She's who I would have picked for him."

"Is she converting?" Zayde said.

"No," Richard said.

"I never thought I'd live to have Christian descendants," Zayde said.

"You never thought you'd outlive Mom," Richard said.

"I've outlived everyone," Zayde said. "No one alive knows my first name."

The Goldsmiths, including Zayde, insisted that Ruth call them by their first names.

"We don't do Mom, Dad, or Zayde for anyone but the boys," Mrs. G. said to Ruth. "No poaching on their territory."

Ruth laughed. "Nico will have to call Mom and Gran Ms. Ann and Ms. Ruth until the cows come home. They wouldn't like being called by their first names. They'd think it disrespectful. They have the sensitivities of the respectable poor. Lila notices things like that too, who gets called by their first name, who doesn't." She told them the Podsnap story.

The McGowans liked Nico, a turn of events they found disconcerting and consoling.

"She's marrying a doctor," Ann said to Gran. "Not a Podsnap doctor."

"She's not converting," Gran said. "Maybe she'll let us baptize the babies in the kitchen, just to be safe."

"The Goldsmiths don't object to him marrying a Christian girl," Ann said. "Jewish people are often touchy about that."

"I don't think the Goldsmiths worship anywhere," Gran said. "Ruth said the boys can't read Hebrew."

"He loves her," Ann said. "I didn't have that. You didn't either."

"We're not dead yet," Gran said.

• • •

THE GOLDSMITHS THREW AN ENGAGEMENT party at Vinegar Hill. They took a private room. There were a dozen guests: five Goldsmiths (Nico, Xander, Richard, Kathy, Zayde); three McGowans (Ruth, Ann, and Gran); and four Maier-Pereiras (Grace, Lila, Joe, Frances).

"The Maier-Pereiras have to be there," Ruth had said to Nico. "They are my other family." She laughed. "Your family used to be my other family but now they're my real family. I seem to need more family than most."

"Making up for the Bateses, maybe?" Nico said. "I'm sure it will be fine. I'll ask."

"We'd love to have them," Richard said. "I'm wearing my boots and my white suit."

The party went on for hours. Everyone had a good time, except Zayde: the food was too rich, the chairs too hard, the cocktail hour too long, the company too snooty, the toasts too risqué, the laughter too raucous. At the end of the toasts, he turned to Richard, seated on his left, and whispered loudly. "That horse laugh of yours could raise the dead."

Richard eyed his father for several seconds. "I wish Mom were here," he said.

Zayde shrank back into his chair. "She'd have had a better time than me. She could get along with anyone, the garbage man, the mayor, anyone." He surveyed the table. "That tall, old lady, Frances, she wouldn't give me the time of day."

"Did you introduce yourself to her?" Richard said.

"I was nearby," Zayde said. "She didn't ask me who I was."

"Let me know when you want to go home," Richard said. "I have a car ready."

"I'm too old for parties," Zayde said.

"I wonder if I'll get to ninety," Richard said.

"God forbid," Zayde said. "I didn't understand a word of Alexander's toast."

Xander's toast was affectionate. Most of it was spent comparing him and his brother. Nico was unruffled. Xander was ruffled. Nico was scientific. Xander made things up. Nico was excellent husband material. Xander was still working on his boyfriend skills. After each comparison, he shot a look at Grace, who was sitting across the table. They'd gotten off to a bristly start. Grace had asked him how his show was doing. Xander told her, then kept going with stories about college and Hollywood.

Seven minutes in, Grace tapped her watch. "Ahem," she said. "You've been rattling on for several minutes. Is this how men talk to women in L.A.?"

Xander sat up, startled. "I thought you were interested."

"In your senior thesis?" she said, her eyebrows rising. "There's a protocol. I ask you a question about your work, then you ask me about mine. I didn't need the potted Nietzsche lecture. He's like boxing, a male sport."

Xander nodded. "Prefix confusion. I wanted to IM-press you. Instead, I OP-pressed you."

Grace gave him a half smile.

"Thank God," Xander said, taking a note card from his pocket. "For my toast." He wrote: *Nico is comfortable with everyone. I'm barely comfortable in my own skin.* "I'm a fidgeter and a fiddler. Nico's more like Mom, I'm more like Dad, which is shorthand for: Mom is calm, Dad is racked by anxiety." He nodded. "You're right. I've got to learn to shut up. It's not the . . ." He caught himself. "I was relaunching. Ruth said you write for *The New Yorkist.* She called it the Oligarch beat. What are they like?"

"When I started out, I thought they were like the Mafia," Grace said, moving on as Lila would, "corrupt, ruthless, exploitative, menacing, quick to take offense and revenge, but with smoother edges, more money, and better-looking wives and girlfriends. It wasn't an original comparison, only a sexy one." She looked sharply at Xander. He nodded. "Now, they seem to me to be more like the tech billionaires, Zuckerberg, Gates, Bezos, Tesla guy. They've adapted to their environment. They're arrogant, obnoxious, smarmy, entitled, careless, greedy. They don't pay taxes. Their children go to Ivy League schools. They think they did it all on their own, and the people who don't make it are lazy and without ambition."

"All rich men are alike," Xander said. "Every poor man is poor in his own way."

Grace gave him another half smile. "I may steal that," she said.

"You have a great stealth smile," Xander said.

Grace raised her eyebrows. "Don't be fooled," she said. "I'm famously cranky. A family outlier. My sisters are mind-bogglingly cheerful. Papagena and Papagena."

"What's next," he said, "after *The New Yorkist*?"

"I've been working on a novel, three years in my head, three months on paper, autofiction, I think they call it, based on my mother's life." She nodded toward Lila. "It's in outline form. I'll need a job for years. And you, what's next after *Florida Men*?"

"I'm working on a novel too, a potboiler, based on a Hollywood lot," he said. "Danielle Steel meets Raymond Chandler. I also have another TV idea, this time for a limited series. *Smithies,* about Smith College women. Some big names went there: Margaret Mitchell in the twenties, Julia Child in the thirties, Madeleine L'Engle in the forties; Senator Tammy Baldwin in the eighties. I'm still doing research." His finger started tapping the table. "I'm trying to get Reese Witherspoon interested. Women own television these days. You can get any actor you want. Residuals." Hearing himself, he stopped. "I'm talking too much. It's me, but it's you, something about you."

"I don't think so. I think it's you," Grace said. "I'm no Ruth, the listener nonpareil."

"Maybe, I'm tired," he said. "I took the red-eye, and then Dad wanted to play golf. He likes to play with me when I'm wiped out. He wins." He shook his head. "Nico and I applied to Chicago. He got in. I didn't. We both got into Columbia. He's a great guy."

As the party was breaking up, Ruth sidled up to Grace. "What do you think of Xander?"

"For the first time, I understand why Jo married the old German professor instead of Laurie," Grace said. "Do you think Mr. G. was like Xander when he was younger? I didn't think a Southerner could talk so fast."

THE DAY AFTER THE GOLDSMITHS' party, Ruth and Nico's engagement announcement appeared in *The Tallahassee Register*. At 9:00 A.M., Jacqui Bates phoned the McGowans.

"How could you let your daughter marry a Jew?" Jacqui said.

"Who's calling?" Gran said.

"Mrs. Bobby Lee Bates, Jr.," Jacqui said.

"I believe you have the wrong number." Gran hung up.

"Who was that?" Ann said.

"A fundraiser," Gran said. "Bubba's Church of the Crusader."

19

Stuck

AFTER A YEAR AND A HALF AT *THE NEW YORKIST*, GRACE DECIDED TO look at her notes for *The Lost Mother*. She opened the file and gulped. *Nothing here but names.* She had thought about the book, without putting anything on paper. *I'm truly Hope-less,* she thought. *A writer who doesn't write isn't a writer.*

She decided to start at the end, with Zelda. Lila's story, she told herself, would pour out of her. Her own, too. Zelda's story was the sticking point. There was no story except the one in her head. She would have to make it so riveting, the reader would either believe it or not care that she'd made it up.

Ruth was baffled. "What's in it for you," she said. "The first novel is a bildungsroman. Fiction 101. What does Zelda have to do with you?"

"I know I'm right," Grace said. "Zelda didn't die back in 1968, though she may now be dead. Her story is the origin story of our family. Everything follows from her escape."

"What about Aldo?" Ruth said. "You've never acknowledged the horror of Lila's childhood. The story isn't the missing mother. It's the violent father. You've concocted a matrilineal inheritance of desertion: first, Zelda abandoned Lila, then Lila abandoned you." Ruth squinted at Grace. "Where are the fathers? Think of the huge difference between Aldo and Joe."

"You're not getting it," Grace said. "Before Zelda left, Aldo beat her, not the children. After she left, he started beating them. Zelda fled to save herself. Lila could hold out against Aldo's violence but not against his violence *and* Zelda's desertion, her dereliction, her betrayal. It would have torpedoed her. Zelda had to be dead." She nodded several times, punctuating her speech. "Lila has no memories of Zelda. Clara says the few she recalls made her cautious and distrustful. She won't say what they are. Polo remembered her. He would talk about her. He was five when she was hospitalized. I've always thought he knew she wasn't dead and it torpedoed him."

"Do you want to torpedo Lila," Ruth said. "Is that your plan?"

"I'm making it up. I'm writing a novel. Mostly," Grace said. "She won't know more than she knew before."

They were sitting in Ruth's tiny apartment in the East Village, a box, twelve by fourteen, with a kitchen the size of a closet, and a bathroom the size of a smaller closet. Ruth had moved to New York in the New Year, to be near Nico. She was living on her savings, working on *Elephant Memories*. After several weeks interviewing people she knew and people who knew people she knew, she started interviewing strangers. She'd approach them in parks, coffee shops, museums, department stores, and ask them if they'd be willing to be interviewed. "As long as it's quiet, you can pick the venue. Public libraries are good," she'd say. "Bring a friend if you want." Most agreed. Some of the interviews worked out, some didn't. She kept going. She played them for Nico, no one else.

Grace was so happy that they were living in the same town again. They saw each other at least twice a week, usually at Ruth's place. Grace would bring wine, pizza, and Lila-snacks, M&M's, pretzel sticks, potato chips. They'd sit on the trundle bed and catch up.

"Is there a plot?" Ruth said.

"It's very rough," Grace said. "Current scenario: Zelda runs off. She thinks she's pregnant. She steals money from Aldo. She goes to her doctor. He does a D & C and ties her tubes. She changes her name, finds a husband, a widower, works as a travel agent, joins Hadassah. No children, of course. Husband slaps her now and then. When she's old, she goes into a nursing home on Medicaid."

"Hmm," Ruth said. "Not much going on."

"It's hard," Grace said.

"What is Zelda's personality like in her new life?" Ruth says.

"She's standoffish, she doesn't trust people. Anyone could betray her. She makes up a story about what she did for the seven years she was married to Aldo. She's living a lie, in every way. She tells people the tragedy of her life was that she could never have children."

"I think it needs some juicing," Ruth says.

"Someone in the nursing home recognizes her? A former neighbor?" Grace said.

"Doesn't that come too late to make much of a difference?" Ruth said.

"If it came earlier," Grace said, "wouldn't it seem too coincidental?"

"Coincidence is the engine of novels," Ruth said. "That and 'backward glances.'" She laughed. "Speaking of which, what about Aldo," she said. "What's he up to?"

"I'm calling him Fredo in the book. Good, no?" Grace said. "He makes up a story, like the one Aldo told Lila except different."

"How does Hope find her?" Ruth said. "Genealogies?"

"No," Grace said. "Old-fashioned shoe leather searches. Birth certificates, death certificates, wedding licenses, divorce decrees, voting registration."

"But she does find her, right?"

"If she's alive."

"The plot fizzles if she's dead, Fiction 101," Ruth said. "Even I know that."

"I'm not good at building suspense, only surprise, which could be disappointment," Grace said.

"Have you actually done any searching?" Ruth said.

"I told you," Grace said. "It's a novel. It's a story. It's a theory I've had my whole life. I suppose I don't want to know the truth any more than Lila does. I'm going for truthiness."

"You're having your cake and eating it too," Ruth said.

"I need an editor," Grace said.

"How does it end?" Ruth said. "Do Lila and Zelda fall into each other's arms?"

"I don't know," Grace said. "Maybe. Probably."

THE END OF GRACE'S AFFAIR with Morgan came deus ex machina, in late June, before they'd tired of each other and said mean things. Felicity Turner was in town for the George Polk Awards. *The Globe* had been nominated for their stories on the afterlife of the Spiderlings. She saw Josh and Grace at breakfast at the W Hotel. She was there with a New York friend. The air of intimacy between them set her teeth on edge. *What's this?* she thought. *Payback time.*

That afternoon she called Grace at *The New Yorkist*.

"I'll get to the point quickly," Felicity said. "I saw you with Josh Morgan at breakfast this morning." She paused. "I had an affair with him. You must have been my replacement after he moved to New York. He almost ruined my career."

Grace was silent.

"I think he's getting back at your mother," Felicity said. "He's a bounder and a louse." Grace was still silent. "Did you hear me?" Felicity said.

"Yes," Grace said. "Why are you telling me this?"

"I love your mother," Felicity said. "I can't watch him going after you to hurt her."

"Not to get back at him?" Grace said.

"My heart isn't pure," Felicity said, "but he's bad news. Ask your mother. Ask Doug. Ask Sally Alter. Ask anyone at *The Globe*."

"I don't think I want to thank you for this information," Grace said.

"I restrained myself from going over to your table," Felicity said.

"My mother wouldn't be hurt by our relationship," Grace said. "Maybe annoyed, surprised. Lila doesn't do hurt."

"Don't you believe me?" Felicity said.

"You make it sound like *Les Liaisons Dangereuses*," Grace said.

"You make me feel sorry I told you," Felicity said.

"I'm not grateful," Grace said, "if that's what you were expecting."

"Maybe he won't turn on you," Felicity said. "He turned on me. The end of our relationship ruined everything that came before. He was so cruel."

"I'm going to go now," Grace said.

GRACE CALLED JOSH AT HIS office. "Can we have a drink one night this week?" she said.

"What's up?" he said.

"I'm breaking up with you," she said. "I want to do it in person."

"I knew this day would come," he said. "You've given me a year. I took it."

They met the next evening at the Algonquin Bar. "Liquor is called for," Grace said. She ordered a margarita. He ordered a scotch.

"I always ordered wine for us," he said. "Domineering."

"You were on a mission to civilize me," she said.

"So, why are we here?" he said.

"I'm stuck," she said. "Our relationship has no future, only a perpetual present. We don't go anywhere, we don't have mutual friends. It's only ever the two of us. And waiters. I haven't even told Ruth. I feel I'm selling myself short. I should be with someone my own age. I have to go."

"Did something nudge you?" he said. "I've spent months breaking up."

"Felicity Turner," she said. "She made me feel fungible."

"I was terrible to her," he said.

"She wanted to protect Lila," she said. "She wasn't doing it to protect me."

"I had bad motives when I called you," he said, "but that changed the first time we had lunch. You wouldn't let me pay. Then you added to the tip."

"You tipped better after that," she said.

"I don't know that you made me a better man," he said, "but I was a better man with you and I liked that man better. I got off on the wrong foot with your mother, my fault. I should have apologized. I didn't. Ask her sometime."

Grace shook her head. "I'm going to stick to my memories."

He smiled. "Were we ever in love? I don't know. I do know that I like you more than any other person I've ever known."

"I like you too," Grace said.

"Is there someone else?" he said.

"Possibilities," she said.

"Can I call you?" he said. "Can we have a drink now and again?" Grace shook her head.

"You're talented," he said. "*The Lost Mother* is going to be great." The waiter came with the drinks and the bill.

"This one's mine," she said. She put down four tens.

"You go," he said. "I'm going to have another drink."

She got up, leaned over, and kissed him on the cheek.

He watched her walk out. She didn't turn around.

20

Onward

CONTEMPLATING RETIREMENT, DOUG DECIDED, IN LATE SPRING 2020, to start a podcast. He hashed it out with Lila. "I'll have to do something when I step down as publisher, and I'll be ready to step down when you go in three years. I'm already seventy. I don't want to abuse the publishers' privilege."

"Does it have a name?" Lila said.

"I'm calling it *The Press Gang*. It's a *Globe*/WAMU partnership. Do you want to be a part of it?"

"Like *The New Yorker Radio Hour*?" she said.

"Less decorous," he said. "It's a *Globe* offshoot, after all. More sausage making."

He started with ten employees, his own Pirates, half *Globe*, half WAMU. More than a hundred people had applied for the jobs. "The romance of start-ups," he said. "They could all be furloughed in months."

They were a motley crew, no two alike. "Our stories will be 'ripped from the headlines,'" he said at the first group meeting, "but also the features pages, the fashion pages, the sports pages, the business pages, the obits." Taking his cue from Lila, he added, "No political analysis, no editorializing. Podcasting is now. All kinds of shows are online. We'll do short form and long form, interviews, reported pieces, personal essays, reviews. We'll cover the news, but our real purpose will be going behind the news." He slowly scanned the group, looking hard at each of them. "I expect a high level of professional behavior. I will need to know all your sources and their bona fides." He smiled. "We'll have a good time with this."

XANDER WAS PLANNING A TRIP to New York in the new year. He called Ruth. "I'd like to see Grace when I'm there. Could the four of us go on a date?"

"Do you have a place to stay?" Ruth said.

"Aren't you jumping the gun?" he said.

"My place is small and Nico's place is small," she said. "We can't put you up."

"Oh," he said. "I'm staying at the William Vale Hotel in Williamsburg."

"What would you like to do?" she said. "Why aren't you setting this up with Nico?"

"I find Grace irresistible and difficult," he said. "I've never liked a girl so much and I barely know her. I thought you might help me navigate the high waters. She's . . . testy."

"We can eat somewhere around Union Square and then you and Grace can take the L train to Williamsburg," she said.

"My treat," he said. "The studio's paying. I'm taking meetings."

"I'll say we're having dinner with you and could she join us," she said.

"Could you mention somewhere that I want to see her?" he said.

Ruth laughed.

"Do you believe in love at first sight?" he said.

"Yes," she said.

"True love, not infatuation?" he said.

"Yes," she said.

"Don't you think she's beautiful, too?" he said.

"Yes," she said.

THEY HAD DINNER AT CASA MONO, sitting practically in the laps of their table neighbors, in the halcyon pre-Covid days. They talked about college, arguing whether Columbia was more rigorous than Chicago. "In your dreams," Grace said. They talked about television and podcasting, about artificial limbs, and oligarchs. The reservation was for 9:00 P.M. They stayed until midnight, Xander ordering multitudes of expensive wines to keep the waiters happy.

Grace invited Xander to her place. He suggested his hotel. "Very posh," he said. "Room service and a spa."

"Will you take me home, if I decide not to stay over?" she said.

"Without question," he said. "I'm not a brute."

It was after one when they got to the hotel.

"I'm hungry and hungover," Xander said. "I could eat something." He had a suite. The living room was comfortable and soothing. There were two oversize beige sofas, a huge television, and three lamps with low-wattage bulbs.

"They assume no one reads unless it's on a screen." Grace sank into the sofa cushions. "Comfy."

"Are you hungry? We could order room service," he said.

He's tall and thin and gangly, Grace thought. *Like Joe.* "Breakfast," she said. "Lila says it's every hotel's best meal. She also says at a diner, order a BLT with mayo on white toast."

Grace ordered poached eggs, bacon, English muffins, fresh orange juice, and coffee. Xander ordered blueberry pancakes, bacon, a side of scrambled eggs, a strawberry-banana smoothie, and coffee.

"I'm impressed," Grace said. "Can you really eat all that?"

"When you're six-two," he said, "you can eat a whole lot, though Dad says I can't keep going this way once I turn thirty-five. He says I'll get a pot. He has a pot, which he's resigned himself to. He's always telling me to learn from his mistakes. Nico, being a man of discipline and sense, needs no such advice."

"Do you think Nico and Ruth are too much alike?" Grace said.

"I think I know what you mean, placid waters, but only Nico, not Ruth," he said. "She's not as unflappable and sensible as she 'presents.' With Nico, she can tie herself in knots, overthinking, overplanning, overworking, overdoing. Nico's always the same, tolerant, flexible, good natured. He works hard and he's steely when roused, but he'd always rather get along." He laughed. "I'm more like Ruth than he is, though she has it better under control." He took a bite of pancake. "Delicious." He squinted at Grace. "I'm betting from what I've seen, you're a lot like your mother. You don't overthink. You get on with it."

"Not always an admirable quality," she said. "I often act without considering the consequences. Lila is more careful on that score. Joe says I'm self-absorbed, 'solipsistic' is his word. He says I'm a late bloomer, stuck in adolescence." She laughed. "He says it not unkindly, but as a fact, there for everyone to see. I tell him twenty-six is the new seventeen, which reassures him that I recognize the problem." She picked up her coffee cup. "I'm working on it, in my crab-like way, but it's hard to get outside yourself." She took a swallow of coffee. "I recently ended an inappropriate relationship. He was much older and married. I never thought about his wife, what she would feel. He was a notorious bounder. I must have been Girlfriend No. 16. Maybe she messed around too. He was good to me." She took another swallow. "I sound unfeeling, but I'm not, not completely. It's a delayed reaction."

Xander took in a big breath. "I've had three longish relationships since I moved to L.A.," he said. "They were all nice women, sporty and hardworking, with good jobs and long silky hair that was always getting in the way."

"But," Grace said.

"They weren't funny," he said. "Correction. They didn't laugh at my jokes." He took a bite of his eggs. "I should have ended all three relationships after the first year. The women all talked about freezing their eggs. I felt guilty, I knew I wasn't going to marry them"—he picked up his cup—"but I liked them. They finally threw me over in year three."

Grace lowered her eyebrows. "It's easier when they do the breaking up."

"Our first date," he said, "and we're talking breakups."

IN FEBRUARY, LILA CAME DOWN with what she thought was the flu. When after a week, she couldn't breathe, Joe called an ambulance. She was diagnosed with Covid, one of the earliest cases in D.C. More irritated than concerned, she was a noncompliant patient. She told both Joe and Doug, who was a trustee of Johns Hopkins, that under no circumstances was she to go on a ventilator. "I'm not dying in an iron lung." Joe backed her up. "If she survives," he told the doctors, "she'll be mad at me and madder at you." They gave her oxygen and steroids. She wound up spending three weeks in the hospital, two of them in the ICU. Except for the first three days, when she was too breathless to lift her head, she worked every day.

Doug had special permission to visit her. She was all business. "What are we going to do when the city tells us to close down?" she said.

"We won't close down," he said. "They can't close us down. We're the First Amendment."

Not wanting to argue, she rephrased the question. "What are we going to do *if* they close us down. You need to get the tech people working. FaceTime can't handle it. People won't come into work."

"How do you know this?" he said.

"Don't you see how exhausted the doctors and nurses are, how understaffed this place is," she said. "How many people at *The Globe* called in sick today? I'm betting close to ten percent if not more. We want to get the paper out every day. You need to figure out how we can do it remotely, electronically. People who work at home can work when they're contagious." She coughed. "And don't forget to ask the printers what they're doing. Get in there now, ahead of *The Washington Times*."

"Anything else," Doug said, reeling from her instructions.

"Ruth McGowan, Grace's great friend, is developing a podcast. She could use help. Take her under your wing, would you? She's special, very smart, very hardworking."

"Is that it?" he said.

"If I die," she said, "no Fox people at my funeral, no Rupert Murdoch or Lachlan Murdoch. Elisabeth and James can come. No Newt Gingrich. No Webbs or Spiderlings. No Mitch McConnell. No billionaires who don't pay taxes. I'll make a list. Nancy Pelosi should sit down front, in the family section."

The Press Gang launched in late spring. Everyone worked remotely. The early shows were not half bad. The pros at WAMU asserted themselves, not wanting to embarrass the station. Within two months, the show was going "gangbusters." Doug decided to stream it. Ruth was his thirteenth hire. He called her "to chat," he said. "Lila recommended you and that goes a very long way with me. Can we Zoom?"

The chat quickly turned into an interview. "Why should I hire you?" he said.

"Have you listened to the podcasts I sent you?" she said.

"Yes," he said. "They're good. They're not polished, but that may be part of their appeal. I particularly liked the one on earliest memories, the old gent who said he walked in on his parents having sex. 'I was three, three and a half,' he said. 'I probably had earlier memories but that one obliterated them.'"

Doug sat back in his chair. He was enjoying himself. He liked talking to Ruth. *Something about her,* he thought. "What do you bring to the table?"

"I love people's stories. I've wanted to do podcasting since forever. I'm a late adopter. I was a classics major at Chicago, which may explain it." She raised her shoulders. "I'm a Southerner. I was born when my mother was seventeen. She was born when her mother was eighteen. No dads in the picture. Mom and Gran are Republican Baptists."

"You don't have a Southern accent," he said.

"It took a lot of years and work to suppress it," she said.

"How would you describe your interview style?" he said. "I don't hear you much in the podcasts. You let them speak."

"I was brought up a 'good girl' and I've spent the last nine years working on burying her. I'm never rude, I'm never mean, I never step on someone's answer. I don't mind ruffling feathers but I draw the line at creaming someone's corn. I ask a question and I wait. Lila taught me that. I take out the pauses. Once, I waited two and a half minutes. I have a clock with a second hand on my desk. I almost gave in."

"What did the person finally say?" Doug said. "Was it worth the wait?"

"Yes and no. She said she had three breasts, like Anne Boleyn. She asked me not to use it. I obliged."

"I'd have been tempted to use it," he said. "Not Lila."

Ruth nodded. "I talked it over with her. I don't like gotcha moments."

"How come you don't say 'y'all'?"

"That's a recent Northern appropriation that makes me flinch," Ruth said. "When someone says 'y'all,' I get this picture in my mind of Bull Connor letting loose the dogs on the Birmingham protesters. I could no more say 'y'all' than I could 'ain't.'" She gave a half smile. "Except I do say 'Ain't I,' like Sojourner Truth, but that's because 'Am I not' sounds like something only the Lord would say."

"What do you want from me, from the show?" he said.

"I want to make wonderful podcasts and I can't do it alone," she said. "I need a mentor, I need colleagues. The interviews have gotten better, but I need direction, criticism, encouragement, equipment. None of the podcasts I've made have been on the air. I'm stockpiling them now."

"Do you play well with others?" he said.

"I get along," she said. "I'm good at work-arounds. I'll come in the back door if the front door is locked."

"I'll give you a try," he said, "a six-month paid internship, five hundred dollars a week. If you work out, I'll hire you." He smiled. "What was your earliest memory?"

"When I was two, a wild hog broke through the fence in our backyard and tore up the kitchen garden. I was outside. Gran heard the noise and came running out. She scooped me up and ran inside. That scared me more than the hog, which was fat and nimble and committed. It's a family story so I don't know if what I remember is the scene itself or the telling. Gran was shook up. I have to say it colored my view of *Charlotte's Web*. My admiration for Charlotte was boundless, but my sympathy for Wilbur was at best halfhearted."

Doug smiled. "Wilbur was some pig." He nodded. Ruth saw the interview was over. She waited. "You can start on Wednesday, six months' probation," he said. "I always have new employees start midweek. A whole week is too exhausting for a newcomer. You can stay in New York for now."

"Thank you, Mr. Marshall," she said.

"Doug," he said.

Doug would often say Ruth was not like Lila but, after Lila, she was the young reporter he most enjoyed working and talking with. "She's direct," he said to Lila. "She answers the question you put to her, not the adjacent one. She's never manipulative. She tells me when she thinks I'm wrong, and more tactfully than you would. But then she's tactful with everyone. Have you ever seen her blow her top?"

"No," Lila said, "though she can be bracingly stern with Grace."

"Ah, Grace," Doug said. "Grace is wonderful and exasperating. She's just a late bloomer. She'll be fine. I have sympathy with late bloomers. I didn't bloom until my thirties."

"Ruth and I didn't have the luxury to bloom late," Lila said. "Another middle-class privilege."

Within a month of working on *The Press Gang*, Ruth was embedded. After three months, Doug hired her full-time, benefits and vacation, but, explicitly, no overtime. No one got overtime. "For reporters, editors, and producers in the news business," he'd say, "overtime is regular business hours."

Doug didn't show favoritism toward Ruth, not in any public, discernible way, but their conversations were far more ranging than those he had with the other staff. Doug noticed the gaps in her knowledge, smart as she was, and saw one of his responsibilities to her was to fill them in. They talked about evolution as fact and theory, the uses of psychoanalysis, Communism and Fascism, deconstruction and close reading. He told her to read Hofstadter's *Anti-Intellectualism in American Life* as well as *The Paranoid Style in American Politics,* Trollope as well as Dickens, the *Daily Mail* as well as *The New York Times.* "Out of school, someone, parents likely, told these things to your friends at Chicago before they got there," he said. "Not all of them, but many of them."

He was more boss-like with the other reporters, trying to get them to stop talking on the show the way they talked to friends. "This isn't Millennial Radio," he'd say. "You can keep your cultural references but you can only speak Adult." Ruth didn't need to clean up her language. Between Latin and Greek and the Southern accent purge, she never used "um" or "uh" or "like" or "you know" or "awesome." When she dropped occasional southernisms, he let them stay. "They're regional not generational," he'd say.

After six months, Doug had her do stories as well as interviews. "You need to stretch yourself," he said. He had her work with the directors, editing others' stories. "Editing is the glue," he said. At the end of her first year, he made her an occasional host of the show. "You need to learn to drive," he said. If she was terrified, she didn't show it. Lila had taught her that. "Fronting."

XANDER UNDERSTOOD THAT SEX WAS easier for Grace than love. He took issue with Joe's assessment. "You're not so self-absorbed as closed in," he said to her on their fifth date. He came to New York at least once a month, ostensibly on business but really to see Grace.

"She's . . . difficult," he said to Ruth in a call planning his sixth visit. He always arranged for the four of them to have a great dinner somewhere. Grace was at her most relaxed, most comfortable, most playful in Ruth's company.

"Yes," Ruth said, "but once you're in, you're in."

"Is she difficult with everyone or just me?" he said.

"Everyone," she said.

"I don't know why I've fallen so hard for her. She's so hard to get, in every way. Maybe that's it." He started fidgeting in his chair. "She's an original. I can never guess what she's going to say next."

Ruth laughed. "Joe says that about Lila."

"Am I like Joe?" he said.

"If Joe were ever anxious," she said.

He laughed. "Do you always tell the truth?"

"To those I love."

"Thank you," he said.

"Of course," she said.

"You think I'm anxious," he said. "You can tell?"

"When you're in new or particularly hard places," she said, "you're like a cat on a hot tin roof."

"Really?" he said. "I thought it meant a woman who thought she was losing her man."

"If it made her anxious," she said.

"Do you think she could love me?" he said.

"I do," she said. "Keep on keepin' on."

XANDER DIDN'T LAY SIEGE TO Grace. He just kept turning up, injecting himself into her life, becoming a regular presence in their Gang of Four. They talked on the phone at least weekly, sometimes for hours. Xander always made the calls but she always picked up.

"She's got to know I love her," he said to Nico in a call.

"Only one way to know," Nico said.

"She's too skittish."

"Maybe she's skittish because you're holding back."

"I'm almost thirty-five, and I've never been in love before."

"I know exactly how old you are."

"Maybe you or Ruth could tell her."

"'Are you a man or a mouse?'" Nico said, falling into one of their old routines.

"'Put a piece of cheese on the floor and you'll find out,'" Xander said.

AFTER HER BOOK CAME OUT, in late 2022, Grace was embarrassed around Doug. Ruth, who had come to love him, told her to say something to him.

"What do I say?" Grace said.

"You know what to say," Ruth said.

"When's the best time to call him?" Grace said.

"Make an appointment with his assistant," Ruth said. "Zoom."

"You're kidding," Grace said. "Face-to-face?" *No way,* she thought. *I'd rather stay embarrassed.*

"Don't be a ninny," Ruth said. "You need to *mensch* up."

Grace made the Zoom appointment.

Doug was Doug.

"How are you, Grace," he said. "I've been reading some of your pieces in *The New Yorkist.* You're the best writer on the staff. You could move."

"It's harder than you might think," she said. "I want to do print journalism. All the jobs are online."

"What can I do for you?" he said. "You'd be great for *The Globe* but we're not hiring, we're laying off."

"I called to . . . say . . . I wish I hadn't made up the affair," she said. The last words dribbled out. "Lila spent all her time at *The Globe*. So did you. It had a kind of irresistible pull on my imagination."

"It upped my reputation," he said. "Lila Pereira was not your run-of-the-mill popsy."

Grace jerked back in her seat. *I can't believe he said that,* she thought. *Who's writing his lines, Nora Ephron?* "I wanted to tell you."

"Lila never apologized. She got away with it. Most people can't. If you're apologizing," he said, "and it's hard to tell, you should apologize to Joe."

Grace nodded. She could feel the tears gathering. *He's been judging me this whole time,* she thought. *He thinks I'm a horrible daughter.*

"We're square, you and I," Doug said.

"Thank you," she said. "I wish I hadn't written the book."

"Spilled milk," he said. "How many times have I heard that?"

XANDER COULDN'T TELL IF HE was making any progress with Grace. He decided he would declare himself in a phone call. She could hang up if she wanted to.

"I'm crazy about you," he said.

Grace was quiet for several seconds. *What's my problem?* she thought. *Why can't I believe him? Joe says I'm lovable. Difficult but lovable. Say something.*

"Thank you," she said, frozen in her seat.

Xander reported the "transaction" to Nico and Ruth.

"You need to do it in person," Nico said.

"If she said thank you to me in person," Xander said, "I'd cry."

Nico handed the phone to Ruth.

"Keep on keepin' on," Ruth said. "I've never known two lovers like you and Grace."

"Are we lovers?" he said. "Maybe it's just me."

"You're lovers," Ruth said. "You have to trust me."

Two months later, Xander tried again.

"You're the one for me," he said to Grace in a call. "I knew it the first time I saw you."

"Love at first sight, really?" Grace said. "Like Joe and Lila."

"What did Lila say?" Xander said.

"She said it took her a month," Grace said. "And that was before they even kissed."

"Will you get back to me in a month?" Xander said.

Grace laughed. "Soon," she said.

PART III
Zelda

21

Telephone Calls

IN MID-APRIL 2023, A MONTH AFTER LILA'S MEMORIAL SERVICE, GRACE
made herself sit down at her computer and begin *The Quest for Zelda.*
Her heart was sore. She was sorry she had written *The Lost Mother.*
She'd upset the family, even Clara, the kindest of them all, and she'd
hogged attention that should have gone to Lila's retirement. A reporter
on *The Globe* recently said to her face, "You didn't kill your mother. You
didn't even kill her reputation, much as you tried."

She was racked with regret. "I was only twenty-seven when I
wrote it," she said to Ruth. "I thought you were forgiven everything
you did before you were thirty."

"In the world I was raised up in, only by God," Ruth said, "and
then, you had to get down on your knees."

The book had made a lot more money than Grace had expected.
Every newspaper in the country, it seemed, wrote about it, and it
spent a week on *USA Today's* bestseller list. Several publishers con-
tacted her agent asking whether she had another book. She swore
she'd never write another novel, *if it was a novel,* she thought. She'd
begun to refer to it as a novelization.

"I don't understand why it was reviewed everywhere," Grace said to Lila, instead of apologizing. Lila was unperturbed.

"Book section editors have a tough job," Lila said. "The usual problem—other people. Editorial houses push their books. That's their job. The paper's staff lobby for their friends to be reviewed and also, when the book is a howler, their enemies. The masthead editors want 'the big, important' books reviewed so they can score interviews with the authors. The publisher wants the top sellers to be reviewed. They mean ads. I get it, I get it all." Lila shook her head. "Yours was an easy choice. Everyone loves newspaper stories. There's all those movies and books. *All the President's Men, She Said, His Girl Friday, Citizen Kane, The Journalist and the Murderer.* Throw in Cinderella and Mrs. Danvers, and you're on the front page."

"I thought it was you," Grace said. "They all wrote about you."

"It's a mistake to take things personally," Lila said. "Good or bad."

LILA'S LAST LETTER, WHICH AT first seemed a gift, was becoming a curse, as if Lila was saying: *If you think she's alive, find her.* Grace could not imagine a satisfactory outcome. *What do I get out of it?* she thought. *What's the difference now between Zelda alive and Zelda dead?*

She called Clara. "Lila sent me on a quest for Zelda. I feel like I'm looking for Kurtz."

"I know," Clara said. "We talked about it when your book came out, and again when she was dying. She thought her belief that Zelda was dead had in some way—loyalty, fear—held you back from looking for her." Clara stopped to collect her thoughts. "Here's what I think. Instead of finding out the truth, you asserted your belief." She stopped again. Unlike Lila, who'd shed her Midwestern identity when she left for D.C., Clara remained a Detroiter. She spoke not so much slowly, as carefully. "It seemed to me," she continued, "that Lila was saying 'She died,' and you were saying 'She ran away,' but neither of you wanted to know the truth. Lila wanted Zelda dead, to protect herself. You wanted her alive, to . . . I don't know why you did it, to prove something, I guess."

Grace started. *Geez,* she thought, *that's a comeuppance.* "I should drop it, shouldn't I?" she said.

"No," Clara said. "You should honor Lila's letter, if you can." She paused. "Come what may."

Grace started again. "Oh, God," she said, "I never thought what *The Lost Mother* would mean to you. Did you think Zelda was dead?"

"I split the difference," Clara said. "I told people my mother had disappeared when I was four."

"Would you help me then?" Grace said.

Clara was silent for several seconds. "Let me think about it," she said. "Come back in a few days."

"How will you feel if she's alive?" Grace said.

"I don't know," Clara said. "I don't think I'd be furious that she left, not the way Lila was. As far as I'm concerned, it all lies on Aldo's head." The line went quiet.

"Are you still there?" Grace said.

"Lila ran away too, you know," Clara said. "She left Polo and me behind."

"I never thought about that. Did Lila see it that way?"

"Yes," Clara said. "The day after she and Joe moved to D.C., she started pressing us to leave. They would underwrite the move."

"Were you tempted?"

"Never," Clara said. "We had our careers, our friends, our house. We had each other."

"I've often wondered why neither of you married."

Clara was quiet. *Oh, God. I stepped in it,* Grace thought. "I shouldn't have said that."

"It's okay," Clara said. "Marriage was dangerous for us. Whatever safety we felt, we felt with each other."

"Did you miss having children?" Grace heard her question with horror. *I've become a blurter. Was I always? How could I have asked that? She's my aunt, not a source.* "Ugh," she said. "That was a horrible Barbara Walters question. You needn't answer."

"No and yes," Clara said. "Maybe if I'd fallen in love with some-

one like Joe. Polo and I would joke about it. We couldn't do it without someone like Joe. Do you know how lucky you were to have Joe
for a father?"

Grace felt her brain combusting. "Sometimes, not enough," she
said. "I was too tied up thinking how unlucky I was in my mother."

"Grace, Grace, Grace," Clara said. "You've got to grow up. Lila
was unlucky in her mother. I was unlucky in my mother. You were
lucky, so lucky."

Grace closed her eyes. *I'm a vortex of solipsism.* In Latin, it
sounded less awful.

Chastened by her conversation with Clara, Grace briefly played
with the idea of hiring a private eye. *Let's get this over with,* she
thought. She googled "Private Investigators." The listings stunned
her. No more gumshoes. PIs had morphed into high-tech profession-
als, with advanced degrees and bespoke suits. She couldn't do it. Lila
would see it as a gross violation of the Scarface rule. "Do it first, do
it yourself, and keep on doing it." Grace mentally squared her shoulders. *It's my mess to clean up,* she thought.

She googled "How to find a missing person." Google spat up
pages of stories of runaways, mostly children and girlfriends. She
regoogled: "How to find a person missing for 50 years." Pages of dead
bodies and cold cases. She googled a third time: "How to find a living
person missing for several years." Pages of women who'd been abused
by husbands and boyfriends, mostly living in Florida or California.

Grace called the Starbirds.

"I need help," she said in a joint call. "After Lila died, Joe gave me
a letter she'd written to me, telling me to find out what happened to
Zelda. What do I do?"

"This is straight up, or down, our alley," Stella said. "Bread-and-
butter work for divorce lawyers."

"Though we're more likely to look for missing fathers," Ava said.
"Not being sexist, only factual."

"Part one, the paper trail. Start with a death certificate," Stella
said. "That will settle the matter quickly, so long as she died in Mich-

igan. The other place to begin is at the Eloise. Find out if she was hospitalized and/or died there."

"Next up, a police record of a missing person," Ava said. "Aldo may have filed one, though who knows when. He may also have filed a death certificate after seven years."

"You'll want her birth certificate and marriage license," Stella said. "You'll need her maiden name."

"Look for marriage licenses, plural," Ava said. "If she flew the coop, she's likely to have married again. No other means of support."

"Then, look for divorce decrees, from Aldo and any other husband she may have acquired," Stella said. "Of course, she might have remarried without a divorce, not wanting to ignite Aldo."

"You should also get a copy of your birth certificate, to show the connections between the generations, to establish your bona fides, if anyone questions you," Ava said.

"You should be able to get these records, the copies," Stella said. "They're public, but you never know. You're dealing with gatekeepers whose only discretionary power is the power to say no. I'd say, straight off, I was looking for my grandmother who disappeared under mysterious circumstances. It's an appealing story for people whose jobs are beyond boring."

"You might check out the archives on Ancestry.com," Ava said. "They are the best, the most thorough, the most extensive, though maybe not for people who are trying to stay hidden."

"Part two, Aldo," Stella said. "You need to talk to him, if he'll talk to you. If he's still alive."

"Why are you doing this," Ava said, "besides Lila's letter?"

"I want Aldo to know we know his wife left him," Grace said. "When we find her."

"Only if she's dead. He could track her down," Stella said. "Take someone with you when you see him. You don't want him charging you with harassment."

"Take Clara, if she's on board." Ava said. "Is she? She'd be useful in every way."

"Part three," Stella said, "A DNA search. If Zelda had other children, one of them or their progeny may have done it."

"You should ask if Clara would be willing to do it," Ava said. "Genotyping grandparents and grandchildren is more complicated than parent and child."

"This sounds like a full-time job," Grace said, "and I have a full-time job."

"Hire someone to find the records," Stella said.

"But only you can do Aldo," Ava said.

"Time to go," Stella said. "Pregnancy is hard on the bladder. Also on the feet and ankles."

"When are you due?" Grace said.

"Six weeks for me," Ava said, "seven for Stella."

"We didn't get pregnant together on purpose," Stella said. "Everyone seems to think that."

"Both boys," Ava said.

"What are an aunt's duties?" Grace said. "I'm no Clara."

"Buy them soccer balls," Stella said.

"When they're eleven, watch *Ted Lasso* with them," Ava said.

"Thank you for your help," Grace said.

"We're off," Stella said.

"Good luck," Ava said.

They hung up.

"She said 'thank you,'" Stella said.

"Should we help her?" Ava said.

"If she asks," Stella said. "Only if she asks."

GRACE CALLED JOE.

"I just got off the phone with the Starbirds," she said. "I asked them to tell me what I needed to do to find Zelda. They gave me so much homework, birth certificates, death certificates, marriage licenses, divorce decrees. I don't even know Zelda's maiden name."

"Did you ask them to help?" Joe said.

"I was hoping they'd volunteer," Grace said.

"You're almost thirty, Grace," Joe said. "If you want something, ask for it. That's how it works."

"We're not close," Grace said. "I only see them on Thanksgiving."

"Look," Joe said. "They're also Zelda's grandchildren. They're interested. It's a good story, however it ended. Better than the one you wrote."

"Are you going there again?" Grace said. "I wish I hadn't done it."

"The real story would make a good article, if you want to go down that dark alley again," Joe said. "You start with your book's version, then the search, then . . . your findings. I prefer *The Search for Zelda* to *The Quest for Zelda* as a title."

"I suppose I'd have to make a mea culpa," Grace said.

"No doubt," Joe said.

"No thanks," she said. "I'll bail."

"Good call," he said.

"Do you have copies of my birth certificate and Lila's?" Grace said. "The Starbirds said I should get them."

"I doubt it. Maybe yours. God knows where," Joe said. "Listen, I'm glad you called. I was going to call you. Frances is failing. Her heart. She hates the way she feels. Tired, breathless, swollen feet. She can't wear her Ferragamos anymore. She's wearing Crocs. I'm going out to see her this weekend."

"Should I go with you?" Grace said.

"No," Joe said. "We should stagger the visits, drag them out, give her something to look forward to. I'll go, then you, then Ruth. Clara calls and visits regularly. The Starbirds will zoom. I'll set it up."

"Lila's death did it," Grace said. "Frances hates that she outlived her."

"She's outlived most of her friends," Joe said. "She's sick and she's lonely. I tried to get her to move to D.C. She wouldn't have it."

THE NEXT DAY, GRACE CALLED her grandmother.

"Joe says you're not taking care of yourself," Grace said. "That's not acceptable."

"Acceptable to whom," Frances said. "On the subject of me, I decide what's acceptable."

"Unless you want an abortion, or meth, or a death with dignity," Grace said.

"Oh, the government," Frances said. "I don't worry about them. The only government agency interested in me is the IRS."

"Speaking of which," Grace said, "wasn't it great, G-men raiding Webb's wine cellar. Someone got it on video. I saw it this morning, on *Morning Joe*. Boxes on boxes being carried out. Do you think Big Chuck whupped him for taking all those gifts home? There was a gold Rolex worth a quarter of a million dollars. Saudis, of course. Poor Big Chuck, he thought he'd swan through the rest of his life, picking up the perks of being the ex-president's father." She laughed. "Maybe he will. Even five years after he was booted out, Spiderman is still gold in Texas."

"I wish Lila had lived to see it," Frances said. "She'd have loved it."

"Do you think she was happy?" Grace said. "Did she have a happy life, once she left Detroit?"

"I don't think being happy was something she thought about, or even cared about," Frances said. "She wanted life to be interesting, challenging. She loved her work. I miss her dreadfully. If I were a Christian, I'd have the consolation of seeing her again in heaven. Perhaps you could find a willing Mormon to baptize me posthumously," Frances said. "Like Anne Frank."

"Don't you want to live long enough to see Ruth married?" Grace said.

"I told her last Thanksgiving, I'd love to give her a wedding, but she has to stop dithering, I'm too old for dithering."

"You're not too old," Grace said. "You're just old."

"I've lived a long time," Frances said. "Too long. Every day is a slog. Breathing gets harder and harder. I won't even mention stairs. I'm ready to go." She paused. "I'd like to see you married."

"Have you stopped eating?" Grace said.

"You're a sharp one," Frances said. "Not yet." She paused. "If it comes to diapers . . ."

"First Lila, then you," Grace said. "That would be hard."

"Would you accept my death if I were ninety-five, ninety-eight, a hundred and one?" Frances said. "I'm old enough to die. Lila wasn't. I would have died for her."

"So instead, you're going to die in addition," Grace said. "Thanks loads."

Frances laughed. "I see your point."

"Did you hate *The Lost Mother*," Grace said.

"No," Frances said, "but I don't understand why you made up the grandmother's escape and the mother's affair. The story ran close to the truth and then it veered off. You wanted people to believe your version, and you made it easy for them. Everyone at the club believed it."

"I'm sticking to reporting other people's stories from now on," Grace said.

"Good," Frances said. "Joe said you're going to visit in two weeks. He's planned it all out, to keep me alive as long as he can."

"It's a conspiracy," Grace said. "We're all in."

"We'll see," Frances said. "I'm off now. Time for my late morning nap, which falls between my early morning nap and my early afternoon nap."

"You're the best," Grace said.

"No, you're the best," Frances said.

AT 9:00 P.M., 6:00 P.M. PST, Grace called the Starbirds at their office.

"After we spoke yesterday," Grace said, "I panicked. I am out of my depth. Would you be willing to help me find Zelda? I haven't a clue where to start looking for all those licenses and certificates."

"Yes," Stella said. "I've been thinking about Zelda since you called. If she escaped, I bet she's a bigamist."

"If she's dead, do you think she has a tombstone?" Grace said.

"Do you remember Lila telling us she walked the Jewish cemeteries for several weeks, after Aldo said she'd died, looking for the grave."

"She stole money for the bus fare from Aldo. I remember that," Ava said. "I also remember she took her switchblade along, 'just in case.' She was big on 'just in case.'"

"There was a lot of Aldo in her," Grace said. "I don't know anyone tougher."

"She was brave," Stella said. "Brave but not suicidally brave." They fell silent, remembering Polo.

"We'll do the document search," Ava said. "You talk to Aldo. You better get going. He's, what, ninety-five. And, Zelda, if she's alive, must be eighty-five."

"Finding her would be a coup," Stella said. "Also a coup d'état. You could blow up her second family."

"I hadn't thought of that," Grace said, mentally slapping her forehead. *The things I don't think of outnumber the things I do. I don't think therefore I am.*

"Let's think positively," Ava said. "Luck, we need luck."

"'Better to be lucky than smart,'" the three of them said together.

My sisters, Grace thought, sniffling. "You guys are bricks," she said. "I've asked Joe if he has Lila's birth certificate. It might have Zelda's maiden name."

"Good thinking," Stella said. "Well done."

"Keep us posted," Ava said. "And vice versa."

"If the babies come," Stella said, "we may get backed up."

"We've got two associates who could take over," Ava said. "They'd be thrilled."

"Do you have names for the boys?" Grace said.

"Felix," Stella said.

"Dominic," Ava said.

"Good names," Grace said. "I'm sorry I call you the Starbirds."

"The husbands call us the Starbirds," Stella said. "So do many of our friends."

"We think of ourselves as Romula and Rema," Ava said. "Raised by a shewolf."

"We're too much alike, we know that," Stella said, "but, at this point, it's beyond repair."

"Real twins would have struggled to distinguish themselves," Ava said. "We weren't, so we didn't bother."

"Remind me again why you're pursuing this," Stella said.

"Besides Lila's letter," Ava said.

"If Zelda's alive, I want her to know we know," Grace said.

THE NEXT TWO DAYS, GRACE worked. On the third day, she called Clara.

"I've come back," Grace said. "Would you help me in my quest? *Ask up-front,* she thought. *No pussyfooting.* "The Starbirds are searching for birth certificates, marriage licenses, divorce decrees, hospitalization records."

"Is it legal?" Clara said. "I'm not like my outlaw siblings. I'm not a swashbuckler." She laughed. "I hated my switchblade. Lila said I had to carry it. I wasn't safe without it. The gang would turn on me. I'd run home from school and stay inside. Better to die than to kill."

"Scylla and Charybdis," Grace said. "I'm on the kill team."

"Of course you are," Clara said. "So are the Starbirds. Joe is probably on my team, which isn't to say we would never kill. I'd kill to protect you."

"How did you turn out so human?" Grace said.

Clara was quiet for several seconds. Grace wanted to count but didn't. *Lila wouldn't like it,* she thought.

"Bubbe, I think," Clara said. "She looked out for me. She never kissed me or hugged me, but she petted me, patted my head. When I went shopping with her, she held my hand." She paused. "But there was no escaping Aldo's poison. I'm timid. I'm fearful. I'm needy, things Lila wasn't. I'm not independent or self-sufficient. Lila said I should be a doctor, not a nurse. She would pay, Joe would pay. I couldn't do it. I didn't want the responsibility. I didn't want the power or the attention." She paused again. "Five years of therapy went into that explanation. Not something Lila or Polo would have done." She laughed. "What is it she always said. The unexamined life is the only one worth living."

"I'm sort of like that, not by principle but by mental defect. I don't think ahead." Grace fell silent. *This is another grown-up conversation with a relative,* she thought. *How did that happen?*

"What would you like me to do?" Clara said.

Grace jumped to. "Would you help me with Aldo? I want to interview him. Would you ask him if he'll see me, and then, if he agrees, would you come along?"

"I can do that," Clara said.

"I thought of asking the publisher to send him a copy of my book, but decided against it," Grace said. "I'll send him a copy afterward. He's not going to like my version of Zelda's departure."

"No," Clara said. "He still talks about Zelda's hospitalization and death. Maybe that should have been a clue. Protesting too much."

"One other favor," Grace said, "down the line. If we don't get results from the document search, would you be willing to take a Genealogies test? It's easier with mother and child."

Clara didn't answer.

"I know it's a big favor, intrusive and consequential," Grace said. "I can do it if you don't want to."

"Let me think about it," Clara said. "I thought this might be in the offing. Suppose we find her and she won't see us. Suppose she sees us but denies everything."

"I understand," Grace said. "It's okay if you don't do it. There are always work-arounds."

"I'll phone Aldo next week, in the morning, before he starts drinking," Clara said. "It's amazing he's still alive. Drinking, smoking, living in a house riddled with asbestos. I'm sure that's what got Lila.

Bubbe would fake-spit, pppt, after she said his name. 'Like his father,' she'd say. 'Cockroaches.'"

"I'd like to have talked to Bubbe," Grace said. "Don't you have stuff belonging to her? Do you think there might be any papers that would be useful, letters, photos?"

"Oh, God, I forgot, probably on purpose," Clara said. "When she was dying, she gave me a large cardboard box, sealed with duct tape. She said I might want to look through it. I never opened it. Pandora's Box. I have her will. She made sure I got it, and not Aldo. He was enraged she left us money and not him." She paused. "I'll send you the box."

"Thanks," Grace said. "What was Bubbe's name?"

"Marta but she used Martha," Clara said. "If I had had a daughter, I'd have named her Marta."

GRACE WORKED ANOTHER TWO DAYS and then called Ruth.

"I'm calling about Frances," Grace said.

"Joe called," Ruth said. "I'm going out after you." She paused. "I could stay on. I work remote most of the time." She paused. "It's a privilege, an honor, to sit with the dying."

"She'd rather see you married," Grace said.

Ruth was quiet for several seconds. "I don't know why I keep putting it off," she said.

"Cold feet," Grace said.

"No," Ruth said. "I feel I have to be launched before I get married. I can't be dependent. Gran and Mom would like to see me married too."

"Is it money or work?" Grace said.

"Work," Ruth said. "I want a podcast of my own."

"How does Nico feel about this?" Grace said.

"He understood when he was doing the bioengineering Ph.D.," Ruth said, "but now he says it's time. He's making a good salary. He'll probably get tenure. He says I'm overthinking. Again. He says I could take a leave from *The Press Gang* and go all out with *Elephant Memories.*" She paused. "I've learned a ton as a producer on *The Press Gang* and they've offered to stream some of the podcasts, a tryout. I've got thirty episodes in the can—not all with friends and relations— but I keep thinking I need more, and I can't get them done, not with the job." She paused again. "I've boxed myself in nicely."

"What does Doug say?" Grace said.

"He has this quote from Randall Jarrell, which he's lately been hammering me with," Ruth said. "'And yet, the ways we miss our lives are life./Yet . . . Yet . . ./to have one's life add up to *yet!*'"

"Killer," Grace said.

"Do you think I'm missing my life?" Ruth said.

"Not yet. It's more like pathological postponement. Joe tells this story. When I was little, I didn't like help, especially when I needed it most, like putting on my shoes or eating with a fork. 'Self,' I'd say, swatting his hand away. You seem to be in an acute 'self' stage."

"I keep thinking, if I depend on Nico and something happens to him, to us, I'm stranded."

"Listen," Grace said. "Your mom didn't do it by herself. She depended on Gran. And Gran depended on her." She paused. "We had Frances. We still have her. We've engaged in a conspiracy, all of us, to keep her alive."

"I love Frances," Ruth said. "She's been wonderful to me. I didn't tell you. She bought me a Bottega Veneta wallet for my thirtieth birthday. She cut me off before I could protest. She said she was allowed to give me a present for my birthday, 'just not for nothing.'"

"Joe and Lila supported me for three years when I was earning peanuts at *The Town Crier* and, at first, at *The New Yorkist.* I didn't like it, but I didn't want to live with a roommate who wasn't you."

"What about Xander as a roommate?" Ruth said. "He loves you. He's told us multiple times."

"I don't know," Grace said. "He's calmed down a lot. He has a job. He makes me laugh."

"Frances's rule," Ruth said. "'Marry a man who makes you laugh, they all make you cry.'"

"I don't think Joe ever made Lila cry," Grace said. "No one ever made her cry except Eminem."

"Xander wouldn't make you cry," Ruth said. "You're likelier to make him cry."

"Joe is my idea of what a husband should be, and a mother for that matter," Grace said. "Can you imagine Xander as a father? He would love the kids, I don't doubt that, but he'd get caught up in a project, wander off, and forget to meet the school bus."

"He could forget to pay the electric bill or pick up the dry cleaning. He wouldn't forget his children," Ruth said. "Anyway, that's beside the point. I didn't think you wanted children."

"I'd still want a husband who would make a good father," Grace said. "Okay, enough prancing. Why won't you marry the man you love?"

"What if I fail with *Elephant Memories*?" Ruth said.

"So what," Grace said. "'Ever failed. No matter. Try again. Fail better.'"

"What question would you recommend for my inaugural podcast?" Ruth said.

"The one where you asked for a story about a grandparent," Grace said.

"Ah," Ruth said. "Zelda, the family ghost."

AT DINNER THAT EVENING, RUTH told Nico she was finally ready to get married. He leaped from his chair and kissed her.

"After five years, she suddenly makes her move," he said, sitting down. "I'd have waited forever."

"You've been great, never pushing it," she said, "I was spinning my wheels, finding reasons that made sense but weren't true: we'd known each other a short time when we got engaged; most people our age marry in their thirties." She leaned over to kiss him. "I felt so insecure about the podcasts. I couldn't enter a marriage without being self-sufficient. Suppose you died."

"Whoa," Nico said. "You've made yourself a widow before becoming a wife."

"It's the belt-suspenders syndrome," she said, "especially when it comes to money. I don't ever want to be poor again. It's humiliating."

He took her hand. "What made you decide?" he said. "You haven't launched *Elephant Memories.*"

"Grace read me the riot act. She said a five-year engagement was excessive, if you weren't a movie star. She said it was time to launch *Elephant Memories.* And then, Frances is dying." She stopped, her eyes tearing. "We could have a small wedding, the usual suspects, at Tara. Frances told me she wanted to throw it but she can't unless I stop dithering." She looked at Nico expectantly. "Sometime later, we could have a party in Tallahassee or New York."

"I'm in," Nico said. "Frances can throw it. I'll marry you anywhere. When?"

"As soon as we can arrange it," Ruth said. "Frances will be in her element." She started tearing again. "No Lila."

Nico reached across the table and took her hand. "Let's move on it," he said. "Wherever we marry, we want Frances there."

Ruth called her mom, her gran, the Maiers, and Doug. Nico called his parents, Zayde, and Xander.

Ruth's mom and gran laughed and cried. "This is the best news," Gran said. "A blessed event," her mom said. "Will you convert?"

"No," Ruth said. *They're happy for me,* she thought, her eyes watering.

"It's okay if you do," Gran said. "Judeo-Christian, after all."

"One catch, or not," Ruth said. "Frances wants to throw the wedding. She says she's not doing me any favors, she's only doing it for herself. She can't travel so if we had it in Tallahassee or New York, she couldn't come. Of course if she throws the wedding, she will insist on paying for everything, transportation included, for inconveniencing everyone." Ruth paused. "She's dying. She says it's a dying wish. She says she can never repay you both for bringing me into the world and into her life." She paused. "She wants you to fly up to Chicago a week before the wedding and go wedding dress shopping. She's buying and she has a tailor who can do all adjustments in two days. She's a steamroller. She'll put everyone up at Tara." Ruth paused again. "I know it's a lot to ask of you."

"Do rich people do this?" Gran said. "You're not kin."

"I love her and she loves me," Ruth said. "You've always told me to fill my life with people who love me."

"Who's going to marry you?" Her mom's voice was shaky, tentative.

"Doug Marshall, my boss at *The Press Gang,* my mentor, has offered. He's been so good to me. Without him, I wouldn't have podcast prospects. I wouldn't have been employed these last four years." She wanted to say he'd been like a father to her. "He's a Protestant. He'll use the King James Bible. I thought you'd like that. He's got an internet license and great presence. He was Lila's best friend. Would you each read a Bible verse, your choice?"

"I'll read the Wedding at Cana," Ruth's mom said, her voice excited, then tentative. "Is it too Christian?"

"It's perfect," Ruth said.

"I'll read from the Old Testament," Gran said. "The Jewish Bible."

Ruth hung up and cried. An hour later, she called Grace.

"Mom picked the Wedding at Cana, Jesus turning water into wine at a Jewish wedding. Sounds good, right? Then there's the last line, 'The first of his signs, Jesus did at Cana in Galilee and manifested his glory, and his disciples believed in him.' Every Christian gets married with this verse."

"We all know you're a Christian," Grace said. "None of the Jews will object. The Starbirds married Christians and their mothers-in-law picked that verse. No malice meant. Affirmation of who they are, not who we're not."

· · ·

NICO CALLED HIS PARENTS AND brother.

"Finally," Richard said. "Best news."

"Nothing could make me happier," Kathy said.

After hanging up, Richard said, "Frances made this happen. It's like a Jewish grandmother joke. 'I'm dying, grant me this one last wish.'"

"It was Lila's dying," Kathy said. "It's killing everyone she won't be there."

Xander whooped at the news. "Ruth is great. You're great. You two will be transcendently happy."

"Your turn now," Nico said.

"I always thought I'd be married by the time I was thirty," Xander said. "Now, I wonder if I'll be married before I turn forty."

"Have you asked her?" Nico said.

"With Grace, you wait for the signal," Xander said. "I can't propose. She's not that sort of girl. I'd have to say something like 'Maybe we'll get married someday.' Or 'Do you think we should get married?'"

"Have you ever said you loved her?" Nico said.

"To her face, you're kidding," Xander said. "She'd laugh me out of the room, not to say her life. I've said it, on the phone, albeit without using the word 'love,' and I tell everyone else, so the message gets through. I tell Ruth almost daily."

"You need to tell Grace," Nico said. "She won't laugh. She may shudder. I think she wants to be loved."

"By me?" Xander said.

"Yes," Nico said.

"I don't think she'll say she loves me," Xander said. "I don't think she's said it to anyone. Maybe Joe and Frances. Has she said it to Ruth? We know she loves Ruth."

"Ruth is easy to love," Nico said.

"Grace says she'd make a terrible mother," Xander said. "At worst, she'd be like Lila."

"And better than Zelda," Nico said.

"So, which school are you?" Xander said. "She died or she ran away."

"She ran away," Nico said.

"Me too," Xander said.

THE STARBIRDS GAVE BIRTH IN mid-June two days apart, Ava first, then Stella. Like their mother, they were back at work in two weeks. They had married men willing to raise the children with the help of many nannies. Joe flew to California to meet his grandsons, Felix Joseph and Dominic Joseph.

He called Grace to give a report. "They're perfect babies. I'm tempted to say they're Pereiras except the husbands look so much like the Starbirds, it's not an easy call."

22

Beginnings

RUTH WAS MARRIED AT TARA, ON LABOR DAY WEEKEND, FIVE MONTHS after Lila's death. Frances arranged everything. Everyone else, even the bride and groom, especially the bride and groom, floated in her wake. The Starbirds, who had had their weddings arranged by Frances, warned the couple against resisting.

"She'll say, 'Yes, of course, sweetheart,' then do exactly what she wants," Stella said.

"If surrender is inevitable, surrender at once," Ava said. "Lila's advice."

"She'll take care of everything," Stella said, "and, believe it or not, you'll have a wonderful time."

"Wonderful times are her specialties," Ava said.

The wedding preparations took two months. Frances bloomed.

"You won't believe this," she said to Joe, two days before the wedding. "For the first time in eight months, I squeezed my feet into my Ferragamos. Do you think I was somaticizing with my pregnant granddaughters?"

The guest list was short: three McGowans; five Goldsmiths;

eight Pereira-Maiers—the Starbirds' babies stayed home with nannies; one Doug Marshall; and Frances's six-pack, "the Remnants" as she called them, the last of the Bloomfield Hills Club Women, straight-backed nonagenarians like her, with strong opinions and large houses. "They'll be so pleased to be invited to a wedding," she said to Ruth. "They haven't been to one in a decade. They haven't been anywhere except the club in a decade. None of them are Republicans."

Ruth didn't invite Artie Brinkman. She called him. "Lucky fellow," he said. He and his wife had separated. "No children, that's the good news. You were right not to marry me. Lousy husband but a pretty good doctor."

ON THE MORNING OF HER wedding, Ruth got up very early. Frances would be at breakfast and Ruth wanted to waylay her before anyone else showed up. *Unfinished business.*

A hotel breakfast was laid out on the sideboard. Frances was alone, sitting at the head of the table, drinking coffee and reading the paper.

"You're up early," Frances said.

"We need to talk." Ruth poured herself a cup of coffee.

"Don't thank me," Frances said. "I hate being thanked."

"I'm not going to thank you," Ruth said, sitting down next to Frances. "I want to know about George, the boy you didn't marry. We need to close the circle."

Frances picked up her coffee cup and took a sip. "Hot," she said.

"You said it was a story for another day," Ruth said. "Today seemed the right day. Here I am, a lapsed Baptist, marrying a Jew."

Frances took Ruth's hand in hers. "You're a miracle."

Ruth smiled. "Are you trying to distract me?"

Frances smiled. "I know better than that. You're the elephant in *Elephant Memories.*"

"You don't have to answer, Lila's rule," Ruth said. "Just say, no thank you."

"I was widowed when I was thirty-four," Frances said. "I thought I'd remarry. I had offers, but I didn't want to settle again." She took another sip of coffee. "I was fond of Marty, very fond, but I didn't need to be married, like some women. I was fine by myself." She put down her cup. "Today, you can find someone on the internet in ten minutes, but back then, in the sixties, seventies, and eighties, you had to hire investigators. I couldn't do that. Too demeaning. And what would I do if they found him? He was probably married, a father. Maybe he drank. Maybe he played around. Maybe I was lucky not marrying him." She looked at Ruth. "You're not eating."

"I'll wait. I want to listen." Ruth smiled. "Like Lila, I can't multi-task."

Frances set down her cup. "In 2000, on my seventieth birthday, George called. He was not halting or tentative, but he wasn't confident either. 'I remember you,' he said. We talked for two hours. His wife had dementia. She was being cared for at home. It had been going on for seven or eight years. When his wife didn't recognize him, he decided he would call me. He'd been wanting to. He was fond of his wife. She had been a good partner, a good friend. They had had four children, two girls, two boys. All settled. Nice people married to nice people. He told me he wasn't calling me because he was lonely, though he was. He called because he wanted to know if I remembered him." Frances cleared her throat. "My heart leapt. At seventy, I didn't think it possible. He was living in Connecticut. We started seeing each other. He bought a cottage on Lake Michigan, he called it his escape house. It was very small, two bedrooms. His children understood how hard it had been for him. They never visited. He'd go there regularly. I would join him. We did this for four years. He died during open-heart surgery. His wife outlived him by a year. One of his daughters called me the day he died. She thanked me for being his friend and companion. He had told her about me the day before he went into the hospital. We've met a few times. She was his favorite. Her husband is Jewish. Her mother had been unhappy about that. George had been supportive."

Frances took her hankie out of her pocket and blew her nose. "If I had married him, there would be no Joe, no Lila, no Starbirds, no Grace, no you. It was too late to reimagine my life with him, but they were some of my happiest years." She squeezed Ruth's hand. "Late-life happiness is a gift." She stood up. "Now, go get your breakfast."

Ruth stood up. "What happened to the escape house?" she said.

"When he bought it, he put it in both our names, a joint tenancy. It didn't pass under the will. How did you know to ask?"

"Who else could he possibly have left it to?"

RUTH WORE A VERA WANG dress, a silky, palest pink gown, ballerina length. She didn't wear a veil. She didn't carry a bouquet. Her mom and gran, also in Vera Wang, walked her down the aisle. Kathy and Richard walked Nico. Grace and Xander were best persons. Ann, as planned, read from the New Testament, the Wedding at Cana. She spoke in a low, clear voice. Her heart had opened to her Jewish in-laws. "Your church buries the truth," Ruth had said to her. "Jesus was a Jew. He worshipped their God." Ann heard her.

Gran read from the Old Testament. "I'll be reading from the Hebrew Scriptures, specifically the Ketuvim," she said.

"What's the Ketuvim?" Richard said in a loud whisper. Kathy shhhed him.

Gran cleared her throat. She was excited and nervous. She'd never spoken in public before. "I'm going to read from the Book of Ruth," she said. "I am also named Ruth." She took in a large breath and let it out slowly. "The story of Ruth is as familiar to Christians as it is to Jews. The line runs from Ruth to David to Jesus." She looked up at the guests and nodded. "Ruth and her mother-in-law, Naomi, have been widowed. Naomi is a Jew, Ruth is a Moabite. After living for years in the land of Moab, Naomi decides to return to Bethlehem, where she was born. Against Naomi's entreaties, Ruth insists on going with her." She cleared her throat again. "*And Ruth said, Intreat me not to leave thee, or to return from following after thee: for whither thou goest, I will go; and where thou lodgest, I will lodge: thy people shall be my people, and*"—her voice broke—"*thy God my God.*"

The room wept, even Frances, who had known what Gran would read. Gran had rehearsed with her.

Doug performed the ceremony. The vows were simple. He had lifted them from *The Book of Common Prayer.* He loved the seventeenth-century service, with its gorgeous language, especially its final pledge, now fallen out of fashion and rarely included. As Nico and Ruth exchanged rings, they recited together: "With this ring I thee wed, with my body I thee worship, and with all my worldly goods I thee endow."

Grace and Xander exchanged glances, wide eyed, electrified.

Frances's posse were surprised to see Doug take a central role. They'd all read Grace's book and knew about The Affair. At the champagne reception, they whispered among themselves.

"It was very understanding of Joe and Frances to have Doug play such a big role."

"Perhaps too understanding."

"Frances says there was no affair."

"She says Grace made it up."

"That wasn't nice."

"No, but it's a better story."

Ruth had asked Joe if it was all right. "He's been so good to me," she said.

"Of course," Joes said. "He's perfect for the job." Since Lila's death, he and Doug, always cordial, had become friends, linked in their consuming grief. They started taking walks together on weekend mornings. Doug's idea. In the beginning, they talked mostly about Lila.

"I couldn't stay mad at her," Joe said. "She'd make me laugh."

"I couldn't stay mad at her," Doug said. "She didn't care. 'Roll with the punches,'" she'd say.

"Punch-rolling, a specialty of hers," Joe said. "She never thought of herself as a victim or a survivor."

"I don't think she thought about herself at all," Doug said. "I remember once talking to her about psychotherapy. Some article extolling its virtues. She wanted to scrap it. She understood if someone was mentally ill, bipolar, schizophrenic, psychopathic, 'brain sick,' she called it, but otherwise she believed in repression. You might say she was a Freudian essentialist."

"She refused to acknowledge anything like an inner life," Joe said. "Forward and outward. Grace is like that too, except when it comes to Lila."

At the rehearsal dinner, Lila was in everyone's thoughts but not their toasts.

"There's an embargo on Lila toasts," Grace said, performing her emceeing duties. "Only Joe is allowed one."

Joe's toast to Lila was short. "What wouldn't I give to have her here."

Frances had hired a string quartet to play at the ceremony, and a small band to play at the party. "Two groups?" Ruth had said. "'Such much.'"

Frances waved her hand. "Music makes a party," she said, "the same way music makes a movie. You'll see."

The band started off playing standard tunes, tunes to dance to. Everyone obliged. The Starbirds and their husbands danced with Frances's friends. Ruth danced with Zayde, Richard, Joe, and Doug. Nico danced with Ann, Gran, Kathy, and Frances. There were no wallflowers.

The Remnants were giddy. "What's next," one of them said to Frances. "The hora? I danced with Stella's husband. What a good-looking boy with muscles."

Frances smiled at her, then nodded to the bandleader.

The music tempo speeded up, then swerved into the overture of

A *Chorus Line*. Everyone stopped dancing. Some tapped a foot, some clapped in time. From a side door, Stella, Grace, Ruth, and Ava sidled across the floor in sparkly tap shoes and high hats.

"Ready, girls," Frances said. They nodded. Frances turned to the room. "Everyone, please take your seats."

The band struck a note, then burst into "One." Tipping their hats, their smiles broad, the four young women, Rockette style, broke into song and dance. The choreography was jaunty, stamping and stomping, high kicking and hat tipping, mostly in unison. They'd rehearsed under everyone's nose. Three of the four sang in tune.

The performance had a boffo ending, the Starbirds, on the ends, doing splits. The guests leaped to their feet, even the Remnants, cheering, clapping, whistling, applauding. The wait-staff went around pouring more wine. The band started playing swing and sixties favorites. Everyone hit the dance floor. Ruth and Nico hadn't done the first dance, they waited and did the last, a tango, so deeply romantic, seductive, and elegant, everyone sat hushed and enchanted. At midnight, the band played taps.

Frances's posse went home, tired and merry. The rest of the party went into the living room. Frances had drinks and snacks laid out and a fire burning. Slowly, over the next two hours, the "grown-ups," except for Gran, wandered off to their rooms. She stayed to the end, listening to the eight young people talk.

At dawn, the "youngsters" went outside onto the verandah to watch the sunrise. They stood together, arms around each other, swaying, laughing, crooning "Auld Lang Syne." Gran gently squeezed Ruth's hand. "I can't imagine a happier day ever," she said.

THE WEDDING HAD RECUPERATIVE POWERS. Frances lost the will to die. She knew better than to ask Grace if she and Xander were ever going to get married, but she asked Joe.

"Ruth's wedding was a tonic," she said to her son. "I think if I had another one to plan, and a year to do it, I could live to a hundred."

"I have another idea," Joe said. "Why don't you help Grace with her search for Zelda?"

"What could I do?" Frances said.

"Ask your GM acquaintance what else he knew," Joe said. "The one who said Aldo was alive."

"He didn't exactly say Aldo was alive," Frances said. "He said he wanted to meet him. It was at your wedding. He thought it hilarious that Aldo was a lineman. I just waved my hand, as if indicating he was somewhere around. I shouldn't have invited him. Not a nice man. There were about a hundred people I shouldn't have invited."

"Do you think he knows more?" Joe said.

"He was head of HR," Frances said.

"You didn't say anything to me for forty-three years?" Joe said.

"It wasn't my business," she said. "People have their reasons."

"Did he say anything about Zelda?" Joe said.

"He asked if Lila's mother had come too," she said.

Joe started. "Why would he think Zelda was alive?" he said. "What did you say to him?"

"I just waved my hand again and shooed him away. I told him I had four hundred guests to look after." She was quiet for several seconds. "He probably looked at Aldo's federal withholding form, to see if he had a spousal dependent."

"Bingo," Joe said.

"Only a guess," Frances said.

"You should have been a lawyer," Joe said.

"No. I don't like conflict, and that's the lawyer's lot." She gazed at her son as if sizing him up. "Whatever I should have done, I should have been the boss."

THE TALLAHASSEE TIMES PUBLISHED a write-up of Ruth and Nico's wedding, with a photograph of the two of them standing on the front porch of Tara. It appeared on the front page of the local section and ran seven hundred words. Ruth's mom and gran had notified the society editor, who went to town. "It's sort of like Kate Middleton marrying Prince William," she told the editor in chief, who at first balked at the length. "People will love it and hate it." The prose was pale purple.

> Last Sunday, in Michigan, as the sun was setting, Ruth McGowan and Nicholas Goldsmith, Tallahassee natives, were married at Stony Field, the Bloomfield Hills estate of Frances Maier, the daughter of the late Henry Fieldstone, the first Comptroller of General Motors. Douglas Marshall, the Publisher of *The Washington Globe,* officiated. The bride is the daughter of Ann McGowan, a nurse-practitioner with the Apalachee Medical Group, and the granddaughter of Ruth McGowan. The groom is the son of Kathy Goldsmith, a beloved English teacher at Chiles High, and Richard Goldsmith, who needs no introduction.

THE PHOTO CAUGHT JACQUI BATES's eye. She instantly recognized Ruth from her graduation and engagement photos previously published in *The Tallahassee Times.* She felt affronted, ill-used. The Local section was her section. She never read national news. She was only interested in stories about Tallahassee people, her people. *Why is this girl always getting written up,* she thought, *like some low-rent Scarlett O'Hara?* She had pushed Ruth out of her mind.

She called Jeff Bates. "Did you see your niece's picture on the front page of the Local?" she said.

"Yes," he said. "Did you read it?"

"No," she said. "I'm not interested."

"Well," he said, "you should. We knew she was marrying a Jew, but her husband is not just any Jew. I didn't pay much attention to the engagement story. It turns out her father-in-law, Richard Goldsmith, is the biggest, most important lawyer in town, in the state maybe. He's a trustee of UF. He's on the State Board of Ed. He's on the Symphony Board. He's everywhere but my living room." He waited for Jacqui to laugh. She didn't. "But that's not all. The editor of *The Washington Post,* the Watergate newspaper, performed the ceremony, and she got married at the mansion belonging to the chairman of General Motors. GM, you ever hear of that? Twenty bedrooms. They didn't rent it. The owner was the host, a close friend. This girl has major league connections. I think it said she wore a Dior dress. What's your daughter going to wear?"

Jacqui didn't say anything.

"Did Bobby Lee see it?" he said.

"I don't think so," she said. "He doesn't want anything to do with her. Sleeping dogs and all that."

"I wonder what will happen when your kids decide to do one of those DNA tests?" he said.

"We'll act surprised," she said.

"What if they contact her?" he said. "She knows, you know."

"She won't want to have anything to do with them, with us," she said. 'She probably thinks she's better than we are."

"No foolin'," he said.

GRACE HAD A WONDERFUL TIME at the wedding, "I think it may have been the best time of my life," she said to Ruth, "though the threshold in that category is low." They were back in New York, having dinner at Lupa.

"What made it best?" Ruth said, ignoring the down in the mouth qualification.

"Just about everything, everyone," Grace said. "The ceremony, the chorus line, the tango, the sleepover party with Gran, Frances's posse, the vows—'With my body, I thee worship.' Holy cow. Those Jacobeans."

Ruth smiled. "Anything, anyone else?"

Grace picked up her fork and picked at her salad. "Xander," she said. "He sort of proposed, a backdoor proposal. He said I was the one for him. He said he knew it the day we met. He said . . ." Grace cleared her throat. "He said I was the smartest and most interesting person he'd ever met. Not woman, person." She cleared her voice again. "He said he loved me."

"What did you say?" Ruth said.

"I was too dumbfounded to speak," Grace said, her eyes wide, "so I kissed him. The best I could muster."

"Later did you get around to saying 'I love you, too,'" Ruth said.

Grace shook her head.

"You need practice," Ruth said. "You can start with me. I know you love me but you've never told me. I've told you."

Grace poked her salad again.

"I've had a lot of practice," Ruth said. "Mom and Gran regularly say they love me, especially Gran, and I say I love them." She smiled. 'I love you' practically rolls off my lips. I told Nico I loved him, I told Artie Brinkman. I told Kathy and Richard. I told Xander. I told Joe. I told Frances. I told Doug."

"Did you ever tell Lila?" Grace said.

"When she was dying," Ruth said. "She squeezed my hand."

"I said it too," Grace said. "I don't know if she heard."

"Are you going to tell me you love me?" Ruth said.

"You're putting me on the spot," Grace said.

"Yes, I am," Ruth said. "Don't say it if you don't mean it."

Grace took in a big breath. "I love you," she said.

"I love you," Ruth said. "Now you can say it to Xander."

"It's hopeless," Grace said. "He needs to work in Los Angeles. I can't work there. I hate having to drive everywhere and *The L.A. Sun* has lost its way. It changes editors more often than I change my underwear."

"You can still call him up and tell him you love him," Ruth said.

"I sometimes think the four of us are a debased modern version of *Pride and Prejudice,* the one with a disappointing, twenty-first-century ending," Grace said. "You and Nico are Jane and Bingley, and Xander and I are Darcy and Lizzy, except I'm Darcy."

"Maybe he won't answer, maybe you can leave a message," Ruth said.

"It's not as if I'm the only one foot-dragging," Grace said. "You were engaged to Nico for years before you got married, and now you keep putting off the launch of *Elephant Memories.*"

"I'm not one to talk, is that what you're saying." Ruth narrowed her eyes. "Okay. Don't call Xander. Don't see what newspaper jobs there are in L.A. Don't have another 'best time of your life.'"

"I heard you," Grace. "You didn't stop."

"Tell me to stop," Ruth said. "Don't hound-dog me."

Two days later, Grace called Xander. She got his voicemail. *Xander Goldsmith here, I'm on a shoot. Leave your name and number. Say them slowly, clearly. I'm tired when I pick up my messages.*

There is a god, Grace thought. She left a message. "Hi, Xander, Grace here. I called to say . . . to say . . . I love you too."

Xander called the next morning at seven EST, four PST. "I got home at eleven, California time," he said. "I waited by the phone until sunrise in New York."

"It would have been okay if you called then," Grace said, surprising herself as much as Xander.

"You made me very happy." He paused. "Does this mean you'll marry me?"

"We can say we're thinking about marriage," she said.

"Can I buy you a ring?" he said. "Beautiful but versatile, not a dedicated diamond engagement ring. You can wear it on any finger."

"What could I buy you?" she said.

"A watch," he said.

"We can go shopping together," she said. *Did I really say that,* she thought.

"I can get away to the city in a few weeks," he said. "Does that work for you?"

"Maybe I should go to L.A.," she said. "I hardly know it and what I know I hate."

"The Grace I know," Xander said, laughing. "I was worried for a moment you'd been Stepfordized."

"I get crankier as the day goes on," she said.

"I noticed," he said. "I get more anxious."

"I noticed," she said.

"I love you," he said.

"I love you," she said.

They fell silent for several seconds.

"Okay," Grace said, embarrassed and happy. "I have an early appointment. I have to get dressed and eat breakfast. I can't keep talking."

"Excellent phone etiquette," he said. "You didn't say, 'I'll let you go,' as if I was the one who wanted to hang up. I never answer the phone. All calls go into messages. I call back. I learned early I do better when I initiate the call. I'll answer your calls."

A WEEK LATER, GRACE FLEW to L.A. for a week. Xander had a house in Venice. It was small, by L.A. standards, 1700 square feet, but voluminous by New York's. Grace's jaw dropped. It had a modern but small kitchen, a rectangular living room/dining room, two bedrooms, an office, two bathrooms and a powder room, a washer and dryer, four large closets, a pantry, a small deck, and a front lawn. Its lines were clean, spare, but not austere. An architect had been consulted. The furniture was Scandinavian and Italian high design. Xander had a cleaning service come weekly.

"I wasn't expecting this," Grace said. "My place is a pit."

"ADHD," Xander said. "I need order. Clear spaces."

Xander had made a list of touristy things to do. They went to MOCA, Disney Hall, and Santa Monica. They ate at four first-rate restaurants and one weird one, a vegan egg restaurant. "L.A. is weird," he said. "It must be faced."

Grace ordered a tomato omelet and coffee. "What am I eating?" she said to Xander as she surveyed the plate. "What do they make this out of?"

"Tofu," Xander said, "or tofu substitute."

They went ring shopping and watch shopping. Xander had done some reconnaissance at Sotheby's and found an emerald-cut emerald ring, six carats, in a platinum setting, with flanking diamond baguettes. He thought it looked sporty and classy. Grace started when she saw it. She never imagined having a ring like that. "It goes with anything, everything," he said. It was a size seven, a tad loose on her finger, but she liked the way it looked, the way it slipped around.

"Would you like it made smaller?" the saleswoman said. "Either way, it works."

"As is," Grace said. She looked at her hand. "I've become a Californian," she said. "The Starbirds will have a field day."

"Yes," Xander said, "and they'll be proud of you."

Grace bought Xander a Tank watch with a steel band. She had asked him if he wanted a Rolex. Frances would front the money. He shook his head. "They're watches for admirals and studio heads and basketball players," he said. "I couldn't afford the insurance, and someone would steal it the first time I wore it on set."

They had been efficient and successful. They went back to Xander's house happy with their gifts, happy with each other. Sitting on the sofa, they admired their purchases.

"It's very beautiful," Grace said holding out her hand. *I'm becoming mush,* she thought, *and I don't seem to mind.*

"You're very beautiful," Xander said.

"Do you want children?" she said.

"I think so," he said, "but I don't need to have them."

Grace leaned in to kiss him. "Will we be all right?" she said. "We're not easy people."

"I stick," he said.

The next day, they went to the lot to watch the filming of *Smithies,* Xander's miniseries. He'd settled on five alums: Anne Morrow

Lindbergh '28, Betty Friedan '42, Jean Harris '45, Sylvia Plath '55, and Gloria Steinem '56. It had taken him four years to get a green light. Reese Witherspoon was producing. Nicole Kidman agreed to play Lindbergh. Xander was the showrunner.

"I'm not sure Smith will like it," he said, "but I think the audience will."

Each episode focused on one of the women and a catalytic event in her life: the kidnapping and murder of Lindbergh's baby, with a side glance at Anne's proto-fascist husband, Charles, the famous aviator; Friedan's writing of *The Feminine Mystique* and the middle-class revolt she launched; Harris's murder of her faithless lover, the Scarsdale diet doctor; Plath's marriage to Ted Hughes, her poems, and her suicide; Steinem's undercover assignment as a Playboy Bunny for *Show* magazine.

Grace had never been on a film set. It was bedlam. Everyone was yelling when they weren't shooting. They were filming the Plath episode. Elle Fanning, in a brown pageboy wig, was playing Plath. Jake Gyllenhaal was playing Hughes. Grace couldn't figure out where to look, so much was going on, the least of it involving the actors.

"Does she bite him in the cheek the first time they meet?" Grace asked Xander.

He nodded. "It comes so early in their relationship," he said. "A shame. We tried to build to it but really, she just went at him." His eyes panned the scene, as the camera might. "I wonder what it's like to be the kind of man who drives a woman to bite him."

"Wanton intensity and pheromones," Grace said. "Everyone said Hughes reeked of sex."

THE PRESS GANG PODCAST GROUP aired *Elephant Memories*. They promised Ruth they'd continue to broadcast the show once every two weeks, as an offspring of theirs, for ten episodes. If *Elephant Memories* caught on, it could become one of their regular podcasts. They'd underwrite her for six months and help her hire staff. Ruth agreed in principle. No contracts were signed. She didn't want a big staff. She thought most podcasts were overproduced.

"I'd like some better equipment," she said to Nico, "but I want to be the Fred Wiseman of podcasts, me and the sound engineer."

"Only the first year," Nico said. "After that you'll want a platoon of gaffers."

The maiden podcast to air was, as Grace suggested, about grand-mothers. The first guest was Tito Solas, a Puerto Rican actor friend from Chicago, who was raised grudgingly by his grandmother. When he was two years old, his mother ran off with his step-grandfather. Mima, his grandmother, had mixed feelings and hard feelings. She didn't blame Tito but she did. He wasn't angry or sad, he was spirit-less. He warned Ruth when she asked him to sit for an interview that he only came to life when he was acting. "Pretend you're Tito Solas," she had said. Her last question elicited a wrenching answer, surpris-ing both of them by its intensity.

"If you met your mother, what would you do?" she said.

"I'd turn my back on her and walk out. Mima calls it reciprocity." He laughed dully. "I call it physics. For every action, there is an equal and opposite reaction."

The second guest was Grace. "Her story," Ruth said in her intro-duction, "is a kind of variation on Tito's, another disappearing act, but a generation removed. Tito was an abandoned child. Grace is the daughter of an abandoned child, her mother, Lila." Ruth paused. "This story is a muddied one. There is disagreement within the fam-ily whether Lila's mother, Zelda, died, as her father, Aldo, told her, or ran off. Grace believes Zelda ran off."

Grace began to speak. "This is a ghost story. Whether Zelda died or lived, she haunts our family. In the beginning, Lila was suspicious of her father's story—there was no funeral, no grave, no death certificate—but she soon accepted it. She didn't want to believe her mother could have left her children in the hands of their brutal and violent father." She paused. "When I first heard of Zelda's disappear-ance, I too was suspicious, but unlike Lila, with no stake in the official version, I've held on to it. You might call it gut instinct, but I don't trust gut instincts. Too much like wishes." She paused. "Last year, I published a novel, based too closely on my family. In it, the grandmother, called Zelina, had run off. Not long after, my mother died. On her deathbed, she wrote me a letter, telling me to find out, one way or the other, what happened to Zelda/Zelina. She was writing, one reporter to another. I felt I had no choice but to look for her." Grace took in a big breath.

"My grandmother's married name was Zelda Pereira. I don't know her maiden name, I'm working on it. She would be eighty-seven years old if she's still alive. I've been told she was beautiful, like my mother, my aunt, and my sisters, a short curvy blonde with pearl white skin and blue eyes. She lived in Detroit at the time of her disappearance, on Grand Street, a Jewish neighborhood in those days. The name is Sephardic, but over the generations, the family intermarried with Ashkenazic Jews, and Yiddish, not Ladino, was the lingua franca. I'm doing all the standard things, combing official records, taking a DNA test, but I keep thinking there are people out there who know or knew my grandmother. I'd love to hear from you. Send an email to Ruth. She'll forward it." Grace took another big breath.

"You may be asking why I've made such a big deal of this," she said. "After all, Zelda is not my mother, but my grandmother. I'm prepared to be proven wrong, but I don't think I will be." She paused. "I like to think I want to exorcise the family ghost, but then, maybe it just comes down to the fact I'm a reporter and I want to get the story."

Two weeks later, Scott Simon interviewed Grace on *Weekend Edition*. He had known Lila and he had read Grace's novel. One of his producers had heard Ruth's podcast. Simon's last question was one Grace had avoided asking herself. "Do you think Zelda, if she's alive, will be happy to hear from you?"

Grace took a few seconds to answer. "As a reporter," she said, "I work hard not to write the ending before I finish the investigation."

After the interview, Grace called Ruth.

"Did you hear my bit on *Weekend Edition*?" she said.

"Yes," Ruth said.

"What did you think?" Grace said.

"It was slick," Ruth said, "the same way the end of the podcast was slick. Grace Maier as the thoroughgoing professional. It makes no difference if the missing person is her grandmother or Podsnap's grandmother; she gets the job done. I know that's harsh but that's what I thought."

"What did you expect me to do?" Grace said. "If I'd been honest, whatever that entails, I'd never get another newspaper job. The reporter can't be the story, only the storyteller."

"What does being honest entail?" Ruth said.

Grace was silent for several seconds. Ruth waited.

"I've made a mess of things and there's no way out except going forward," Grace said.

"Do you want Zelda to have died or escaped?" Ruth said.

Grace again fell silent. "I want her to have died," she said. "If she escaped, I'll hate her for not taking her children with her."

23

Investigation

GRACE CALLED CLARA FROM CALIFORNIA. "I'M GOING TO MARRY XANder. I don't know exactly when. He didn't propose. He didn't get down on a knee. We decided together. He bought me a gigantic emerald. I bought him a spiffy watch. He has a big job and a jewel of a house. I'm applying for jobs in L.A." She paused. "I suppose that means we're engaged."

"Wonderful news," Clara said. "Xander's good for you. Like Joe. He's crazy about you." She paused. "How long has it been? Have you broken it off yet?"

"Xander said I couldn't break it off for six months," Grace said. "He said we have to get used to it, give it a chance. He's much calmer. Success helps. He runs three days a week and meditates the other four, or vice versa. And then, just to be on the safe side, most days he takes half of a tiny white pill. He needs to be pulled together at work." She paused. "I don't think I've ever seen him lose his temper."

"The same can't be said for you," Clara said. "Snap, snap."

"I don't so much lose my temper," Grace said, "as give in to it."

"What did Joe say?"

"Joe was relieved. He thought I'd blow it."

"I have news too," Clara said. "Aldo's willing to talk to you, for two thousand dollars."

"Is that 'ask' take it or leave it?" Grace said. "Shouldn't I counter? He'll think I'm a pussy if I don't."

"I'd offer three hundred tops," Clara said, "and tell him he has to deliver."

"Would you do that for me?" Grace said. "Next week, Monday or Tuesday if that works for you. I'll spend the weekend with Frances. Why don't you come too?"

"Bring cash," Clara said.

"Thanks so much," Grace said. "I can't wait to meet him. The only person I'd rather interview is Zelda but . . ."

"He's cunning, but not clever," Clara said. "He was a Webbite. He had a sign in the front yard. He's got a union pension and votes straight Republican."

"Great party story," Grace said. "'I paid three hundred dollars to talk to my grandfather.'"

ALDO STILL LIVED IN THE house on Grand Street. He'd paid off the mortgage when he was fifty-five, and since then, he had paid for a new roof and a new boiler. When he turned ninety, Clara's conscience, a constant nag, moved her to pay for a housekeeping service once a month. The first time, four cleaners spent two days chucking and two days scrubbing. Clara had to rent a small dumpster. She insisted that Aldo shower before they came. He regularly proposed to one or the other of them. Clara had them come the Friday before the interview. "I think we should sit in the kitchen," she said to Grace. "The rooms with stuffed furniture are harder to clean. As far as I can tell, he hasn't bought anything new since Bubbe died."

Aldo was sitting on the porch when Clara and Grace arrived. He was wearing black work boots, a black parka, and a black hat. He slowly stood up as they got out of the car and pulled off his cap. He was vain about his hair. It was thick, white, and curly. Other men his age were bald. He hadn't shaved, but he looked as if he'd showered in the last two days. His skin was florid, pockmarked, and wrinkled; his nose was flat, like a boxer's; his mouth turned down; his eyebrows needed trimming, as did the hair in his nose, which was black, not white. He had more teeth than Grace had expected. He was short and sturdy. Grace was at least six inches taller than he was. As she walked carefully up the steps, he snorted. "You're not a Pereira, that's for sure."

Grace held out her hand. "Grace Maier," she said. "Lila's youngest daughter. My sisters are Pereiras." He ignored her hand and walked into the house, grinding his teeth.

They sat at the kitchen table. Grace and Clara had stopped at Starbucks and bought coffees and blueberry muffins. They kept their coats on.

"Did you bring the money," Aldo said. "Three thousand dollars, in tens and twenties."

"I brought three hundred, as agreed," Grace said. She reached in her purse and pulled out a wad of twenty-dollar bills. She started counting them out. When she reached two hundred dollars, she handed them to Aldo.

"I'll give you the rest at the end of the interview," she said.

He picked up the cash on the table. "I want the rest now," he said.

"I'm paying for your information," Grace said, "not your hospitality. Shall we start."

"What do you want?" he said.

"I'd like you to tell me about your marriage to Zelda, the early days," Grace said. "Why did you marry her."

"She was a real looker and she had a bit of money," Aldo said. "Dead parents. No in-laws. I treated her like a princess. My mother lived with us. She did all the cleaning and cooking and looking after the kids. The wife spent her days reading novels and eating chocolates." He grinned at Grace. "We had sex all the time. I could do it again and again and again. Clean sex mostly. Me on top."

"Were you happy with her?" Grace said.

"Yeah," he said, "except when she was pregnant, too pregnant to have regular sex. I made her do dirty things then, standing and sitting. She didn't like it, but a man has his needs." He made a crude gesture. "Do you like dirty sex?"

"When did she leave the house?" Grace said.

"After Lila was born, she cried all the time. She didn't want to have sex. I made her, of course, my right, but she cried the whole way through. I threatened to hit her if she kept crying. A man doesn't want sex that way. She'd stop for a while, long enough. She knew I meant it."

"Did she ever stop crying?" Grace said.

"No," he said. "After two years, I'd had enough. I took her to the Eloise and asked the doctors to make her stop crying. She cried there too. She cried twenty-four hours a day. They said they'd keep her for a week and see if they could treat her."

"Did they treat her?"

"Nothing worked," he said. "She stayed in the hospital for years. Electric shock helped and then it didn't. Then she started a fire in her room and killed herself."

"Did you ever visit her?"

"Twice," he said. "She screamed the whole time. Out of her mind."

"I haven't been able to find a death certificate for her," Grace said.

Aldo showed his teeth. "The Eloise, was like a lot of loony bins back then. They buried their patients in the back fields. Dead infants too. Patients' babies. They didn't tell the authorities. The relatives didn't care." He leaned in and grinned. "She might have been dissected by medical students." He nodded. "They did that with some of the bodies. What's the word?"

"Cadaver," Clara said.

"That's right," he said. "She might have been a cadaver. The only useful thing she ever did. They didn't send me no death certificate. I didn't care. She ruined my life. I wasn't sorry she was dead."

"Did you ever hit any of your children?" Grace said.

Aldo glanced quickly at Clara, then turned away. "Every father hits his kids sometimes. They do bad things. They lie, they steal your money, they talk back. Ask Clara," he said.

"I've already interviewed Clara," Grace said. "This is your interview."

"Polo and Clara were like regular kids, not Lila. She had a mouth on her." He took a bite of his muffin. "She took the beatings, she knew she earned them, and look what they made her." He took another bite. "University of Michigan, big-shot Washington newspaper editor, married to a GM millionaire." He took a swig of coffee. "Never visited. Never called. The day she left for college, she stole Bubbe's jewelry. I never saw her again. She never sent me no money. She never called. She didn't invite me to her wedding. She came back to Detroit, lots of times. Ungrateful." He took another swig. "I spit on her memory." He leaned over and spit on the floor.

Grace stood up. "Thank you," she said, handing him the second stack of bills.

He took the bills and grinned at Grace. "I outlived her," he said.

In the car, Grace sat quietly for several minutes. Clara waited.

"Did you notice," Grace said, glancing quickly at her aunt, then looking straight ahead, "he was fluent when he talked about Zelda, who he never named, but fidgety and twitchy when he talked about Lila, who he did. The Zelda story has been told many times. It's practiced. The Lila story has not. It's raw. It stings." She turned again toward Clara. "Did he ever talk about Lila?"

"Interesting," Clara said. "He talked about Zelda periodically, always the same, the crying, the Eloise, the electric shock, the burning bed."

"Like Jane Eyre," Grace said.

"I never heard about her cadaver before," Clara said. "Someone must have recently told him about the law on unclaimed bodies. They now turn them over to the Wayne State Medical School for the students to dissect. If he mentioned Lila, it was only to call her a selfish ingrate, not to everyone, just us."

"He was very dexterous discussing the beatings," Grace said.

"He says it, he believes it, he's always in the right," Clara said. "The catch, he couldn't brag about Lila. He never got any money out of her. After her wedding, a neighbor asked if he was proud of her. He scoffed. 'She don't show no respect to her father. All I did for her. No respect.' I only heard him say it once. He saw it made him look bad, like a man who earned no respect. After that, he'd just shrug." Clara started the engine. "The marriage did up his status. He got a better job at the plant. Some of the men called him 'Big Shot,' but there was no payoff." She released the parking brake. "No Cadillac parked in the driveway."

CLARA SENT GRACE BUBBE'S BOX. "I can't bear to look at it," she said to herself.

She pushed it into a corner. *I'll open it tomorrow, or the day after, or the week after, or never.*

She opened it four days later. Xander was visiting.

"What's that?" he said, pointing to the box. It looked like a refrigerator box that had been cut down. "Sears went bankrupt years ago."

Grace explained.

"Let's open it," Xander said, pulling the box toward the sofa and sitting down.

"I don't want to," Grace said. "Lila wouldn't want to." She stood across from him by the kitchen.

"I'll open it," he said. You sit across the room and watch. Do you have a box cutter?"

Grace got him a knife. "Be careful," she said. "It's got a spring opening." She sat down next to him.

Xander pushed the latch. The blade flew open. He lurched back, stunned. "What the hell is this," he said. "I could have killed myself."

Grace shook her head. "Maybe cut yourself, that's all. Lila's switchblade. She didn't have jewelry, only knives. My sisters have them too. This is an early model. She carried one on her, wherever she went. She always wore pockets."

"I didn't really know her," Xander said. "Nico and Ruth's engagement party. That was it."

"A mother like no other," Grace said. "Here, give me the knife."

She cut the tape and opened the flaps. "Come look," he said, peering inside.

Grace shook her head.

He reached in and lifted a picture frame. He turned it toward Grace.

"This must be Zelda," he said. "She looks like the Starbirds and Lila."

Grace looked at the picture. "She's so young. It must be her high school photo." She peered into the frame. "Oh, look," she said. "She's wearing the chain Lila always wore." She put the frame down next to her. "I'm going to cry now."

Xander gently pulled her close to him. She buried her head in his shoulder. He stroked her hair.

"Do you have a handkerchief?" she said. Joe always carried one on him.

"I do," he said. He pulled it out of his pocket. "'R.G.' Dad likes monograms. When we were kids, Nico and I got them for him every Father's Day. That and Old Spice."

Grace wiped her eyes. "I can blow, yes?" she said. Xander nodded.

"I wasn't expecting a photo," she said.

"It's not just one photo," he said. "There are several, also some newspapers and books and I don't know what else. Memorabilia. It's a memorabilia box."

Grace reached in and pulled out another frame. It held a photo of Zelda and Aldo, dressed up. He has his arm around her waist. She was staring straight ahead. "He looks sort of like Paulie Walnuts, don't you think, the boxer's squashed nose," she said. "She's so young, so young and unhappy."

"I think she's pregnant," Xander said.

"Polo," Grace said, tearing again. "This is very hard. I didn't know I was such a sap."

"Hard for anyone," Xander said.

"Look," she said, reaching into the box. "Lila's wedding invitation, with Bubbe's name written in. Marta Pereira. Frances hired a calligrapher." She laid the invitation back in the box. "She never made it to the wedding."

Xander gingerly pulled out a fistful of photos. He handed one to Grace.

"That's the three of them, when they were little," she said.

"Clara and Lila could be virtual twins, like the Starbirds," he said. "Polo looks very serious." He took out another photo. "Is this Bubbe?"

"I'm guessing it is." Grace stared at the photo. "I think she's wearing her Sabbath dress, stiff black silk. Lila asked her once why she always wore black to synagogue. She said she was mourning. Lila asked who she was mourning. 'Me,' she said. She died the spring before Lila's wedding. Clara said they should all move out and live together. Bubbe said she'd think about it. She died first."

Grace put the photo down. "What books are in there?" she asked.

Xander pulled out *Exodus*.

Grace picked it up. "This must have been Lila's." She opened the book. On the title page, Lila had written in her barely legible hand: *This book was stolen from Lila Pereira*. Grace laughed. "Lila didn't lend books. She'd buy you one if you asked to borrow it."

"You're wearing your ring," he said.

"I sleep in it," she said. He stroked her hair.

"If I can't sleep," he said, "would you mind if I rifled through the box some more? It's a time capsule. I wish I had known Lila."

"Look all you want," Grace said. "If the box was someone else's story, I'd stay up all night rummaging in it. Lila brought nothing with her from Grand Street except stories, which were set in amber by the time my sisters and I heard them." She teared. "Have you been to the Holocaust Museum in D.C.? It was the pile of shoes that did me in." She wiped her nose. "I don't know why I'm so weepy. You can curate it for me."

The next morning, over donuts and coffee, Xander asked Grace if she wanted to go through the box. "I was up at four," he said. "I found some more photos. Look, here, the three children with Zelda. She looks like a zombie."

"That must be Lila," Grace said, pointing. "She can't be more than eighteen months." Zelda was seated in a chair, holding baby Lila. Polo was standing on one side of his mother, Clara on the other. "D-day looming." She tucked the photo in her purse.

"Look at this," he said. He handed her a small pile of report cards. "The top one."

It was Lila's fourth-grade report. In the comment section, the teacher had written, *Lila is very intelligent, very observant, but she won't talk in class. I asked her why. She said, "My father said I need to zip it."*

"There was no self-pity in her stories, only an undercurrent of anger." Grace put the card down. "Children's Protective Services never came by. They didn't think Jews beat their children . . . or their wives."

Xander put his arm around her. "Look at this," he said. He handed her a copy of *The Secret Garden.*

Grace opened the book, smiling. In the inside cover, she saw the stamp, Detroit Free Library. She pulled the take-out card from the envelope. "Lila took this book out a dozen times, in 1967."

"And then she kept it," Xander said.

"And then she kept it," Grace said.

THE STARBIRDS REPORTED IN. THEY'D found Zelda's marriage license to Aldo, identifying her as Zelda Pessoa, Spinster. They also found a pair of birth certificates, which were identical except for the first names. One was for Zelda Pessoa and the other was for Frida Pessoa.

"I'm guessing a name change, Zelda to Frida, not twins," Stella said.

"No death certificates for either," Ava said, "at least not in Michigan."

"No divorce decrees," Stella said.

"We're checking for a marriage license for Frida Pessoa," Ava said.

"Clever and simple," Stella said. "An uncontroversial name change and suddenly, you're reborn.

"Like Don Draper," Ava said.

"We couldn't get copies of the originals," Stella said. "If they still exist."

"Spinster," Ava said. "Don't you love it? Seventeen years old."

Two weeks later, the Starbirds called again.

"Frida Pessoa married Herbert Berman, in 1960," Stella said, "the year Zelda was hospitalized."

"We googled around," Ava said. "They lived in Farmington, twelve miles west by southwest of Frances."

"Herbert's dead," Stella said. "Two thousand eight. He was ten years older than Frida."

"They belonged to Temple Israel," Ava said. "Herbert was a Rotarian."

"There's an accounting firm, Berman & Glasser, CPA," Stella said. "We're checking it out."

"We haven't found any children yet," Stella said. "I'm thinking Temple Israel may be a source."

"Hold on," Grace said. "You talk so fast. I need to write down the names. Could you give them to me again?"

"Frida Pessoa married Herbert Berman," Stella said.

"In 1960," Ava said.

24

Unraveling

NO ONE THOUGHT HERBERT BERMAN WOULD EVER MARRY. IN 1949, when he was twenty-four, he proposed to a girl. They'd been on three dates. She didn't laugh at him, not to his face, but she made him feel three inches tall.

"We've never kissed," she said. "We've never necked."

He apologized and left her house, his face red, his shirt damp with sweat. His parents hired a matchmaker. The girls were plain and older than he was. *First I'm humiliated,* he thought, *then I'm insulted.*

He wished he had been drafted. The vets, especially the ones who'd served overseas, got all the best girls. He had been called up, but he failed the physical. He was so nearsighted, he could barely make out the large "E" on the eye chart. "Blinder than a bat," he'd say. "More like a mole." His glasses were like the bottoms of Coke bottles. Even the doctors were impressed.

"How do you navigate?" one said to him.

"I'm a talented interpreter of blurs," he said. He was not without a sense of humor, though until he married, he showed it only with men.

He told his parents he wanted to wait to marry until he was more settled in his work. He had graduated from Wayne State with a BS in accounting. He worked two years for a medium-size accounting firm, then left to open his own, with a college classmate, Irving Glasser, in Oak Park, his hometown. They built their business, Berman & Glasser, using their connections at the synagogue, the Brotherhood for the businessmen, the Sisterhood for the widows. No person was too poor, no company too small. They bet on growth.

The business grew steadily. They had a solid reputation. They believed not only in good work but in good service. Word got around. After the Jews, the Catholics came, then the Protestants. By the time the business was ten years old and Herbert was thirty-five, the company employed five junior accountants, two secretaries, and a messenger. It grossed $200,000 in 1955, giving them enough profits over expenses to buy their building. Herbert and Irving each took home $25,000. Herbert joined the Jewish Country Club and played golf on Sunday. His handicap was sixteen. He was tall with long arms. He could just see the ball on its tee and if he connected with it, it flew. He drove an Oldsmobile and bought his suits at Brooks Brothers. Just before his thirty-fifth birthday, he bought a brick colonial house for himself in Farmington and a ranch for his parents in Oak Park. He had offered them a house in Farmington. They turned him down. "Who would I play mahjong with?" Mrs. Berman said. The mothers in town began to think he was a catch.

When Hilda Pessoa called Mrs. Berman to ask if Herbert was ever going to settle down, Mrs. Berman moaned. "From your mouth to God's ear," she said. "My greatest wish. He's such a good son."

"I have a girl, beautiful, only twenty-four, Jewish, of course, my niece, Frida Pessoa," Hilda said. "She's staying with me. Her parents died when she was seventeen, and she was living as a companion with a great-aunt on her mother's side, an invalid. The old lady died a week ago. I took Frida in. She's family. She needs to get married. Her great-aunt was very selfish, like the rest of that family. She didn't do anything for the girl. I immediately thought of Herbert. She's very shy, quiet. She's lived like a nun. She needs a man who will take care of her, a good man, a kind man. Not a boy."

"Is she really beautiful?" Mrs. Berman said.

"You know that actress Veronica Lake," Hilda said. "Prettier. Prettier too than Lana Turner. Why don't you come over and meet her?"

Mrs. Berman went around to the Pessoas' that afternoon. They sat in the parlor, only used for important occasions. Frida was as lovely as her great-aunt said. Mrs. Berman was very direct.

"Are you interested in getting married?" she said.

"Yes," Frida said.

"My son is tall, nice looking, but he has very bad eyesight," Mrs. Berman said. "Still, if he stood close to you, he'd see how . . . pretty you are."

Frida smiled and put her head down.

"He's much older than you," Mrs. Berman said. "He's thirty-five."

"His character is the most important thing to me," Frida said.

"Have you had other boyfriends?" Mrs. Berman said.

Frida shook her head.

"Her great-aunt wouldn't let her go out of the house alone," Hilda said. "It was a kindness on her part to look out for Frida, an orphan girl, but selfishness too. Frida had no life of her own."

"Did you keep kosher?" Mrs. Berman said.

Frida nodded.

"Can you cook and keep house?" Mrs. Berman said.

Frida shook her head. "My great-aunt had a housekeeper."

"That's honest, at least," Mrs. Berman said. "Herbert can afford a housekeeper."

"Why don't you go to your room, Frida?" Hilda said. "Mrs. Berman and I need to talk."

"It was very nice to meet you, Mrs. Berman," Frida said. "Thank you for coming."

Mrs. Berman smiled as she watched Frida leave. "Very lovely," she said, "and modest and polite. Maybe not so useful, but you can't have everything. Does she have any education, any skills?"

"Her great-aunt took her out of high school, her senior year. So selfish. She never graduated. She's working on her GED," Hilda said. "She likes to read. She's reading *Exodus*."

"Do you have a photograph I could show Herbert?" Mrs. Berman said.

Hilda took an envelope off the coffee table and handed it to Mrs. Berman.

Mrs. Berman looked inside. "A very good likeness." She looked sideways at Hilda. "Is she a virgin?"

"What a thing to think, let alone ask," Hilda said. "She's been living like a nun."

"Herbert deserves a virgin," Mrs. Berman said.

"Only the best for Herbert," Hilda said. "So?"

"I'll tell Herbert that you and I had tea today and I met your niece who's staying with you. I'll tell him about her and see if he bites. I won't show him the photograph until we've talked it through." She smiled at her friend. "I've got this feeling, a tingling in my fingers. This might work out."

Herbert and Frida went on three dates. On the second date, he kissed her. On the third, he proposed. He bought her a diamond ring. Frida gasped when she saw it. "Really?" she said. "For me?"

He nodded, smiling, and kissed her again. They married a month later.

People weren't surprised. "Rich men get beautiful girls," Mrs. Irving Glasser said to her mother-in-law. "I bet a lot of mothers are grinding their teeth now."

Herbert and Frida went on a honeymoon to Bermuda. She came back pregnant. Herbert hired a cleaning woman. A son, Dennis, was born six months later. He weighed four and a half pounds and spent a month in an incubator, learning to breathe on his own. When he came home, Herbert hired a baby nurse. Frida felt desperate.

"He's still so small and I'm so incompetent. I can't even nurse. I think he's starving," she said. She started to cry. She cried often in the early days. "From happiness," she said, "and fear it might go away."

Herbert took out his handkerchief and wiped her tears. "Not to worry. There's formula." He stroked her hair. "I always wondered why I worked so hard. For you."

Two years later, Frida gave birth to a second child, a girl, Heidi, larger, full term. This time, Herbert hired a housekeeper. Lenore stayed fifty years.

"I'm not very motherly," Frida said to Lenore when she interviewed her. "Is that unusual?"

Lenore laughed. "That's why I have a job," she said. "Many perfectly nice women aren't cut out for motherhood."

Frida was fond of her children, but she wasn't a hands-on mother. She made sure the family ate dinner together. She had read somewhere that was good for children. She went to their games. They were both good athletes, Dennis especially, though he was short, like Frida. Herbert was sanguine. "Blessedly," he said, "he didn't get my eyes."

After Heidi was born, Herbert taught Frida to drive and bought her a car, a Chevy Caprice station wagon, for the carpools. Frida drove Dennis to school. Lenore picked him up.

When Heidi started nursery school, Frida saw an opportunity.

"What would you think," she said to Herbert, "if I went to college? It would make me more interesting. I have a good head for numbers. I could understand your work better." The one household task she had taken on enthusiastically was the family checkbook. The first year Herbert checked it against the statements. After that, he left her to it. She was careful with money. She opened savings accounts for Herbert's retirement and the children's college education.

"If that will make you happy," he said. It was his standard refrain with Frida. She made him happy. It seemed only right that he should return the favor.

Frida enrolled in Wayne State. She made friends with the other students, most of them a decade younger. "I don't feel older, except for the dating and drinking," she said to Herbert. "They have so much more experience of life." She lowered her voice to a whisper. "They have sex outside marriage." She graduated cum laude in six years, with a BS in accounting.

Herbert was so proud. "What are you going to do now?" he said.

"I thought I'd take the accounting exams and then, if you agree, get a job," she said.

"You could work for us," he said. "I'd hate to see some other company get the benefits of your services. They might exploit you."

"Would Irving mind?" she said.

"No," he said, laughing, "but Marcy Glasser would. She's so jealous of you, getting your degree. Irving is not as open-minded or forward-thinking as I am, not at work, not at home."

"Would I get a salary?" she said.

"Of course," he said, "the starting rate, more when you pass the exams. We have high standards, but I know you'll meet them."

"I don't know how I got so lucky," she said, "marrying you."

"It wasn't luck," he said. "It was Hilda, God help us."

Frida passed her exams on her first try. She got a raise. She and Herbert decided she'd work only twenty hours a week, to try it out, but after a year, she went full-time. "The children don't need me around," she said to Herbert. "They certainly don't want me around." Dennis was thirteen, Heidi, eleven, both teetering on adolescence, embarrassed by everything their mother did.

She did an audit the first year, a local business with a hundred employees. She never did another. The day she started, the vice president hung around her desk.

"He got fresh with me," she said to Herbert that evening.

"What did he do?" Herbert said, thinking he'd have to fire the client.

"He was paying me all kinds of compliments, how pretty I was, and then insulting me, saying a pretty girl shouldn't work so hard." She pursed her lips. "I told him if he wanted to chitchat, I'd have to explain to my boss and probably his too, why I got so little done in six hours. 'That could be awkward,' I told him. He skedaddled." She looked at Herbert, her forehead furrowed, her bright blue eyes wide open. "I like doing taxes better."

"How did you know how to handle the situation?" he said. *She's remarkable,* he thought, *in every way.*

"Some of the Wayne State students would get a little fresh with me, hang around, wanting to flirt and chitchat," she said. "I'd tell them I was in college to work. I thought they were too. After that, they were very respectful." Her face fell. "The VP could give me a bad report."

"I'll cut him off at the pass," Herbert said. "I'll send someone else tomorrow. Someone who isn't pretty."

BY THE END OF HER third year, Frida was the income tax expert in the firm. She kept up on the changes in the law, state and federal, and taught her clients how to keep their records. The widows liked working with her. She took her time with them, especially those who knew nothing of the family's finances.

For her fortieth birthday, Frida asked Herbert for a set of golf clubs and golf lessons. "Good for business," she said to him. "If I get good, maybe you'll play with me."

It was a happy marriage, unexpected for both. The only blight on it was Hilda. Herbert called her "the rain cloud." She made incessant demands for attention. If they weren't met, she huffed and sulked and phoned Frida four times a day, calling her ungrateful and selfish.

"I think some of her demands are unreasonable," Herbert said.

"Of course they are," Frida said. "Are we going to say no?"

Hilda had insisted that Heidi have an "H" name, "one similar to mine, so everyone knows you named her for me."

Herbert was thrown. "We name our children after dead people."

"I can't wait until I'm dead," Hilda said. "Anyway, we're Sephardic. You can do it if you're Sephardic."

Hilda came to dinner every Friday night for the Sabbath, and for all the other holidays, Shavuot, Rosh Hashanah, the Yom Kippur break-fast, Chanukah, Purim, Passover.

"Purim, too?" Herbert said to Frida. "No one over twelve celebrates Purim."

Hilda's demands reached a crisis state after Dennis's bar mitzvah, when Frida told her the family wasn't going to keep kosher any longer. They had joined a Reform synagogue. More of their country club crowd went there.

"Don't tell me," she said. "That hoity toity 'temple' for atheists. They don't even call it a synagogue."

"We're not atheists," Herbert said. *Would atheists put up with you?*

"What am I supposed to eat when I come to your house?" Hilda said.

"We'll make you a plate," Frida said.

"It won't be as good as your meal," Hilda said.

"We'll serve fish when you come," Frida said. "We'll all eat the same thing."

"I don't like fish," Hilda said.

"We'll serve macaroni, without meat," Frida said.

"It won't be tasty," Hilda said.

"But we'll all be together," Frida said. "Isn't that the point?"

"You can cater it from Schlomo's," Hilda said. "Brisket this Friday."

Hilda insisted that Dennis and Heidi call her Nana. At Dennis's bar mitzvah, she made sure he thanked her. "You wouldn't be here if I hadn't played matchmaker with your parents," she said. She then turned to Heidi. "You too, miss."

Every year, over the Fourth of July weekend, the family took a cottage on Lake Michigan. Hilda came along.

"She'd have tested Job," Herbert said.

"She can't live forever," Frida said. "Bite my tongue."

When Hilda got pancreatic cancer at sixty-nine, Frida and Herbert took her in. "It will be short," Frida said. Hilda lived another eighteen months, long enough to make Herbert and Frida throw her a seventieth birthday party at Schlomo's. "They'll do it right, kosher," Hilda said. "I know you want to do this for me."

She left Frida her house. She explained the gift in her will: "Frida knows what I did for her."

"I think she wanted me to be more grateful to her for our happy marriage than to you," Frida said to Herbert.

"Let's go to a movie next Friday night," he said.

DENNIS GOT HIS BS AND JD degrees from Wayne State. He was a diligent student. He worked hard. Heidi got her BS and JD degrees from the University of Michigan. She was an excellent student. She worked hard. Their parents were proud of their children. After law school, Dennis clerked on the Detroit District Court. Heidi clerked on the Michigan Supreme Court. When the time came to get jobs, they opened a practice together in Detroit, wills, taxes, and divorces.

They both married in their early thirties, Dennis to an accountant who worked for his parents, Heidi to another lawyer, another woman. They had thought of practicing in Ann Arbor, Heidi loved it, but they knew they'd have more opportunities in the greater Detroit area, and they wanted to be closer to their parents and, theoretically, their nana. They invited Hilda often to their homes, but she wouldn't go. "Not if Heidi's person is going to be there," she'd say. She thought Detroit was a cesspool of crime and disease and homosexuals. Dennis and Heidi ceded the Jewish holidays to Hilda, claiming Thanksgiving, Christmas, and Easter for themselves and their families.

"First my family fled Europe, then they fled Detroit," Hilda said. "Where do we go from here?"

"Boca," Heidi said.

The law practice did well. Like their parents, they paid attention at work. Heidi was a better lawyer than Dennis, but she was better at everything they did.

"Why aren't I?" he asked one day.

"You were premature," Heidi said. "You've done great, and anyway, I'm no genius."

"I wish there were more of us," he said. "Relatives. When Mom and Dad die, there will just be us."

"And our children and grandchildren when they come," Heidi said.

"But no people in our generation," he said.

"We might have second cousins or third," Heidi said.

"I don't know," he said. "Our Berman grandparents never had anyone over and neither did Hilda. Sort of pathetic."

"Why are you thinking like this?" she said.

"A client was in today, to make out a will. She had three brothers and two sisters. Her mother was one of six, her father one of eight. She had a zillion cousins." He laughed. "There were a hundred people at her wedding, sixty-five of them were family. She said it was the best party ever."

"I'm guessing she wasn't Jewish," Heidi said.

Herbert died on the golf course, at the seventeenth hole. A heart attack. Boom. He was eighty-three.

"I wish he could have finished the round," Frida said when the club pro called. "He went the way he wanted to. He never gave anyone any trouble."

She was sad and sometimes lonely, but she had her work. She took over the management of Berman & Glasser. "I can't imagine my life without work," she said to Heidi. "Mothers who stay home must feel like prisoners. Children don't stick around. One day, they're crawling, the next, they're off to college."

She retired at eighty-two and sold the business to Irving Glasser's daughter. "She's smarter than her brother," she said to Heidi. "Not as nice, but smarter."

"Like me and Dennis," Heidi said.

"Like Dad and me," Frida said.

Three years later, during a snowstorm, she slipped and broke her hip. The bone healed but the accident took away her confidence and, she told Heidi, a lot of brain cells. "I used to be tactful, not now. I say what I think, and sometimes it isn't nice. I suppose eighty-five years of good manners is all you can expect of a person."

She became reclusive. She hardly ate. Lenore looked after Frida as best she could, but she was older, with bad knees and hips. Heidi hired a cleaning woman to look after them both.

"A housekeeper for the housekeeper," Lenore said. "The Berman solution."

When Lenore said she wanted to retire, Heidi and Dennis persuaded Frida to move into an assisted living complex.

"I'll go if Lenore goes with me," Frida said. "I'll pay."

"She wants to live with her daughter, not with you," Heidi said.

"Do I know anyone at Halsted House?" Frida said.

"Marcy Glasser," Heidi said.

"Marcy hates me," Frida said.

"You'll make friends," Heidi said.

"Better, still," Dennis said, "you'll be taken care of as long as you live—which I hope is a very long time."

"I'd prefer shorter than 'a very long time,'" Frida said. "You're a sweet boy."

Frida went into the unit with the lowest level of care. She was good at covering up missteps and she was still pretty. People were attracted to her. She had a two-bedroom apartment nicely furnished with her own things.

"Spare me the dementia floor," she said to Heidi, the day she went in. "That's all I ask of you."

"I want you to join the Scrabblers and the reading group." Heidi said. "You want to keep your brains."

"So bossy," Frida said. "Since when?"

"You were a good mom," Heidi said. "A good role model."

"Not so good," Frida said. "I won't play Scrabble. Boring. I'll try the reading group."

Shortly after Frida arrived, the group picked *The Lost Mother.*

Everyone at Halsted was talking about it. "It's a Detroit story and a Jewish story," Marcy Glasser said. "What could be more perfect? Someone said the author's grandmother was Frances Maier, Henry Fieldstone's daughter. I didn't like the violence. Do you believe the editor's father was really such a monster? I can't believe there are Jews who beat their wives and children."

"Of course there are," Frida said. "And not only poor ones. Remember Hedda Nussbaum and Joel Steinberg. He killed their adopted daughter. She didn't stop him. She saved herself."

"I'll bet she's a better person now," Marcy said. "What doesn't kill you makes you stronger."

"What nonsense," Frida said. "What doesn't kill you makes you desperate, scared, and cunning."

"How would you know?" Marcy said. "Did Herbert ever try to kill you? I don't think so."

"I've met people with PTSD," Frida said. "You need to get out more."

When the group met, they spent most of the time debating whether Zelina had died or run away. They were evenly split.

Frida sided with the "runaway" contingent. "The husband was a liar," she said. "I don't believe his story. Too complicated. Shock treatment. A burning bed. No body."

"It was a terrible thing she did," Marcy said, "leaving those little children behind."

"The children lived, didn't they? They didn't become ax murderers." Frida glared at Marcy. "Maybe it was for the better. Look at the author's mother, a big-time newspaper editor."

DENNIS DECIDED TO DO A Genealogies test.

"Why?" Heidi said. "Why now?"

"I don't know. I keep thinking when Mom dies, I'll . . ." He looked away. "I feel alone."

"Cousins are the solution?" she said.

He shrugged.

"You have your children," she said. "And Linda."

"That's different," he said. "I'm talking about my family of origin. Isn't that the word?"

"What's going on?" she said.

"I'm short," he said. "I'm not smart."

"I think you're wonderful," she said. "You're the best big brother ever."

"The shortest big brother ever," he said.

"You're a Pessoa," she said. "Good looking, like Mom. Me, I'm a long drink of water."

The DNA results were as he expected. "No hits," he said. "I'm related to no one. Except you. At least, I think we're related. Why don't you get tested?"

"Are you nuts?" Heidi said. "The FBI, Interpol, the Detroit Police Department, the Michigan State Police, they ransack these repositories to find criminals and sell your data. Then there's Facebook and Google, who sell them to Amazon."

"You're cynical," he said. "I think it's from doing all those divorces."

Heidi shook her head. "I got it from Mom," she said. "DNA."

25

DNA

IN EARLY NOVEMBER, CLARA AGREED TO DO A DNA TEST. SHE AND GRACE were sitting in her kitchen, drinking coffee, talking through next steps.

"Test results take four weeks," Grace said. "You can opt in and opt out whenever you want. When you're in, relatives can see you, you can see them. When you're out, no one sees anything."

"I'll opt in for a while, look around, and opt out," Clara said. "If no one turns up, I'll try again in a few weeks. Okay?"

"Do Genealogies," Grace said. "It's the biggest."

"Do you think Frida is my aunt?" Clara said.

"I think she's your mother," Grace said.

Clara stirred her coffee. "I didn't care at first whether Zelda died or walked out, not like Lila," she said, "but after Polo died, I wanted her dead." She lowered her head and started crying. "Lila thought she was responsible, taking the beatings for him and me. He felt he should have stood up to Aldo, fought back, defended his younger sisters."

Grace reached across the table and took her hand. "I'll do the test too," she said. "I'll stay in. Maybe none of Frida's children have tested, but her grandkids might have. They'd be at least in their twenties."

"Is this a good thing we're doing?" Clara said.

"No," Grace said. "My fault."

"Lila egged you on," Clara said.

"The only story she didn't pursue," Grace said.

"Will there be closure?" Clara said.

"No one really believes in closure," Grace said, "except, maybe, if there's revenge."

CLARA'S RESULT CAME FIRST. SHE had one hit.

Clara called Grace. "I have a full brother in Detroit."

Grace inhaled sharply. "What's his name?"

"Dennis Berman," Clara said.

"Frida married Mr. Berman," Grace said. "Ergo . . ."

"Ergo," Clara said. "We'll talk later. I have to lie down. I'm getting a headache."

"I'm sorry," Grace said. "Truly."

"Maybe it's better we know," Clara said.

"It would be better if she had died in the Eloise," Grace said. "There, I said it."

The next morning, Grace sent out an email broadside to Joe, Stella, Ava, Xander, Ruth, Nico, and Frances.

November 29, 2023

News. Clara spit in a test tube and had a hit. She has a *full* brother, Dennis Berman, living in Detroit. Upshot. Zelda ran away pregnant, changed her name to Frida, married Herbert Berman, and gave birth to Dennis. If she passed him off as Herbert's son, which I'm guessing she did, he's likely two years younger than Lila, 62 or 63. I googled him. He's a lawyer, in practice with a Heidi Berman, who is his sister, or his half sister, or his adopted sister, or . . . For now, Clara's going to see if he contacts her. He took the test first. I'm guessing it will be cataclysmic for him. It must be for Clara too but she feels worse for Dennis than she feels for herself. I've also spit in a test tube. Waiting on those results.

DENNIS CHECKED HIS GENEALOGIES PROFILE every few days. When he saw he had an unknown sister, he was shaken. He showed the results to Heidi. They were at their office, in the conference room, going over the day's schedules. "Did Dad have a love child before he married Mom?" he said.

Heidi looked at the results. She was quiet for several seconds.

"Well," he said. "What do you think it is?"

"This Clara person," she said slowly, drawing out her words, "she's your full sister. Same father, same mother."

"How can that be?" he said. His face flushed, he felt damp, clammy, his heart started racing.

"Well," Heidi said, "likeliest case, you were adopted."

"Adopted," he said. "I knew something was off. I knew, I knew. Why wouldn't they have told me?"

"I don't know," Heidi said.

"Do you think it's a mistake?" he said. "Would you take the test? Are we even related?" He put his head on the table. Heidi walked around to his chair, leaned over and hugged him. "I think I'm going to be sick," he said.

Heidi looked down at the page of results. "Clara Pereira," she said. "The name sounds familiar. Why don't you contact her?"

"I wasn't looking for a secret sister," he said. "I have a sister, I thought I had a sister." He threw his head back. "My life has exploded."

"Go home. Talk to Linda. Take a Xanax. I'll take care of things here." She looked at him. His face was the color of parchment. "I'm calling an Uber. You shouldn't drive."

She walked him outside, holding his hand. "We'll get through this," she said, helping him into the car. "I love you." He nodded. "You're my brother. You'll always be my brother."

Back in the office, she lambasted herself. *I blew it. I wouldn't have treated a client that way. I didn't think. I should have let him figure it out for himself or not figure it out.*

She googled "Clara Pereira." Lila's obituary in the *Detroit Free Press* popped up. The famous editor, she thought. *Her sister.* Her mind ran ahead. *Also Dennis's sister.* She googled "Lila Pereira" and found obituaries in *The Globe* and *The New York Times*. She clicked on the *Times's. They'll be less respectful, more gossipy.* She read slowly, making a list of the family names: Joseph Maier, Stella Pereira, Ava Pereira, Grace Maier. *Where did I hear that name?* Polo Pereira. *The millennial fireman. Terrible.* Frances Maier. *The Fieldstone Maier. Funny. The obit doesn't mention Lila's parents.* Toward the bottom, she came to *The Lost Mother. Ha. Mom read it for the Halsted Reading Group.* She looked up a review.

She sat back. *Time to move.* She ordered a copy from Amazon— *the hardcover, I can probably get it signed*—and then she ordered a DNA kit from Genealogies. *For Dennis.*

She asked the office manager to cancel all appointments for the day. She drove to Halsted House.

Frida was in the art room. She was painting with oils on a large canvas, a New England scene, a white clapboard church on a village green.

"When did you start painting?" Heidi said as she walked in.

"Recently. You meet a better class of person in the art room," Frida said. "Most of the others spend their days watching television, buying things on Amazon, gossiping. The gossiping is the worst. People they don't even know. Princess Di, who's not even alive, and Kim somebody. They don't read anything, not even a newspaper or magazine."

"What about the reading group?" Heidi said.

"Once a month they read a book about Jews," Frida said. "Herman Wouk is their god."

"What about *The Lost Mother*?" Heidi said. "Was that Jewish?"

"Jewishish," Frida said. "It's really about fathers. She should have called it *Fathers Who Stay*." She shrugged. "Your father was the better parent. Warmer. Nicer."

"What do you think of the mother, running away, leaving the children behind?" Heidi said.

"Fathers do it all the time," Frida said. "Why is it worse when the mother does it?"

Heidi shrugged.

"Your children have two mothers," Frida said. "If one of you had left, they would still have had a mother. Would that have made them luckier than children with a mother and a father if the mother left?"

"This is getting philosophical," Heidi said. "I need a flow chart."

"The mother in the book, not much of a mother," Frida said. "More like one of those Handmaidens. A breeder."

"You seem caught up in the story," Heidi said.

"Not the story so much," Frida said. "People's reaction to it. Very judgey."

"What happened to the mother when she left?" Heidi said.

"A repeat. People don't change. Too hard," Frida said. "She got married again, to another man. Completely boring. She wanted safety."

"What do you think really happened, with the writer's grandmother?" Heidi said.

Frida grinned. "She shot him."

THE FOLLOWING EVENING DENNIS AND Linda and Heidi and Sarah went out for dinner.

Heidi had called Linda. "We need to talk it out," she said. "Dennis won't answer his phone."

"He says there's no point," Linda said. "He says nothing has a point." She paused. "I see his point." She paused again. "I feel so bad for him. Such a good man, such a kind man."

Sarah and Linda both ordered a glass of Chardonnay. Heidi ordered a martini, Dennis a double scotch straight up. They sat nursing their drinks for several minutes, darting glances at each other, then looking away.

"Did you tell your kids?" Heidi said to Dennis. He looked at her, stricken.

"No," Linda said. "I told him they'd want to know. They're grown up, well, almost grown up." She took a swallow of wine. "So, what are you feeling?"

Heidi looked at her brother. "I was stunned, but whatever it means to me is nothing to what it means to you. I love you and I always will."

"Can you sort this out for us?" Linda said, glancing sideways at Dennis. "I don't know how to read the results."

"Dennis and Clara Pereira have the same mother and father," Heidi said. "I see two possible scenarios. One, you and Clara were both adopted, or two, she wasn't adopted, only you were." Heidi looked at Dennis.

"Couldn't our mothers have been sisters, identical twins?" he said. "They have the same DNA."

"Maybe," Heidi said, "but that doesn't solve the father problem."

"Dad confused the twins and had sex with the wrong one," Dennis said. "She seduced him."

"Very biblical," Heidi said.

"I'm just saying," Dennis said. "You're jumping to conclusions."

"What do you want to do?" Heidi said.

"I want you to get tested," he said.

"I ordered a test," she said. "What about Clara Pereira?"

"Let's see what your test says," he said.

"Aren't you curious about her?" she said.

"I don't want her to be my sister," he said. "I thought cousins would be nice. I thought I thought that."

Heidi took the test. The result came in three weeks. Dennis was her half brother. They had the same mother, different fathers.

"At least we're related," he said. They were in the office conference room. Heidi had put off showing him the results until the end of the day, when the two of them would be alone.

"What do you want to do?" she said.

"I want to go back in time," he said. "I want to undo the tests."

"You can let it lie," Heidi said.

"I don't sleep anymore," he said. "I don't think about anything else."

Heidi didn't say anything.

"We don't look alike," he said. "You look like Dad, I look like Mom."

"That's not unusual in families," she said.

"I always hated that you were taller than me," he said.

"You were premature," she said. *Or not,* she thought.

Dennis didn't say anything.

"She's my sister, too," she said. "Well, half sister."

He reached for a tissue and blew his nose.

"You could get in touch with Ms. Pereira or you could ask Mom," she said.

"I can't ask Mom," he said. "That would be so insulting."

Clara and Grace waited three weeks to hear from Dennis Berman. When he didn't get in touch, they decided Clara would write him a letter to his law firm. Grace wrote a draft.

December 22, 2023

Dear Dennis Berman,

I don't know if you've checked your Genealogies results, but you've been identified as my full brother. It is a mystery to me how this happened. Perhaps you have the answer. Could we talk? You may not wish to and if I don't hear back, I won't contact you again. These kinds of results can be shocking and shattering.

Yours,

Clara Pereira

Grace added Clara's cell number, email address, and home address.

"Why did you say 'shocking and shattering'?" Clara said.

"I think he's shocked and shattered," Grace said, "and he's more likely to respond if he thinks you feel the same. The letter doesn't say you were shocked or shattered."

"I am sad for him," Clara said. "He must be reeling."

Four days later, Dennis sent Clara an email. He asked if they might meet. He would bring his sister—his half sister, also her half sister. She might want to bring someone too.

Dennis, Heidi, Clara, and Grace met at the Berman law offices, the first week in January.

Clara explained that her mother and his was hospitalized in 1960, the year he was born, and ostensibly died in 1968. "That is the story my father told me and my sister and brother. We never saw her after she went into the Eloise."

Clara showed him the birth certificates for Zelda Pessoa and Frida Pessoa, with the same parents, same birth dates, same minute of birth.

"See," he said to Heidi. "Identical twins. Same DNA."

"We have the same father, and he isn't Heidi's father," Clara said.

Dennis put his head on the table.

"I'm so sorry," Clara said.

He lifted his head. His face was wet with tears. "I'm a bastard, an illegitimate bastard." He stood up. "Thank you for coming." He walked out of the conference room.

"I'm assuming your mother is still alive," Clara said to Heidi.

Heidi nodded.

"I'd like to meet her," Clara said. "We've come this far." She pursed her lips tight together. *I'm going to throw up,* she thought.

"I read your book," Heidi said, turning to Grace. "Your grandfather was a brute." She looked at Clara. "It was terrible for you and your sister and brother. Dennis escaped that, but for now, he's inconsolable. I feel bad for him. He's such a decent person. I would have taken it better. I do the divorces. I see this a lot. He does the taxes and wills."

"My sisters are divorce lawyers, in practice together," Grace said. "They look like Dennis, like my mother and Clara, and like the pictures of Zelda." She handed Heidi Bubbe's photo of Zelda with the three children.

Heidi put on her glasses. "Looks just like Mom," she said.

"Will Dennis mind, if we visit her?" Clara said.

"She's my mother, too," Heidi said. "Bring the birth certificates and photo."

GRACE CALLED THE STARBIRDS TO tell them the news.

"Frida's children are very nice," Grace said, "but she's going to hate Clara and me."

"How is Clara feeling?" Stella said.

"She must feel awful," Ava said, "finding the mother who abandoned her."

Grace took in a large breath, then exhaled slowly. "It's been hard for her. She doesn't want to talk about it. She feels sorry for the man, Dennis, who discovered he wasn't his father's son. I feel sorry for him too." Grace sat back, surprised, then relieved by her admission. *It's good I said that,* she thought, *though it would have been better if I'd said it to Dennis.*

"I'd visit late morning, before lunch," Stella said. "After lunch, everyone's too tired to confront their past."

"Don't beat around the bush," Ava said. "She'll take one look at Clara and know who you are."

"Don't lie," Stella said. "No matter how useful it would be."

"You can keep quiet, the best tool in the toolkit," Ava said. "Lila called it 'sweating them out.'"

FRIDA WAS IN THE ART studio, facing a large canvas, her back to the door.

"Mom," Heidi said, "I'd like you to meet Clara Pereira and her niece, Grace Maier, Lila Pereira's daughter."

Frida put down her brush and slowly turned around. She had been working on a painting of a nondescript suburban house. "A commission," she said. "I charge two hundred dollars."

Clara clutched Grace's arm. Her legs felt shaky. Her stomach was churning. *She looks so like Lila,* she thought.

Grace grasped Clara around the waist, holding her steady. *She looks like Lila, like Clara, like the Starbirds,* she thought. *Case closed.*

"Let's go to your rooms," Heidi said.

"I'm eighty-eight," Frida said. "Very forgetful. What are your names again?"

Clara and Grace reintroduced themselves.

"Pereira," Frida said. "Is that Portuguese?"

"Yes," Clara said.

In the apartment, Frida bustled around the kitchen. It was open to the sitting room. "I'll make coffee," she said. "I'll be with you shortly."

Heidi, Grace, and Clara sat in the sitting room. They talked quietly to each other. Heidi pointed to a book on the coffee table. "The Reading Group read it," she said. "Frida read it."

"Is she surprised we're here?" Grace said.

"I think so, though the book may have tipped her off in some way," Heidi said. "She's working out her story."

"Will she lie?" Clara said. *How can she lie?* she thought. *It's there, on her face. What am I doing here? I shouldn't be here.*

"Her life has been built on a lie," Heidi said. "Why would she undo it now?"

"She's gutsy," Grace said. "Lila would admire that."

"She's smart, too," Heidi said. "She wasn't motherly. She was nice and she was there. Our father was our mother."

Like mother, like mother, Grace thought, shooting a look at Clara, who gave a slight nod.

"Do you want to lead?" Grace said.

"Let's wait and see," Heidi said.

Frida brought the coffee on a tray. "I'm afraid I haven't any milk or sugar. I never have guests in. They never leave. They stay and stay, nattering about nothing." She looked at Clara. "Are you thinking of moving in? You're too young. You don't want to get stuck in here with all these old people. I was getting forgetful and my housekeeper retired. Heidi, here, and her brother strong-armed me into coming. Painting saved me."

"Clara isn't moving in," Heidi said. "Grace, Clara, do one of you want to start?"

Grace nodded. "I am hoping you can help me, Mrs. Berman. Did you ever know anyone by the name of Zelda Pereira, maiden name Zelda Pessoa?"

"Pessoa was my name," Frida said, "before I married Herbert."

"Did you know Zelda?" Grace said.

Frida smiled at Grace. "I'm sorry, what's your name again?"

"Grace. Grace Maier. Zelda was my grandmother."

"Pessoa was a very common name in our neighborhood," Frida said.

"Do you know about DNA testing?" Grace said.

"What's DNA?" Frida said.

"It's a blood test to find out who you're related to," Grace said. "Clara and I were tested and the results showed that she was my aunt and I was her niece."

"Nothing good comes of that," Frida said. "I've never even been fingerprinted."

"Dennis got tested, too," Grace said.

"He's a sweet boy," Frida said. "He gives blood regularly."

"The tests showed that Dennis and Clara are brother and sister," Grace said.

"How could that be?" Frida squinted at Clara. "Why are you making trouble?"

"Are you my mother?" Clara said, startled by her outburst. *Why do I feel like a monster?*

Frida didn't say anything. She closed her eyes. A minute passed. Two minutes. Heidi grew anxious. She started to speak. Grace shook her head.

After five minutes, Frida opened her eyes and stood up. She glared at Grace. "Why didn't you leave?" she said. "I'm an old woman." She sat down.

"Why did you leave?" Clara said, unable to stop herself. *How could you do that?*

"You're still pretty," Frida said. "I bet you were a beauty when you were young." She smiled. "I was a beauty. It helps, being beautiful helps."

"Why did you leave?" Clara said again. She thought she might faint. It was very warm and the air smelled stale, like old books. *Like old people,* she thought.

Frida stood up again and started pacing. She talked as she paced. "I tried to kill myself, twice," she said. "The first time, I put my head in the oven. Bubbe found me. The second time, I went into the garage and turned on the car's engine. I was pregnant again. I woke up in the Eloise. Aldo had committed me." She looked out the window. "There were no windows in the Eloise, not in the inmates' rooms, did you know that? Jumpers. After a week, they wanted to send me home. I told the doctor I'd keep trying to kill myself until I succeeded. He said he'd help me. Bubbe told him about my aunt Hilda. Two months later, I married Herbert Berman."

She sat down. "Is that what you wanted? Are you happy now?" She squinted at Grace, then turned toward Clara, her face forbidding. "One way or another," she said, "I was going to abandon you."

. . .

HEIDI, CLARA, AND GRACE WALKED slowly to the car. "Let's get a drink," Heidi said. "Let's get drunk."

"I'm sorry," Grace said, biting her lip, then going on. "When I started, I didn't think there would be someone like you at the end, or someone like Dennis. I should have but I didn't. I'm ashamed. My mother was dead. I had this bee in my bonnet." She turned toward Clara. "I'm sorry for doing this to you."

Clara shrugged, still sorting her feelings. *Anger, am I angry?*

"Water under the bridge," Heidi said.

"Blood over the dam," Grace said.

Heidi squinted at Grace. "My mother could have said that," she said.

They sat in a booth, Grace and Clara on one side, Heidi on the other. The seats were hard, the backs were straight. They caught the waitress's eye and ordered drinks.

"For now," Heidi said, "before we plan any family reunions, the only thing I care about is Dennis. I'll give him the book. It might help him to understand that Frida, in saving herself, saved him. No one ever hit him. Both our parents were kind to him."

"Do you think your father knew?" Clara said.

Heidi shrugged. "In the deepest recesses of his mind, I don't know." The waitress brought the drinks. "He wouldn't have wanted to know. He loved her so much. They were happy together."

"Why did Dennis take the DNA test?" Grace said. "Most people take it to find a missing link."

"He felt like an outsider. I was smarter. I was taller. Mom and Dad were very successful in their way. He never felt successful."

"Why did you go into practice with him?" Grace said. She inwardly sighed with relief. It was easier talking to Heidi than to Clara or Dennis.

"I love him. I wanted to work for myself. I wanted a life outside work." Heidi drained her glass and gestured to the waiter for a glass of water. "He's a good lawyer, conscientious, hardworking, but I worried about him holding a job. He needed a safe landing. His insecurities dog him." She leaned back. "I've had a good career working with him. I was never sorry. Our parents worked together in the accounting firm." She took a swig of her drink. "He was born at about six months, or so everyone said. He spent a month in an incubator. His lungs were compromised. Maybe his brain too. Oxygen deprivation. I'm thinking now it was the carbon monoxide when he was in utero." She took in a big breath and let it out slowly. "What might he have been."

"Dead," Clara said. *Oh, God,* she thought, *I sound like Lila. Like Frida.*

Heidi stared at Clara. "I thought I was tough," she said.

"I was an ER nurse for forty years," Clara said.

Grace ordered a second round for the table.

"Mom had an aunt, Hilda. She was a Pessoa, Mom's father's sister. A gorgon. She took Mom in, then played matchmaker with our dad. Mom catered endlessly to her. Hilda would say how much Mom owed her. I think Mom was worried Hilda might spill the beans. Now we know. A bigamist with a violent first husband. In 1960, I'd have been worried too. I was named for Hilda. She insisted, a name that sounded like hers. Mom said she wanted to call me Lia, L I A. Her mother's name. My older daughter is Lia. My younger is Mara, named for herself. I'm Lia's birth mother, my wife is Mara's. We had to adopt each other's babies." She took in a large breath and let it out slowly. "The sisters are close. They're only a year apart. We used the same male donor, which means they have different mothers but the same father. I said that to Dennis yesterday. He admitted he always thought of Mara as my daughter, his niece, but he insisted his case was different. 'I was deceived,' he said." She slouched in her seat. "I don't know what to think. I've had a good life. Dennis too. We wouldn't be here if . . . our mother hadn't run away." She half-smiled. "I almost said Frida. I often think of her now as Frida."

Heidi ordered a third drink. "Today's problem, figuring what to say about Zelda-Frida's suicide attempt. He hasn't seen her since he got the test results."

"As much truth as he can bear to hear," Clara said, *if any of it is bearable.*

"And what about you and me?" Heidi said. "We're sisters, half sisters, and Dennis is your brother."

"You and Dennis need to figure out what you want from us," Clara said. "I'm the only one left of your generation. I doubt Dennis wants to meet Aldo."

"I wish Aldo were dead," Heidi said.

"We've all been wishing him dead for years," Clara said. "We don't pray. That might be more effective, but you can't ask God to do your dirty work."

"Would you mind if we visited Frida again?" Grace said.

"No," Heidi said. "I'll put you on the visitors' list."

"Would you want to come, too," Grace said, "to make sure we don't cross any lines?"

"Mom can take care of herself," Heidi said. "You saw that."

"Lila would have looked like Frida if she'd lived into her eighties," Grace said, blinking back tears.

"I can't hate her," Clara said, her mind lurching to the mass killings, where the relatives of the victims almost immediately forgave the shooter. *I couldn't have forgiven them,* she thought, *but I wouldn't hate them. It's enough of a burden hating Aldo.*

GRACE WANTED TO SEE FRIDA again. Clara was reluctant. They were sitting in Clara's kitchen, having breakfast, going over the events of the last few days. Her house, minimally furnished, had no personality, except for family photos, mostly of Polo and Lila.

"It's too late to think of her as my mother," Clara said, "especially since she doesn't think of me at all."

Grace nodded. "I'll go alone."

Clara shook her head. "You can't. She isn't trustworthy. She doesn't like us."

"I don't like her, either," Grace said.

"I don't want to sympathize with her, I don't want to understand why she abandoned us, why she escaped without us," Clara said. "I'm susceptible on that score."

"Lila always thought she would hate her," Grace said. "I don't know if she would."

"I'm not good at hating," Clara said. "We are who we were: Clara, the Guardian. Polo, the Knight. Lila, the Hoodlum."

Grace's eyebrows met. "Frida, the Motherhoodlum."

Grace and Clara timed their visit for late morning, an hour before lunch.

Frida was in the art studio, working on another house portrait.

"What are you doing here?" Frida said. "Don't come again."

"Could we go somewhere quiet to talk?" Grace said. "We won't stay long. Just a few questions."

Frida put down her brush. "Follow me." She led them to a small seating area, under a large window. They each took a chair. Grace moved hers so that they sat at angles to each other.

"Did you know about Polo's death?" she said.

"Yes," Frida said. "It was all over the Detroit papers. A torrent of grief. Like Princess Di's death. It had nothing to do with him. It just made everyone, except the family, I imagine, feel good."

"Did you know that Lila was an important editor?" Grace said.

"Oh, yes," Frida said. "Local girl makes good. The *Free Press* fawned over her."

"Did you know Lila married Henry Fieldstone's grandson?" Grace said.

"Of course," Frida said. "If you were a Jew living in Detroit, you knew about that marriage. GM Mechanic's Daughter Weds GM Heir."

"Did you worry about Aldo finding you?" Grace said.

"Not Aldo, he wasn't smart." Frida looked hard at Grace. "I was smart. I had drive. What good it did me. He got me pregnant. The first time he took me out. I didn't know what he was doing." She paused. "I used to wonder what might have been if I hadn't been trapped into marrying him. I bet I could have been a contender, a somebody, like your mother." She turned to Clara. "You're so pretty. I looked like you once. Heidi looks like her father. Dennis looks like me, coloring, size, but not the way you do." She turned to Grace. "Any more questions? This is getting tiresome."

"Did you ever think about your children with Aldo?" Grace said. "Did you wonder how they were?" She paused. "Did you miss them, have regrets, feel guilty?"

"No, no, and no," Frida said. She stood up. She was done. "You aren't stupid, why do you ask stupid questions?" She scowled at Grace. "If I looked back, I couldn't go forward."

26

Roundup

GRACE WAS PREGNANT. "AN ACCIDENT," SHE SAID TO RUTH. "LIKE mother, like child. I was crying all the time. I thought I was crying for Clara and Dennis and Heidi. So unlike me but maybe . . ." She was calling from L.A. She'd given up her New York apartment and moved in with Xander.

"What does Xander think?" Ruth said.

"He thinks it's great if I think it's great. He doesn't think it's a disaster. He said the decision was mine. I can't see raising a child in Los Angeles. Everyone's too in touch with their feelings."

"You were a happy accident," Ruth said. "Why not mobilize Frances and get married in the next few months?"

"We talked about that," Grace said. "Xander said he'd like to be married when the baby comes, if it comes."

"What did Joe say?" Ruth said.

"He said maybe the baby would look a little like him. My sisters' children are Pereira replicants." Grace paused. "Lila said there's never a good time to have a baby. You either wanted it or you didn't."

"I'm with Xander. It's great if you want it," Ruth said. "You can always move back to New York. There's a lot of television in New York."

"I can't tell if it's a disaster," Grace said. "We could marry, I could find a job after the baby is born. I'm still on staff at *The New Yorkist*." She paused. "I'll keep it until I get something here. I need to work. I'm like Lila that way." She paused. "I don't think she spent ten minutes thinking about what life would be after she retired. And then, she didn't have to."

"How's the current job going?" Ruth said.

"I'm working on an article on cases I'm calling for now 'Medical Malpractice by Amateurs,'" Grace said. "So far, I've found two mind-bogglingly dangerous ones. The first involves two old women sharing a hospital room. One of them is unconscious and breathing through a ventilator. The other, Ms. Mengele, unable to sleep with the machine's thrumming, gets out of bed, switches it off, and goes to sleep. A nurse, alerted to the disconnect, reconnects it and, having deduced the male-factor, speaks firmly to Ms. Mengele, telling her, in no uncertain terms, that the machine cannot be turned off. It's a matter of life and death. The nurse leaves. Ms. Mengele switches the machine off again, this time seriously compromising her roommate's health and recovery." Grace shrugged. "I'd call that a case of extreme privilege. I'm trying to find out what happened to Ms. Mengele. The police were called."

"And the second case?" Ruth said.

"A baby is gravely ill. He needs a blood transfusion. The parents refuse to give permission unless he is transfused with blood from unvaccinated donors. The hospital goes to court to get temporary custody." Grace's voice rose in indignation. "One way or another, those parents seem hell-bent on killing their baby."

"Where do you find these stories?" Ruth said. "You aren't pinching them from *The Daily Mail*, are you?"

"I know someone inside," Grace said. "No HIPAA violations. There was a police report and a court filing."

"Artie Brinkman," Ruth said.

"I'm afraid I can't reveal my source," Grace said.

"How is he?" Ruth said.

"Sweet and sad," Grace said.

"His parents were rotters," Ruth said, "not only that last terrible time."

CLARA CALLED HEIDI. "I'D LIKE to write a welcoming email to Dennis. I hope you feel welcomed."

Heidi laughed. "I'm glad I like you," she said. "Yes, write the email. I told my daughters, Lia and Mara. They'd like to meet you sometime, down the road."

Clara's email went through many drafts. She didn't show any of them to Grace. Each draft got shorter.

January 15, 2024

Dear Dennis,

I hope we can be friends if not brother and sister. My sister and my other brother died. I have nieces and great-nephews, but no one left of my generation. I'm glad you didn't have to grow up in our house. I'm glad you had such a supportive and loving sister. I know it's been a terrible blow but the truth is, Frida saved you in saving herself.

I can be a good friend.

Yours,

Clara Pereira

Dennis wrote back straightaway.

January 16, 2024

Dear Clara,

It's been very hard for me, I'll admit it, but in the great scheme of things, you had a much harder time. I see that now. Frida abandoned you. She kept me, "saved" me, as you wrote. Your father was a monster. My father was the kindest man. I hope one day to feel as lucky as I know I should. I read Grace's book. Polo and Lila were larger than life, especially my life, which couldn't have been any more ordinary. I was a nice Jewish boy who grew up to be a nice Jewish man, or so I thought. I haven't been nice to you. I'm working on it. That's my way. I work at things. I was looking for cousins when I did Genealogies. I found a sister instead. Sometimes we get more than we thought we wanted. Thank you for writing. You're very kind. That makes everything easier.

Yours truly,

Dennis.

P.S. I have two daughters and so does Heidi, a bit younger than Grace. More nieces.

GRACE CALLED FRANCES. "I'M PREGNANT, weepy and pregnant," she said. "We're planning on getting married quietly. We'll come to you, so you can be there, but we don't want a wedding, just a brief ceremony and a dinner. We'll have a party afterward, probably in D.C. A wedding party–baby shower."

"Perfect," Frances said. "Exactly the tonic I needed. I've been tired all the time, as if I were getting ready for the Big Sleep. I already feel more alert."

RUTH'S PODCAST TOOK OFF. DOUG had scheduled the episodes to drop every two weeks. The first one got five thousand hits in a week, ten thousand in two weeks. The second got thirty thousand in two weeks. When the third reached over fifty thousand hits in two weeks, Doug formally invited her to join *The Press Gang* podcast group. "Exponential, like an earthquake," he said. "If this keeps up you could have over a million in a year. Heart, they're full of heart. People want that now."

At Joe's urging, Ruth hired an IP lawyer who was working at his firm. The young woman was ecstatic to have a client of her own.

"You want one who's a digital native," Joe had said.

Ruth was rattled and excited. "How do I get paid? How much do I get paid?"

"We'll figure all that out," the young lawyer said. "Look at Substack. You might want a newsletter to go along with the podcast. Subscriptions there too."

Nico, after many consultations with experts, bought Ruth state-of-the-art recording and editing equipment, along with a digital cinema camera. "For TikTok and Instagram," he said. "You need a visible presence on social media."

"I thought it would take time to catch on," she said. "I thought the audience would grow slowly."

"The project grew slowly," he said, "and then like a desert cactus, it bloomed. Six years in the making of an overnight success."

"I'm not ready," Ruth said.

"You have to run with it now, and then, when you hit a hundred thousand listeners, maybe we might try for a baby."

"Do you think so?" she said.

Nico took her in his arms. "We could buy a second apartment, in this building or one nearby, and install your mom and gran there," he said. "Ann said she was ready to move. Her August electric bill was four hundred dollars."

"When did she tell you that?" she said. "Did I hear right, you called her Ann, and not Ms. Ann?"

"Yup," he said. "I asked. She said, 'Of course.'" He nodded. "She called to talk. She wondered if Grace's pregnancy made us think about having a baby."

"She didn't say that to me. She doesn't want to put pressure on me." Ruth half-smiled. "I'm almost twice as old as she was when I was born."

"There's a lot on your plate," he said.

"Including the Bates sibs," Ruth said. "Why did I ever do Genealogies?"

The day after the second podcast went up, Ruth received an unexpected email.

January 20, 2024

Hi Ruth McGovern,

I'm writing for me and my brother Jackson Bates (Stonewall Jackson Bates). We found you through Genealogies and then Google. We did it as a joke, with friends, never thinking we had a half sister. We have the same father, Bobby Lee Bates (Robert E. Lee Bates). We asked our dad about you. He said he was sixteen when you were born. He didn't know about you until you did Genealogies years ago. I think he was embarrassed and ashamed. Mom was ticked. They separated a couple of months ago. She's living now with his brother, Jeff Bates (Jefferson Davis Bates). I listened to your podcast about missing mothers and grandmothers. Did your friend find her grandmother? I don't know if you're interested in meeting us. We'd like to meet you sometime, maybe on your next visit to Tallahassee. We've never been to New York City. I'm a teacher. I teach Spanish at a middle school. Bill works with Dad at his nursery. We're both married. I'm expecting my first baby. He will not be named after a Confederate General, if you were wondering. I hope to hear from you.

Yours sincerely,

Scarlett O. Bates Newton

"What do you want to do about them?" Nico said.

"I'll think about it," Ruth said. "It's a careful letter. That family specializes in careful letters." She smiled wryly. "She misspelled my name."

"Careful but cordial," he said. "What about Bobby Lee? She's set her mom up as the bad guy."

"You mean a Quest for Bobby Lee, like the Quest for Zelda?" she said. "If he reaches out, maybe. I don't want to hurt Gran and Mom."

"The interesting thing about Frida is how much Grace said she sounded like Lila." Nico gave a slight headshake. "If that's true, then she also sounded like Grace, at least before she got pregnant. She seems to be mellowing."

"I'd like a baby, too," she said. "If it's a girl, could we call her Lila?"

GRACE AND XANDER WERE MARRIED at Tara, on March 1, 2024. The bride was four months pregnant. The wedding was quiet and small, Joe, Frances, Clara, the Starbirds, their husbands and babies, Kathy, Richard, Zayde, Ruth, Nico, Gran, Ann, the Remnants, down to five, and, with Joe's blessing once again, Doug, who performed the ceremony. Grace didn't invite Heidi or Dennis Berman or Josh Morgan, but she wrote them to let them know.

"I like Heidi but I don't feel any kinship," she said to Xander, "and I barely know Dennis." As for Josh Morgan, *the fox among the pigeons,* she thought.

She had asked the Starbirds if the babies might come. "Frances hasn't met them," she said. "I could practice holding them and feeding them."

Frances hired a string quartet and a small band for dancing. "A wedding without music is like a kite without a tail," she said. "No lift." She left the rest of the details, the dinner, the cake, the flowers, to her housekeeper. Grace wore Ruth's dress. She had it adjusted to accommodate her bump. Ruth had offered, then insisted. "You can't wear the dress you wore to my wedding, which is what you'll do. I know you."

Grace and Xander hadn't registered. "It seems like a grab when you're rich," she said to him. "Let's tell everyone we want them to pick out a gift they like and think we would like."

The Remnants gave them twelve settings of Georg Jensen's Cactus silver pattern.

"Don't even think of protesting," Frances said when Grace, spluttering, called to tell her. "That would be insulting. They all agreed

Ruth's wedding was the best time they had in years. They're back for another best time." She paused. "When I got married, I got mounds of silver, most of it monogrammed so I couldn't return it. So spiteful. Even back then, we didn't need silver grapefruit bowls or swan candelabra. A nice set of cutlery, horse of a different color. Use it every day. Celebrate daily life. It's so much more important than any holiday." She paused again. "I have a set of Royal Copenhagen for twelve, the ones with blue flowers, never used. I was given four other sets of dishes. Would you like it? Very beautiful."

"Thank you," Grace said. "I have chipped Ikea. Xander's are up market. Maybe Williams Sonoma."

Doug gave them the complete Oxford English Dictionary, twenty volumes. Josh sent Grace a first edition set of Mencken's newspaper trilogy and Xander a first edition of *The Last Tycoon*. Gran knit six beautiful, brightly colored baby sweaters, running from a two-month size to a two-year size. "I want to frame them," Grace wrote her. Joe gave Grace Lila's gold chain necklace. "Oh, Joe," she said. "You're the best."

At the dinner, Grace made the toast to Lila. "What wouldn't I give for her to be here."

All the toasts were short.

"I'm marrying Xander," Grace said, "because he makes me laugh, even when I'm cranky. Also, it's in his kiss."

"I'm the luckiest man ever," Xander said, "living a life with Grace."

She and Xander danced to Sondheim's "Send in the Clowns." Afterward, the band played Viennese waltzes, starting with the "Drinking Song" from *The Student Prince*. Grace and Joe waltzed, crying quietly. The evening ended early. Throughout her pregnancy, Grace had morning sickness, which often ran into the afternoon and evening. "I only threw up twice," she told Xander the next day, "and none of it got on Ruth's dress."

"They're a good match," Joe said to Doug, who had had three wives, all jealous of Lila. "They feel lucky in each other."

. . .

GRACE GAVE BIRTH ON JULY 16, 2024.

"It's a girl," Xander said to Frances. He called to let her know she had a great-granddaughter. "We want to name her after you. Is that all right. Frances Fieldstone Goldsmith Maier, Frankie for short. The next one gets my last name."

Frances cleared her throat, fighting tears. "I'd be honored," she said. "So many names, like royalty. Is she dark haired and skinny, a proper Maier?"

"She's twenty-two inches, seven pounds, red faced, and bald," he said. "Apgar score 9. She took her sweet time. We didn't know we were having a girl. We wanted to be surprised."

"What about the other great-grandmother," Frances said. "Does she know?"

"No, Grace hasn't seen her since their last interview. She feels guilty and remorseful. She discovered she had been right and saw the damage she did."

"How's work going for her?" Frances said. "Still with *The New Yorkist*?"

"More good news," Xander said. "Two days before she went into labor, she was offered a job at the *L.A. Sun* writing obituaries. The best part of the job is interviewing big shots while they're still alive. She starts in two months. She asked if she could include funny stories. The editor told her to shelve her East Coast sense of propriety. 'This is L.A., sweetcakes,' she said. 'Nothing's sacred.'"

FRIDA DIED TWO WEEKS LATER on the back page of the Temple Israel newsletter. The write-up noted her achievements, the first woman accountant in Farmington, the first woman owner, with her husband, of a prominent local business. "Women didn't do those things back then," Heidi was quoted as saying. "I always wonder what she might have done had she been born thirty years later. Law and politics, I'm thinking. I could see her as the CEO of an investment company."

Heidi had called Grace and Clara the day Frida died. "The funeral's at Rose Memorial Chapel. Burial follows. Then a two-day shiva."

Clara went to the funeral, burial, and shiva. *Why do I do this?* she thought. *Why do I do all three? I am therefore I do.* After the burial, she stopped by Aldo's. She let herself into the house. She could hear him scuffling in the kitchen.

"Hello," she called out.

"What are you doing here?" he said, shuffling unsteadily into the living room.

"I brought you something." She handed him a copy of Grace's book.

"I don't need a book," he said.

"It's about our family, about Zelda and Lila and Polo and me and Bubbe and you, lots of you," she said. "The names have been changed, to protect the guilty."

"I don't read anymore," he said.

"In the book, Zelda escapes the Eloise. She doesn't die. She runs away," Clara said. "But you always knew that."

"Get out of my house," he said. He lifted a whiskey bottle and shook it at her. "Don't come back."

Later that evening, Clara called Grace. "We buried Frida this afternoon," she said. "It was a small gathering, a few of the Halsted inmates, some people from the synagogue, Heidi and Dennis and their families. Heidi was glad I came. So was Dennis. He seemed less of a sad sack. He thanked me."

"Did anyone ask how you were connected to the family?" Grace said, shifting in her seat. Frankie was lying in her lap, making gurgling noises.

"No," Clara said. "If anyone asked, I was going to say Frida was a distant relation."

"It was kind of you to go," Grace said. "Generous, too."

"Is that Frankie I'm hearing?" Clara said.

"Yes," Grace said. "She gurgled and burped."

"How is it going?" Clara said.

"Better than I expected. I'm not scared of her anymore."

Clara laughed.

"I've been thinking a lot about your mother and mine," Grace said. "Having a baby does that to you. Your perspective changes. Like the secretary becoming the boss." She cleared her throat. "No one protected Lila from Aldo, but no one protected Zelda from him either."

"Which means . . . ?" Clara said.

"They did what they had to. They did what they could."

Acknowledgments

It takes a village to raise a writer. I want to acknowledge and thank the following people and organizations for their support and encouragement, above and beyond anything I had ever hoped for.

- My editor, Whit Frick; my agent, Kathy Robbins; and my husband, David Denby, the *sine qua nons*.
- My original editor, Susan Kamil, the guiding spirit who launched the book, loved and missed.
- My friends Jean Howard, Richard Cohen, Joanna Cole, Joseph Finder, Mary Cohen, and Jane Booth—early readers who made the book better.
- The Dial Press team, the best in the business.
- The Robbins Office, the top of the line.
- The Ragdale Foundation and the Hannah Judy Gretz Fellowship, the residency program that gave me the luxury of time to plot.

I would also like to acknowledge the sources of several unattributed quotations I buried in conversations. They may not be exact. People misremember. The authors are:

- Hunter S. Thompson
- Edgar Allan Poe
- Matthew Arnold (?) (Someone said it or something like it; he comes closest.)
- Bill Bradley
- Sigmund Freud
- Jonathan Lethem (a play on his book title)
- William Shakespeare (twice)
- Frank McCourt
- Herman Melville
- Daniel Okrent
- Rick in *Casablanca* (a play on his words)
- e. e. cummings
- Samuel Beckett

If you find them all (and any I missed), let me know.

About the Author

Susan Rieger is a graduate of Mount Holyoke College and Columbia Law School. She has worked as a residential college dean at Yale and an associate provost at Columbia. She has taught law to undergraduates at both schools and written frequently about the law for newspapers and magazines. She is the author of *The Divorce Papers* and *The Heirs*. She lives in New York City with her husband David Denby.

About the Type

This book was set in Fairfield, the first typeface from the hand of the distinguished American artist and engraver Rudolph Ruzicka (1883–1978). Ruzicka was born in Bohemia (in the present-day Czech Republic) and came to America in 1894. He set up his own shop, devoted to wood engraving and printing, in New York in 1913 after a varied career working as a wood engraver, in photoengraving and banknote printing plants, and as an art director and freelance artist. He designed and illustrated many books, and was the creator of a considerable list of individual prints—wood engravings, line engravings on copper, and aquatints.